To John William Edward Mepham,
Grandad, a true romantic.
I miss you.

15th November, 1920 ~ 7th February, 2012

Chapter One

New York City, March 31ˢᵗ

Elizabeth Ward eased back the blinds and peered into the quiet street that ran alongside the apartment building. Rain streaked the windowpanes, drops running together and fracturing in the orange glow of the streetlights. A dark-colored Lincoln crouched like a shadow next to a squat, black and silver hydrant. Her former colleagues from the FBI's Organized Crime Unit sat in that car. Watching. Waiting. Her so-called protection.

Betrayal burned the edges of her mind like battery acid.

The grandfather clock in the hallway chimed five times, making her jump.

Five a.m.

Nearly time.

Her fingers gripped the edge of the window frame. Night's gloom clung to the red brick of the Victorian tenements opposite, its weak edges and cold breath eating into what should have been springtime.

A drunk wove his shopping cart down the back alley, searching for a safe spot out of the killer wind. Even Midtown's exclusive neighborhoods were scattered with down-and-outs, hunched behind dumpsters, curled up between parked cars. A community of desperate souls, listless, gaunt, and stinking like the dead.

She envied them.

She wanted to be that invisible.

Swallowing past the wedge in her throat, she counted to ten and slowly inhaled a lungful of air. She'd done her job, and done it well, but it was time to get the hell out of Dodge.

She sat at her computer in the darkened room and signed in to an anonymous email account. Wrote two messages.

The first one read, *Terms of contract agreed. Proceed.*

There was more than one way to skin a cat.

Her teeth chattered, but not from cold. A rolling shake began in her fingertips and moved up through her wrists—whether from rage or fear she didn't know. She clenched her hands together into a hard fist, massaged the knuckles with her interlocked fingers, grateful for the unyielding gold of her signet ring that bit into her flesh.

Pain was a good reminder.

She pulled her shoulders back, typed carefully, *Beware the fury of a patient man.*

Baiting the tiger, or the devil himself.

Bastard.

A tear slipped down her cheek, cold and wet. She let it fall, blanked the searing memories from her mind.

Elizabeth logged off. Reformatted her hard-drive, erasing every command she'd ever received, every report she'd ever sent. Letting the computer run, she headed into the stylish bathroom of the apartment the FBI had leased for her undercover alter ego and prepared for the final chapter of her New York life. She leaned close to the mirror and put in a colored contact lens.

One eye stared back, frosted iced-blue, the other looked eerily exposed, its pale green depths shining with fear. With shaky fingers she put in the second lens and made up her face. Heavy foundation hid the dark circles under her eyes and translucent powder covered her rampant freckles. Blood-red lipstick and thick black eyeliner dominated her face, making her look harder, bolder.

"Hello, Juliette." She knew the old fraud better than she knew herself.

Blush emphasized cheekbones sharp enough to cut, and mascara elongated her thick lashes. She pinned her hair back into a neat bun, tight to the nape of her neck. Pulled on a wig that was similar to her own dyed, red hair, but cut shorter into a bob that swung just beneath her chin.

She was ready to die now.

Her lips curved upward. Her cheeks moved, her eyes crinkled, but there was not an ounce of happy to buoy it up. The façade held, despite the escalating internal pressure.

FBI Special Agent Elizabeth Ward had sat quietly when the Assistant DA had informed her that mobster Andrew DeLattio was being allowed to turn state's evidence. Then she'd excused herself and thrown up in the restroom.

Lines of strain etched her eyes and mouth. Her pulse fluttered.

Truth was she didn't mind dying, but she wasn't going to stand on the sidewalk with a bulls-eye tattooed to her ass. Juliette Morgan was a target for every organized-crime family in the US and Elizabeth intended to make her disappear.

Permanently.

She walked through to the main bedroom, pulled out a scarlet Versace pantsuit and a tangerine silk blouse and walked back into the bedroom.

Can I really do this?

Yes! The answer screamed inside her head. How else could she reclaim her life? And if she died trying? So be it.

She dressed. The red and orange clashing violently in an eye-catching display of high fashion—exactly the effect she was going for.

Satisfied, Elizabeth walked through to the lounge and took one last look at the stylish Manhattan apartment. She was done with it, burned out, wasted, with no future to speak of and a past full of regrets. Time hadn't diminished her fury; if anything it burned brighter and stronger every day. DeLattio owed her and Witness Protection or not, she was going to get her revenge.

Forcing herself to move she stopped before she'd gone two paces. Her eyes caught and held an old sepia photograph staring at her from the hall table. A young couple grinned at her from their perch, affectionately hugging two tiny figures between them.

It knocked her sideways, the lifetime of grief locked up in that treasured photograph. She swallowed three times before she could catch her breath.

Ah, God.

Elizabeth blinked to kill the tears and slid the photograph into her purse, next to her Glock. Hiding behind dark sunglasses, she picked up her keys and left without a backward glance.

***

Triple H Ranch, Montana, April 3ʳᵈ

In the open doorway of the ranch house with his old dog pressed against his side, Nat Sullivan gazed up into the inky depths of the night sky. No moon shone tonight, though stars glittered like tiny diamonds against the blackest coal.

It was two a.m. and his eyes hurt.

A thin layer of fresh snow covered the ground, gleaming like exposed bone. The storm had been a quick blast of fury, totally unpredicted, but not unexpected, not this high in the mountains. Trees popped like firecrackers deep in the heart of the forest.

A dull throbbing poked at his skull like a hangover. Not that he'd had the time or luxury to get drunk. The headache was the lingering aftereffect of a difference of opinion he'd had with a couple of repo men that afternoon. They thought they had the right to come to the ranch and steal his property. He figured they'd be better off dead.

Stroking the silky fur that covered the old dog's skull, tension seeped from his stiff neck as his muscles gradually relaxed. He let out a breath and his stance tempered, shoulders lowered as the tightness slowly eased.

Peace, finally, after a day of almighty hell.

The Sullivans had been granted a temporary reprieve when his mother suffered a heart attack. A life-and-death version of the silver-lined cloud.

Nat tried to force a smile, found the effort too great, his jaw too damn sore to do it justice. Last time he'd seen his mother she'd been pasty gray, her hair standing on end, lying flat on her back in a hospital bed.

Still giving out orders.

Old. Weak. *Cantankerous.* His mother would go to her grave fighting for this land. He could do no less.

Absently, he played with the silky fur of Blue's ears. The Triple H was nestled in the foothills of the Rocky Mountains, a lush valley butted up close to the Bob Marshall Wilderness. Settled by his great, great grandparents, it was as much a part of his heritage as his DNA. A few hundred acres of prime grazing land, carved over millennia by the friction of ice over rock.

Nat had had his adventures, traveled the world, seen more than his fair share of beautiful country, but now he was back to stay. Montana was in his bones, the backdrop to every thought and the oxygen of every breath. He leaned against the doorframe, looked out at the mountains and welcomed the fresh clean air pressed close against his cheeks.

It was sacrilege to think the ranch could be taken from them.

A shooting star plunged across the night sky, falling to its death in a brilliant display. Nat drew in a sharp breath at the flash of beauty. The dog stiffened beneath his palm, a low growl vibrating from its belly all the way to its teeth. Nat cocked his head, ears tuned in, attention focused. A low humming sound grew louder, like the buzz of a honeybee getting closer.

A car.

Heading this way.

"Quiet, Blue. Go lie down." He didn't want the dog making a racket and waking his niece. Pulling the baby monitor from his pocket, he checked it against his ear to make sure it was still working, and turned back to the open door.

Could be nothing.

Could be Ryan driving home drunk even though he knew better. But Ryan didn't always show good judgment after a bad day. Didn't sound like Ryan's truck though. Nat flicked off the baby monitor.

Hidden Hollow Hideaway was remote and secluded, with mountains surrounding and enclosing the ranch on all four sides. Miles off the beaten track it was hard to find even in daylight. At night it was damn near impossible. People did not just pass by and they weren't expecting any paying guests for at least another week. Troy Strange was their only neighbor for miles and he was more likely to visit smallpox victims.

Trouble was coming—Nat smelled it, almost tasted it at the back of his throat.

Cursing, he grabbed his rifle and ammo off the gun-rack above the kitchen door and loaded it, chambering a round. He moved quickly outside to stand in the deep shadows besides the big Dutch barn. Cattle lowed behind him and a wolf's howl echoed through the hills to the east.

Prickles crept up Nat's spine. Were the repo men coming back for another shot at his horses? Despite all his attorney's fine words?

The car was cresting the rise a hundred yards from the main house. It sure as hell wasn't Ryan's truck. Nat's heart thumped hard against his ribcage and adrenaline banished tiredness. He hugged the side of the barn as headlights cut deep into shadow. The rig, a Jeep Cherokee, pulled into the yard in front of the main house, cut the lights, cut the engine.

Silence resonated around the granite peaks like a boom in his ears. Nat breathed in and out. He smelled the exhaust fumes tainting the pure mountain air, listened as silence combed the darkness, as if nothing existed except the colorless wasteland of night. Just time and universe, cold and rock.

Anticipation sharpened every sense as he waited, balanced on the balls of his feet. Nobody moved. Nobody crept out of the Jeep. Nobody sneaked into his stable to steal his prize-winning Arabian horses.

Nat's breathing leveled off, his heart rate slowed. He relaxed his stance and adjusted his grip. Waited.

The repo men had brought a truck this morning.

Nat waited another minute, then another. His eyes grew gritty with fatigue and he fought back a yawn. This wasn't the repo men. He didn't know who it was, but it wasn't them. Cold seeped into his hands from the frigid metal of the gun; his trigger finger was freezing up.

"Damn it all to hell."

He wasn't about to leave some stranger hanging around his property in the middle of the night.

Though it was pitch-black, Nat's eyesight was sharp and well-adjusted. He knew every inch of ground, every stone, fence, and broken-down piece of machinery on his land. Picking out shades of gray, he moved towards the car. Flicked off the rifle's safety and peered in through the frosted-up glass. It was like trying to see to the bottom of a riverbed in the middle of winter. He couldn't make out a damned thing.

With one finger, he lifted the handle of the driver's side door. It clicked open, but no interior light came on. Nat took a step back and peered inside, made out a bundled up figure in the back seat, curled up, unmoving.

Gripping his rifle he felt the tension crackle like static on a dry day. The fine hairs at his nape sprang up, tensile and erect.

"Drop the rifle, mister." The voice was softly feminine.

"Now why would I want to do that?" he asked.

She was silent. He could feel her apprehension; almost see her weighing her choices in the concealment of the Jeep.

His teeth locked together. "I don't think so, ma'am." He might have been raised to be polite to women, but he wasn't dumb. "Not 'til you tell me why you're sneaking onto my property in the middle of the night."

She shifted slightly. He heard the rustle as she pushed aside the blankets.

"What's your name?" she asked. There was a lilt, some sort of accent in her voice that sounded both warm and aggressive at the same time. It undid some of his irritation and sparked a glimmer of curiosity.

"Well, ma'am." Pitched low, Nat's voice was steely with courteousness. "A better question would be what the hell's yours?"

***

It was a good question. It was a great question. But Elizabeth had been working undercover for so long now she'd begun to wonder herself.

13

She'd followed the directions she'd been given by the woman over the phone, gone wrong a dozen times before God had decided she needed an even greater challenge and had given her a flat tire. All in all, she'd been driving for three days with limited stops and hadn't eaten in eighteen hours. Fear and exhaustion had turned her into an amateur.

Stupid.

Instead of blending in she was sticking a gun in an innocent man's face.

Doubly stupid.

She slid the Glock back into her purse. Slowly, noiselessly. She didn't want to alarm him, didn't want to get shot by some trigger-happy nut-job citing the second amendment. She had enough trigger-happy nut-jobs to worry about.

Her vision blurred and her reflexes moved like glue.

The rancher didn't sound too chipper himself. But what had she expected, turning up in the middle of the night? She pressed her lips together into a rigid line of self reproof.

Irritation seeped through the darkness in a palpable wave of hostility. The cowboy was seriously pissed.

She'd screwed up.

"I'm Eliza Reed. I booked one of your holiday cottages for next month?" Her voice came out surprisingly light and airy. "I took off earlier than expected. I was hoping to just sleep in the Jeep tonight and beg a room in the morning."

Making herself out to be an idiot wasn't difficult at this point in her life. She cleared her throat, watched him carefully. Noted the way his chin dipped, even though the rest of him stayed as still as a mountain. Silence stretched as she held her breath waiting for his response. His silhouette was dark and looming—unrelenting.

Shit.

He was going to send her away.

She tried to moisten her throat, swallowed repeatedly, but it didn't help. She could not drive any further tonight. Her stomach rumbled, but she couldn't face food. She just needed about a million years of rest. Her eyes closed and her body swayed. She caught the headrest in front of her, squared her shoulders and lifted her chin.

"You can stay," he said, finally.

His voice was deep and carried a lazy drawl that reminded her of a childhood spent watching westerns on Saturday morning TV. That childhood had died along with her parents.

"Thanks. Thank you, so much."

Babbling was not a good sign.

She glanced up as relief washed through her, took a deep breath and tried to relax.

"I'm going to get out now, okay?" She nodded toward the rifle, waited for his curt acknowledgement, sensed the slight relaxation in his stance like the uncoiling of an angry snake as he pointed the rifle at the ground and flicked on the safety.

She raised her eyes to his face, made sure her hands were clearly visible before she moved. They shook badly, but that was okay. Between the cold and the adrenaline rush, he'd never know why she was really scared.

"You frightened the devil out of me opening the door like that." She forced a nervous little laugh, realized it came naturally. Fluttering a trembling hand to her breast, she added, "I've heard all these horror stories about grizzly bears and wolves."

Like anyone ever heard of a wolf opening a door.

The man didn't move. Didn't speak. It was as disconcerting as hell. Her gaze hooked on a shadow that dented his chin, all she could make out in the darkness. Her balance cart-wheeled with nervous fatigue and suddenly she couldn't breathe.

Air. She needed air.

Blankets trapped her legs, made her panic. She pushed them away and clambered out of the Jeep. The man hadn't moved an inch and she found herself eye-level with that dented chin.

He had a strong, firm mouth and she didn't like it.

A lungful of frigid mountain air iced up her insides and she shivered with cold, let out a deep gulp of breath and watched, mesmerized, as it curled up to brush past the cowboy's cheek. He moved a fraction, as if to avoid the ephemeral contact.

Annoyance radiated from him in waves, from the set of his shoulders to the rigid way he held his arms.

Battling her cool reception, she tried again. "I'm really sorry, I would have phoned, but I lost my signal..." She could tell he was frowning at her.

Fear skittered along her nerves. Fright clogged her vocal cords and paralyzed her muscles. Suddenly, she couldn't speak. Nobody knew she was here. Nobody knew she was on a remote ranch in the mountains, only an inch away from a big, angry cowboy.

And wouldn't that be one of God's little ironies?

Murdered while on the run.

Frozen, she jammed the edges of her jacket closer together, wrapped herself in its protection. Fingered the big, round, buttons, and concentrated on their smoothness. Wished to God she'd put her Glock in her pocket rather than her purse, or thought to wear her backup weapon. Stupid, stupid, stupid.

Relax. Breathe. Relax.

She'd been a good agent once—better than good. Now her heart thundered like a raging river and sweat broke out along her spine. She wanted to flee. Run and never look back. But she had nowhere left to go.

Every sense strained as Elizabeth tried to gauge the stranger's intent. Her eyesight had adjusted to the starlight and her right hand itched for her weapon. He surveyed her carefully, as if trying to make up his mind.

Whether to shoot her or send her packing?

A nervous laugh hovered at the back of her mind—exhaustion making her punchy. His jaw clenched so tight she could see it flex despite the dim light. She took an involuntary step back, found herself pressed against the frigid steel of the Jeep.

"Guess I should welcome you to the Triple H Ranch, ma'am." His voice was pitched low and soft, so soft she had to strain to hear him. He extended one hand in front of him while the other gripped the rifle. "Nat Sullivan."

The reluctance in his voice made her lips curve in a wry grimace. The background check on Nat Sullivan suggested he was a straight-up sort of guy. Single, early thirties, he'd given up a promising career as a wildlife photographer for National

Geographic to come home and run the ranch when his father died.

But background checks didn't always tell the whole story...

"Thank you," she said, reaching out to take the hand he offered, determined to be brave. But the touch of his rough skin on her fingers sent a shockwave screaming through her nerves like a blast of fire. She jerked away, wrapped her arms tightly around her waist and pasted a smile on her face with the last scraps of her energy.

She hadn't been prepared for that. *No, sir.*

She hadn't expected some weird chemistry to jump out and bite her on the ass. *No. Sir.*

Maybe the earlier adrenaline rush had left her hypersensitive. Maybe exhaustion made her jumpy. Or maybe that came with the million-dollar price-tag on her head. Her smile slipped a notch and she couldn't quite force it up into her eyes.

The heat of him, even without physical contact, was like a solid wall of energy that emanated from his body. She wanted to steal some of that heat. Coldness moved inside her like a glacier now.

He adjusted his grip on the rifle and she flinched, a small flicker of movement, but enough to remind her she was a victim. Fear made her weak and that was one thing she was determined not to be. She swallowed the hard lump in her throat, fought the haze of emotion that threatened to choke her. She'd made a mistake coming here tonight— should have gone far away. But even the moon was too close when you were running from memories.

What a bloody mess.

"Keys?" he demanded.

"Pardon me?"

18

"Where are your keys?" Each word was drawn out slowly, as if he was holding on to his patience by a very thin thread.

She glanced towards the ignition, jerked back as he moved to retrieve the keys that dangled there.

Oh, crap.

The cowboy wheeled and stalked away.

Elizabeth swayed on her feet, baffled and confused. The breeze snatched at her jacket, tugged at her hair as she watched him go. Her thought processes clicked slowly, one synapse at a time.

What was he doing? Too tired to even put one foot in front of the other, she just watched him go, grateful she wasn't dead.

***

Nat cursed, knocked off balance. He opened the cargo hold, stared unseeing into its depths as a puny bulb cast a dim glow over the interior. After his day from hell, he'd been irritated that she'd turned up early, unannounced. But he'd been goddamned thunderstruck when he'd got a load of her face.

It wasn't just that she was pretty. *That* hadn't fazed him. But for one brief instant, when she'd first stepped out of the car and raised her face...she'd looked like Nina. And his heart had damned near pounded itself to death.

He rubbed his eye socket with the heel of his hand, winced as he caught a tender bruise one of the repo guys had landed on him earlier. Darkness had leached the color from her eyes, but not their shape. Big and wide, tilted like a cat's at the outside edge and topped by movie-star brows—just like Nina's had been.

But she wasn't Nina.

And while her eyes were pretty they were also heavy with fatigue, lashes drooping, drifting shut, as though gravity alone would put her to sleep.

He heaved a long sigh that lessened the tension in his chest and slung the rifle over his shoulder.

The woman wasn't Nina. But she was trouble. Beautiful women always were. Not what he needed in a life already as complicated as sin. If he hadn't desperately needed the money he'd have sent her packing, no matter how goddamned tired or pretty she looked.

Damn.

He hauled out a couple of tote bags that might've contained clothes or bullion. Picking them up, he felt the newly healing skin of his knuckles split as the weight settled against his fingers.

Maybe next time he'd remember he was too old for fighting.

And maybe next time he'd grow another head.

"Better sleep in the ranch house tonight." He looked over his shoulder at the woman who hadn't budged. "The cabin takes a good few hours to warm up."

At least with his mother in the hospital there was space in the main house. That silver lining thing was happening all over again.

His lips twitched.

The woman stood looking at him, dark hair peeking out from under a shapeless beanie, big eyes blinking shut. Not that she'd sounded tired when she'd told him to drop the rifle. *Hell, no.* She'd sounded like a goddamned army general then. Nat scowled, hefted one bag onto his shoulders and turned away, headed toward the front door of the main house.

She still hadn't moved.

He turned back to her. "You coming?"

Her hand reached out, palm up. Then her eyes rolled and she collapsed to the frozen earth.

She hit the ground with a solid *thwack*. His mouth fell open as his jaw dropped. His legs wouldn't work, not that he was close enough to catch her even if they did.

Dropping the bags, he ran over and checked for a pulse. Her face was paler than the snow, but her skin was soft and warm beneath his fingertips. The pulse in her neck beat strong and steady, thrumming rhythmically.

He heard a soft noise and stared, uncertain. He'd already had one emergency dash that day, didn't need another. Again, a steady sound. Light, but resonant.

Grinning, he realized Miss Gorgeous was fast asleep and snoring. He leaned back on the heels of his cowboy boots, and debated what to do. There was no emergency. The woman seemed fine other than collapsing with fatigue, but he couldn't just leave her here in the snow. She looked so serene, the gentle rise and fall of her chest, peaceful and relaxed. Nat didn't have the heart to try to wake her. He leaned over and scooped her up in his arms.

Despite her height, she was lightweight. Her long legs dangled over his elbow, her head rested against his shoulder, tucked neatly beneath his chin. Ignoring the softness of her breasts and the curve of her backside against his arm, he headed toward the house. Didn't need reminded that she was a beautiful woman, or that it had been a long time since he'd held one close.

He shifted her higher in his arms, smelled her scent, natural and unadorned. It triggered a response deep within him that he wanted to ignore and explore, all at the same time. He pushed the thoughts away.

Bare-naked lips were half-parted in rest and her breath caressed his cheek like a lover's whisper. He looked up, not wanting to think about her lips.

Moving carefully through the darkened homestead, he carried her up the stairs. He hesitated at the top before entering his room and placing her upon his bed where he pulled off her boots and hat.

She didn't stir.

He smoothed the dark hair off her forehead, felt it slip between his fingertips like satin.

Drawing the top cover over Miss Eliza Reed's sleeping form, he stood back and watched her. Told himself it was concern that made him stare. Her breath was deep and regular, her face relaxed and starting to lose its deathly pallor. She twitched in her sleep, her hand creeping beneath the pillow.

A laugh stirred in his chest and took him by surprise. The day had been a complete disaster and life kept getting weirder and weirder. But at least this time, weird involved having a beautiful woman curled up in his bed.

Chapter Two

Something jumped her at six a.m.

He'd found her. *Damn it.* She lunged for her weapon—came up empty. Desperate, she swept her hands beneath the pillow, searched and ripped at the sheets. Sweat rolled down her face as she braced herself for his laugh, that bitter twist of sound that froze her heart and echoed through her nightmares. Her breath hitched and jammed as she fought a scream, let it ricochet through her mind but never made a sound.

She would not scream. Not this time.

Enveloped in blackness, she couldn't breathe, couldn't see, couldn't break free of the covers trapping her. Hot, stale air suffocated her, sweat ran into her ear and her fingers were useless pieces of sponge.

A kick to her left kidney left her gasping and was closely followed by a sharp jab in the ear. She wheezed and choked, fought to get out of the heavy blankets to fight back.

Where am I?

A glancing smack on the nose made pain explode in her eye sockets.

Lights went on further down the hall and a soft giggle penetrated her terror. Elizabeth fell back onto the pillows as a smiling cherub peeped over the top of the covers. She'd finally gone insane.

Hallelujah.

At least it wasn't *him.*

The child was beautiful. Gossamer fine curls and big dark blue eyes. Elizabeth reached out to touch a silky tress. Jerked her hand away when she realized the little girl was flesh and blood, not a figment of her imagination.

The child spotted Elizabeth at the same moment and her mouth turned into a round 'O' of confusion.

"Who're you?" the child asked in a high-pitched whisper. "Where's Unca Nat?"

Elizabeth groaned, rubbed her hands over her face as she remembered what had happened last night. Uncle Nat must think she was a freaking nutcase.

The little girl pulled at the bedclothes, searching for her missing uncle.

"I can tell you right now he's not down there." Elizabeth gave up the tug-of-war with the covers. The creak of a floorboard warned her someone was approaching the room. Her muscles froze, her breath lodged in her chest.

A large silhouette loomed and she realized it had to be Nat Sullivan. The missing Uncle. She relaxed slightly. He hadn't hurt her last night when she'd been as vulnerable as a newborn babe—*stupid, stupid woman.*

Leaning against the doorjamb he wore a pair of old denims and an unbuttoned shirt that hung loosely over broad shoulders. The shirt gaped briefly over a lean torso that was ripped with muscle before he started to slowly do up the buttons. She averted her eyes, uncomfortable with the rush of awareness that flooded through her and left her breathless.

"Morning, ma'am."

The smooth tones of his voice sent warm shivers

down her spine. Good shivers—nice shivers—normal shivers. It had been a long time since she'd felt any of those things.

Glancing up, she caught his gaze. Sleep-rumpled and tired-looking, he'd recently been in a fight, she realized. One eye socket was blackened and a series of yellow-blue bruises ran over his jaw and a nasty-looking graze darkened his full lower lip. Dark eyes, the color of square-cut sapphires, twinkled at her, amused. A wide forehead, heavy blond brows and a thin blade of a nose complemented a mouth that looked both sensual and reserved.

He dragged a hand through his hair, made it stick up in blond tufts, then rested his hand against the doorframe.

"Feelin' better?" His voice curled through her, with that slow, sexy drawl. Moving into the room, he smiled an easy smile at the little girl who sat playing peek-a-boo with the covers, and then looked back at Elizabeth.

Fear shot through her system faster than a lightning strike. Where was her gun...? *Damn it!*

Her stomach roiled as she looked down at the child who played on the floor. Thank goodness she hadn't had it.

Nat Sullivan came further into the room, blocked the light as he got closer. He was big enough to fill the space.

Panic raced over her skin like a thousand dancing ants. Elizabeth scooted up the bed and hunched her knees beneath her chin. She wrapped a hand around each ankle as she visually weighed him.

Could she take him?

Too big, too strong. All lean sinew and balanced toned muscles. She forgot to breathe, caught off-guard as he reached the bed and stood beside it, hands hooked in the back pockets of his jeans.

Frantically her gaze searched his face, but there was no malice. No dark intent. The blue eyes sparkled with laughter and despite the firm, hard jaw, his mouth curved into a smile that looked...bruised.

"Where'd you get the shiner?" Her voice was croaky from disuse, or maybe nerves.

One side of his mouth kicked up as if he'd forgotten about the bruises or maybe hoped she wouldn't notice. They must have hurt like hell.

"Let's just say I had a slight disagreement with a couple of guys." He rubbed his bristled chin with a thumb and index finger and she watched, transfixed.

Nodding, she ran her tongue over dry lips, but shrank away from the interest in his gaze as his eyes followed the movement.

"I think your mother gave me directions. Does she live here too...?" She strived to sound casual, knew she'd failed when Nat Sullivan straightened and took an offended step away. Annoyed and backing off.

Thank God.

"She's in the hospital just now, but yeah, she lives here." His brows lowered over don't-flatter-yourself eyes that no longer looked amused. "My sister Sas stayed there last night after her shift finished—she's an ER doc. And Ryan, my brother...well, he's not back yet."

She tried to keep a lid on her alarm, chewed at her bottom lip. "So it's just you and me."

She stiffened as he threw back his head and laughed.

"You, me," he pointed to the little girl who was pulling books off the shelf at the side of the bed. "Tabitha. Couple hundred head of cattle, seventy-six horses, three dogs, two barn kittens, a donkey and a couple hamsters." He laughed again and the deep sound filled the room with warmth. "You're never alone on the Triple H. We've got a couple of hands who live out in the bunkhouse and Sas and Ryan'll probably roll up in time for breakfast. Make the most of the peace and quiet." He made no secret about looking her over now. "It won't last."

Tabitha broke in, her small piping voice loud in the pre-dawn stillness. "Unca Nat?"

Elizabeth remembered to breathe as Nat's attention switched to his niece. Hunkering down he caught her small hand in his, "Yes, Tabby?"

"Is this your girlfriend?"

The quiet laughter had a hard edge that made her shudder, and his glance flickered over her as if he'd spotted her reaction.

"No, Tabitha Rebecca Sullivan, this lady isn't my girlfriend, and *you*," he pointed his finger at her belly and wiggled it, "shouldn't be in here hassling our guests."

He tickled her briefly before he scooped her up under his arm.

"What you doing, Unca Nat?" Tabitha asked between giggles and shrieks.

"Looking for you, Squirt." He tickled his niece again. "And checking up on our guest," his voice was low and warm as he smiled, "making sure she's still alive."

If you only knew.

The tension ebbed as Nat Sullivan turned to leave the room. She relaxed with a sigh that turned into a groan as the big wooden headboard pressed unforgiving against her spine.

"Come on, Tabby. Mizz Reed here looks like she needs more shut-eye. Let's see if she can stay on her feet for the whole day this time, huh?"

Ignoring the heat that flooded her cheeks, Elizabeth pulled the covers back onto the bed and glared at him for no other reason than it made her feel better. He winked at her, ignored her scowl even as she felt her blush spread down her neck. He hoisted his niece over one shoulder and strolled out of the room as if he didn't have a care in the world.

She should be so lucky.

She slumped back into the covers, both bemused and annoyed by Nat Sullivan. "What the hell am I doing here?"

Her hands cradled her forehead and she closed her eyes. Turned her face to the coolness of the pillow and nearly cried at the thought of getting up.

It was 6:10 a.m.

For the first time in months she let herself drift off, sleep stealing her awareness and lulling her into a light doze. The warmth and security of Nat Sullivan's bed provided a sanctuary that she needed more than her life's blood.

***

Federal Plaza, NYC, April 3rd

Marshall Hayes, Special Agent in Charge of the Forgery and Fine arts Division of the FBI held the SAC of the Organized Crime Unit in a two-handed grip, suspended against a wall in the latter's plush NY office. Nicotine laced Ron's breath and Marsh was close enough to see the stains on his teeth. Ron's face pulsed blue-purple, the sort of color that spelled oxygen deprivation and skyrocketing blood pressure. Short legs kicked uselessly off the floor.

Marsh's forearms hurt from the strain of lifting dead weight and his biceps vibrated as muscles began to give. He sucked in a deep, deliberate breath, relaxed his hold a fraction and let the fury dim.

The whites of Ron's eyes were blood-shot and highlighted the dirty blue of his iris's. Pudgy fingers clasped Marsh's wrists like manacles, an intimate embrace between two men who didn't even like each other.

Marsh stepped back, jerked his hands away, fingers stiff with residual tension. Ron clung to him as he slid down the wall and landed with a thud. Marsh shook him off, backed away and listened to the heartbeat in his ears go *thud, thud, thud.*

Ron Moody wasn't worth a murder charge. He wasn't even worth a new suit. Marsh reached down, picked up the gun off the thin beige carpet. Nobody had drawn a weapon on him in years. The type of criminals he dealt with usually used deception and paper trails, not firearms. Ron had been fumbling with his holster from the moment Marsh had opened the door.

Things must be even worse than he'd realized.

Marsh flicked the safety on the weapon and stuck it in his jacket pocket. Slumped in the chair opposite Ron's messy desk, suddenly deflated as adrenaline crashed. Ron was a moron, a classic blue-flamer, who didn't care who he burnt on the way to the top.

"If she's dead, I'll bury you." Marsh kept his voice low as he stared at the view dominated by the Brooklyn Bridge. He turned his head, leveled a flat stare at the man on the floor. "I may even kill you first."

Ron gave an ugly mutt scowl. He breathed heavily, his hands wigwaming on the carpet on either side of his hips.

Marsh reached across the desk, pressed the old-fashioned intercom. He needed information, but first he needed caffeine.

"Can I get a coffee, Alice, please? Better get your boss one, too."

Marsh watched Ron silently. The other man's neck looked too thick for his starched collar; the flesh bulging against the stiff cotton. Ron inserted a stubby finger and leaned back to suck in more air. After a moment, he rose unsteadily to his feet, holding onto the wall for support. He stumbled, just enough to be convincing, before he sank into the black leather throne behind his desk.

Face beet-red, eyes pitifully distressed, Ron rubbed his throat as he waited for Alice to bring in the coffee. Everything about the man confirmed Marsh's deeply held belief that you should never judge by appearances.

After she'd left, Ron cleared his throat. "Elizabeth's not dead." His voice was raspy and coarse.

Marsh waited. Sipped his coffee.

Ron loosened his tie, undid the top button of that constricting shirt.

"DeLattio was looking at twenty years minimum with what we had on him. He had no chance." Ron chuckled, leaned back in his chair with a satisfied rocking motion.

Callous bastard. Marsh clenched his fists tighter, trapped the emotion inside and honed his wrath. To Ron, Elizabeth was nothing more than a means to a career-making arrest.

"Once we accessed his computer, we found more evidence of money laundering and embezzlement than we'd ever suspected. Hundreds of millions of dollars worth." Ron pulled a handkerchief from his suit pocket and swabbed the sweat that streaked his brow. He glanced quickly at Marsh, eyes skittering away before their gazes connected. "But all the players were entered in code. Without DeLattio's help we couldn't pull the evidence together to make the arrests."

Silence hummed between them. Marsh didn't want excuses; he wanted a lead, anything to tell him where his agent had disappeared.

"He's smart." Ron shifted in his seat, held Marsh's gaze for about half a second. Getting braver. "We could find nothing else to pull this thing together, okay?"

No, it wasn't okay. It was not, freaking okay.

Ron crumpled the grubby linen handkerchief under his right hand. "With DeLattio looking at jail time, there was no way he was talking. The DA brokered a deal and now we can wipe out an entire generation of criminals playing the money game. Do you know what that could mean?"

Marsh knew what it meant all right. *Elizabeth hung out to dry. Screwed three ways to Sunday.* He let Ron talk, giving the man enough rope to hang himself.

"Those files contained information on not just

the Bilottis, but South American drug-lords, terrorists, government officials, even dirty cops." Looking calmer now, his color back to a ruddy brick-red, Ron carried on. "Everything went to plan. He never once suspected a woman would have the balls to infiltrate his family's organization. The bugs she planted worked brilliantly."

Marsh knew that Moody was as surprised as the mob that a woman had led the sting on the Bilotti's. Ron still had a hard time dealing with women on equal terms.

Marsh gripped the arms of the chair so he didn't lash out. He kept his voice level, reasonable. "You *screwed* up, Ron." He didn't give a rat's ass about the mob or Ron's bureau credibility. "You sacrificed an agent, *my agent*, who'd repeatedly risked her life for *your* cause."

His agent. His friend. A woman he'd dragged into the bureau when she'd been too young to know better. Marsh clamped down on the self-recrimination that tormented him. He should have looked after her. And she should have damn well known better.

Ron stared back at him with small dense eyes, rat-like—scheming and barely hiding it. The Organized-Crime Unit had used Elizabeth like a tissue and discarded her like garbage. His molars clamped together so tightly his jaw ached. Placing one palm on each thigh, he pressed them down with the full weight of his shoulders. All to keep from punching Ron in the face.

It would definitely make him feel better.

But it might not get him what he wanted.

"Look, Hayes, I know DeLattio is pissed at Elizabeth right now, but he has more important things to worry about than revenge. He still doesn't know she's an agent. *Was* an agent," he corrected quickly. "He just thinks she's a vindictive bitch with more money than sense."

"Who else knows she was working undercover?" Marsh asked. He'd insisted the information had remained need-to-know. His department relied on long term undercover work that unwary agents could blow with a single careless action.

"McCarthy. A couple guys in the DA's office." Ron picked up a pen and tapped it on the desk, on his coffee mug, on his knee. "Johnston may suspect. He's sharp. And his partner, Valdez. The rest of the office thinks she turned state's evidence."

"She thinks you've got a leak in your division, Moody."

"That's bullshit, Hayes, and you know it. We rounded up the mob guys without a hitch. If we had a leak, word would have gotten out." Ron leaned back, sweat once again glistening on his brow.

Marsh didn't agree. He took another drink of coffee and placed the cup back on the floor beside his chair. Leaks could be as low level as a typist or service tech, even the janitor if the agents got sloppy. Or it could be a smart agent knowing when to push the boundaries and when to hold fire.

"Look, I know you're angry, but it's not my fault she bolted." Ron rubbed his bald spot, irritation showing through with each jerk of his hand. Ron Moody wasn't used to placating anybody. His voice was a low rumble as he leaned forward, his eyes narrow beams of annoyance.

"The bottom line is that more people want Andrew DeLattio dead than Jews hate Hitler. If the mob gets him, he ends up drinking the East River. So he testifies, gets a face transplant courtesy of the U.S. government, and lives out the rest of his miserable life in WITSEC." Moody's shoulders dropped as he rested back against his fancy chair and took a slurp of his coffee. "He doesn't have the time or the resources for vengeance."

Marsh rapped short fingernails on the arm of his chair. DeLattio had been bred for violence. Despite his ivy-league education, he'd lived and breathed it, every day of his life. He must have stashed away millions at some point—he'd have been a fool not to. DeLattio didn't strike him as a fool.

Marsh's eyes narrowed.

Ron owed him.

The press coverage had blown two-years of solid undercover groundwork; Elizabeth's life, both undercover and real, was fucked. He stared at Moody without blinking. A cheap trick, but he wanted Ron off-balance.

Ron ran a single digit around his shirt collar. Marsh didn't crack a smile.

"Look, I know the press and the mob want a piece of her, but our sources suggest they don't know any more than we do." Ron hesitated and Marsh knew he was hiding something.

"Spill it," Marsh said.

Ron stared down at his hands that were now on the desk, strangling a pen.

"Rumor has it Peter Uri flew into La Guardia the same day Agent Ward disappeared. We don't know for sure that she was his mark, but we're pretty sure he flew on to Mexico."

"And you just let him go?" Marsh sat up straighter in the chair, too wise to the games of the bureau to be surprised, but horrified just the same. The implications...

Uri was one of the most wanted professional assassins in the world, a shadowy figure with a reputation that was clinical, ruthless and deadly.

"It was only a rumor."

Marsh leaned forward. Grabbed Ron by his fat blue tie and dragged him halfway across the desk with papers flying. Ron knocked his mug, spilled his coffee, eyes pin-balling the damage as he yelped. "Those were my orders, okay? You wanna know why? Go ask your pal Lovine!"

Brett Lovine was the youngest director the FBI had ever had. He was Marsh's boss, but he was also a close personal friend of the Hayes' family. And without Marsh's father, General Jacob Hayes' personal backing, Brett would never have made it past Assistant Director.

Damn straight Marsh would ask him—in private.

Marsh released Ron. His top lip curled with disgust at the sight of the man before him. Ron made him want to put his fist through a wall.

"So what are you going to do now, Ron? Sit on your fat ass and contemplate promotion?"

"What do you want me to do, Hayes? Take off after her myself?" Ron's ruddy jowls wobbled with indignation. Maybe he'd do them all a favor and keel over dead of a coronary. "Special Agent Ward was offered protective custody, but she refused. She resigned. I couldn't detain her, for Christ's sake. We even offered her Witness Protection. Your precious agent told me to shove it where the sun don't shine."

"You offered her the same protection you

offered DeLattio?" Marsh leaned forward, smelled Ron's sharp and acrid fear. "You miserable little prick."

"Now you just listen to me..." Ron spluttered, trailed off, remembering the ease with which he'd been overpowered earlier.

Marsh held perfectly still. He waited as anger bubbled and popped below the surface of his skin, raised an eyebrow to make sure he had Ron's full attention. "No, you listen to me. I want every piece of information you have on Special Agent Ward's disappearance. Every photograph, report and sound-bite. And I want it today, before I leave this building. Before I talk to Director Lovine."

Ron's Adam's apple bobbed convulsively, like he was swallowing string.

Marsh felt no pity. This man had left his agent at the mercy of a monster. Elizabeth could have easily ended up on a slab in the morgue with the protection Ron had offered her—maybe she would have preferred that.

Ron managed a sickly smile. "No problem."

Marsh knew better.

Ron stood up and pulled on his crumpled jacket. Marsh followed him into the inner sanctum of the largest field office in North America.

Chapter Three

Quantico, Virginia, April 3ʳᵈ

"**I** want to know where that bitch is and I want to know now." He slammed his fist into the metal table, wanted to pound it into the floor. Wanted to crush and twist and damage it so desperately he could barely think.

Beware the fury of a patient man.

Give him ten minutes alone with her, and he'd carve the letters onto her flesh.

The email message Charlie had passed on had to have come from her.

Who the fuck did she think she was?

His Italian suit was rumpled and grimy, his tie and belt removed for personal safety reasons. His scalp itched. His unwashed hair was greasy, and three days worth of beard stubbled his chin. Andrew rubbed the uneven bridge of his nose, remembering. It had hurt like fury when he'd finished with the bitch, but not all the blood had been his.

And he still wasn't done with her.

He made his lips curve. The skin on his face crinkled around his eyes, even though he wanted to maim.

He'd first spotted Juliette Morgan at a gallery opening by some up-and-coming nobody from the Lower East Side. To him the pictures had looked no better than blood splatters on a wall. He'd kept his opinions to himself, smart enough to know that the feds were chasing him harder than ever now he was on Wall Street.

He leaned back in his chair. Examined his fingernails; cleaned them with the edge of his teeth.

She'd been smiling at some fat art critic, but not for long. The critic had scuttled away when Charlie had told him to get lost. The critic had known who Andrew DeLattio was. Juliette hadn't had a clue.

He pushed dried cuticle down his thumbnail. Bit away the dead skin. The bitch had looked down her perfect nose at him, elegant eyebrows raised in inquiry, looking like a freaking movie star.

And he'd wanted her. Totally, mindlessly. In every fucking way. He slammed his fist against the table, lowering his eyebrows to hide the hate. She'd hooked into his bloodstream like opium and the more she'd spurned him, the more he'd been determined to have her.

Andrew kicked back on the orange, plastic chair, one foot balanced on the metal table in front of him. The ugly table and chairs provided the only furniture in the utilitarian room. He was being held at Quantico in the heart of the American justice system, protected from his friends and family by Marines.

The irony might have amused him if his uncle, second-in-command of the Bilotti crime-family, hadn't put a contract on his life for a cool five million. Right now Andrew was glad of the protection.

He pulled a cigarette from his pocket and lit it.

His life was ruined because Juliette had opened her big fat mouth, and to think he'd once wanted to marry the bitch. Blowing smoke from his cigarette, he narrowed his gaze at his lawyer. The man treated him like a recalcitrant schoolboy rather than a millionaire businessman with mob connections.

"I've already told you, Andrew," Larry Frazier repeated slowly, like he worked for a dim-witted child. "Juliette Morgan has disappeared without a trace. The FBI has said so, and so have your own sources," the calm tones continued. "Let's move on here, we've a lot of ground to cover."

"You seem to forget that you work for *me*, Larry." Andrew's temper flashed to mercury and he stabbed his finger into his chest. "I am telling you to find out where that bitch is hiding."

He'd grown up with stone-killers for best friends and gangsters for family. The strong ruled, and the weak bent over and took what was coming to them. His birdlike lawyer needed to know that.

"My job is not that of a lackey, Mr. DeLattio, nor that of an accessory." Larry sat back primly in the hard, plastic chair.

Andrew watched the lawyer shuffle his papers with offended efficiency. As if Larry had any real power. As if he could threaten him. Andrew leaned forward, almost amused. The old man was dynamite in the courtroom, but he still didn't get it. Andrew would never get near a courtroom.

Placing his hand over the lawyer's arthritic one, he spoke in a low conversational tone, like an old, trusted friend. "How is Dorothy, Larry? How're the grandkids?"

The man's movements stilled, his watery blue eyes slowly rising toward his client.

"My wife and grandchildren are fine, thank you, Mr. DeLattio." Subtly he tried to break the grip that stayed his hand.

Andrew smiled with genuine amusement.

"I've seen pictures of your girls, Larry," Andrew said. "They look real cute. Your wife is a little old for my taste, you understand...no offense." Fingers crushed bone, releasing a wave of satisfaction that made Andrew's heart pound and the cigarette in his other hand tremble. "You have to take real good care of your family, Larry, especially those cute little girls. Something could happen, something really bad."

He took a drag on the cigarette as the old man's joints cracked under his grip. His lawyer's skin was parchment thin, and felt like it might split if Andrew pressed too hard.

Control was the key.

Larry's gaze faltered. Words locked inside a mouth that opened and shut quickly. Larry had reviewed all the evidence the FBI had on him and knew what he was capable of. *Well, some of it.*

Andrew always kept his promises, something Juliette Morgan was going to find out. He'd promised to slit her throat if she said a word to the cops.

Larry nodded, his fear palpable, which pleased Andrew more than anything had in a long time.

"I'll do what I can to find out Ms. Morgan's whereabouts, Mr. DeLattio. Now you'll have to excuse me, I have to go. I have a court appearance at one." The words were stuttered, voice high-pitched.

Andrew released his lawyer's hand, watched him nurse his sore bones against his chest.

"We still have some time left." Andrew laughed, easy now he'd flexed his muscles, used his power. "We have to go through a couple of things first." He crushed out the cigarette and kicked back

40

in his chair. There was one set of business associates that he hadn't given up, nor would he.

"I want *complete* immunity from prosecution before I say another word to the F—B—I." The letters were stretched out mockingly. "Signed by a federal judge." Andrew smiled like a shark, showing plenty of teeth. "For all the crimes I've committed, *prior* to today."

***

"What's she like?" Ryan caught up with Nat long enough to ask.

Only a full-blown inquisition would satisfy his brother, so Nat kept right on saddling Winter, his white Morgan, and Morven, a quiet bay mare, and shrugged his shoulders. "She's okay."

After an early morning visit to the hospital, he'd gotten a late start. His mother was fine, but now he had cattle to check before dark and the twins were like a couple of dynamos when it came to nosing around for gossip. He'd already had a bellyful from Sas.

"Okay hot or okay ugly?" Ryan asked, rubbing Winter's thick snowy mane and peering at him from under the rim of an old felt hat.

Nat tipped his hat low enough to cover his eyes and prepared to mount up. "Plain, mousy," he lied straight-faced, "not your type."

Ryan looked disappointed and kicked a stone that skittered along the frozen yard.

"Looking for an easy lay, Ry?" Nat tried to keep the bitterness out of his voice. Since Becky had died, Ryan had backfilled the emptiness with beer and sex. While it wasn't for him to judge, some days he figured his little brother needed a good kick up the ass, for his daughter's sake if nothing else.

"Hell," Ryan said, pushing his hat to the back of his dark head. "Couldn't hurt."

Nat swung onto Winter's back with an easy stride. "Yeah," he grunted, "like you don't get enough."

His gut tightened at the thought of Ryan getting it on with Eliza Reed and he didn't know why. No way was he jealous.

"Look somewhere else, Sunshine," Nat told him. He took a deep breath and tried to let go of the tension he couldn't shake. "Hitting on the customers is bad for business."

That sounded reasonable. He let the idea sink in while he checked out the sky. Snow was on the way and he had to get moving.

Eliza Reed bothered him. He didn't have time to start chasing around after some city girl and that bothered him too. He wasn't a monk, so when had life gotten so freaking grim?

About three years ago—chasing around with some other city girl.

Damn.

"She's bad-tempered," Nat said, letting a hint of a smile escape. He tapped a finger against the side of his skull. "Maybe a little crazy."

Ryan squinted up at him, as if the snow was too bright, hooked his thumbs into the front pockets of his jeans. "Why's she still here then?"

"We need the money." Nat's sigh was big enough to make the horse flick back its ears. "Last night, she claimed she thought I was a bear." Nat paused for a moment, adjusted the reins and rubbed a fleck of mud from Winter's withers.

42

"A bear?" Ryan's attention locked onto him.

"Yep," Nat looked over toward the house and nearly groaned as Sas escorted Mizz Eliza Reed out onto the porch. Nat sighed. "Or a wolf."

With the exception of her woolly hat, jacket and boots, Mizz Reed was decked out in his clothes, reminding him he'd forgotten to take her bags up to her room last night. Instead he'd stuffed everything back in the cargo hold of the Jeep. Not that it mattered, her figure filled out his old denims better than he ever did. His heartbeat kicked up a notch and nerves that hadn't twitched for years, started to dance. Her body was curvy, but lean, dark hair pulled back from her face emphasized her bone structure and she was as leggy and sleek as a cat.

Hell, she looked good enough to eat.

Sas handed their guest a pair of riding gloves and waved him over.

It looked like he had no choice but to spend some quality time with Eliza Reed. The ranch hands were out fixing fence-lines down by the reservoir and Sas was on duty at the hospital in a couple of hours. After the conversation he'd just had with Ryan, he sure as hell wasn't going to let *him* entertain their visitor.

Nat turned Winter with pressure from his calf muscles and led Morven out of the paddock toward the main house.

"A wolf, huh?" Ryan's tone was dubious. Climbing onto the bottom rung of the paddock gate, Ryan swung on it as it closed shut. Finally he laughed and shouted just loud enough for Nat to hear. "So you're a wolf, and she's plain and mousy? I'm just trying to figure out which of you is more short-sighted."

***

"Can *I* ride?" Elizabeth muttered as her eyes shot darts into Nat Sullivan's broad back.

He'd stared down at her from that beautiful, gray horse and issued a challenge she'd just had to accept. She'd sent him a look designed to quell any more stupid questions.

'Of course I can ride,' the look had said, *'do I look like a dummy?'*

She sniffed. Dug a tissue from deep in her pocket and blew her nose. She was an idiot. A teenager having weekly English-style riding lessons on well-trained hacks, in heated indoor arenas in Ireland, was a far cry from riding western through the frozen wilderness of Montana. She stuffed the tissue back in her pocket and kicked the horse on.

The mountain air was reminiscent of Christmas, cold and fresh, a hint of crushed pine with a heavy twist of horse and leather. Snow fell lightly. Large cotton-puffs sank slowly down to earth, like down-feathers after a pillow fight.

It was beautiful, but didn't change the fact she was miserable.

Despite the gloves Sarah Sullivan had given her, her hands were numb and she couldn't feel the reins with her fingers. Luckily, Morven followed Nat's stallion like the biddable mare she was.

No match for the weather, Elizabeth's trousers were damp where the snow had melted against the mare's dark coat, and her thighs were rubbed red-raw. The tip of her nose was frozen, lips chapped and cracked. And her butt ached, not just a small ache, but deep spasms in muscles that had been awakened after more than a decade of dormancy.

"Can I ride, huh?"

"Say something?" Nat reined his horse aside and took a long look at her. The hot, vivid, wild-fire of his eyes pierced her like a knife.

Elizabeth managed to hold his gaze and shook her head. Unfortunately, despite the bruises, Nat Sullivan had a handsome face. In fact, the yellow and purple wounds made him better looking, less perfect, more human, sexier. She held back a shudder. Noticed the way weak sunlight stroked the dark blond hair that showed below his cowboy hat, highlighting flaxen streaks. His jaw looked carved out of stone. Strong sculpted cheekbones. Deep grooves bracketing a wide mouth.

And for some reason when he frowned at her the way he was doing now, she simply couldn't put a coherent sentence together. She didn't know if it was fear or exhaustion that affected her, so she kept her mouth shut. Elizabeth willed her lips to curl upwards, but they were frozen in place and might crack if she tried too hard. *Frozen, inside and out.*

"Just one more pasture to check, then we can head back. Can't afford to leave any sick animals out in this weather," Nat said.

She nodded, wishing desperately she hadn't come. The man seemed impervious to the cold, but then he wore chaps and a thick sheepskin coat.

She tried to concentrate on the scenery. The Flathead Range stretched as far as the eye could see, over the Continental Divide and into the eastern Rockies. Magnificent; nature at its most beautiful and most unforgiving. Big pines and Douglas firs were draped with heavy stoles of snow, their lower branches bowed sharply under their burden. The whole world was silent. A hard silence that amplified any noise they made, like wearing high-heels in church.

Not a creature stirred, not a soul moved.

Except them.

The horses kicked up plumes of white snow as they carefully picked their way through the trees. Morven's breath came out with small puffs of steam that condensed and drifted away on the breeze. Elizabeth sniffed and wiped her nose, listening to her saddle creak, a gentle rhythmic sound that reminded her of those early riding lessons and lost childhood dreams.

The world was monochrome, the sky pewter, the jagged mountains a deeper shade of slate. She had no idea where she was or how far they'd ridden. They'd been out for hours and she was completely disoriented with a man who amounted to a total stranger.

Under normal circumstances she could take care of herself.

But she'd learned to expect the unexpected.

Numb fingers gathered the reins in one hand and she rapidly opened and closed the other hand to try and warm it. She switched hands, determined not to succumb to the harshness of the elements.

Her sidearm was still in the Jeep.

Dumb.

Not that Nat Sullivan seemed like a threat—not the way DeLattio had from the first moment she'd felt him watching her. Like a cat watched a mouse before it dug in its claws. Her heartbeat accelerated. Breath tightened in her throat as images burned through her mind. Christmas lights. Music. Champagne. Whirling darkness until she'd woken up tied to her own bed.

She jerked as Nat pulled to a halt at the edge of a pasture. Cattle huddled together beneath a sturdy wooden shelter, tucked into the far edge of the meadow. They munched down on bags of hay that had been strung out for them.

"Stay put," Nat said, nodded towards a thick belt of yellow pine, "it'll be more sheltered here."

"I'm okay," Elizabeth said and smiled to try to prove it.

Nat looked at her as if for the first time. His eyes pinned her where she sat, stripped away the layers of expression and flesh, bone and bitter determination.

She licked her lips, swallowed and looked away, suddenly scared by what he might see. A moment later she heard him head off. He turned the gray, opened the gate without dismounting, and cantered across the pasture. Morven nosed around the thicket that edged the fence-line, looking for anything edible to chew. Embarrassment and awkwardness forced doubts through her mind, but nothing she wasn't used to. The poor little rich girl, always left behind for the holidays because her family was dead.

At least working for the FBI had given her a reason to live. A purpose.

Determined to cut off self-pity before it overwhelmed her, she watched Nat Sullivan. Noted the graceful way he rode the gray, making even a trot look smooth. The gentle touches of reins against the horse's neck, subtle shifts of his long legs that guided the horse around obstacles and those big broad shoulders that looked big enough to carry the world.

He was handsome. But Andrew DeLattio had been handsome too.

She lifted her chin against the frigid wind, ignored the hair that danced across her cheeks. It would have bothered most people, but she welcomed the veil.

Nat Sullivan probably thought she was a bad-tempered bitch; she'd been so surly.

An old tin bath sat just outside the shelter and she watched him smash the ice in the trough. Then he dismounted and went inside the lean-to, disappearing from view.

Shivers started, wracked her body. She curled up as tight as she could over the pommel and tucked her hands under her armpits in an effort to maintain warmth. Huddling into her jacket, she tried to imagine a desert island where the sun was hot enough to feel the UV burn.

Time drifted.

She wrenched her head up as the grind of the gate warned her Nat was back. He looked at her from beneath the rim of his snow-covered cowboy hat.

"Everything okay?" His blue eyes assessed her and seemed to find her wanting.

Elizabeth straightened her spine. Felt each vertebrae realign.

"Of course," she lied.

Nat snorted. One side of his mouth kicked up into a wry smile and Elizabeth realized he knew exactly how 'okay' she was feeling.

The sonofabitch was waiting for her to crack. Her eyes narrowed into twin beads of annoyance.

Nat leaned over the horn of his ornately carved saddle, his voice soft and warm. "Just one more field to check—"

"What?" The word cannonballed out of her mouth before she could stop it.

He laughed and she watched open-mouthed as he tried to hide it, to turn it into a cough behind his leather-clad fist.

"Sorry, just kidding, couldn't resist." His mouth turned rueful, blue eyes softened. "You look colder than an ice-cube in the Arctic. You should have said something—I'd have taken you home."

Angry heat spiked through her system and Elizabeth didn't know whether to hit him or thank him.

"We're heading back now. Got about a ten minute ride back to the ranch house from here."

"What?" Elizabeth repeated, stupidly.

"Ten minute ride." He looked at her closely, not missing a thing. "Think you can make it?"

Elizabeth nodded. She didn't trust herself to speak. Sometimes she thought if she opened her mouth and started talking, she wouldn't be able to stop until all the blackness and bitterness spilled out like tar. She kicked-on the horse after Nat, who already led the way.

Ten minutes. She just had to survive another ten minutes. Morven brushed past a branch that whipped back and dumped its load of snow straight into her lap.

Damn.

Frantically she brushed at the snow, stood up in the stirrups, holding onto the raised pommel. She did not want a frozen crotch.

Next thing she knew she lay flat on her back on the ground, looking up at the snowflakes that drifted out of the gray sky. Great white dots that got bigger and bigger, brighter and whiter as they got closer.

For a blessed moment she could hear nothing, feel nothing, taste nothing.

Then her head reeled and white pain exploded inside her brain. Iron flooded her mouth. Her eyes were blinded and dazzled. She wanted to retch, but she couldn't move.

She'd ridden straight into the branch of a huge cedar. Her vision cleared slowly, dot by dot. She watched suspended from reality as Nat turned back towards her, a look of resigned panic on his face. His mouth moved, but she couldn't make out what he said over the ringing in her ears.

He bent over her, gently kneading her limbs. His lips moved soundlessly as she waited for the fear to overtake her, to strangle reason and paralyze her with dread. She couldn't explain the cheated feeling that seeped through her when it didn't happen.

"Can you hear me?" He squatted on one knee beside her. No longer touching, but carefully watching.

Probably wondering why on earth she hadn't moved.

Crap.

She held herself very still while she regained her equilibrium. Found herself staring into eyes so blue they looked like you could dive right in.

"I'm okay," she managed. Her voice came out croaky, like some geriatric smoker. She forced herself up onto her elbows and her stomach recoiled.

Nat leaned back on his haunches and gave her a slow look she couldn't decipher.

"You ever been anything but *okay*, Miss Reed?"

Too observant. Too perceptive. Elizabeth

TONI ANDERSON

swallowed and nodded once, briefly. Tears burned her eyes, but she forced them away. She couldn't afford to be weak now, couldn't cope with sympathy. She'd made mistakes and she dealt with them the only way she knew how.

Alone.

Struggling to her feet, she flailed in the deep snow. Nat held out his hand and she hesitated only briefly before reaching out and letting him pull her to her feet. He held her hand in his, gently, but firmly.

Touching him, even with gloves on, was like touching fire. Heat and energy scoured her down to her toes.

Uneasy, she jerked away and felt even more foolish than she had before. She busily swept snow off her clothes. Out of the corner of one eye she watched the cowboy. He stood about a foot away, hat tipped to the back of his head, regarding her critically. He grinned openly when she brushed the snow off her backside.

"You could ride up behind me, you know," he said, "if you're not feeling too good."

She forced a smile. Everything she'd been through, everything she'd suffered over the last few months pressed against her mind and tried to shut down the pretense.

"I'm okay." The response was automatic and she grimaced.

"Sure, you are." He pulled his hat forward before turning away to fetch the horses.

And she fought the urge to cry.

Tears did no good.

He stood behind her as she tried to remount Morven. Not touching her, but waiting, as if to catch her if she fell. She could feel his eyes bore into her back and knew he was waiting to give her a leg-up. If only she said the word. If only she asked.

She clamped her lips together. She didn't want to need anybody. Didn't want anyone's help. She especially didn't want to have Nat Sullivan's hands on her body reminding her of heaven and hell with one simple touch.

Her head thumped and she felt lightheaded.

On the third attempt she managed to haul herself into the saddle with more luck than grace. Relief shunted through her body with a huff and the smile she gave him was brilliant.

"Made it."

Nat held Morven's reins as if judging her competence. She raised her chin a fraction, combated the wooziness by concentrating on the jagged edge of the distant mountains.

"From the depths of hell," he said finally.

Chapter Four

Boston, April 3rd

Like a switch being thrown, Marsh figured out Elizabeth had gotten herself a decoy.

He'd captured stills from surveillance footage taken in the days prior to Elizabeth's disappearance, and run them through in-house image-recognition programs.

Someone had spent a day impersonating Elizabeth in her role as Juliette Morgan, before the decoy too had disappeared. It was simple, but clever. Agent Ward had gained herself twenty-four hours before every mobster from here to San Francisco realized she'd slipped the noose.

Now he had a lead. All he had to do was track down the decoy, Josephine Maxwell.

Sounded easy.

He sat behind his utilitarian wooden desk in his neat and tidy office in his division's headquarters. Laid out in front of him was everything he needed to know about Josephine Maxwell, except her current whereabouts.

Eighteen years ago, a nine-year-old girl had been knifed in Queens. Badly knifed if the reports were to be believed, and the doctors hadn't expected the child to live. They'd fingerprinted her routinely—to distinguish hers from those of her attacker on the knife that had pinned her to the ground. And because she was a runaway, her prints

53

had gone into the system.

The phone rang, but he ignored it.

He'd met Josephine once, briefly. Recognized her from the surveillance photos only after he'd put the pieces together. She looked seventeen and acted twelve. She was tall, as Elizabeth was tall, but willow-slim like a wraith. She must have worn body padding under the flashy suit she wore in the photographs. Her lips looked soft and full, the top one larger than the bottom, another subtle difference between the two women.

Breathtaking.

Her eyes held the essence of her beauty. Bright blue, full of mystery. A woman with the face of a princess and the temper of an alley cat. She'd loathed him on sight, not a reaction he usually got from women. He placed both fists carefully on the table and stared at the file.

He was missing something.

From the age of six, Josephine Maxwell had been in the system, removed from an alcoholic father. But every time she was placed in foster care, she bided her time and escaped back to the slums.

Marsh had an address for Josephine's father but had no idea if he was still there. Sighing, he rubbed his fingers through his short hair. He'd check it out.

The police report from the knife-attack contained a photograph of a thin, hollow-eyed girl. He chewed on the end of a pen as he stared at the photograph. She was an enigma, a sewer rat with the looks of a supermodel and the wits of a street fighter. A beautiful blonde, who was about as far removed from a bimbo as cat food was from truffles.

He brought his mind back to his current

problem—how to find Elizabeth. Elizabeth was thorough, smart, and she'd had plenty of time to set things up. She was also as rich as Rockefeller and a creature of habit. She was doggedly loyal to those she cared about and liked having backup plans. They both did.

And she liked to nail the bad guys.

Andrew DeLattio had destroyed the girl he'd known, the girl Marsh had recruited for the FBI and turned into a damn good undercover operative. Unlike OCU's surveillance, his team would have protected her.

He pressed his fingers to his temples and leaned back in his chair. Marsh would only find Elizabeth if she wanted him to. Josephine Maxwell, however, was another matter.

***

"We gonna lose her?" Cal asked.

"Not if I can help it." Nat's teeth were clenched so hard the words escaped in a hiss. He knelt in fresh hay next to a chestnut mare. Hands resting on her heaving flank, he tried to soothe her with gentle words of encouragement. The foal was breech. If he stretched his hand far enough inside the mare, he could just feel tiny hocks. A rare event in equine labor but not insurmountable.

But that wasn't the real problem. The real problem was that Banner, the ten-year-old Arab brood mare, was exhausted. She'd labored hard for close to sixteen hours and the foal hadn't moved more than an inch. Nat had watched her from outside the loosebox for most of the day. Things had started okay, but as time crept on, he'd realized the mare was in trouble.

The lights were dimmed. A strip-light further up the center aisle of the stable block cast strong shadows.

Nat needed this foal. His fist curled over sweating palms as the mare bore down with another contraction. His pulse-rate accelerated until it was an unremitting roar in his ears. He needed this foal to live. He needed something to hope for.

When it had become obvious they were in for another freezing cold night in Montana, he'd turned on the heat. Spring hadn't sprung in the Treasure State yet. He just prayed the utility company didn't cut them off. They had a backup generator in the root cellar, but that only supplied the main house.

Most of their horses were kept in the horse-barn next door, but nursing and pregnant mares were cosseted here, in separate boxes with individual feeding regimes. The stable block was smaller than the horse-barn, built on concrete foundations that were easy to clean and maintain. Each of the twelve loose-boxes were floored with fresh hay and foam mats, more comfortable for the mares to stand on, they could be hosed down after mucking out.

Five years ago, it had been state-of-the-art.

His father had been building up the brood-stock and getting the facilities ready to turn the Triple H into a stud farm. It had been a dream they'd all shared. Now Jake Sullivan was dead and his medical bills had wiped out their finances. Paint peeled off the walls, the foam mats were ragged around the edges and the woodwork was in dire need of a coat of varnish. But there was no money for the little things.

"Veterinarian coming?" Cal stroked the mare's

sleek cheek, looked at Nat with sharp hazel eyes that had seen too much. Cal was more than just a hired hand; he and Nat had been friends since they were boys, through thick and thin.

Nat snorted. "Vet said he was pretty busy."

Cal cursed a blue streak. Nat compressed his mouth into a thin line as he reined in his own temper. He'd phoned the vet five times and got nothing but the damned answering machine. It couldn't be a coincidence. The vet wasn't a local man. He was a newcomer from LA who'd just bought the practice in town. He had a penchant for shiny toys. Toys like the silver BMW Troy Strange had reputedly given him as a 'thank you' for saving his golden Labrador after it had chased a lone wolf up into the foothills. Damn dog was too stupid to live, but somehow the vet had saved it.

Figured. Seemed it was no longer survival of the fittest, instead it was survival of the richest.

The games his neighbor and his sex-crazed wife played were becoming more than just burrs in Nat's side.

The mare was in second stage labor. The placenta had ruptured with a gush of yellow-brown liquid three hours ago. Nat had been buoyant, optimistic, but his mood had darkened as time had dragged on.

Normally second stage lasted twenty-to-thirty minutes.

Nat left the loose-box to fetch a length of thick cord. He scrubbed it in a bucket of hot soapy water and hoped to hell he knew what he was doing. The mare was suffering and wouldn't last much longer.

"Called Logan." Nat wiped sweat from his brow with his shirt sleeve, swallowed sawdust along with despondency. "He can't get here for at least another hour."

Logan Ryder was the former vet's son, a friend from way back, who ranched down near Hungry Horse. His old man had died last spring, but Logan had spent his youth helping out his father and had more foaling experience than anybody Nat knew.

"One of his kids cut themselves on some broken glass," Nat said.

"Serious?" Cal asked.

"The kid?" Nat looked up from scrubbing his hands. Shaking his head, he moved his hair out of his face with an impatient swipe. "Nah, Logan said she was okay, just needed a bunch of stitches."

Cal nodded towards the cord. "What you gonna do?"

"Gonna get this foal out before Banner dies trying."

Despite the chill, Nat was stripped down to his undershirt, sleeves rolled up. He soaped his hands, rinsed them well and soaped them again. Sweat gathered on his brow and ran down the sides of his face. His hair was damp with perspiration, his clothes rumpled and stained. Exhaustion weighted his muscles like water drag.

Nat made a noose with the cord and waited until the mare finished a contraction. Banner had gotten weaker, head lolling, her breath shallower after every muscle action. He inserted his hand, pushing the rope before him, then nudged the loop out in front of his fingers as he pushed against thick vaginal walls. His arms screamed with tension as he reached fully into the mare and felt just the tip of a sharp little hoof kick against his hand.

A spurt of energy buzzed around his body. At

least the foal was still alive. Forcing himself to go just an inch further, he bit down in pain as another contraction hit and his arm was squeezed in a vise. Bones and joints compressed, pain shooting along nerves from his fingers to his elbow. He concentrated on the foal, not the pain, gritted his teeth and breathed out through his nose. The contraction stopped and Nat pressed forward and managed to loop not one, but two tiny hooves.

Hallelujah.

A fierce grin contorted his face as he pulled the coil tight, dragged the hooves back toward him. When he leaned forward again, he could just get a grip on the foal's fetlocks.

"Get the rope," he urged Cal.

Cal knelt behind him in the hay, gathered the slack as Nat tightened his grip on the foal. There was no time to waste.

"Next time she has a contraction, heave," Nat said. He braced himself against the mare's flank.

"Now!" Nat felt the muscles begin to bear down on his arm. He and Cal pulled as hard as they could while the contraction lasted. The mare kicked uselessly, clearly in agony, but too weak to fight.

The foal *had* shifted towards them.

He sensed rather than heard someone slip into the stable block and walk down the center aisle towards the stall. Pungent smells of horse and sweat filled the air. The wind rustled the skinny branches of the quaking aspens in the nearby forest so hard they rattled.

"Sas?" Nat shouted. He desperately needed some medical help.

"No," Eliza Reed said. "It's me."

Nat looked over his shoulder and saw her peer

uncertainly over the top of the half door.

The woman would be suspicious of water. He turned back to the mare. He didn't have time to play tour-guide right now. Banner and her foal were dying.

Cal braced his knees on the ground as Nat prepared for the next contraction. Banner's head lay still against the fresh hay, her breath a thin thread of steam from her nostrils.

"What's going on? Where's the vet?" Eliza Reed's voice rose accusingly, clipping the Irish to a hard edge.

"Foal's stuck." Nat stroked the mare's coat with his free hand. "Vet's busy."

He concentrated on the struggling mare. He'd bet a hundred-to-one the vet would have come to the aid of the likes of Mizz Eliza Reed.

"What do you mean the vet's busy?" Her hoity-toity voice was outraged.

"Too busy for the likes of us," Nat said not looking up. "That's what I mean." It was a damned shame. Banner was one of the most beautiful horses he'd ever known. Even tempered, but brave. She had pure Egyptian bloodlines and was worth thousands of dollars, but even that didn't matter now. He just wanted this beautiful creature and her foal to live.

Another contraction began.

"Come on, Banner!" Nat urged.

Nat and Cal heaved with all their strength and again the foal shifted toward them. His teeth came together with a snap of anger. He'd seen so much suffering and death in the last few years he was sick to his stomach of it. *Please God, spare the mare.*

"Come on girl."

She was gonna die.

She was gonna die because their damned Texan neighbor had some twisted desire to force them out.

Eliza Reed slipped into the stall, skirted around them, and went to kneel beside Banner's head.

He and Cal gathered for another effort. Banner was beginning to lose consciousness, her head laying still, her sides going lax.

Eliza placed a hand on the mare's broad cheek, softly, like she was afraid to touch.

"Can I help?" Her luminous green gaze locked on his. Nat looked away, but was drawn back reluctantly. There was something terribly vulnerable about the fierce determination he saw there. Something he didn't want to acknowledge.

"Only if you believe in miracles," he said.

Eliza's eyes went flat. She shook her head.

Banner stopped breathing for a second. Nat's stomach coiled like a snake in his gut.

"Come on, girl," Nat shouted, "Come ON!"

Time had run out. They had to get the foal out of there. Cal grabbed a bucket of cold water and doused the mare's back. She jolted and another contraction hit. Nat pulled on the cord with all his might, sinew stretching and muscles bulging with effort. Eliza joined him, straining against the rope, her breath coming in broken gasps behind him.

The foal was stuck fast. The mare shuddered violently and then lay still.

"Damn it to hell!" Nat's bellow reverberated around the stables, but the mare didn't stir. He bowed his head, fighting back the sense of defeat that threatened to overwhelm him.

The mare lay motionless, her sides unmoving, her breath finished.

Dead.

Banner was *dead.*

They'd needed a miracle but it hadn't come.

Eliza Reed was staring at him, wide-eyed, on her knees in the damp straw.

Nat's teeth were clenched so hard they could have been fused. He swallowed. It was too late. Banner was dead. Numb on the inside, he took out his hunting knife, the blade six inches long and as sharp as a scalpel.

"What are you doing?" Eliza asked.

Kneeling next to the mare he put his hand on her warm flank, said a silent prayer for forgiveness and cut. He cut deep. Deep enough to expose the mare's insides.

Despite death, the muscle contracted violently against the action of the knife. It curled up like heated plastic at the edges. Nat ignored the life-like spasms and cut quickly, careful not to slice into the unborn foal. Finally, with a whoosh of amniotic fluid Nat pulled the foal out.

It wasn't breathing.

"Fuck." He was vaguely aware that Cal and Eliza watched him with open-mouthed expressions of horror and distaste, but he didn't care. Blood soaked the ground, soaked his clothes.

Nat cursed again, cleaned the mucus from the newborn's nostrils. He clamped his left hand over the mouth and lower nostril and blew a big breath through the top nostril, deep into the tiny animal's lungs.

Nothing.

He wiped his mouth, prayed and did it again, and again, compressed the tiny ribs down with a solid push—once, twice, three times. The foal coughed, gagged and opened its eyes.

Nat couldn't believe it.

Holy damn, he'd actually done it. His neck muscles strained so tight his tendons felt like they'd snap and his heart drummed like a marathon runner on the home stretch. Overwhelmed, he stared at the tiny creature as it started to breathe on its own. Body shaking crazily, hands trembling with palsy, Nat realized he'd saved the foal. With his hand over mouth, he stumbled to the corner of the stall and threw up.

Tears slid down his cheeks, unchecked, emotions raw and exposed. Wiping his mouth, he looked over his shoulders at the foal. The colt was pure black, not an ounce of color in his midnight hide. He had a perfect dished profile, huge liquid eyes and wide nostrils that flared wide with each breath.

Nat couldn't move, couldn't even reach out his hand to touch the newborn. The foal tried to stand, four delicate legs teetering beneath him like twigs in the wind. Cal bent down to remove the rope from the foal's legs and rubbed him with fresh hay, getting rid of the damp mucus and blood.

"You saved him." Eliza Reed's voice was rough, no more than a whisper in the shadows.

Relief hit him. Then raw grief settled in as he looked at the mare. His mouth turned arid as he caught Eliza's gaze, her green eyes huge and brilliant with tears. His own eyes burned again, but he forced himself to get on with the work. He had to clean up Banner, feed the foal.

"Hey?" Shouts echoed down the stable block.

"Nat?" A door banged and footsteps approached.

"You in there?" Logan's deep voice cut through the darkness.

"Back here." Nat forced the words past shaky vocal cords.

"She okay?" Sas ran down the aisle, bundled up in a thick down-jacket, carrying her black doctor's bag. She drew to a halt and her eyes went huge as she stared at the colt. "He's beautiful. Oh, Nat, he's gorgeous." Then she saw the mare, lying cut open beside him. "Sweet Jesus."

Nat crawled around to the mare's head, touched her cheek. "She didn't make it."

Grief hit him like electric rain—stupid because she was just a horse. But she'd been beautiful, and hadn't deserved to die like that, in pain, and desperate. No animal did. He was a rancher and a wildlife photographer, knew the twists and turns of Mother Nature better than most, but nothing had prepared him for such an unnecessary death.

A vet could have saved her.

The foal nosed his hand with velvet lips and Nat looked into the tiny creature's midnight eyes. The little fellow was hungry and wondering where his mama was. He had to get the foal to a surrogate soon, or he had months of bottle-feeding to look forward to.

The door of the stable block banged shut and Nat was surprised by the flash of disappointment he felt when he realized Eliza Reed had left the barn.

Shrugging, Nat turned and watched Logan examine the foal. He broke the umbilical with a sharp jerk, checked the heart rate with the palm of his hand against the thorax.

"I had to resuscitate him." Nat's voice was gruff, the walls of his throat tight with anguish.

"Looks pretty damn good to me. I'll give him a couple of shots, just in case." The big rancher covered the tiny animal with a blanket to keep him warm. "Got a mare lined up?"

Nat nodded, and prayed to God that the mare would accept a second foal.

"Bumped into Logan at the end of my shift," Sarah explained. "He told me Banner was having problems and the vet couldn't get up here."

Nat nodded. Bitterness wouldn't do him any good, but he couldn't let it go.

"I'll remember that if I ever come across the SOB in a road traffic accident." She swore softly. Sas might look tiny and sweet, but she was just as ornery as the rest of them. She went over to stand next to the foal, stroked his inquisitive black nose and hugged Cal loosely with her other arm.

"What're you gonna call him?" Logan asked softly.

Tonight should have been a time to rejoice, but death and hardship tempered it. Nat said nothing for a moment. There was still work to be done and he'd be lucky to see his bed before dawn.

"Redemption." Nat looked at the delicate black form. "Red, for short."

"He looks like a Red to me," Cal said, keeping his arm tightly clasped around Sarah's waist.

"An awful big burden to put on such tiny shoulders." Sarah softly stroked the foal's quivering nose.

"He'll grow into it." Logan came to stand next to Nat, clapped him on the back. "He's gonna be a champ, just like his papa."

Nat said nothing and prayed.

He hoped it was enough.

***

Tears ran down her cheeks, great ribbons of emotion that flowed like rain, and dripped from her chin. She'd never seen birth before nor death. Never beheld that pure moment when all promise and expectation crystallized into something as wonderful as a newborn foal. Or experienced the agonizing void of helplessness when life ceased. She stumbled out of the stable, barely able to see where she was going. She could hardly breathe, hardly draw the air past her constricted throat as she tried to control the sobs. Blindly, she reached out as a fence loomed in the darkness.

The training ring.

She'd seen violence and evil, wickedness and corruption. But there was more power in that single moment of birth than in everything she'd witnessed while working for the FBI. Power so huge it was staggering. Humbling, heartbreaking, real.

She climbed the rungs and sat astride the top, letting the solitude embrace her, crying her eyes out as she stared sightlessly at the stars above.

She'd loved working undercover at first, before it had sucked out her soul, leaving her as empty as an actor in a never-ending stage play. A grand adventure for a lonely girl with too much money and not much of anything else. She held the top rail between both hands, squeezed the unrelenting wood as hard as she could. She'd had a boring, lonely childhood, raised in the very best private schools, visiting her aunt in America only for the longer breaks. Money was a poor substitute for friendship—a hollow family to love.

Special Agent in Charge Marshall Hayes had approached her during one of her trips to Boston. She swiped at the tears that rolled down her cheeks. His mother and her aunt had been matchmaking— trying to consolidate the family fortunes no doubt. He'd been handsome, exciting. A real live FBI agent.

And he'd pursued her all right. Cornered her in his home office and shown her the FBI recruitment website. With her dual American/British citizenship and master's degree in Art History she had the perfect background for his team. He wanted her. She just had to pass her basic training.

She pulled a tissue from her pocket and blew her nose. She'd worked her balls off to get through the sixteen weeks of boot camp. Reveled in the challenge—loved the excitement and the sense of danger, longed for the chance to finally prove her worth beyond her bank balance.

But what she'd discovered was that, on the scales of justice, her worth barely registered.

Life sucked. Then you died.

A wolf howled high in the hills. The sound echoed off the outbuildings and reverberated around the yard. A lonely, mournful sound that felt fitting somehow.

She'd been scouting out the ranch, checking the outbuildings and vantage points from within the trees. She'd even had her cover story all worked out before she'd realized these people wouldn't care if she snooped around, investigated the place. They had nothing to hide. They'd just think she was plain, old-fashioned nosey.

She rubbed her thighs against the cold as loneliness stole over her, made her think about the things she didn't have, couldn't have—like family. She had a few friends, but none she could turn to now. To involve anyone else in her life was too dangerous.

Josie was safe enough as long as she stayed low, and she was street-smart.

Elizabeth wiped the tears from her cheeks with the cuffs of her jacket. She missed Marsh, and Dancer, and all the gang from the Forgeries and Fine Arts Division. But she couldn't go to them. Marsh had warned her not to get involved with the Organized Crime Unit's investigation and told her to steer clear of DeLattio. She'd ignored his advice and plowed on. Thought she could handle it. Thought she was clever.

She hooked a strand of hair behind her ear. This was her problem, her mess and she'd clear it up.

A noise behind her startled her and made her jump. She fell off the top rung into the soft sand of the training ring. Her hand slid to the shoulder holster she'd started wearing again, hidden beneath her jacket.

"Sorry," Nat Sullivan said out of the darkness, "didn't mean to startle you."

"No, no, you're all right." Elizabeth pulled her hand away from her gun. The man made her nervous, but she wasn't scared of him. Most men made her nervous nowadays. "Sorry." She wiped her eyes again embarrassed to be caught crying. "I've never seen anything like that before." Elizabeth found words to try to cover her emotions. "I've never seen anything born before."

"Well," his voice was troubled, eyes pensive, "I'm not so sure he was born so much as ripped out."

He stood a yard away, watching her through the gap between the top rail and the next one down, blood-soaked, dirty and rumpled, in his shirtsleeves on a freezing cold night.

He didn't even shiver. Didn't appear to feel the cold.

She wrapped her arms tight around her body and wished she had even a fraction of his warmth. He stood absolutely still, but she could feel his energy vibrate through the air. His eyes shone with dark emotions—exhaustion, frustration, grief.

She understood the darker side of life, understood the nature of guilt.

"He'd have died if you hadn't cut him out." She spoke quietly. Mindful of the dead.

"Yeah," he said, "probably." He placed his hands on the wooden rail between them, leaned closer. "Thanks, for your help."

"I didn't do much good." Elizabeth swallowed, felt the tears burn again. She wanted to reach out and clutch those warm capable hands. There were some days when she needed refuge, isolation from the slightest touch, others, like today, when she wanted to be held so desperately she ached.

She didn't move.

"I'm sorry," she managed, "about the mare."

He nodded, lips twisted. "Me too." Half turning away, he hesitated and looked down at the ground.

"Your accent..." he tilted his head to look at her, "where'd you say you were from?"

Blindsided, she sucked in a quick, startled breath. "I didn't say." The words were too sharp, too hard. "I mean, it's not a simple answer." She came from everywhere and nowhere. It would take a lifetime to explain.

He nodded, smiled as if she'd said something amusing.

"It's beautiful—wherever it's from."

Surprise jolted her on the spot. He turned back toward the stables and as she watched him walk away, the breeze chased him as if it already missed his company. It whipped her hair across her cheek and rustled the branches of the trees behind her.

She shivered as the night closed around her, pressed against her like a wet blanket. She wanted to follow Nat back into the stables, absorb his warmth and discover what really went on behind those vivid blue eyes

But she didn't have the guts.

The wolf howled again, lost and lonely. Another wolf answered, then another, and another. The eerie cries picked up and echoed off the trees, through the ditches and valleys, across the wide-open spaces.

She climbed the fence, kept a close eye on the caliginous forest as she made her way back to her cabin. Touching the Glock holstered beneath her jacket, she reminded herself she was safe for now. Wild things wouldn't hurt her, but it wasn't wild things she was worried about.

Ten minutes later, she huddled up in the cottage's double bed wearing a New York Giants T-shirt that came almost to her knees. One hand crept under the pillow, an inch away from her Glock as she tried to fall asleep.

Nat Sullivan's face formed in her mind, glowing eyes with that half smile of his that warmed her from the inside out. She wanted to touch him so badly that her hand actually reached out, but she let it fall back down to the cool sheets. She fell asleep and dreamed. The foal gamboled about, the mare's eyes pain-filled, but accepting. Accepting death.

Suddenly she was running fast, lungs bursting with the effort, her body slick with sweat, stumbling, unable to see through the fog that crawled over the ground. She couldn't see him, but he was close. Too close. Right on her heels. Dogging her.

Shadows shifted and he was straight ahead. Whirling away she lurched suddenly over the edge of a cliff. Fear scraped at her throat as she wheeled again, but there was no escape. He was there. At the edge of the shadows. Watching her. Reaching for her. Shapes shifted, black and gray then coalesced into a solid malevolence. She watched, frozen, as a man began to form out of the fog.

"Daddy," she cried and thrust her arms towards the shadow. But the shadow turned black, and laughed.

Blood-stained hands grabbed at her, and she whirled and threw herself over the edge of the cliff. She screamed as the air whipped past her face, falling and falling. She heard his laughter and screamed again.

Elizabeth jerked awake, the scream echoing through the cabin. Tangled sheets pinned her down. She fell back onto the pillows, her breath harsh in the cold room.

The fire had gone out.

Sweat turned to ice on her flesh as she realized where she was.

It was just a dream. Just another dream.

Gritty-eyed and tired, she huddled in the blankets and tried to think of nothing. Not blood, nor death, not fear nor pain, not humiliation, not rape and not Andrew DeLattio. But it didn't matter

how hard she tried, her mind just kept replaying the
videotape.

Chapter Five

Breathing hard, Elizabeth bent over and rested gloved hands against jean-clad thighs. The cold air burned her lungs as she snatched in huge gulps of it. The bright blue sky stretched out like a canvas above her, broken white clouds splotched across it like a child's painting. No ominous gray clouds today, though Sarah Sullivan had told her that could change in a heartbeat.

Elizabeth's eyes hurt; she hadn't slept much last night—nothing unusual in that. Stretching up, her muscles loosened and eased. She rested her hands on her hips and looked around. The mountains reared up before her, snow covered granite that looked as unforgiving as broken glass. It looked a barren place near the summit of those spiky peaks. Swathes of conifers stretched dark green across the lower reaches of the mountain, cut off sharply at the tree line. Pine, fir, larch and aspen slowly merged on the far side of the meadow, breaking up the monotony of the landscape.

She didn't need to go much further.

Trudging across the meadow she was grateful for the snowshoes Sarah had given her; they made walking in the deep powder much easier. She followed a trampled path into the trees and looked down among the underbrush where she could see the tracks of wild things crisscrossing the snow. Recognizing bird and rabbit tracks, she spotted much larger prints that could only belong to a mountain lion, and prayed it wasn't hungry.

Nervous, she pulled out her .30-30 Marlin from its carry case and inserted rounds into the tubular magazine that ran the length of the barrel. She chambered a round, inserted another cartridge into the magazine, just in case. She'd bought the rifle in a backwoods town in northern Ontario. She'd wanted a backup for her Glock, but hadn't wanted to call attention to herself by buying another handgun. The little lever action rifle was compact and easy to carry, but it packed a powerful punch at close quarters. Elizabeth left the hammer half-cocked and carried on walking, taking big steps in the cumbersome shoes, holding the gun barrel pointed toward the ground.

She reached a small clearing at the foot of a heavily forested hillside. This would do for her purpose. She stopped, shucked off her pack and laid the rifle carefully on the ground. Sitting on a half-rotted tree stump, she pulled out some brightly colored balloons from her knapsack and started blowing them up to the size of footballs. She tied each one off with long pieces of twine, thankful there was no wind to scatter them around the glade. The balloons looked garish against the white background—unnatural in the pristine wilderness. She stopped to catch her breath, eyed the surrounding thicket suspiciously.

Satisfied with the targets, she gathered the strings, pulled a staple-gun from her pack, and marched 100 yards further up the gentle slope.

Snow flicked over the top of her boots, but the thick socks she wore helped keep it out. After that first day's ride in the snowstorm with Nat, she'd sworn she'd never leave the warmth of the cabin again. But doing nothing had given her time to think, and that was the last thing she'd wanted. She'd rather freeze.

Elizabeth came to a felled pine near the edge of the forest. She removed her gloves with her teeth and dropped them to the snow at her feet. With quick efficient movements she stapled the target balloons along the length of the tree trunk where they bobbed gently in a long festive line that looked both jolly and sweet—like a birthday party.

She'd be lucky to see another birthday. But she wouldn't die alone.

Blowing out a cloud of icy breath, she smiled grimly at her little soldiers and walked back to her pack and then stood, absorbing the atmosphere of the mountain. It felt like nothing she'd ever experienced before. Even the air was different up here, sharper, clearer. They called Montana 'Big Sky' country and now Elizabeth knew why. You were so close you could almost reach up and touch it.

The silence was all encompassing. Tangible.

Her heartbeat slowed. Tension eased out of her shoulders, releasing her neck from its iron grip. There was a deep sense of solitude here that embraced and held her. Recognized her for what she was, and didn't care about the bad parts, the imperfections.

An eagle soared high above the valley, on meager thermals, surveying its kingdom of ice, tree and granite.

There was power here, in the eagle and the land.

The savage strength of the ocean had often called to her as she'd watched storm driven seas and seen the fury of waves that pounded surf and rock.

But this power had a different feel. Older, dignified, like inner peace. The backbone of the world forged by molten heat, time and patience. For some reason, that conjured an image of Nat Sullivan. He was big and beautiful with an underlying core of strength.

When she'd first seen him in the stable last night she'd barely recognized him. Fiercely intent, there'd been no twinkle in his eyes, no good humor teasing his mouth. He'd been sharp-edged with desperation.

Watching the mare die, and seeing the foal born, had been one of the saddest and most poignant moments of her life—an emotional whirlwind of sorrow and joy. It had taken courage to cut the foal out of its still warm mother. Decisiveness and action.

A bird twittered in a nearby tree, jumping excitedly from naked twig to naked twig with dexterous hops. Shaking her attention back to her objective, Elizabeth looked across at her targets. Latex bubbles lined up in the snow, waiting to party. She braced her feet one behind the other, a stride apart, her weight balanced evenly on the balls of her feet. Taking a calming breath, she raised the rifle to her right eye and closed her left, took in the slack of the trigger and slowed her breathing. She exhaled and squeezed smoothly. The rifle recoiled and the balloon vaporized as the shot echoed around the hills, shattering the silence.

***

Nat swore under his breath as he tightened the cinches on Winter's saddle before mounting up. *Goddamned poachers on his land.* Poachers who sneaked up into the mountains and killed whatever they wanted, regardless of the law. Regardless of nature's rhythm.

There was nothing in season this time of year.

Nat's mind raged as he thought of the lowlifes who left piles of trash blowing in the wilderness as a sign of their contempt. Well, after the week he'd had, he was more than ready to deal with them.

Shots rang off in the distance again.

He checked his Remington .308 and ammunition. Looked up into the woods—his woods, his land, his mountain.

For now...

These guys were too close for comfort.

Normally, he would have waited for Ryan or Cal to join him, but they were busy moving cattle in from the lower pasture near the river and he couldn't afford to wait. Clouds were gathering against the northern horizon, moving fast. More snow was on its way.

He kicked-on Winter and they headed out at a ground-eating canter. Nat narrowed his gaze as if he could see past the trees with sheer willpower. His wolves were up in these hills. They used this part of the mountain to den-up and raise pups each spring.

People in these parts held wolves in about as much regard as serial killers and maybe a pack would take out the occasional sick steer, but most cattle were too big and strong to be tackled by the elusive creatures. His father had been a nature lover—recognized early the threat people were to the natural predators that lived in the parks nearby. Nat had only ever hunted them with his camera and had spent years photographing this particular pack.

Goddamn

Urging Winter on with his heels, he rode faster, up the gentle rise of the meadow with the reins wrapped loosely around the saddle horn, the horse moving with little instruction from him.

Winter was a Morgan, the oldest American breed, and standing at just under sixteen hands, he was bigger than average. His short, pricked ears faced towards the gunshots, his fine intelligent head held high on alert. The straight, clean legs and deeply muscled shoulders worked tirelessly to plow through the deep snow.

They were close to the shooter now. Nat could smell the gunpowder tainting the pristine mountain air. He approached carefully from well behind the direction of the shots, frowning as he looked down at the ground and noticed a single set of tracks of someone on foot. Unless someone else had flanked the area, there was only one hunter to deal with.

Nat smiled, nudged Winter forward. *One wouldn't be a problem.*

The horse picked his way through the thick snow with barely a sound. Nat judged the shooter to be about a hundred yards away behind a stand of trees. He slid off Winter's back and left the horse loose in the clearing.

Cautiously, Nat inched forward, careful not to step on any buried branches that would trip him up or snap and give his presence away.

He hunkered down and kept the thick trunk of a Douglas fir between himself and the shooter. He didn't want to end up stuffed on somebody's mantel.

Leaning against the trunk, he peered cautiously around the tree and jerked back with surprise as he spotted Miss Eliza Reed, computer specialist from

New York, shooting targets.

She wasn't exactly camouflaged in her red and black lumberjack coat, standing out in plain view, and Nat figured by the steadiness of her stance and confidence of her bearing that she knew what she was doing.

Sonofabitch.

At least she wasn't a poacher.

Using the old 3-9 Redfield scope on his rifle, he checked out her progress. She hit each balloon dead on, over and over. Despite himself, Nat was impressed. She was a good shot—for a computer nerd.

Nat lowered his rifle, stood silently in the protection of the trees as he watched her put the Marlin through its paces. There was a mechanical fluidity to her movements, a rhythm in how she took the shots and reloaded. She looked like she'd done it a million times before. The action wasn't rushed, and nothing was forced.

He didn't trust her. Knew she was hiding something beneath that porcelain-fine exterior. He looked down the scope, admired the curve of her cheek, the slight pull of her lips to one side as she concentrated on a shot.

Not that he wouldn't mind tasting those lips...

Christ.

Just because he'd found the woman he'd loved in bed with a bartender only hours after he'd left to visit his dying father, didn't mean he'd sworn off sex. *Hell, no.* Just because he'd been a fool once didn't mean he didn't occasionally enjoy what women had to offer. Not that Mizz Elizabeth Reed was offering. Unlike Troy Strange's wife.

Hadn't that been fun. He rested his forehead

against the tree trunk, pulled his lips back in a grimace.

Marlena. That damned woman had to be the reason Troy Strange was putting the squeeze on them. What the hell had she told her husband about him?

A woman scorned.

A couple of weeks ago he'd gone into town for supplies and stopped by the *Screw Loose* for a drink on the way back home. He'd bumped into Marlena in the parking lot. She'd asked him for a ride home as her Porsche wouldn't start. It wasn't out of his way and even if it had of been there wasn't a person in the world he'd have hesitated giving a ride to. Except this one. She was model thin and exotically beautiful, but he didn't care for her. Didn't trust her, didn't like her. But ingrained manners had had him saying 'sure' before he could get the word 'no' past his stupid lips.

She'd gone for his zipper five miles from the ornate security gates of Strange's ranch. Nat had damned near crashed the truck into a Douglas fir. By the time he'd pulled over she'd had him in her mouth and he'd damn near come on the spot. The tiny portion of brain that hadn't been in her mouth had wondered what her angle was.

Not that his body had given a damn. Turned on just thinking about it, he shifted uncomfortably from the memory. It had been a long time since he'd been with a woman and a hell of a long time since he'd had a blowjob. And for the first few seconds his body had been praising the Lord and doing Hallelujah cartwheels, but even his steam-fogged brain had realized he couldn't do it. Even though his body screamed for release, he couldn't do it. She was a married woman and he didn't like her.

Removing her hot mouth and manicured claws from his dick had been a dangerous procedure, and he'd been damned proud of himself for doing it.

But she'd been pissed.

He'd forced her out of the truck while she'd screamed and spluttered and then he'd got the hell out of there, abandoning her on the side of the road. Should have known she'd cause trouble. Maybe he should have just fucked her, like every other guy in town. He blinked as the sound of another shot rebounded off the granite peaks.

An idea sprang into his head. It was crazy and she'd probably shoot him, but right now he didn't give a damn. Slowly he crept out of his hiding place and moved silently through the thick snow. He counted off the shots. Figured the rifle should be empty. Got about three feet behind her and waited for her to lower the weapon to reload.

"Howdy ma'am." He tipped his hat and grinned as she jumped a mile into the air, swinging her rifle around and pointing it straight at his heart.

"Holy Mother of God!" she shrieked, her green eyes glittering. "You scared the shit out of me, you crazy—"

Nat kept a wary eye on the rifle. *Should be empty, but you never know for sure.*

"Didn't ya hear me walking on over here?" He scratched his chin and stretched his accent, added a little cowboy color.

Looking thoroughly pissed, Elizabeth Reed narrowed her eyes, obviously seeing through his ploy. The woman sure was pretty, even when she was spitting nails.

"I could have shot you, you *idiot*."

Nat raised the brim of his hat off his head and ran his hand through his hair before settling the hat firmly back in place.

"Way things are going," he nodded towards the rifle that was still pointed at his heart, "figure you still might."

***

Elizabeth lowered the rifle with a snort. Damned cowboy could have been shot. That would be all she needed. And he'd nearly given her a heart attack, creeping up on her like that. As if she wasn't spooked enough by the wildlife and the price tag attached to her head.

She wrapped her fingers around the stock and the barrel, held the rifle loosely in front of her. She wasn't scared of him, not *that* way, and that freaked her out. But she was determined she wasn't going to look at every man from a victim's viewpoint. As if nightmares and insomnia didn't already make her one.

"Don't tell me..." Nat squinted down at her, those midnight blue eyes almost black in the shadow of his ash-colored cowboy hat, "...it's that bear thing again, right?"

She found herself smiling, could feel bubbles of laughter spill from her mouth. She'd kept her emotions locked down tight for so long she didn't know how to deal with simple things like laughter or joy anymore.

Her heart rate began to return to normal and the adrenaline rush was receding. She hadn't heard a thing before he'd announced himself. Even in the thick snow. Now that was scary.

"How's the foal?" she asked, noting the lines of strain that etched Nat's face. His bruises were fading, but he still looked tired.

Nat tipped his hat to the back of his head, rested his hands on his hips. "Got a young morab mare feeding him. Little devil went straight in there and tucked into dinner. Never really gave her the option to say no."

He shrugged, smiled, looked up at the sky. Eliza followed his gaze and noticed for the first time that it had clouded over to a tin metal gray.

"Shame about the mare though," she added and Nat nodded, looking away.

Something rustled in the bushes and she instinctively reloaded her weapon. A snowshoe hare hopped out, unconcerned by their presence, burrowing away at the snow looking for something to eat. Elizabeth turned back to Nat and found him watching her.

She shivered, but not from cold. There was something about Nat Sullivan, with his long rangy legs and broad shoulders that made her nerves quiver. Not to mention those sapphire-blue eyes that twinkled with hooded amusement blended with something else she couldn't quite decipher.

"Where'd you learn to shoot like that, if you don't mind me asking?" Nat looked past her to the balloons that dotted the pine tree.

She did mind, but she answered anyway. "Gun club."

Despite the easy smile and charming manner, Nat Sullivan wasn't as *country* as he wanted her to think. Those laser blues missed nothing, even if he was too polite to comment.

"Why?" Nat asked.

Maybe he wasn't so polite.

Elizabeth glared at him, irritated by the questions that forced her to lie—if he just minded his own damned business. "Because I wanted to."

She was being rude again, but it didn't seem to faze him. He just curved his lips into an amused smile and changed the subject.

"How 'bout a wager?" he asked.

Elizabeth rested the gun over her shoulder and looked up at him suspiciously. "What sort of wager?"

"A dollar," Nat said, his smile grew wider, "we take it back another fifty-yards and give it the best of three."

She really hated that smile of his. It dazzled her like the morning sun.

Another fifty yards would be about the limits of the range of the Marlin. She eyed his rifle and knew if he were any good, he'd wipe the floor with her. But the balloons made for big targets. She might be able to take him.

Elizabeth was doomed and she knew it. If she had a weakness, and God knew she had many, it was the inability to back down from a challenge. That was how she had gotten into this mess in the first place.

She nodded and watched satisfaction light up his face. Stuck out a hand. Nat spat in his palm and shook hers before she could stop him.

Yuck!

"That's how we do it in the mountains," he said. The sparkle in his eyes suggested he meant to rattle her any way he could.

Elizabeth handed him her rifle while she went to set up more balloons. Her Glock was hidden under her jacket. Walking back to him, she smiled and felt the skin stretch tightly over her cheeks in the cold air, but she was in top form and she intended to whip his ass.

"How you wanna play it, ma'am?" Nat asked. He tipped his hat to the back of his head.

The 'ma'am' thing was beginning to irritate her. Like she was his granny or something.

"You take your three shots, then I'll take mine," Elizabeth offered.

Nat shook his head and waved his hand. "Ladies first."

"Alternate shots then," Elizabeth suggested, watching Nat handle his rifle—like he'd been born with it.

Oh, shit.

Nat nodded.

Elizabeth offered him a warm up, but he declined. She swore under her breath. He was getting to her all right.

Elizabeth stood for a good minute, settling herself down and getting used to the new distance. She recalculated the trajectory in her head, took control of her breathing and balanced her body. Then she took the first shot. The balloon burst with a crack and she stood back waiting to reload.

Nat's eyes followed her. Revealed nothing as she moved away to stand behind him.

At the mark, she watched him cycle the bolt, raise his gun to his cheek and settle his breathing. He let his breath stop, body still and then took the shot. The bullet went straight through the center of the balloon, smashed into the slope behind the targets.

Nat moved away and didn't say anything. The

competition was on.

Elizabeth walked back to the mark, loaded and cycled a fresh round into the chamber. Her next shot bounced the edge of the balloon, effective enough to make it burst. She turned around, disconcerted to find Nat standing right next to her, like a second shadow. Startled, she jerked back, dropping her rifle into the snow as she stumbled.

Shit.

Nat caught her with his free arm before she hit the ground.

"I've got you," Nat said, steadying her on her feet.

His arm wrapped around her waist and held her firmly against him. She could feel his heat and hated herself for craving that warmth. Shivers ran all the way down to her toes. She found herself staring into the bluest eyes she'd ever seen, deep aquamarine like the ocean, framed by pale lashes and heavy brows.

"S-sorry," Elizabeth said, unnerved. She stepped out of his embrace, frustrated that she'd let him unsettle her. If she wasn't annoyed at him, she was apologizing. Or falling over or tripping up or tumbling off things. She'd turned into a goddamned klutz, her cool self-possession a thing of the distant past.

He nailed his second shot through the middle of the balloon with less effort than it took to raise his head.

Elizabeth was acutely aware of him, but he didn't seem even vaguely disturbed by her. She didn't want this sexual awareness, not with him and not with any man.

Damn.

Despite the frigid air, she unbuttoned her jacket.

The bottom line was that Nat Sullivan bothered her, put her on edge. She didn't fear him physically; it was her mental health that worried her. She tried to settle her breathing, but her concentration was shot. She snatched the trigger and the bullet pulled low and right. The balloon bobbed about with cheerful mockery.

Swearing under her breath she moved away and let him take his final shot. This time he clipped the balloon, but it burst nevertheless. Elizabeth was sure he did it just to make her feel better.

She huffed out a big sigh, and though she hated losing, she had to admit he was one hell of a marksman. She checked to make sure her gun was unloaded and turned towards him.

He was watching her. Intelligence lit up his eyes—shining with questions, and the answers he'd found.

The wager had been some kind of test and Elizabeth realized she'd just failed it. She'd been worried about being attracted to the man while he'd been sizing up Elizabeth Reed, IT specialist.

Her low self-esteem and lack of confidence had her measuring her worth in terms of physical abilities and old skills. She was a damned good shot, but he was better. This wasn't just some hick cowboy from way out west and she'd do well to remember that.

"You're a hell of a shot, Mr. Sullivan."

***

"So are you Mizz Reed, so are you." Nat had thought she'd go off in an angry snit. Hell, he'd wanted her to go off in a snit. Elizabeth Reed had been outgunned six ways to Sunday and she knew it, but she'd still taken him on.

He tipped his hat and eyed her thoughtfully, watched her hand slide down the smooth denim of her jeans and into her pocket. She brought out a shiny silver dollar coin, held it out toward him.

"Your dollar, Mr. Sullivan."

Was that her lucky coin?

Freckles stood out like constellations against pale skin, her green eyes flecked with tiny pieces of glittering gold. It intrigued him that someone from the city could shoot the balls off a rat at two hundred paces. 'Course, there were plenty of rats in the city.

Reaching out, he curled her fingers back around the coin. He wouldn't take anyone's luck, even though he could use some.

Ryan would have swapped the coin for a kiss...

"Keep it, and call me Nat." Her hand was cool within his grasp and he tried not to think about kissing her.

At six foot three, it made a nice change not to have to stoop down to talk to a woman. Nina had been tall too, and cocky, and beautiful. Unconsciously his grip tightened.

Jerking her hand away, she stuffed the coin back in her pocket. "Eliza, call me Eliza. I hate being called Mizz *or ma'am.*" She looked startled by her declaration, a flush rising along her cheekbones and her green eyes going wide.

"Eliza." Nat thumbed the safety on the rifle, slung it over his shoulder and watched as her eyes widened before she avoided his gaze—again. *She was as jittery as hell.* He grinned, never having

88

encountered a woman like her before, *deadly and jittery*—a perfect combination if you wanted to get your head blown off.

She raised her gaze from a spot in the snow and their eyes clashed and held. He stared and watched the shutters come down. A mystery, an unknown. A beautiful woman, full of secrets and contradictions—just passing through. His brother's prayers answered.

Nat stared at her lips and wanted to kiss her. He'd wanted to kiss her from the moment he'd first seen her standing in the pale starlight. Hell, had this been his fantasy, they'd already be lying back making a four-legged snow angel. But this wasn't his fantasy and the frozen look of fear in Eliza's eyes held him still. Fear didn't belong in a woman's gaze.

It shook him.

A snowflake drifted past her cheek, then another. Big fat flakes that floated down lightly, catching eddies and twirling around like ballerinas. One landed on her cheek. He brushed it away with his thumb without thinking. She flinched, breaking the spell. Looking up at the sky, she backed away from his touch. He glanced up at the burgeoning heavens and swore softly. This winter was never going to end.

"Better get back," he said, as if nothing unusual had passed between them.

***

A snowflake landed on her bottom lip, a sharp pinprick of cold that jolted her senses.

A bit like touching the cowboy.

She went and grabbed her gear, shriveled up pieces of balloons and the empty casings. She'd been terrified that Nat Sullivan was going to kiss her—terrified of how she'd react.

When she glanced over her shoulder, he'd disappeared. She ran a shaky hand through her hair, trying to keep it out of her eyes as the wind picked up. She stuffed everything into her rucksack, placed the rifle back into its case and pulled it across her back, grabbed her snowshoes. Turning, she found Nat waiting for her on the back of the gray stallion.

Looking like a Nordic God.

She swallowed, uncertain, as he proffered a hand to her.

Any normal person would jump at the chance of a ride down the mountain, but this man unsettled her more than anyone she'd ever met and she couldn't afford to get close to him.

Another snowflake hit her nose, melting with a burst of cold, and a moment later she let him pull her up behind him. The snow began to fall in earnest, so thick that she tucked her forehead against Nat's back as they headed down the mountainside through a dense forest of lodgepole pines. He felt solid and strong and safe. She clutched at his jacket with cold fingers, belatedly realizing she'd forgotten to put on her gloves.

Nat reached down, took her naked hand and placed it between the buttons of his coat, safely inside his jacket—cocooned in warmth. Beneath her fingertips his shirt felt smooth, the muscles hard and flat under the press of her palm. Staying absolutely still, as if the spell would be broken if she so much as breathed, she absorbed his stolen heat.

A raccoon stood between the trees watching

them as they rode past, one foot raised as if he'd been interrupted mid-step.

The steep slopes and slippery footing meant she had to hang on tight and she gripped Nat harder. She could smell leather and horse, and the faint scent of sandalwood beneath. The gray slipped over the uneven ground, haunches bunched, muscles straining, and then found better purchase in the gently sloped meadow. The energy of Nat's body seeped into hers with each step the gray took.

It unnerved her.

It warmed her.

Truth be told, it scared the bejesus out of her.

Desperate to remove herself from Nat's touch—not because she didn't like it, but because she did—she scooted off the back of the horse as soon as they passed her cottage.

She sensed his eyes on her as she ran with her head-down through the blizzard, up the three wooden steps and across the porch into the cottage. She threw him a quick smile and a 'thanks' before closing the door firmly behind her. She was running again, only this time it wasn't from the mob.

Chapter Six

The smell of lemon polish and saddle-soap overwhelmed even the odor of horse in the small tack-room at the far end of the horse-barn. Bent over an ornately carved western saddle, Elizabeth rubbed the soap into the leather with a soft cloth.

Shaking her head, she blew her bangs out of her eyes. She'd spent the morning being shown the horses by Sarah Sullivan, who wasn't on duty at the hospital until the afternoon. Sarah impressed the crap out of her. Though small and slight, she was a ball of energy coping with her demanding job, her family, the ranch chores, and on top of that, acting as hostess for their ranch holidays.

Elizabeth sat back and admired the sheen in the dark leather.

The horses were beautiful. The ones she'd ridden had been well schooled and gentle, but she'd been knocked-out by the magnificent Arabian stallion dancing and twirling around a wide corral, showing off to the fillies in the next field. She was entranced and so were the fillies.

There was something incredibly potent about the way the black stallion moved, the fluid grace with which he ran. Muscles flowed like living steel, pouring into each great stride. His neck arched and his long mane danced, the color of midnight against the snowy backdrop. His finely chiseled head and delicately pricked ears shook from side to side as he whirled and chased from one end of the corral to the

92

other.

He was, quite simply, perfect.

Rubbing hard, she buffed the saddle, wrinkling her nose at the smell of polish and enjoying the ache in her muscles from the physical labor.

A creak had her jerking around, knocking a hoof-pick onto the floor with a clatter. Cal Landon stood outlined in the open doorway carrying a saddle, with a bridle draped over one shoulder. Even though it was only mid-afternoon, Elizabeth realized it was getting dark outside. The barn behind Cal looked gloomy and forbidding.

"Sorry, ma'am." He tipped his battered black cowboy hat and backed up a step, "Didn't know you were in here."

Cal didn't have the startling good looks of the Sullivan men, in fact, if anything, he might be best described as plain or rugged. About five-nine, the same height as Elizabeth, he was whipcord thin from a lifetime of ranch work, or so she assumed. He looked maybe thirty-five, but it was hard to tell, the sun had carved his face heavily, forming those insidious creases that added character to men, and age to women. He had sharp features with bright hazel eyes and short cropped hair that was patchy in color, parts being dark brown like sable and others glinting like dull gold in the sun. He looked like a mongrel—a mongrel in snakeskin boots.

She smiled as she kept a wary eye on him.

They'd come to an unspoken agreement. He didn't treat her like an idiot and she didn't expect to be entertained. He didn't bother to charm or beguile her, the way Ryan did, and he didn't seem to give a damn about who she was or where she came from. Maybe that was the reason she'd managed to relax around him. Or maybe it was something else she'd noticed in his ultra-calm eyes.

She raised her eyebrow in inquiry. The cowboy was quiet to the point of being mute and this was the first time she'd been alone with him.

"More snow coming," Cal said, scratching the side of his head.

Elizabeth nodded silently, encouraging him. He still hesitated.

Keeping her eyes locked on him, she reached down and stroked one of the ranch dogs.

Cal moved forward into the small room, leaning close to heft the saddle onto its bracket on the wall. His obvious discomfort with her in close quarters made her own nerves quiet. He had to stand right behind her and almost throw the saddle into place. The saddles were bulky and heavy and she ducked down and tried to make herself as small as possible to give him more room.

Despite the cold, Cal was in his shirtsleeves. The saddle started to slip and Cal lunged forward to catch it before it fell and hit her. He caught it, but not before Elizabeth got a full view of the tattoos that covered Cal's lower arms.

She froze.

Standard prison issue.

Cal was still stretched across the workbench hoisting the saddle into place when he followed her gaze and muttered an oath. Shoving the saddle into position, he moved back from the bench, rubbed his hands over his face and blew out a big frustrated sigh. "Damn."

"So, do the Sullivans know?" she asked. Being a dumbass, she'd left her weapon in the cabin. *Stupid.*

Cal blew out a hard laugh and nodded. Ex-cons

94

never admitted their crimes, but she wanted to hear what he'd say.

"What did you do, fiddle your tax returns?"

Concentrating on hanging up his bridle on the rack opposite, he said nothing for a long moment. Then he turned and looked her dead in the eye.

"Killed my step-daddy." Cal shifted from foot to foot, watching her warily. He must have noticed her sudden tension because he reached out and touched her shoulder, gave it a gentle squeeze. Flinching, she shrank from his touch and Cal withdrew. The guy looked down at his boots as if wondering where the shine had gone.

"I was fourteen years old..." He faded off like it was a story he didn't want to tell, his voice flat, achingly, annoyingly flat. "Anyway, it doesn't matter. I did my time."

He turned and walked back into the main part of the horse-barn, Elizabeth sat absolutely still, absorbing what he'd said. During training, and before she'd gone undercover, she'd met her fair share of cons. She'd also seen her fill of tragedy and circumstance. She knew bad people when she met them, had smelled the taint of DeLattio long before she'd seen the man.

Fingers clenching so hard they hurt, she had a death-grip on the saddle she'd been cleaning. She let the saddle go, leaned back in the wooden swivel chair for support and wondered what had turned a 14-year-old boy into a killer. Some people were born bad, others...

Empathy sliced her like a knife. Christ, she was no saint. Maybe she was a sucker, but the Sullivans trusted Cal Landon and they seemed to be pretty sane people. She got to her feet and followed Cal out into the barn. Horses stood in small groups in the wide pens that lined either side of the aisle. A palomino mare tried to nose her arm for a treat, but Elizabeth didn't stop. She wanted to find the cowboy. Cal was rubbing down two horses in one of the empty pens near the front of the barn.

Warily he turned to face her. Probably figured she was gonna make trouble for him.

Elizabeth looked outside, through the small opening in the slide-door of the barn and realized the snow was falling faster than ever. All it ever seemed to do here was snow.

She hesitated one second before she asked, "You need any help getting the stock in from the fields?"

Cal's flat-eyed stare turned surprised and then flickered to grateful.

"If you're up to it." He nodded.

"I'm up to it," she said, putting her hands in her jeans pockets. Befriending a convicted murderer didn't seem like such a dumb idea. In her mind's eye, she'd put a gun to DeLattio's head a thousand times. Pulling the trigger was as easy as swatting flies and that scared her a lot more than Cal Landon ever could. They weren't so different after all.

***

They worked as quickly as the horses would allow. Despite the rattles of feed buckets and the ever-increasing chill of the wind, some of the fillies seemed reluctant to move from the freedom of the meadows into the warm confines of the horse-barn. Hair blowing in her eyes and ears feeling so cold she feared they might snap off, Elizabeth threw a rope halter on the last recalcitrant female. She led the squirrelly horse down to the barn, chiding it all the time for being mischievous. Cal followed with the Arab stallion, which danced on the tips of his shiny black hooves. Cal turned the stallion out into a large loose-box at the end of the aisle where the horse could hang his head over the split Dutch-doors and watch his harem.

Ryan Sullivan rode up out of nowhere and straight through the open door of the horse-barn. He was handsome like his brother, but he didn't have the same effect on her that Nat Sullivan did. He jumped off his mount and immediately went to work saddling another while Cal took care of the first animal.

As Ryan worked, snow began to drip off his dark Stetson onto the muddy stone floor at his feet. Elizabeth studied him. He had the same killer blue eyes, but where Nat was blond, Ryan's hair was black as coal.

"How're you doing, Miss Reed?" Ryan asked, without looking up from tightening the cinch on the saddle. He finished the first horse and began saddling a second pony just as efficiently.

"I'm fine, thank you," Elizabeth said. God, she sounded like some prim and proper schoolgirl. She watched him throw a saddle-pad followed by a plain western saddle onto the back of a roan. The cowpony stood placidly waiting to go to work, like a commuter on the subway.

She leaned back against the wooden rail and wished she could sink right back into it. She liked Ryan, despite his flirting ways, much the same way she liked Cal, but she still didn't want to get too close. They were both polite and easygoing, respectful of her privacy, not overstepping the boundaries she set up, but she suspected Ryan had a dark side, whereas Nat seemed blindingly pure and bright.

"So what'd ya think of the Triple H so far, Miss Reed?" Ryan asked. He'd finished saddling the second horse and turned towards her, brushed some of the melting snow off his jacket.

"Call me Eliza." One of the horses nudged her from behind and she laughed, turning slightly to stroke a soft brown nose. "It's beautiful. Cold, but gorgeous."

"Yeah, well cold we can do, though it usually isn't this bad." Ryan's voice flowed like raw honey, an obvious sales-pitch, but one laced with pride. "But it's pretty and if you're around long enough to see the summer, well now, that's one of the most beautiful experiences a human-being can have."

She pinned him with a direct look, but kept her mouth shut. It wouldn't take much to encourage Ryan Sullivan and he looked like a man who knew all about beautiful experiences.

The wind howled outside the sanctuary of the barn. Listening to the blizzard rage, Elizabeth realized she'd like to see a summer here. She'd like to watch the flowers burst forth, to enjoy the hot lazy days, to see the horses run wild and the cows bellow in the high meadows.

She might not live that long. She shrugged. "Maybe. Who knows?"

Ryan's smile was full of satisfaction. He'd make a great salesman.

"I'd better get back to work before Nat comes in here and hauls my ass out into the snow. Wanna come?" He looked her over speculatively, like maybe she wasn't up to it.

The wind howled like a banshee and it was as cold as the pits of Arctic hell. Her spine stiffened. Cal started to mutter something, but she ignored him.

"Sure," she said, straightening up.

Ryan glanced at her critically. He looked around the side of the barn door and found a pair of sturdy leather work-gloves to protect her hands. Then he took a wide-brimmed hat that had been hanging on a peg just inside the door, gave it a quick whack to clean off the dust and stuck it on her head. Next he found a pair of suede chaps and showed her how to put them on.

"Keep the barn in sight and call it a day when you get cold."

She was already cold.

Gritting her teeth, she squared her shoulders and headed off through the stable doors like they were the gates to purgatory.

Horizontal snow hit her in the face like baseballs; the soft flakes of before replaced by fierce little creatures that stung. Elizabeth followed Ryan who led the two horses to just outside the barn.

"This is Tiger," he said, shouting against the howling wind. He patted the docile roan affectionately. "Stay on her back and you won't get lost. Or hang on to me if you like." His face was close to hers.

She snorted, making her choice obvious.

"Then what?" she said loudly enough to make her voice heard over the screaming wind. She gritted her teeth against the rush of cold air into her lungs, kept her head low behind the horse's back to gain a momentary respite.

"We're herding loose cattle into the shed here." He pointed to a big red Dutch barn the other side of the yard from the horse-barn. "Just make sure they don't sneak past you, up onto the road."

It sounded easy enough. She declined his offer of a leg-up and watched him jump onto the other horse. Sticking her foot into the stirrup, she hauled herself onto the back of the mare and followed Ryan.

The cowboy disappeared into the swirling snow almost immediately, but she kept the huge red barn close-by. The light was fading, turning the world into a whirling mass of monotonous white on gray.

It was an easy job for the most part, except for the cold that numbed her fingers and froze her nose. When a spooked cow did something stupid like dive past her, Tiger acted more or less of her own will to curb the beast and change its direction. When that failed, Blue, one of the ranch dogs, nipped at their heels and sent them lumbering back towards the security of the well-lit barn. All Elizabeth had to do was stay on.

Tiger dived left, cutting off a frisky heifer.

Taken by surprise and numbed by the cold, Elizabeth's center of gravity shifted out of sync with the horse and she took a nosedive to the right. Her ankle twisted and caught in the stirrup. She tasted snow and grit as she landed face first. She was busy hanging from the saddle and spitting out dirt when two strong arms enfolded her.

"What the hell are you doing out here?" Nat Sullivan shouted directly into her ear.

She hadn't seen him since yesterday afternoon, but he felt warm and solid and Elizabeth hated herself for being so relieved to see him.

"Helping out," she shouted back, although hanging upside-down by an ankle that was being torn in two by pain might not look that way to him. Holding back a cry of agony was getting harder and harder.

Nat picked her up and hoisted her into his arms like she weighed nothing at all. The screaming pressure on her ankle eased and suddenly she found herself nose to nose with a furious male. She could feel every hard inch of his body pressed from her chest to the top of her thighs. She swallowed.

He glared at her, his mouth bracketed by hard lines. "Are you crazy?"

Elizabeth figured it was a rhetorical question.

Blue danced anxiously around them, his old legs skittering about in the snow. Nat told him to sit and the dog immediately sat, his tail churning up fresh snow like a windshield wiper.

She cried out when Nat tried to pull her foot from the leather stirrup. Her boot was stuck fast. He shifted her weight until she was almost all the way over his shoulder like a sack of grain. Elizabeth ignored the pain and the sensation of his hands moving across her body as he manhandled her. Tears threatened to overwhelm her, but she wouldn't let them fall. She already felt like a fool.

***

Fury rose through Nat as he tugged at Eliza's boot. He was going to kill Ryan when he got his hands on him. Despite the freezing wind that drove the snow down the mountains, a sweat broke out on his brow. Elizabeth Reed could have died out in this weather.

An inexperienced pony could have dragged her off into the blizzard. He swore viscously. Ignoring the soft flesh beneath his fingers he shifted her weight higher.

Visibility was down to a hundred yards and once you were disoriented, without shelter, you were as good as dead. Or she could have been trampled, buried under a layer of white death not to be uncovered 'til the thaw.

"Hold tight to me," he said. His voice was clipped and angry, but he couldn't tame it.

Upside-down, she hooked her arms around his back and held on tight.

He ground his teeth and tried to get her boot out of the stirrup once more. It was jammed tight. He pulled harder, but eased the pressure when he felt her flinch.

"Why couldn't you just stay inside? I've got enough trouble dealing with the goddamn stock." He was too tired, too cold, and too goddamned frustrated to be anything but spitting mad.

Finally, Nat worked her foot free and set her down on the soft snow. Her ankle gave way beneath her and she stumbled against him. He held her shoulders, but she reacted like he'd bitten her and jerked away. Her ankle must have been badly wrenched. She staggered and he heard her gasp even though she kept her head down, hiding her expression. She hung onto Tiger's saddle as the horse stood patiently beside her, sheltering her from the worst of the blizzard.

Watching, Nat decided she was the most stubborn female he'd met in his entire life, and God knew, he'd met some damned contrary women. But when she glanced up through a mass of wavy brown hair, he saw tears tracking down her cheeks and guilt slammed into him like a sledgehammer.

Shit.

Without a word, he scooped her up, shouted to Cal to look out for the horses and strode up to the cottage.

Groping for the door handle, he stepped inside, relieved to find the fire blazing and the place cozy and warm. Nat intended to drop Eliza into the easy chair by the fire, fetch Sas and get the hell back to work. The only trouble was Eliza's head was buried under his jacket and he couldn't seem to remove her clenched fingers from his clothing.

Her breath tickled his neck, brushing warmth across his chilled skin, and sent a quiver down every male nerve ending he possessed.

Standing in the center of the room with its cheery yellow paint he nearly groaned with frustration. She was crying, trying not to make a sound—her shoulders shaking just a little.

Hell.

Dampness from her tears soaked through his chambray shirt and turned cold against his skin. That, and her silence, reached out and grabbed at everything within him, touched him where he was most vulnerable, making him want to comfort and protect her.

Easing down into the chair, he cradled her in his arms and let her weep. He didn't have time for this, really he didn't. This was the worst spring for fifty years. He had to get the cows into the barn before those with young froze to death, or before any more cows calved. He needed every single animal on the ranch to pull through this miserable weather if they were to have a chance of surviving the next year.

Absently he slipped his hand beneath Eliza's coat and rubbed the hollow of her back, gently squeezed her shoulders, trying to comfort her. His hands traveled her body the way he would soothe a frightened animal, trying to ease her trembling. He smoothed tangled hair away from her face, stirred up a hint of fragrant lavender that seemed to follow her wherever she went.

"Shush," he murmured, "it's all right." He doubted it was.

Wanting to comfort, he placed light kisses on the top of her head, on her brow, lower, kissing the salty tears from her lashes. His gaze settled on her mouth, her lips half-parted and trembling, watching as her breath hitched and the cloudiness left her exotic green eyes.

Awareness flooded through him as the desire to comfort took on a deeper, more elemental nature. He pulled back and held her away from him with firm hands. "Sorry."

Eliza stopped crying, her eyes watery and wide. Her gaze dropped to his lips and she grabbed his collar with both hands and kissed him full on the mouth. Taken by surprise, Nat hesitated for all of a second, until she slipped her tongue along the crease of his lips.

Sinking into her like a drowning man in need of oxygen, he kissed her back. The heat of her mouth burnt, in stark contrast to her cold skin, and Nat felt seared by the contact. He pressed against the soft curves of her body and realized they fit his like they'd been cast together. He laid her back over one arm, kissed her deeper and deeper, plunging into a mindless whirlwind that reared up and sucked him in. There was a desperation to her kiss, an urgency in the way she responded to him that catapulted his desire to full-throttle in ten seconds flat. He forgot the time, the blizzard and the stock. He forgot everything but the fire that burned his fingers wherever he touched her. Heat built between them, scorched flesh and erased thought. His lips never left hers as his hands raced over her body. Her lean curves begged for his attention. He felt her quiver as his hand slid across her flat belly, down firm thighs and between her legs, cupping her through the denim of her jeans.

Without warning she jackknifed off his lap and stumbled onto the floor, ended up sprawled in a heap at his feet.

"Don't touch me!" she spat. Her hair was a wild storm around her face, her lips pulled back in a snarl.

Nat sat immobile for several seconds, his breath coming in big, harsh gasps. He'd been drugged by passion, aroused so quickly it was embarrassing, only to be doused by ice.

He didn't remind her that *she'd* been the one to kiss *him.* He'd only been kissing her back. Narrowing his eyes, he slowly rose to his feet.

"Don't worry, lady," he drawled. "It won't happen again." He grabbed his hat from where it had fallen on the floor, turned on his heel and left.

Chapter Seven

Elizabeth lay on the hearthrug as frost spread through her veins. Drawing her knees tight to her chest, she curled up into a ball, too humiliated to move, too desolate to cry. She concentrated on feeling nothing—just lay on the hard floor, the rough fibers of the rug scratching her cheek as she hugged herself like a child. Seconds stretched into minutes. She didn't move.

Slowly, stiffly, she uncurled clenched fingers and straightened her legs, stretching them out beneath her and tried to stand. Gingerly, she put her weight on her sore ankle, but pain shot up her leg. She gave up and hopped to the tiny bathroom, using the furniture for balance, and ran the shower while stripping off her damp clothes.

Pulling herself awkwardly into the bath, she knelt beneath the old brass sprinkler and turned the water as hot as it would go. It blasted her skin like a branding iron, but still she shivered. She felt cold on the inside, like hollowed out ice. Grabbing the soap she scrubbed herself, working the lather into every inch of her skin, desperate to remove the taint—the shame.

Not Nat Sullivan. Andrew DeLattio. And herself.

She'd wanted so badly to kiss Nat Sullivan. To prove she wasn't a victim anymore. To prove she was normal.

Ha!

106

Skin glowed red beneath her fingers and still she scrubbed. The water began to cool as the tears came. Hot gushes of pure misery wracked her body with sobs that refused to be quiet. *So ashamed, so stupid.* Blinded, she sank down, curled into a ball in the bottom of the tub, the tepid water beating on her head like doves' wings.

The water ran cold. Shivers turned into great wracking tremors that brought Elizabeth slowly back into herself. Hell was supposed to be burning hot, but Elizabeth knew better. It was bitterly cold.

She got up, leaned heavily on one foot, then slipped and bashed her knee. Swearing, she turned off the faucets and reached for a towel, her movements shaky and deliberately slow. She rubbed her icy skin until it glowed and wrapped her hair in a thick towel. The cold water had actually done her body some good.

Muscles began to heat and warmth spread painfully down to her toes as she moved. She climbed out of the tub, supporting herself on her arms until she got her good foot down. She just managed to reach the toweling robe that hung from the back of the door, before pins and needles attacked her feet in a rush of unwelcome sensation.

She didn't want to feel anything. But even though she concentrated hard on the numbness inside her head, it didn't last. She was so sick of it all.

Wrapping her robe tight around her with quick sharp jerks, even her anger irritated her. She felt as worn out as an old rag. Growing up an orphan had been bad enough, no matter how rich she'd been. Then rape, coming out of nowhere—all her training, all her skills neutralized by a couple of drops of

Rohypnol in a glass of champagne.

Her heart hammered and her fists clenched. She hopped over to the bed and pulled the Glock from beneath the pillow, felt a hundred years old as she sat down on the edge of the mattress.

Worse than the rape, worse even than lying on a gurney under the bright lights of the ER as she was photographed from every conceivable angle, was the betrayal of trust from her colleagues at the FBI. There had been a hidden microphone in her purse the night DeLattio had raped her, and the OCU agents had hung her out to dry. They'd caught the big fish all right. And then they'd protected the bastard.

Tears gathered for another onslaught and she screwed up her eyes in an effort to stop them. When she opened them again she was staring down at the weapon in her hand. She loved her Glock. She retracted the slide to check there was a round in the chamber. Automatically, she popped the magazine into the palm of her hand and peered into the witness hole to see the bullet. Satisfied, she slapped the magazine back in place and ran her index finger along the short black muzzle.

Maybe I should just end it. Stop the chase. Admit defeat.

Every muscle in her body held motionless.

She was on the run from the mob and a brutal rapist out for revenge. The price on her head was seven-figures and rising. There was no one to trust. And her presence alone was endangering the life of everyone at the ranch. Including the stubborn cowboy who'd begun to make her realize just how pathetic and empty her life had become.

She loved her Glock.

Loved it.

Her weapon was reliable, lightweight and virtually indestructible. More like a friend than an inanimate object, somebody to depend on in a tight spot. And only when she wore her gun did she feel she had some measure of control over the madness her life had become. Only then did she feel safe.

Her hands trembled as she looked down the barrel to see the tip of the bullet gleaming in the dull light. Her firearms instructors at Quantico called this the 'pre-suicide technique' for checking that a gun was loaded. She smiled at the irony. They'd been merciless bastards, especially during shotgun training, but she'd liked them. Wanted to be one of them, to fit in somewhere.

She closed her eyes and pressed her lips against the muzzle, then slid the gun into her mouth. Her heart banged so hard against her ribs, she thought it might burst.

It would be so easy to pull the trigger.

Most women shot themselves in the chest, but that was too risky. Her finger pressed lightly against the trigger and she grimaced at the pleasure her death would give DeLattio. That sonofabitch could rot in hell as far as she was concerned. Her revenge was well planned whether she lived or died.

She hesitated. Did she really want to commit suicide? Even the word was distasteful. But it was an option, right? The ultimate way to regain control of her life.

Nat Sullivan's face flashed before her, not angry like he'd been when he'd left the cottage today, but smiling down at her from the back of a white horse, looking like heaven. *Damn, but there was something about that man...*

She took her finger off the trigger.

There would be an unholy mess left behind. Gunshot wounds to the head were never pretty. Taking the gun out of her mouth, she pointed it at the floor. Exhaled a tight breath.

An image of her parents and baby brother flashed through her mind and she wondered what her life would have been like had they not died when she'd been a little girl. She was the last one left of her family, probably the only person in the world who remembered her little brother's single-toothed smile.

Death might be an easy option, but it was still a cowardly escape from a hellish situation. She couldn't do it. She couldn't do it to the Sullivans, she couldn't do it to her long-dead parents, and she couldn't do it to herself.

Besides, why let Andrew DeLattio have that final victory?

Sensation returned to her body and she stretched out her sore limbs. The weight of misery lifted from her shoulders and dispelled like mist. Her grief was spent, her body aching but whole. Being raped and beaten had damn near killed her, but it wasn't the end of the world. There were far too many things left that she needed to do and she'd never taken the easy way out before.

Kissing the barrel of the pistol, she slipped it back under the pillow.

DeLattio would not win. She wasn't going to die a victim. If she had anything to do with it, she wasn't going to die at all.

***

Snow had stopped falling, leaving a world filled with sparkling sunshine and reflected light so bright it dazzled. Nat cleared the snow off the roads with the snowplow hitched to the front of his truck. Normally he'd have given the job to Cal or Ezra, but right now he wanted his own company and some mindless, honest toil. He turned his music up loud, too loud to think.

The valley looked beautiful, like a winter wonderland. Fence-posts made valiant attempts to break free of the shallow drifts, cast spindly shadows like cobwebs over the iced fields. He should really go get his camera and take a few shots. But he was avoiding Eliza Reed and that pissed him off. This was his home and she made him feel uncomfortable in it.

The barn and stables were shrouded with white cloaks that melted as a warm Chinook swept down off the mountain slopes. The thaw began in earnest when the sun reached its zenith.

Finishing up, Nat pulled the truck in front of the ranch house and cut the engine. Quietly, he sat in the quiet sunshine watching the crystal clear water drip rhythmically off the buildings. So what if he'd misread the situation yesterday? So what if he'd thought sticking your tongue in someone's mouth was a come-on signal? So what if he'd been ready to take her in a fury of passion after she'd just wept an ocean of tears in his lap?

His hands gripped the steering wheel, knuckles whitening with strain.

Hell.

That was what he couldn't get past. Yes, she'd kissed him, but she'd been upset, crying. He should have had the strength, and goddamn it, the good sense, to pull away.

He rubbed his fingers over his eyes. Cursed again. The fact that he'd been blown away by a simple kiss just meant it had been way too long since he'd had sex. It did not mean that Eliza Reed was special. Just because she was beautiful, with her stubborn ways and fierce nature, did not mean she was special.

But special or not, he owed her an apology.

He climbed out into the gray slush that carpeted the yard and went in search of Eliza. A pile of snow slid off the sloping roof of the ranch house with a solid 'whoosh'.

There was smoke coming from her chimney, but it was near midday and she'd spent most daylight hours helping out with the horses. He strode toward the paddock, climbed over the wooden rails and headed into the back of the stables, past the piles of hay, hoses and buckets.

Shadow and her foals were in their stall, little Red hiding behind his surrogate dam. The mare nickered as Nat went past, nudged him playfully for a treat. Nat obliged and filled up the feed bucket before he left. He checked all the stalls, but there was no sign of anybody, anywhere.

He heard the soft murmur of voices coming from outside and turned in that direction. Bright sunlight blinded him for a full five-seconds before he could see. Then bile hit his throat and he wished he hadn't bothered to search for Mizz Eliza Reed because at that moment she was stretched out full-length on top of Cal in the middle of the sodden training ring.

His hands fisted tightly as his stomach clenched. Reality blurred. Another dark-haired woman, stretched out over her lover beneath the thin veil of a mosquito net. That time he'd turned on his heel and never looked back, the two-carat engagement ring clutched tightly in the palm of his hand.

He forced out a breath. This time he was damned if he'd run.

***

Elizabeth tried to roll off Cal without crushing any vital organs but knew she'd failed when he cried out in pain as her knee struck a glancing blow off his crotch.

"Oh, God." She tried to sit up and help him, but he was curled up into a ball of pain, his face as white as pure Irish linen.

"I'm so sorry." She tried to pry him into a sitting position, but the man had a grip of iron on his abused anatomy and it was like trying to move a statue.

Christ, first she'd nearly flattened the poor bastard and then she'd kneed him in the balls. She sat back in the mud and knew it was going to take a few minutes before Cal would be able to get up. Though it galled her, she also knew she couldn't stand without his help.

Movement caught her eye and she swallowed her pride as Nat Sullivan approached. She'd been dreading seeing him all morning and he had to choose now to show up.

Well crap, at least he would be able to help Cal up out of the dirt.

She watched him walking towards her, long strides covering the muddy earth with ease. She was mortified that she'd thrown herself at him yesterday, and she owed him an apology.

He looked pristine, not a speck of dirt on his well-worn hide, whereas she looked like she'd been painted gray from the head down, and felt like one big muscle cramp.

She met his gaze, his blue eyes dark and intimidating. He looked pissed.

"Nat..." she began.

"How's the ankle, *Eliza*?" he interrupted. The inflection he placed on her name wasn't pretty, and there was nothing but cold derision in his gaze.

"Fine, thank you." She'd behaved badly yesterday, but she had her reasons. Sticking her chin out, she swallowed and looked him in the eye, trying to ignore the flush that rose up and heated her cheeks.

She tried again, "Nat..."

"Good." He stepped closer and pierced her like a bug on a pin with his steely blue gaze. Leaning down he laid a work-callused finger on the top button of her jacket, resting it just below her throat. Her pulse fluttered and froze, nervous of him for the first time.

"Don't mess with the men on this ranch, Eliza." His eyes drilled into her. "We don't need some goddamned prick-tease stirring up trouble around here."

Elizabeth started to splutter, but Nat walked away, leaving Cal heaving on the ground next to her, and her stranded with a bad ankle and a soaking wet butt.

"Well," she shouted after Nat as he climbed the fence, "I guess that makes you the prick then, huh?"

Cal sputtered a laugh, speculation rife in his eyes as he watched his boss stomp away.

"What?" She glared at him.

"Nothing," Cal croaked.

Elizabeth scrambled to her feet but only succeeded in slipping and thudding into Cal's hipbone.

"Awww," he cried out.

"Sorry." Elizabeth wanted to cry. Again. When she'd woken up, her ankle was swollen to the size of a melon and she couldn't even get her own boots on. Luckily, 'her being so big and all', Cal had said that he had a pair of boots that would fit her.

He'd hoisted her onto the back of Tiger before heading out to check on the cattle. He might have been whipcord thin without a spare ounce of flesh on his body, but he sure as hell was strong.

She'd spent the next two hours trying to rope a damned fence post while the ranch hands had disappeared off to the far-flung corners of the farm to check the stock. Nat had been nowhere in sight.

And she hadn't been able to get off the damned horse.

Some professional she was. For the first hour and a half she hadn't even noticed her predicament. She'd practiced in the small corral that had been cleared of snow. Wheeling backwards and forwards, she'd controlled Tiger with her knees and the lightest touch of the reins against the horse's neck. She worked tirelessly, deep in concentration, round and round the small corral until she was dizzy with it. She'd ignored her sore ankle and applied herself to learning the art of riding western-style and to roping.

'Rope is like a living thing,' Cal had told her before he'd gone off and left her for *two-goddamned-hours*. 'You have to think about it in its entirety, not just the bit in your hand. It's like a flow of energy and you have to become one with the rope, let it become an extension of your arm.'

The Zen art of roping.

Well, she'd sucked at roping.

By chewing the Tylenol she'd packed in her jacket pocket, she'd managed to endure her throbbing ankle and numb butt, and knew she'd hurt like a bitch tomorrow.

Two hours after Cal had left her with 'roping wisdom for beginners', he'd returned full of anxiety, having finally remembered that there was no one else back at the ranch to help her. Sure she could have thrown herself off the horse's back, but she was damned if she was going to wreck the other ankle too. At this rate she'd be leaving the ranch in a wheelchair, *or a body bag.*

But she didn't want to think about that.

Cal had done his best not to laugh at her woebegone state. And, convicted killer or not, she found herself returning his grin, despite the fact that every muscle in her body felt like it had been beaten.

Hell, I should know.

She'd dismounted with all the grace of a shot pheasant, plummeting to earth on legs that had turned into limp noodles. Cal had tried to catch her, but she'd flattened him with momentum.

Then Nat had showed up.

She glanced at the cowboy who was now trying to stand, gingerly clutching his crotch.

"I am *not* a prick-tease," Elizabeth said.

Cal didn't disagree and went back to being mute as he offered her a spare hand up. Pulling her to her feet he surprised her with another grin.

"He's jealous," he said, "me being such a fine catch an' all."

Elizabeth considered that for a moment and discarded the notion. "Jealous, my ass. He's a numbskull, bone-headed jackass."

So much for the apology she'd prepared. Nat could stuff it where the sun didn't shine, all the way up to his tonsils.

Pain streaked up her ankle as she tried to put more weight on it. Cal pulled her arm across his shoulder and placed the other around her waist. Cautiously they moved forward through the slush, like a pair of wounded warriors, covered from head to toe in mud.

She'd made a big step forward today. Being forced to touch Cal, to get on and off the horse, had proved she could still function in a normal situation with a man who didn't threaten her. She didn't always freeze up and freak out.

It felt good being mad. It sure beat the crap out of being miserable.

She blew out a heavy sigh of frustration that Cal interpreted as pain and he tried to take more of her weight to help her back to her cabin. But pain wasn't the problem for Elizabeth. Pain she could deal with.

Lust was the problem.

Lust was supposed to be a simple emotion for the unattached, but she both ached for and feared Nathan Sullivan's touch in equal measures.

Clutching Cal's shoulder hard enough to bruise, she hobbled back to the cottage closely followed by Blue, who wagged his tail as they hopped up the three steps.

"Okay, fella," she said as Cal let the dog in first.

The best plan of action was a hot bath and a long cold beer.

Nat Sullivan could rot in hell.

***

She spent the next few days helping out Ryan and Cal on the ranch. Today she'd been assigned to work the cattle chute. The weather had warmed up considerably and most of the snow had melted off the lower slopes, leaving the creeks full to bursting.

The vacation had been exactly what they'd advertised: backbreaking hard work, no-frills and basic. It wasn't a dude ranch, there was no hot-tub to soak in when you got saddle-sore, no trips to local tourist attractions, no refried beans for dinner. It was a plain and simple 'working holiday', with the emphasis on 'work'. The contrast between ranch life and her urban existence in New York was marked by a gulf so wide they could have been on different planets. Her Fendi furs and Sergio Rossi high heels had been exchanged for Levi's and work boots. Rather than sipping lattés, organizing exhibitions and tracking down fraudsters, she'd spent every minute of daylight looking after the stock or fixing up the ranch. Most evenings she fell asleep on the couch, too tired to move.

She'd settled in. Relaxed.

Nat avoided her altogether and headed up to the mountains to check out the snow in the summer pastures. But just because he wasn't there didn't mean she didn't think about him. She'd mellowed during the week and didn't know whether to be annoyed with him or herself. She'd kissed him and then freaked out, and then he'd jumped to his own conclusions about her cracked personality when he'd seen her lying on top of Cal. The fact that they were the wrong conclusions wasn't really his fault; she was a mess and he was a million times better off without her. Maybe it was better this way, she decided, because nobody would get hurt.

Cal herded a small calf into the chute. It called for its mother, clattered against the railings with instinctive fear. Elizabeth was sitting on an overturned crate with her clipboard on her knee and a red pencil tucked behind her ear. She handled the small Black Angus calves like a pro, now, murmuring reassuringly to them, checking yellow ear tags and weighing each calf individually before freeing them so they could go find their mammas. Some were kept aside for fattening, most were being sent to market.

The work was easy for the most part, but tiring. They were separating out the surplus cattle and preparing the rest of the herd for tagging, castration and vaccination. The rest of the time was spent putting out salt-licks or feed for the cows and exercising the horses.

Ryan had told her that fire destroyed a swathe of upper pastures and the ranch couldn't support last year's herd anymore. Nobody knew if they'd get government aid either because last year's appropriation fund had run out and nobody knew if there was any money in the kitty to spare more beleaguered farmers. Costs were rising all around. And there was the threat of BSE.

Up until a week ago, Elizabeth had had no idea that ranching was so complicated.

Elizabeth tried to put the Sullivans' problems out of her mind. Money had never been a problem for her and she wished she could just hand over a wad of cash and make everything all right. But it didn't work like that, and Elizabeth had discovered a long time ago that money didn't make your problems disappear; it just buried them for a while.

Plus, she liked to keep a low profile about the extent of her personal wealth. She hadn't earned it; she had inherited it at the expense of her family's early deaths. First her parents, and then her aunt, who'd moved to the States when she'd married an American steel magnate. Elizabeth would rather have family—but you couldn't buy family.

Chewing her pen, she mused, maybe she could do something to help the Sullivans financial problems without revealing herself. She could get her lawyers back in Ireland to set something up...maybe.

Old Ezra, the second ranch hand, was a sweet, gnarled old bear of a man, with a corrugated forehead, big ears and a nose the size of a Boeing 747. He smiled easily, despite the look of pain that narrowed his washed-out blue eyes.

He ambled over, his potbelly forcing him to hitch up his pants along the way. He liked chatting to her, always giving her snippets of information he'd obviously read in the morning papers.

"Did you know," he began, "that Australia is the most obese country in the whole stinking world?"

She shook her head and wondered if Ezra thought that made him thinner than all Australians.

"Nat spent a lot of time down in Australia." Ezra spat a wad of tobacco on the ground next to his boot and squashed it into the dirt with his heel. "Said it was as hot as Hades." He rubbed the shiny spot on his bald head as Elizabeth called out and recorded another tag-number and calf-weight, before pulling up the gate lever and letting the calf go.

Ezra looked bothered about something and it didn't take him long to divulge.

"Imagine being real fat in such a hot place. Having to show off all that flab in those skimpy clothes." Ezra stroked his well-defined gut that was thankfully hidden beneath a washed-out navy shirt. "Stinking ugly."

He had a point.

Elizabeth stuffed her pencil into her mouth and tried not to smile, but she couldn't help it. Trying to move on from the problems of exposing too much unwanted flesh, she noted, "You don't curse much do you, Ezra?"

"Never." He shook his head then paused with his head tilted to one side as he considered her question harder. "Well now, I guess I do in my head, but 'stinking' is the word that comes out of my mouth."

"I never used to swear," Elizabeth said, mulling it over. Since she'd attended the academy her language had taken a real nose-dive.

She stood, but staggered on her injured ankle. It was much better, but still weak. "Feck!" Her voice carried and echoed off the hills in a rare moment of silence and everyone looked up from what they were doing.

She grinned at Ezra's appalled expression. "It's not what you think. *Feck* just means damn or heck. It's Irish."

Ezra rubbed his belly before taking his tobacco pouch out of his back pocket and popping a tab into his mouth.

"*Stinking* works better for me," he said, and then laughed a huge belly laugh as he trundled off back to the cattle.

Chapter Eight

_____

Stone Creek, Montana, April 11ᵗʰ

Cal held the saloon door open for Elizabeth and she walked into a solid barrage of bodies with rock blasting from the sound system. She'd braced for country, got rock.

Figured.

Following Ryan's rapidly disappearing back she squeezed between groups of cowboys and pushed when space became tight.

She found a gap at the bar and Ryan miraculously grabbed a stool for her. She didn't need it, but decided it might make a good anchor if her buddies got lucky with the ladies. She ordered a round of ice-cold beer and saluted her new friends before taking a thirst-quenching swig straight from the bottle.

The familiarity of the routine eased her mind. She'd always enjoyed the camaraderie of drinking with the boys and the bar wasn't quite the den of iniquity it looked from the outside. It was full of cowboys wearing their best western shirts, clean jeans, highly polished boots and every size of hat, from ten-gallon to ball cap. The women varied. Most were dressed in western-style clothes, but some of the younger ones were squeezed into Lycra and sparkles.

The *Screw Loose* was a roadhouse on the edge of the small town of Stone Creek about ten miles north of the ranch. It was one big room with a horseshoe bar set against the back wall. A row of booths sat beneath the front windows where customers could eat. A few tall tables were bolted to the floor, stacked high with so many glasses they were beginning to look like crystal sculptures. Peanut shells littered the floor and crunched beneath her boots—at least that's what she hoped was crunching beneath her boots.

A large-screen TV filled one wall; the Canadiens were hammering the Ducks 5:0. Large mirrors lined the back of the bar and added to the chaos, making the place look even more packed than it actually was. The dance floor heaved with energetic bodies writhing and shaking as Nickelback burned it to the ground.

Ryan was nodding to the music, looking for someone to dance with. He looked in her direction

"When hell freezes over." She shook her head when he gave her a puppy dog expression.

Cal pulled up a stool next to Elizabeth and made his opinion on dancing clear. He sipped his beer and slouched backwards against the bar, leaning on his elbows. Elizabeth noted a group of biker boys staring at Cal, throwing him hostile glares.

Back at the ranch, she'd asked him if he'd gotten counseling when inside. Cal had told her, 'cowboys didn't get counseling, they got drunk.'

Right then.

Elizabeth figured it wasn't easy being a convicted murderer in a small town, and wondered why Cal hung around. It would have been easier to make a fresh start somewhere where people didn't know your history. She should know. She shrugged it off, and figured it was nothing to do with her. She and Cal were vaguely friends, nothing more. He had his reasons for living his life the way he did and she had hers. She wasn't about to explain hers to anybody.

Ryan spotted an old girlfriend across the room and excused himself to head off and claim her for a dance. Conversation was impossible so she and Cal just drank their beer and watched the show.

Nat Sullivan had hurt her feelings and dented her pride. Nobody had wielded that kind of power over her for a long time. She was surprised she hadn't packed her bags and left. Maybe she just didn't know where to go, or maybe bullheadedness had her digging her heels in. Whatever the reason, she was glad she'd stayed at the ranch.

A big guy with a long ZZ top beard and small wire-framed glasses came across and spoke to Cal, trying to include her in the conversation. She smiled at him, but didn't answer his questions except for vague mutters that were lost in the noisy bar. She wasn't worried about anyone recognizing her. Her disguise was good enough and the disinformation she'd left behind would take them far from this corner of the United States and only Josie knew where she really was.

She spotted Ryan doing some dirty dancing in the corner with a redhead and hid a smile. That cowboy knew how to party. He acted like an irresponsible teenager most of the time, rarely making time for his daughter, but she knew he'd lost his childhood sweetheart to cancer and that couldn't have been easy. He worked hard and partied harder.

The Sullivans had been a revelation to her. People were always more than you thought, and often less than you wanted.

Elizabeth admired the determination with which Rose Sullivan pursued her recovery from her recent heart attack—like it was just another battle to be fought. And Elizabeth spent a lot of time with Sarah, mostly late in the evening after Sarah came home from the hospital after a marathon shift and Tabitha was tucked up in bed. The woman could talk a mile-a-minute and was nosey as hell, but Elizabeth liked her.

Then there was Nat.

At least she didn't have to wonder what it would be like to kiss him. She knew. It had been like touching the stars from the depths of hell. That kiss—the incredible heat of it stayed locked in her memory, and she could still feel his hands on her body and was damned if she didn't want them there again.

Maybe hot rampant sex with Nathan Sullivan was exactly what she needed.

She thought about him, those sapphire blue eyes and those strong broad shoulders and those long, long legs. Harmless thoughts, now that he was away in the mountains.

At least she didn't have to lie to him.

She'd fielded questions about her past from everyone on the ranch, and she told them the lies that were the closest to the truth, but nevertheless lies all the same. She hated every word of it.

For years lies had been her game, deception and intrigue, sleight of hand and poker face. Now she wanted it over with, finished. But telling the Sullivans the truth would put them in danger and she wouldn't risk it.

It was Friday night and she had cabin fever. It

wasn't the isolation of the ranch that got to her—
she savored that. It was the isolation from
information. The Sullivans weren't hooked up to the
Internet, something Sarah had suggested not so
subtly that Elizabeth, IT specialist that she was
supposed to be, could help them with. Nor could
she get a signal on her cell phone. She'd taken the
opportunity of a Friday night out with the boys to
go into town and check up on Josie.

Thankfully, Josie was fine.

In the cottage, she'd splashed cold water on her
face, but decided against makeup. Juliette wore
makeup, Eliza didn't. She smoothed her wayward
hair back into a loose ponytail, grabbed her
lumberjack coat and dumped her Glock in her
purse.

Now Elizabeth found herself watching the
saloon door like a teenager with a crush. Cal
expected Nat back anytime soon and said if he
wasn't home by morning that he was going up after
him.

The music changed again and this time the
Dixie Chicks declared that *Earl had to die*.
Elizabeth hadn't expected to like country music, but
she loved the Chicks.

She didn't see it coming but suddenly she
pushed sideways off her stool and sent sprawling
onto the gritty floor. She landed between a woman's
legs and was trodden on as the woman's companion
dragged his girl out of harm's way.

Thanks, buddy.

Then all hell broke loose.

Some skinny guy with tattoos snaking down his
arm took a swing at Cal. Cal managed a left hook
that knocked the other guy down, but was grabbed

from behind by some thug with a dirty blond ponytail. He held Cal up like a punching bag and three other guys waded in.

"Damn it." Elizabeth clambered to her feet, rubbed wet, sticky hands on now grimy jeans. Cal was fighting back, but odds were four to one, and they weren't taking prisoners.

Frantically she searched the crowd for Ryan, but the crush of people meant it would take an age for him to break through, even if he realized what was going on.

The guy on the floor got up and the odds were now five to one. Nobody appeared to be siding with the lone man from the Triple H.

Feck. Elizabeth took a deep breath and wished she could draw her gun. *So much for avoiding the limelight.*

She grabbed the guy who held Cal's arms and put him out of action with a single blow to the temple. Released, Cal was at least able to defend himself, but Elizabeth could tell he'd been badly hurt. She swung around to confront the nearest biker, the skinny one with the tattoos. She grabbed his shaggy blond hair and swung him around to face her, smashing the flat of her palm into his nose just hard enough to break it. He dropped to his knees, gasping and choking on blood.

Suddenly, Nat appeared out of the crowd and shouted, "Get the truck." He tossed the keys towards her and leapt into the fray.

Boy, was she glad to see him. She stood for a moment and wondered where the heck Ryan was and tried to work out who was winning the fight. Nat wrestled one guy, who must have weighed two-hundred-fifty pounds, to the floor and held him down in a chokehold. He was good, she'd give him that, but there were still two guys beating the crap out of Cal.

The one closest to her was only about five-foot-eight, but he was stocky and using a beer bottle to inflict damage. Cal went down. Ignoring Nat's instructions, she side-kicked the guy's spleen into his throat. Turning to face her, his eyes blazing with rage and not a little indignation, he lifted the bottle and heaved it at her. She ducked, but it caught her a glancing blow on the temple. She ignored the pain, grabbed his ears and pushed his face into her raised knee. Satisfied, she watched him drop like a stone.

Nat had just finished with the big guy on the floor, but Cal was still fending off one guy who seemed determined to smash him to a pulp. This last guy was a little taller, a little leaner and meaner than the rest of them. One of his hands came behind his back as he prepared to take a swing. Elizabeth grabbed his wrist and elbow, twisted hard and shoved his arm up toward his neck. Then she grabbed his hair and he yelled out in surprise as she slammed him into the bar. He never knew what happened. He fell like a brick to the floor and Elizabeth narrowed her eyes on a face that was now less than pretty.

Cal was slumped against a barstool, breathing hard, his face already swelling. Working on instinct and the need to escape, she grabbed him and threw his arm over her shoulder and started to haul him out. His weight eased off her shoulders and she turned to see Nat take Cal's other arm. Adrenaline still pumped through her body, but relief welled up as she caught Nat's eye and sent him an unsteady smile.

He had a cut lip, but apart from that he looked good. *Christ, he looked great.* They piled out through the crowd into the fresh night air and stumbled across the road to where Nat's truck was parked.

Elizabeth helped Cal into the backseat and then turned to look for Nat, who'd run over to a car parked further down the street. She frowned in confusion, wondering what he was doing as he knocked on the window and a disheveled Ryan popped up his head.

It seemed that Ryan was a faster mover than even Elizabeth had anticipated.

Nat spoke to him and pointed at his truck. Ryan nodded and Elizabeth watched him give a quick kiss to his companion and jump out of the car. At least he managed to do up his pants before he crossed the road. Elizabeth's mouth was open and her eyebrows stuck in her hairline by the time he reached Nat's truck.

"Let's go," Nat opened the passenger door for Elizabeth, which she thought was absurdly old fashioned and polite under the circumstances. She jumped in. Ryan climbed into his own truck and they both gunned the engines for home.

***

Back at the ranch, Elizabeth paced the den while Sarah patched up Cal. The den was rustic and welcoming with bright, Navaho rugs adorning the floors, along with a couple of bleached skulls on the walls that would have looked right at home in a Georgia O'Keeffe painting.

Cal lay shirtless on an old red couch, sharp

features pale and drawn, his hazel eyes unfocused with pain. He was as white as a shroud. Red wheals covered his lean body, and Elizabeth figured at least one of the attackers had worn a knuckle-duster. By tomorrow Cal would be black and blue, and sore all over.

Nat helped him sit up as Sarah wrapped a bandage around his torso. Sarah had given Cal painkillers, but from the look on his face Elizabeth didn't think they'd kicked in yet.

"You might have a hairline fracture," Sarah said, gently probing Cal's chest. "You'll live," she gave him a weak smile, "but tomorrow you're getting an X-ray."

Cal shook his head, but Sarah ignored him and brushed his short hair back from his damp forehead. "Why can't they just leave you alone?"

Cal captured her hand and squeezed. "Leave it."

Sarah rose and turned her attention to Elizabeth, pulling her down to sit in an easy chair so she could examine the wound on her scalp.

"What happened to you? Caught in the crossfire?" Sarah's competent fingers gently examined the cut on Elizabeth's temple.

Elizabeth muttered something noncommittal and would have scowled at Ryan who was grinning at her, but her forehead was too sore. Ryan had been filled in on the action after Nat had roused Sarah.

At least Elizabeth had tried to keep a low profile. *Ex-queen of undercover does local bar fight, rodeo-style.* She glanced up, found Nat watching her with a narrowed gaze that she couldn't decipher. He still had his jacket on, looked like he wasn't staying, looked like he was forcing himself to stand still.

Sarah dabbed peroxide onto the cut and Elizabeth sucked in her breath. She didn't cry out, but she wanted to. Why was the treatment always worse than the injury?

"A flying beer bottle," Elizabeth said and sat back with a jolt as Sarah shone a penlight into her eyes.

"Looks like you may have a mild concussion." Sarah frowned, concern showing in her blue-gray eyes. "You should really go to the ER and have a CAT scan."

"It's nothing," Elizabeth insisted. She wasn't going anywhere.

"Get her coat. I'll drive her." Nat spoke to Ryan like she was blind, deaf and dumb. The pent up energy she'd sensed in him seemed to find a release as he walked over and stared down at her with grim lines around his mouth.

"I'm not going." Elizabeth glared Ryan right back into his seat. Even the thought of an ER room made her stomach pitch. Last time she'd been in the hospital she'd been subjected to a rape kit and she wasn't going back unless they carried her there unconscious and bleeding. *That* image hung all too vividly in her head.

Nat leaned close enough for her to feel his breath on her cheek. His fingers branded her upper arm, his blue eyes glowed with inner fire. "Yes, you are."

"No, Mr. President." Elizabeth shoved his hand away, their gazes colliding like rapiers. "I'm not."

Sarah intervened, shushing Nat when he started to say more. He moved away and angrily shrugged off his jacket.

That's right buddy, back off. She hid her smile,

but lost all sense of triumph when Sarah continued.

"Then you'll need someone to watch over you tonight and wake you every hour." Sarah's pale-brown eyebrows lifted when she saw Elizabeth was about to argue. "That's your choice, Eliza. Hospital or a night-nurse."

Either way, Elizabeth figured she was in for a sleepless night. Great. *Fecking great.*

Sarah moved away to recheck Cal's blood pressure.

Yawning hugely, Ryan grinned and stood. "Remind me never to piss off you city girls, Sugar. I like my face just the way it is."

"So did that redhead, Slick," Elizabeth quipped, hoping to deflect attention away from herself. "Just *what* were you doing to her in that car?" If she'd thought to make him blush she failed miserably.

"If you don't know by now, you never will," Ryan laughed but his gaze flicked uneasily to his sister.

There was a finite pause that stretched into an obvious silence. Eliza followed the brothers' stares. Sarah Sullivan scowled like an upset owl.

"What redhead?" Sarah asked slowly.

"Stacy," Ryan said, standing tall and tucking in his chin.

"Stacy Hopkins?" Sarah asked him, her eyes narrowing like she was drawing a bead.

Ryan nodded.

"You were screwing Stacy Hopkins while Cal and Eliza were being beaten up?"

Elizabeth's eyes popped. She'd unleashed a wildcat.

Ryan looked guiltily towards Cal. "I wasn't expecting trouble."

"No," Sarah replied, "you never do."

She raised her hands to her face and Elizabeth thought for one awful moment that she was going to cry. The whole room held its breath.

"Stacy's not so bad—" Ryan began, but was cut off by Sarah's sneer.

"She's a no-good slut who's always after something that doesn't belong to her." Sarah glared at her brother with rage gathering in her eyes.

"She stole your boyfriend back in high school," Ryan shot back. "Get over it." He walked over to where his sister sat on the couch. "And I don't belong to anyone, not anymore."

Shocked silence echoed around the room for a full ten seconds, until Sarah asked quietly, "What about Tabitha?"

Ryan flinched.

Elizabeth was spellbound. Everybody else might be used to the family dynamics and fireworks, but not her. This was the closest she'd come to seeing a real family operate in years.

Ryan backed off, the anger leaving him as quickly as it had come. Scrubbing a hand over his face, he turned and glanced her way.

"Sorry—didn't mean to cause a scene." He looked battered, emotionally raw.

It wasn't her business, she reminded herself. It was nothing to do with her. She shook her head, shrugged her shoulders. "No problem."

Cal made the effort to stand. He clutched his battered ribs, groaning in pain. Sarah turned to help him with a gentle touch.

"You can take a bed upstairs tonight, Caleb Landon." Sarah ordered, clearly back in control of her temper. "No way you're working tomorrow, so the least you can do is stay here so I can make sure you're all right without trudging up to the bunk house every half hour."

Cal didn't argue. He disengaged Sarah's helping hands and hobbled slowly across the room to where Nat and Elizabeth stood side by side. He stuck his hand out and Nat shook it firmly. Then he stepped up to Elizabeth and did the same.

"I owe you one."

He winced as he clapped her on the shoulder and she had to work hard to smother her sympathy. He looked so beat up that every movement must have hurt like hell and if he did have a cracked rib, he'd be out of action for weeks.

Just what the Sullivans needed.

Nat moved to help him up the stairs, but Ryan was already there. Sarah followed them up, clucking like a mother hen. And suddenly, Elizabeth didn't know how they'd been maneuvered, but she and Nat were alone in the den.

She listened to the others move out of earshot, each squeak of a floorboard and turn of a doorknob marking their progress. When all was silent, Elizabeth wished she was anywhere but alone with this man who made her feel stupid and defensive, and whom she'd kissed to within an inch of embarrassment.

The silence grew tense. Elizabeth glanced up at Nat's face, unsure of his mood. He'd been angry before, now he was...watching her closely, dark eyes narrowed and thoughtful, his mouth set hard.

Crap.

She raised a weary hand to her forehead—tried not to look pathetic.

There was no way she could fight with Nat

Sullivan; she did not have the energy. Normally she was tougher than this, but the brawl had dissipated the edginess she'd felt all day, and now she was sore and exhausted. She'd had enough.

"I'm sorry." His voice had a rough edge as if he were unsure of the right words. His blond hair fell across his forehead; softened the strong planes of his face and made him look younger. He leaned his tall, rangy frame against the oak mantelpiece, crossed his arms over his wide chest and smiled.

Looked way too good for comfort.

Elizabeth walked over to the couch, collapsed onto the soft cushions and closed her eyes against those sparkling blue gems. Paul Newman had nothing on Nat Sullivan.

"Got a barrel-load of excuses, but none of them make a blind bit of difference. I was way outta line the other day and I'm sorry."

She heard him walk towards her, felt the sofa give as he sat down next to her. She tried not to shrink away, but couldn't quite control her tired body. Her mouth twisted into a grim line of self-disgust. The fear was as unstoppable as the tide and she despised herself.

She wanted to tell him to go to hell. To deny the feelings she knew being close to this man would stir up. But she couldn't. After years of deception, honesty was finally taking the upper hand. She held her tongue, forced herself to open her eyes.

Facing her with questions in his blue eyes, he reached out and traced a finger gently along the edge of her wound.

A shiver followed his touch.

"You sure you're okay?"

"I'm fine." A week ago Elizabeth would have

slapped his hand away, instead she let him touch her—as an experiment.

"You're a guest here..." He hesitated, seemed to reassess his words, and took her pale hand from where it lay frozen in her lap. Instinct made her want to jerk it away, but she faltered, fascinated by the contact.

She stared at their linked fingers.

His large hand engulfed hers. She forced herself not to run screaming from the room, forced herself not to hang on too tightly. A callused thumb scraped her nerves as he gently rubbed her palm.

It felt like the most intimate act of all, that cradling of fingers.

She looked up and fell headfirst into a deep blue gaze that seized her and wouldn't let go.

"The other day...I was coming to apologize for what happened in the cabin. For kissing you. Then I saw you lying on top of Cal and I saw red, acted like an idiot." His gaze penetrated and searched her soul for answers, her hand captured in his warm solid grip. "I am sorry." His eyes shone darkly. "I wanted to pound Cal into the ground." He gave a short laugh tinged with irony. "Might have saved the poor bastard one hell of a beating."

"There's nothing going on between Cal and me." She pulled her hand away, immediately regretted the lack of contact.

Nat sat looking so handsome, so bloody perfect that she actually wanted to kiss him again. She needed to go, needed to get out of here before she made a fool of herself. Once she'd been tougher than this, but now she couldn't even force her legs to move.

They sat quietly for a moment, listened to the

silence of the room, interrupted only by the blast of the furnace.

"You called me a prick-tease." Elizabeth muttered, still irritated by that one particular detail.

"Hmm." Nat grimaced like he'd hoped she'd forgotten. "Yes, ma'am, I did."

"I didn't..." Elizabeth stumbled over the clarification, struggling to find the right words. "I'm not," she finished lamely.

"No, I figured that out all by myself." Humor turned his smile into a sexy grin. "I'm a jackass."

"Yes." Elizabeth rose to her feet, needing to be honest. "No. It wasn't your fault. With me kissing you the way I did and then treating you like some kind of...rapist." She stumbled over the word. Looked quickly away.

Nat stared down at his scuffed boots for a long moment before saying quietly, "Well, I guess you had your reasons."

Her heart froze. Silence stretched thin as she blinked at him in noiseless horror. *He knew.* The muscles in her throat constricted and she couldn't move, couldn't breathe. He couldn't know. She wasn't branded on the outside like one of his cattle. But the cowboy looked at her like she was as transparent as glass.

Chapter Nine

Nat watched her face, noted the dilated pupils and bloodless lips. He clenched his fists. Something had happened to her, but she wasn't giving away any secrets. Not that he blamed her.

When he'd first gone up to the summer cabin he'd been angry, furious even, reminders of Nina's betrayal like a knife wound in his chest. But after a day or two of solitude, he'd given a lot of thought to the hot kiss he and Eliza had shared and the way she'd suddenly freaked out when he'd touched her. It didn't take a Ph.D. in psychology to figure she had some hang-ups about sex.

As a freelance nature photographer Nat had been around more than most. Once, he'd been caught up in a bloody civil war where a dream assignment had quickly deteriorated into a nightmare. He'd been lucky to get out alive. Others hadn't been so fortunate. Another time, poachers had threatened his life for documenting their ruthless destruction of black rhino. Only his proficiency with a rifle had saved his ass that time.

Those experiences had carved a hole in his soul that had never quite healed. That man could be so evil toward his fellow man had opened his eyes to the dark side of human nature.

The look on Eliza's face after that kiss had been full of terror and self-loathing. Not teasing. His sexual frustration had clouded his judgment, but eventually, in the quiet of the mountains, he'd acknowledged it and been repelled by his own actions. Then Cal had called him up on the radio. Given him almighty hell for being such a jerk.

Nat didn't want to get involved with another beautiful woman—didn't like the way Eliza Reed stirred up those feelings that had lain dormant for the past three years. But despite her prickly armor and her ability to kick-ass, there was something fragile about this woman. She was dangerous—he knew that, but she had a vulnerability that pulled him, sucked him in and left him wanting to know more.

And if that kiss was anything to go by, the attraction went both ways. So, regardless of her suspicious nature, he was going to see where it led.

Eerie catlike eyes watched him, defiant and proud, and ready to flee.

"Wanna talk about it?" he asked.

Eliza shook her head, dark hair fanning her shoulders where it had come loose from its ponytail. Her narrowed eyes nailed him dead in the eye. "No."

That drew a smile. Unlike most things tonight, *that* didn't surprise him. Eliza Reed was more evasive than a timber wolf, and he had to wonder what the hell she was hiding from.

An abusive husband?

A fist of panic double-punched his gut, both the thought that she might be unavailable, and the thought that someone had lifted a hand against her.

The white sheen of bone showed beneath the skin of her knuckles as she gripped the mantel. Still as a statue and twice as pale, she was as nervous as hell, and he hated it.

"Where'd you learn to fight like that?" he asked,

hoping to move onto neutral territory. She froze again, telling him a lot more than he wanted to know. Another sensitive subject.

A sigh of defeat vibrated low in his diaphragm and he rubbed his chin. At first he didn't think she was going to answer, he could see her mentally weighing the odds of opening up.

"Law enforcement," she said finally, breaking the silence with a giant breath, and putting a tentative hand to her scalp wound. "I used to be in law enforcement."

"Law enforcement?" He rolled the words on his tongue to see how they fit. Not what he'd expected to hear—not in a million years, but... "That where you learned to shoot?" The pieces snapped together.

"Yes." Eliza walked over and picked up her jacket off the newel of the stairs. "And now I'm going to bed."

"Okay. I'm with ya," he said, rising off the couch.

"No. You're not."

"You're concussed, remember?" Nat walked past her, out of the den and down the hall toward the kitchen. He held the door open while Eliza stood and gaped at him.

She followed him out into the hall, her gaze ripe with exasperation. "I don't need anyone watching out for me."

"Yeah, well, Sas said you do and she's the doc." Nat walked back to where she stood, casting her in shadow. "I'll sleep on the pull-out in the other room and wake you every couple of hours."

Eliza held his gaze for a full ten seconds before giving in. She deflated before his eyes, shrank as the anger left her, and brushed past him into the kitchen.

"Eliza." Nat called out softly as she walked away from him. "If I'd wanted to hurt you, I'd have done it the first night you were here. Before anybody even knew you'd arrived."

She stopped with her hand on the doorknob and turned back to face him, her eyes dark bruises that haunted a pale face.

"I won't hurt you." He wanted to shout the words but whispered them instead.

She nodded and headed out the door.

***

He caught up with her just outside the kitchen door. Elizabeth forced herself to walk slowly, not to run away as her instincts urged her to do. Nat hadn't bothered with a jacket. He led her through the cold night wearing only a blue plaid shirt and a pair of old Wranglers. He didn't seem to notice the cold that made her huddle into the warm depths of her coat, her breath condensing on the inside of her collar.

They reached the steps of the cottage and Nat walked right in, held the door for her before going over to fill the wood stove.

Like he owned the place.

Oh yeah. He did own the place. She stifled a giggle with the fingers of her right hand. Maybe she *did* have a concussion.

Blue's tail thumped lazily against the bare wooden floor. Elizabeth closed the door behind her, took off her jacket and stood twisting it in her fingers. The cottage was small but comely, with yellow walls that gave it a cozy feel. The stripped pine and hardwood floor glowed from years of waxing and polishing and she loved the warm rustic charm of the place.

But she hadn't noticed how small it was until now.

Nat watched her, his eyes moving over her like a laser that missed nothing. The lamps she'd left on cast an amber glow across his features and defined the plains of his face, catching pale highlights in his hair.

Beautiful. Gilded in gold.

Somehow his beauty only made her life seem more hideous.

"What was that fight about?" Elizabeth asked, unsure of how to behave with this man in her cabin. Last time she'd jumped him and her cheeks heated with embarrassment.

Nat carried on watching her, but didn't reply. She looked at his big hands filling the wood-burner with large logs of split wood and made a last determined effort, wanting to break the spell he cast over her nerves. "Why did those guys beat up Cal?"

Nat closed the burner and dusted his hands on the front of his jeans before moving toward her. Slow steps that made her want to bolt. She held very still, every muscle tensed. He reached out, took the jacket from between her nervous fingers.

"Cal told you he served time, right?"

She nodded as he hung her coat on the back of the door. She twisted the ring on her finger.

"His step-daddy was one mean old son of a bitch, and used to beat the crap out of Cal and his mother every time he tied one on. I saw Cal a couple of times...afterwards." Nat shook his head. "One day he snapped. He was just a boy, but he hit his step-daddy over the head with a baseball bat and broke the fucker's skull."

Elizabeth swallowed as the graphic image formed in her mind. At the age of fourteen, Cal killed a man. At age fourteen, all she'd been worried about was whether she was going to have to share a room at school and what exam subjects to take. There were worse things in life than being an orphan.

Nat's blue eyes watched her carefully. "One of the guys in the bar was Cal's younger stepbrother. He's still a little pissed at Cal for killing his daddy."

Elizabeth nodded, also understanding the pain of losing a parent to violence. Her own had been innocent victims of the terror campaign that had nearly destroyed Northern Ireland, but she couldn't sympathize with a bully.

Silence hung heavy in the air between them.

Elizabeth stood and shivered, but not from cold. Life was never simple. Everybody had a story. She twisted the gold signet ring on her pinkie, aware her nervous traits were showing through, unable to control them. Those dark-blue eyes of his watched her with a look that was close to caring; it spun magic around her—scared her with maybes.

What would it be like to get involved with a man like Nat Sullivan?

More to the point, could she face a lifetime of regret, wondering what it would have been like to be held in those strong arms and kissed by that beautiful mouth? No matter how short that lifetime may be?

Can I let DeLattio control my life even now?

She could get lost in those blue depths, in the curve of a smile that hooked a single dimple in his left jaw. He lifted his hand and gently brushed a strand of hair from her forehead. Heat bloomed in her cheeks as she retreated an inch. She wasn't strong enough. Not yet. She took a half step back, nonplussed, bit her bottom lip.

"Go to bed," he ordered, as if he hadn't noticed her staring at him with naked longing a second earlier. "I'll wake you in a couple hours."

"Gee, thanks," she forced a laugh, started to turn away. She wasn't ready for intimacy, but God she wouldn't mind a kiss. Better that than the nightmares that usually kept her company.

She hesitated.

"Least I can do. Go." He slapped her on the backside and she jumped in surprise. She wasn't somebody who touched very easily, never had been. People usually kept their distance.

She arched a brow at his grinning face. "You may not have noticed, *Mr*. Sullivan, but I don't like being ordered around." As she said it, she turned her back on his smile. The thought of sex should have made her run a mile, but tonight it tempted.

"Oh, I noticed all right," Nat drawled as she paused in the bedroom doorway and glanced over her shoulder. Then he grinned, looking like a sinner at the gates of Heaven. "But frankly my dear, I don't give a damn."

***

The insistent beep of his wristwatch alarm pulled Nat from a deep sleep. It took him a moment to remember why he was asleep on the couch in the guest cottage, but when he did, he threw off the blanket and sat up.

Blue's legs twitched in his sleep as he dreamed of chasing rabbits.

Nat padded barefoot to the bedroom and carefully opened the door. A slice of soft light filtered through from the lounge where the lamp still shone. It cut across the folds and curves of the covers that outlined Eliza's sleeping form.

She lay flat on her back, her hand thrown up over the pillow behind her head. Quietly, he crossed to the bed, noting her breathing was deep and even, her dark hair tousled around her face. Nat gently pushed it back off her forehead. He told himself he was checking her scalp wound, tried not to savor the softness of the tresses.

"Eliza," he breathed softly. "Wake up call."

Nothing. Not even the rhythm of her breathing changed.

"Eliza," he spoke louder now, "come on, wake up."

Nothing happened.

Nat touched her shoulder, shook her, and called her name again.

Next thing he knew, he was flat on his back on the floor, staring down the muzzle of a matt-black handgun. Eliza's eyes were wide and staring, her breath rapid and shallow.

Nat knocked her hand aside, grabbed her wrist and tore the gun from her rigid fingers.

"What the fuck?" Nat yelled. "You sleep with a gun under your pillow? God! Jesus! *Fuck!*"

Holding onto her wrist, he slid the gun to the floor and stood as Eliza stared at him with naked eyes so defenseless they just about broke his heart.

What the hell had happened to her?

He gentled his grip on her wrist and slid his

palm down until he held her hand. "Eliza, I'm not going to hurt you."

The clock ticked down the seconds as she said nothing, just stared back at him not quite conscious.

Picking the gun off the floor, he turned to leave. Her voice reached him through the darkness, just a whisper of breath, impossibly quiet.

"I didn't know it was you, Nat."

Rage and fury shot through his mind, anger soaking into his soul like a stain. He kept his voice even. Controlled. "It's okay, Eliza. Go back to sleep. I'll wake you in another couple of hours."

***

Quantico, Virginia, April 12th

"That bitch. That mother-fucking bitch!" Spittle flecked Andrew DeLattio's chin. He grabbed the orange plastic chair and slammed it into the wall, pounded it until large shards of jagged plastic flew off into a sterile corner of the interview room.

Larry Frazier stood back out of range, nodding the guards away as they tried to enter the room.

DeLattio's civilized persona cracked a little more each day. Something dark twisted inside him like a feral beast desperate to get out. Juliette Morgan, fed bitch, was going to discover that his first night in her apartment had been just a warm up. He'd make her wish she'd never taken her first breath, never become a government agent, never set foot in New York City.

Irish bitch.

DeLattio swore again. "A fed. The whole time she was a cock-sucking fed." He clutched his hands to his head and laughed hysterically, "Jesus Christ, I nailed a federal agent and those bastards let me do it."

It was the first time he'd felt even a kernel of admiration for the FBI's Organized Crime Unit. They'd never played hardball before. They'd actually made a fool of him.

Larry had the gall to smile.

Andrew's gaze narrowed and Larry's smile turned sickly. The little man started to perspire.

"Isn't that entrapment?" Andrew asked.

"No," Larry said. He shook his head and stood straighter. "You drugged her and entered her apartment illegally. If she'd invited you back, then maybe you could have argued it. Except, given the state they found her in, they could still press charges for assault of a federal officer."

The fact that she was an agent must have been the reason she'd never invited him back to her apartment in the first place. Never let him come upstairs, never once let him touch her outside those perfunctory little kisses that had left him sweating. He'd thought she was sophisticated and discriminating—maybe even a virgin. She had captivated him totally, until she'd dumped him.

A growl worked its way up his throat and he clamped his lips together to stop it escaping. He'd practically had to beg her to go out with him. Woo her with flowers, diamonds and chocolates.

And she'd been playing him like a pro.

Clever bitch. Clever, clever bitch.

'Beware the fury of a patient man.'

He'd show her fury all right.

He wanted to smash down these walls with his bare hands, wanted to smash his lawyer's nose until it split in two. Sweat dripped down his back, hands clenched into tight fists. He couldn't stand it. Could not stand it.

Leaning his head against the wall, absorbing the coolness of the plaster though his hot pores, his rage eased as plans formed.

"What else did you find out?" He took a slow, deep breath.

Larry shrugged his bony shoulders in a quick gesture. "Not much. She's gone on the lam and the FBI is looking for her."

"That bitch set me up." Ruined his life, destroyed his family. He took another deep breath, letting the oxygen calm his wrath.

He knew what he had to do.

"Find her." He held Larry's gaze, told him without words what it would mean if he didn't do as instructed. The lawyer nodded, scurried about collecting his papers.

She'd played him for a fool. Even tied up and bleeding, she'd won the first round. But he was gonna get out of here soon, and when he did, she was going to find out the real meaning of revenge.

***

Elizabeth ran fast through a dark forest, missed her footing and cried out as she stumbled, but was up again in a second. She didn't have time. She couldn't see through the fog that swirled around her, but she knew she didn't have time.

Branches snapped and scratched her face and the bare skin of her arms. Hearing a noise, she pivoted, shadows shifting, and realized he was straight ahead of her. Cold dread pierced her heart and she froze, unable to look away from his glowing eyes. Fear clawed like bile in her throat as she wheeled to run away again.

Run. Run. Run.

She was crying, sobbing and sucking in deep breaths, desperate for oxygen, desperate to escape.

A quiet murmur rolled over her, the soft sound of gentle love. Light glowed and banished the darkness. Her mother's sweet face as she held Sean in her arms, a baby still, gorgeous, with big round cheeks and eyes that sparkled.

Tears flowed, the wet warmth seeping into her marrow. She snuggled closer to the source and smiled. Her mother was here. Nothing could harm her now.

***

Nat woke to bright sunshine and the insistent call of a Steller's Jay. His arm was wrapped tightly around Eliza Reed's waist, pinning her back against his chest. Her head rested on his other forearm, her dark hair curling softly against his skin. She smelled of lavender and antiseptic.

She'd scared the life out of him last night and not just with the gun. The sound of her sobs had woken him from a deep sleep and he'd rushed through to see what was wrong.

He'd found her thrashing around, frantically clawing the air and gasping for breath. The torment that drove her, even in sleep, made him want to break something. Instead he'd held her until the dream had faded and then, when she'd clung to him with desperate fingers, he'd lain down on the bed next to her and drifted off to sleep. He hadn't meant to stay.

But now a certain part of his body insisted it wasn't sleep time anymore.

He shifted backward, trying to escape without waking her. Somehow he knew the last thing she needed was to wake up with a horny male clutching her soft, relaxed body.

Shit.

He eased out of bed and went to get his shirt from the next room. The Glock sat on the floor next to the couch. He picked it up, measured the weight of the deadly-looking pistol against his palm. He preferred a rifle, but the Glock in his hand was a pretty sophisticated weapon. Something a woman in law enforcement might carry.

He ground his teeth and tried not to think about why Eliza slept with a loaded gun beneath her pillow. What was she scared of? Or maybe she was just crazy. But he'd seen her take care of herself in a hostile crowd, knew she wouldn't threaten easily. Maybe she was paranoid after years on the job?

And then again, maybe not.

Carrying the pistol through to the kitchen, he put it down on the worn countertop. Eliza had said she'd been in law enforcement, but that covered a lot of bases. Cops to feds to spooks, even the military had their own brand of law enforcement personnel.

She was running from something.

Too weary to think straight, he set about making coffee to wake up his brain. He'd been gone for three days, checking the snow loads in the summer pastures and taking the latest wolf-pack photographs he'd been commissioned to shoot. The work had gone like a dream, the thaw and warm weather bringing the wolves out of the den to loll in the sunshine.

He'd photographed the pack often over the last ten years, had named them all. Pups were due any day now, the alpha female fat and awkward with her bulging belly. Once he got those shots, he was toying with the idea of putting together a coffee-table book. It wasn't much, but it might keep the creditors at bay for a little while longer.

Out the small kitchen window, he could see Ryan heading to the barn. With Cal out of action he had to get to work. He had four pregnant mares to check and wanted to see how Red was shaping up. He was also thinking about selling the Cayuse ponies to the Wild Horse Research Center in Porterville. Either that or try to get access to some semen from a different stallion. One of the mares was due to come into season soon.

He poured coffee then swept the Glock off the counter, and slipped it into the back of his waistband. He picked up two steaming mugs and walked through into the bedroom.

"Hey, sleepy head, rise and shine."

Eliza sat up slowly. She looked tired and groggy, her green eyes blurry and her hair a mess. He'd half hoped the sight of her first thing in the morning would kill off his desire, but he was doomed to disappointment. She looked shockingly beautiful, fragile and stark without her defenses to hide behind.

Putting down the coffee on the bedside table, he took the gun out of his waistband, laid it next to the mug.

She watched him anxiously, eyeing the gun from beneath dark brows.

There was a photo next to the bed. A man and woman, each holding a small child. He picked it up.

"Who's this?"

The small muscles of her face froze, turning her expression brittle.

"My parents and little brother." Her voice was quiet, loaded with pain.

"They still around?" he asked, even though he knew the answer. People didn't mourn the living.

She shook her head and he didn't think she was going to tell him anything more, but the words trickled out.

"They were killed at a border crossing during the troubles in Northern Ireland." She picked at a thread on the bedspread. "Sean wasn't even two years old."

He looked at the photograph and recognized the little girl clinging to her daddy's knee. She looked seven or eight. Looking at the little boy he realized her parents must have died not long after it was taken. *Hell*. He couldn't imagine growing up without a family.

"I'm sorry," Nat said. She nodded, obviously not comfortable with the emotions, even after all this time. He set the picture down. Changed the subject.

"How're you feeling?" he asked.

"Sore," she admitted, looking grateful to talk about something else.

"Sore where?" He took a big sip of coffee.

"Head, neck, arms, legs, back," Eliza told him, tentatively touching each body part. "Pretty much everywhere."

Nat went to the bathroom, rummaged through the medicine cabinet for Tylenol. Shaking out two tablets, he thrust them into her hands along with the coffee, leaned closer and examined her head wound for signs of fresh bleeding, keeping his perusal strictly professional. He was damned proud of himself for not sneaking a peek down her nightshirt and trying to get a visual on the body he'd held.

There was a thin red welt on her hairline, not too serious. Sarah would check her out later and, if he knew his sister, would have both patients down in the ER before they could blink.

"It's starting to heal over," he said. His eyes drifted down her chest, her nipples clearly outlined by thin cotton.

Hell.

Nat took a step back from the bed and tried not to think about how soft she'd felt in his arms, how feminine. Softness wasn't something he'd associate with women like Eliza Reed.

She stretched her arms over her head, unaware of his thoughts. A Blue Jay's T-shirt fell mid-thigh. The blankets slid lower, and the T-shirt hitched higher, and try as he might, Nat could not tear his eyes away.

His mouth went dry while his heart beat painfully in his chest.

"I, uh, I." He couldn't get the words out.

Eliza shoved her hair out of her face with one hand, and almost inhaled the coffee. She seemed unaware of the effect she was having on him. He should have marked it down as progress, but he couldn't quite muster straight line thoughts.

"Gotta go," he mumbled and turned away to leave.

"Nat?"

He forced himself to stop. Forced himself to

look into her green eyes without revealing a hint of the desire that stretched his nerves to breaking point.

"Thanks," she said and smiled.

Chapter Ten

Brooklyn, New York, April 12ᵗʰ

Marsh hammered on the door of the Brooklyn apartment. The paint on the pale blue door was cracked and peeling with age. The buzzer was broken, but written on the label in faded black ink was the name 'Maxwell'.

Could Josephine Maxwell's father really still be alive?

He glanced down the littered corridor, tried to ignore the smell of filth and urine that rammed his senses. Marsh hammered on the door again and was rewarded by a muffled shout from within.

He held his body tense in anticipation as adrenaline rushed in. Josephine Maxwell could be inside. Marsh stood back as he heard a lock turn and the bolt slide. The door opened a crack and a single eye peered through the gap. The eye was bloodshot, the tiny capillaries fractured and burst. The lone iris was an almost transparent blue with yellow-tinged whites that suggested liver damage. The face was heavily wrinkled and filthy, dirt ground into it like an old doormat.

The apartment loomed dark and empty behind the man, like a warlock's cave.

The man's open mouth revealed yellow, rotten teeth and ruddy gums. Marsh forced himself not to recoil from the stench of hard liquor and decay that came from the rank orifice. He smiled and tried not to gag.

"Mr. Maxwell?"

The eye turned from ornery to suspicious in a flicker. "Who wants to know?" The voice was weak, almost hoarse.

"My name's Hayes. I'm with the FBI."

The pupil dilated. "I ain't done nothin'," the man declared loudly.

"No sir," Marsh said, "I just want to talk to you for a moment." Marsh pushed his ID through the crack, willing the man to open the door and cooperate. They could do this the easy way, or they could do it hard. But the hard way was bureaucratically noisy and he wanted to keep his visit here as unofficial as possible.

"I got nothin' to say to you. Leave me alone." Maxwell thrust Marsh's ID back at him and tried to close the door.

Marsh wedged his Italian brogues into the gap and tried a different approach. Pulling a half-bottle of whiskey out of his overcoat pocket, he waved it enticingly; Maxwell's eyes locked onto it like a ground-to-air missile.

"I just need a couple of minutes of your time, sir. There's no problem, just some routine inquiries."

Marsh jiggled the bottle, his stomach turning as he watched the old man lick dry lips and unchain the door.

"I won't cause you any trouble, sir. Just a few questions and a quiet drink."

Maxwell made a lunge for the bottle, but Marsh tucked it safely back into his pocket and edged past him into the apartment. The squalor hit him immediately, nothing he hadn't seen before, but rank and filthy nonetheless. He walked down a small dingy hall before he entered the lounge. It was dark, except for the flickering of the TV. Marsh snapped on the main lights and immediately wished he hadn't. The couch dominated the room. Old, brown velour, covered with a rancid looking sleeping bag.

The ancient TV sat perched in the corner, switched to one of those talk shows that set people up so they could watch them being knocked back down again. Seemed to Marsh that people watched talk shows because it was easier than dealing with their own problems. Escapism.

Frankly, looking around this place, escapism didn't look like such a bad idea.

The coffee table in front of the couch was littered with food and empty liquor bottles, as was the carpet. Old cartons of half-eaten takeouts lay around in haphazard heaps. Marsh almost heard the roaches licking their mandibles in succulent delectation. He tried to imagine a little girl growing up in this environment, but couldn't. There was no way he'd leave a child here; it curdled his stomach to even think about it.

What had made Josephine Maxwell leave Social Services when all she had to return to was this?

Maxwell eyed the liquor in Marsh's pocket with one arm outstretched like a supplicant. Marsh hesitated, but his small half-bottle couldn't do any more damage. The man should have been dead years ago.

"I need to ask you a few questions about your daughter." Marsh watched the old man's expression shift from wary to crafty in less than a heartbeat.

"What daughter?"

Marsh couldn't decide if this was parental loyalty or if Maxwell was just trying to find out how much the information was worth. Marsh bet on the latter and decided to try the direct approach. "I need to find Josephine. Do you know where she is?"

"Maybe I do." The old man shrugged and began wheezing. "Haven't seen the ungrateful slut in years."

Good. That made it easier to do what Marsh had to. A lot easier. The man would sell his daughter for a drink and now they both knew it.

Marsh put the amber bottle of Bushmills on the coffee table and stepped back. He watched Maxwell approach it, cautiously, as if expecting a trap. His hand reached out hesitantly towards the neck of the bottle.

"Do you know where she is?" Marsh asked.

Maxwell jumped, but grabbed the bottle as he retreated to stand behind the couch like a two-year old who'd been caught doing something naughty. He unscrewed the cap with a couple of flicks of his knobby wrist and took a swig. Slowly, he wiped his mouth, shook his head, smiled as if in pain.

Marsh pulled a couple of hundred-dollar bills from his wallet and wondered why he was so irritated that this man would give up his daughter for money. He was the one paying him.

Maxwell eyed the cash.

"I need to find her," Marsh repeated.

"In trouble is she?" Maxwell looked speculatively at Marsh's smart suit and expensive shoes. The pale eyes sharpened as they focused on the greenbacks. "Always was. Ungrateful little bitch."

Bitterness twisted his features. "She phones but

never visits her old man." He laughed, an unpleasant sound. "Visits the old biddy across the hall, but she thinks she's too good for me. Forgotten where she came from." He wiped spittle from the corner of his mouth with his filthy shirt cuff.

Marsh didn't blame her for not visiting, but he needed a lot more information than what the old man had given him. Maybe he'd try the woman across the hall.

Josephine's father had a crafty look in his eyes, vicious and sly. "Phoned me the other day, out of the blue." Maxwell put his hand to his chin, as if he struggled to remember something. "I pressed that last caller button, you know, the one that gives you the number of the last person who phoned?" He went on scratching his head, but the gleam in his eye was anything but confused.

"Wrote it down somewhere." He glanced around the filthy, cluttered apartment. "Don't know if I could find it."

Marsh placed two-hundred dollars on the table. "I'd be really grateful if you'd take a look for me, Mr. Maxwell." He pulled another hundred-dollar bill out of his pocket, flicked it with his fingers. "Really grateful."

Maxwell took a quick swig of whiskey and headed toward the kitchen, taking the bottle with him. Marsh walked over to the old sideboard and looked through the stack of bills that were strewn across it. He'd bet a hundred-to-one that Walter Maxwell didn't have the wherewithal to pay any of them.

The old man was muttering in the kitchen. Marsh could hear the tip and swallow and tinkle of liquor as Walter Maxwell drank up the nectar that had controlled his life.

A key wriggled in the apartment door, and somebody pushed it open. It bounced against the chain and held. Marsh caught his breath, his hand going to his holster, loosening the straps and preparing to draw his SIG Sauer.

"How many times have I told you not to chain this door first thing in the morning?" A woman spoke heatedly from the hall.

Marsh relaxed slightly and watched as Maxwell went to the door. Instead of opening it up, he stuck his hand through the crack and said, "Give me the damn mail, woman. I don't ask for your help and I don't need it." Walter Maxwell slammed the door in the Good Samaritan's face as if he didn't want anyone to know he had a visitor.

That suited Marsh fine.

Walter Maxwell clutched his meager pile of mail and swaggered back to the lounge. "Nosy old bitch lives across the hall."

"She's the one whom Josephine visits?"

The man shrugged his bony shoulders. "Yeah."

Marsh filed the information away, along with the fact that the 'nosy old bitch' had access to the man's mail.

Walter Maxwell shuffled forward with a scrap of paper in his hands, handed it over, his gaze switching all the time between the $100 bills on the table and the one that remained in Marsh's hand. Marsh handed him the money and looked at the phone number. There was nothing he could do if it was a dead-end, but at least he had a couple of leads to follow now.

Marsh figured he was just one step ahead of the mob finding both Elizabeth and Josephine. If the mob found them first they were dead.

A cockroach crawled out of a Chinese takeaway carton, negotiated cheap disposable chopsticks and scuttled across the floor. Maxwell didn't even blink. Marsh's stomach clenched. It was time to go.

＊＊

Elizabeth closed her eyes and took a deep breath of fresh mountain air. It felt frigid in her lungs as it expanded to fill the spaces within her chest.

The light was fantastic with gold shimmers that dappled the deep shadows of the forest floor, shifting and sighing with the gentle movements of lodgepole pine and western larch.

Nat rode beside her on the gray stallion, looking handsome in ubiquitous Wranglers, a denim shirt and a faded blue sheepskin-lined jacket. His boots were old and worn, a pale-colored cowboy hat was pulled low over his eyes, making him a prime candidate for Marlborough man of the month. Elizabeth found herself watching him—the broad outline of his shoulders, the twitching of those serious lips.

They'd gone on a trail ride. As if she was a real tourist.

He hadn't mentioned last night. Not the fight, not the gun, nor her slip that she'd been in law enforcement. She would have been brimming with questions and curiosity, but he was letting it slide. For now.

The sharp tang of pine mixed with the rising scent of earth churned up by the horses' hooves. They'd ridden for two hours straight in a loose circle around the north perimeter of the ranch. Now they were at the eastern-most edge of the property with the jagged mountains dominating the backdrop behind the trees. Fierce. Imposing. Cold.

Shivering, she drew up her shoulders.

Dense thickets of lodgepole pine blanketed the upper ridges with a dark-green cloak that stopped dramatically at the tree line. The icy peaks had that scrubbed clean look.

Nat grabbed Tiger's reins and pulled Elizabeth to a stop. With his finger pressed to his lips, he motioned for her to dismount. Elizabeth climbed down, withholding the drawn-out sigh of relief that usually accompanied the feel of solid ground beneath her feet after such a long time in the saddle.

Nat motioned her to follow him as he approached the brush this side of the creek. Crouching low, she made her way along, careful not to tread in the mud puddles that had grown as the snow had melted.

She inched between straggly bushes and followed him as quietly as she could, curious as to what he had spotted across the creek. Reaching his side, she held her breath as he turned back towards her with a smile on his face and pointed through a mesh of tangled brambles towards the opposite bank.

Elizabeth dragged her gaze away from his and spotted a tall doe standing guard over two fragile spotted fawns. The fawns' legs were spindly, spread unevenly apart as they stood beside their mother who was drinking from the clean waters of the creek.

Bambi's mom.

Elizabeth pressed closer to Nat, enjoyed the excuse to touch him without worry. The doe raised her head, her ears huge and pricked forward, listening for any hint of danger. Her nose quivered as it sifted the air for trouble, her liquid black eyes scanning the scrub, elegant, graceful and breathtakingly beautiful.

One of the horses snorted and the deer darted into the undergrowth.

"Wish I'd brought my camera," Nat said, rising to his feet, and putting a hand to her waist when she nearly lost her footing in the mud. "Easy," he said.

Elizabeth looked up into his narrowed blue gaze and wished for one crazy moment, that she had the nerve to kiss him. Like a normal woman. Just for once, she'd like to pretend she was ordinary.

Not rich.

Not a target for a mob hit.

Not a rape victim.

His eyes darkened with molten heat, his grip tightened on her arm.

"You gonna freak out if I kiss you?"

She shook her head, her gaze never leaving his mouth as it lowered towards hers. Then she felt his breath just before his lips touched hers, slowly and gently, eking out a response that melted her bones. His hands cradled either side of her face, made her feel like she was the world and everything in it that mattered. She moaned and closed her eyes, her lips straining towards him.

It was a gentle kiss as he probed her mouth lightly with his tongue, but the passion that swelled up swamped and staggered her.

He raised his head and stared at her oddly.

"Well," he said, and took a half step away. "That sure beats the hell out of castrating cattle."

Elizabeth laughed. Startled by the sound, she

looked away. She didn't know the last time she'd felt this happy and that scared her.

"Talking of which, Ryan is going to skin me alive if we don't get back soon, so I guess we'd better move it." His voice sounded rough around the edges.

He fetched the horses from where they grazed the undergrowth beside the creek, and with the slightest touch, he helped her mount.

She wasn't supposed to feel these bursts of anticipation, these little tingles of desire. She was as good as dead, her heart a lifeless weight inside her chest—but she felt them anyway and savored the uncertain tug of attraction and the bittersweet feeling of hope.

***

New York City, April 12th

Marsh took the Brooklyn-Queens Expressway to the Manhattan Bridge, crossed the East River through Chinatown and headed northwest. Passing the trendy craft shops and gaily-colored umbrellas, he turned into the old redbrick tenements on Grove St.

He parked near the building where Elizabeth and Josephine had shared an apartment before Elizabeth had gone undercover, and climbed out of his BMW. It seemed a good area, tidy, with neat little trees starting to bud, protected by green painted cast-iron scrolls. Black cast-iron trelliswork edged the building and numerous window boxes promised brilliant displays come summer.

Marsh stood in the street, lighting a cigarette. He glanced around looking for anybody suspicious, anything out of the ordinary, but it was hard to tell in Greenwich Village. He walked up the front steps and pressed the buzzer for apartment four. He looked up and saw a face peering down at him from the balcony on the top floor. Unfortunately it wasn't the face of a willowy blonde, but rather that of a young guy showing off his hard-earned fake tan, and wearing a black wife-beater T-shirt.

Marsh's smile turned deadly and he crushed out the cigarette with the heel of his shoe.

"Yeah? What can I do for you?" a fuzzy voice came through the intercom.

"I want to speak to Josephine Maxwell."

A slight hesitation, a telling pause. "She doesn't live here anymore."

"You have a forwarding address?" Marsh's voice was hard. He'd had a lousy day.

"Sorry, pal, can't help you."

Wrong answer.

"Listen, *pal*," Marsh's voice rang like steel, his usually endless patience erased by the growing feeling of dread. "I want to speak to you about Josephine Maxwell and I don't want to have to beat down the door to do it. Understand?"

"Look man, I'm calling the cops."

"Don't bother, I'm FBI and if I have to get a warrant to talk to you, I'm going to make your life a living hell." Marsh waited. He could almost hear the wheels turning in the young man's head. *Come on, just open the goddamn door.*

The buzzer went off and Marsh pushed through the heavy outer doors and ran up the three-flights of stairs, adrenaline punching through his system. The young man stood by the open door of the apartment. Marsh ignored his spluttered protests and brushed past him into the living room.

The main room was large and almost blindingly bright. White walls reflected sunlight and huge skylights dominated the ceiling. Exposed oak beams supported the roof and plants flourished every shade of living green. Enormous canvases in vivid hues dominated three of the four walls. The fourth housed a walk-in fireplace that was simple but elegant.

He crossed the polished oak floor and stared up at one of the paintings. It was a fascinating twist of wreathing color, each one melding and evolving like a spirit. It spoke of fire and passion. Smoke and mystery. He found the signature in the bottom right-hand corner. J. Maxwell stood out in neat, stark lines.

Another contradiction.

Marsh turned his attention back to the young man who stood in the doorway. He couldn't say why he'd taken such an instant dislike; maybe it was his pretty boy good looks, or maybe it was the over-sculpted body and trendy black jeans trussed up with a leather belt studded with silver. Whatever it was, he hated the little bastard.

Marsh nodded toward the picture. "Where is she?"

The young man closed the door and followed Marsh into the lounge, glancing toward a room off to the right.

"She's not here." The tone was petulant. "I'm just apartment sitting while she's away."

"Did she say how long she'd be gone?"

The young man shrugged his pecs. "I'm just staying till this semester is over."

Again, that suspicious glance to the room on the

right. Someone was in that room. Marsh walked over to the fireplace and picked up a framed photograph that caught his eye. It was a black and white of two young women sitting on a dock beside a quaint looking boathouse. Josephine and Elizabeth. Marsh thought of the squalid apartment where Josephine Maxwell had grown up; the contrast with this one was like looking at night and day.

He was beginning to appreciate the bond forged between the two women, but that didn't help him to find Elizabeth. They both needed protection and the danger grew every day as the mob trials drew closer. He didn't want Elizabeth killed, nor did he want Josephine Maxwell punished for being her friend.

Ignoring the shout from lover-boy, he strode through the bedroom door, expecting to find a stunning willowy blonde in hiding. The person lying naked on the bed was blond all right, but he wasn't quite as beautiful as Josephine Maxwell. The guy was handcuffed to the bedposts and didn't look pleased to see Marsh standing there.

With great aplomb, he said in a beautifully cultured British accent, "Be a love would you and get the keys? These bloody things are killing me."

Chapter Eleven

Tiger's haunches bunched and swayed as Elizabeth and Nat made their way down the embankment. Elizabeth leaned back, held tightly to the raised pommel, clinging with her legs. She'd enjoyed herself today, had even managed to stay on the horse, so far. Grabbing a branch, she superstitiously touched wood, just as her mother had always done when she'd asked for trouble.

Elizabeth concentrated on staying in the saddle and barely noticed the route they took. The land leveled out, trees thinned and spread across a wide glade, quaking aspen replacing the pines. Nat stopped his horse, stepped down and scouted about as if looking for something on the lush valley floor.

Elizabeth watched him and knew that with every second she spent in his company, she was falling for him, hard, like a meteor plummeting to earth. He cast a spell on her that she couldn't break. It wasn't just the good looks or the tough rangy body, though God knew they fueled her fantasies. It was that solid core of strength, rolled up beneath a subtle layer of tenderness and painted with honesty. Two weeks ago she hadn't even known he'd existed, but now she craved him with every cell in her body.

Fear of his touch was gone. Dissolved like a sugar-cube in water by each subtle glance, each fleeting contact, each soul shattering kiss. Hope grew in her heart; a feeling that she couldn't quell even though it was dangerous. Even though it could kill her.

She had to run before her luck ran out.

But she couldn't leave yet.

Nat shouted, breaking into her thoughts. "Hey, come over here." He held his hand out to one side as she approached him. "Watch your step."

Hunkered down, balanced on the soles of his battered cowboy boots, he stared at a small mound of vegetation that encrusted a rotted stump.

"What is it?" she asked and peered closer at the innocuous-looking plant.

"One of the smallest orchids in the world. Venus' slippers." He scanned the surrounding area for more. "Whole wood will be full of them in a few weeks time."

She leaned closer and tried to take in the detail of the pouty little flower. She'd never thought of orchids coming from the Rockies; they'd always struck her as expensive hothouse plants in need of fussing and nurture.

Nat's calloused fingers glided along her forearm, making the fine hairs rise up on end. She shivered at the contact, but it felt warm and good and normal.

Blue eyes were shadowed beneath his hat. "They burst into flower late spring and then in the summer they disappear." He snapped his fingers. "Like they were never here."

Nat looked down at the orchids, an unreadable expression on his face and she knew, like the orchid, she was going to disappear. But he wasn't a mind reader and she couldn't afford to confide in him. It was too dangerous...the mob didn't play games. All that mattered to them was life, death,

170

and payback. Rising to her feet, she swayed as she tried not to look guilty.

"Watch your step." Nat reached out and caught her arm just as she was about to tread on another small plant. "They're endangered because photographers and naturalists keep trampling them in their search of the perfect shot." He gave her a slanted smile. "One of life's little ironies."

Nat shrugged shoulders that looked massive in his thick coat. They stood like that for a few seconds, his hand firm, but gentle on her wrist. Then he gave her a searching glance before he released her, removed his hat and rubbed a hand through his flaxen hair.

He was going to ask her about her past—she knew it as surely as she knew her own name.

The reprieve was over.

***

"You're lucky to live in such a beautiful place." Her hair danced in the wind as she moved away to gaze out at the valley stretched below them.

She was avoiding him again.

"It's for sale." The words squeezed past the lump of pride that wedged in his throat. "This whole wood goes up for auction in a few days time." He looked around the forest that had been in his family for five generations and forced a laugh. It came out bitter and angry. And he was pissed that he felt sorry for himself. So they might have to sell off some land? *Big fucking deal*. They were hanging on by their fingernails, and he for one had no intention of letting go.

And he'd make damned sure the wildlife people

knew that the orchids were in these woods after the sale went through. Whoever bought the land would have to build around the protection zones that would be put in place. But that wouldn't be *his* problem.

Not anymore.

If his plan made him unethical, tough. He could live with it as long as he could protect the land and keep his family from sliding into bankruptcy.

"Why?" Eliza asked. "Why would you want to sell it?"

"I don't *want* to sell, Eliza, I *have* to." His anger came out hot and loud. "If we don't sell these woods, we'll lose the whole goddamned ranch." His voice echoed across the valley floor and Eliza's uncontrolled flinch had him turning his back, frustrated and unable to hide it.

Shit.

Land was the only commodity he had that could generate sufficient funds fast enough to save the ranch. But it was like cutting out his own heart.

And he was taking out his anger on Eliza.

Damn.

He scrubbed calloused hands across his face. She may as well hear the whole of it. She affected him. He wanted her in his bed, but she wouldn't stay and he didn't want her to, because he had nothing to offer her.

Nor did he completely trust her. Her secrets were stacking up against her like little black marks, but he still wanted her. Turning to face her, he saw she had carefully blanked expression. He'd hurt her feelings.

Guilt made him curse under his breath.

"We've got two-hundred grand's worth of debt

hanging over the ranch and time's running out on the repayments." A Saker falcon hovered over a nearby thicket, pinned to the sky in its hunt for the next meal. "If we don't come up with the money real soon, we're finished." Nat looked down at his boots and kicked a stone out of the grass.

"Is this the neighbor who's trying to force you out?" Eliza asked. She must have been talking to Ryan.

He nodded. How could he doubt it? At first he'd thought Troy Strange just wanted his Arabians. Now he figured Troy's wife, Marlena, was spinning tales. Women sometimes had a piece missing. He'd seen it often enough to recognize the breed. They got what they wanted using sex and if they weren't leading a man around by his dick—they punished him. Nina had been the same, he hadn't even realized until afterwards. She'd controlled him with sex, blinded him with lust. He glanced at Eliza and found her watching him, earnestly, but he wasn't going to fall for that trap again. His lips twisted cynically.

"Can't you expand the holiday business?" Her green eyes lured him as she held her hair out of her eyes with one hand on top of her head, "or run photography courses, nature trails?"

Nat wasn't stupid. He had a ton of ideas for expanding the ranch vacations; photography, fishing, livery, but there wasn't enough time to turn a profit. He told her about his plans, watched her mull over the problem in silence.

"I could give you money," she offered.

Nat nearly fell on his ass. He hadn't expected that.

"No." *The woman had two hundred grand to*

173

give out to strangers? "Hell, no!"

She looked down at her boots. Nat thought he saw a shimmer in her eyes, but it was gone when she looked up at him.

"I just thought—"

"No. We'd better head back," Nat shook his head. He'd had enough of talking about his problems. Talk solved nothing and there was no way he would borrow money from Eliza Reed.

What did he really know about her anyway?

She was beautiful, and rich apparently, could sharp-shoot and fight dirty. She'd told him she was in law enforcement, but she'd been damaged along the way. Did he really want to get involved with a woman as dangerous to his heart as Nina had ever been?

He started to walk away. Remembered that look in her eyes last night when she'd pulled the gun on him. The utter desolation and the nightmares.

He stopped and let her move ahead of him. As he followed her back to the horses, he couldn't help but notice the way the soft denim of her jeans clung to her long legs. He imagined those same legs wrapped around his hips...

Oh yeah, he wanted to get involved all right. He wanted to get *very* involved.

He liked the way she moved. He liked the way she kissed. He'd wanted this time alone with her to gain her trust and he was slowly prying his way beneath the surface, finally seeing behind the mask that slipped over those wide green eyes whenever he got too close. He was learning to read her body language. Not just the signs of physical attraction, but the subtle things, like the way she dragged her hands through her hair when she was frustrated and

twisted the ring on her pinkie when she got nervous.
And the way she unconsciously bit her bottom lip
when she watched him.

Heat kicked uncomfortably into his groin, but he
ignored it.

The woman had a past. She was paranoid
enough to sleep with a gun under her pillow and
flinched at the slightest touch. She sure as hell
didn't need him or his problems. But still he wanted
her.

She stood next to the roan, waiting for a leg up
into the saddle. This concession to him was a big
deal to her, even he knew it.

"I'm sorry," she said as she turned to face him.
"For being nosey."

She was apologizing? To him?

Hell.

Nat brushed a tendril of hair away from her
forehead and leaned down to touch her lips with his.
It was a kiss of reassurance, gentle and
uncomplicated. Nat was determined not to frighten
her by taking things too far, too fast. Even if all he
really wanted was to get inside her.

***

Elizabeth stood for a moment, dazed by the soft kiss
that sent heat spiraling through her veins. It felt so
good she kissed him back, opened her mouth to his
and explored him with her tongue. She rose on
tiptoes and wrapped her arms around his neck, felt
rock hard muscles strain beneath the super-soft
sheepskin. For a single second he hesitated, before
he backed her up against the solid cowpony. She'd
forgotten the raw strength of the man, forgotten the

firebrand nature of their kisses. She felt her knees give way and suddenly he was sweeping her off her feet.

Tiger snorted in Nat's ear and Elizabeth laughed for the second time that day. It was getting easier. Even though life was a bitch, it was getting easier to laugh about it. With Nat.

"Who asked you?" Nat said to the horse. He blew out a big sigh of frustration and placed his forehead against hers. Tiger snorted again and Elizabeth wiped horse drool off Nat's cheek with her jacket cuff.

With a reluctant groan, he slid her slowly down his body and let her feel every frustrated inch of him. Then he held her away.

"So now you know all my deep, dark secrets, Eliza." Nat's blue eyes delved into hers. She froze and knew he felt it.

"I can't promise anything except the here and now." He brushed his thumb across her bottom lip. "No rings, no happily ever after. I've got nothing to offer you, but I want you so badly I can barely stand to let you go." But he did. He released her with a slight squeeze of her shoulders and took a step back. Somehow he managed to look annoyed and considerate at the same time.

Her heart tilted.

She wanted him too.

He'd said he had nothing to offer her but really it was the other way around. She could only cause him misery and sorrow. If she had any decency at all she would leave now. But Nat Sullivan was her chance at salvation, a lifeline thrown at the last possible moment. If she was nervous, it was only that her old fear would paralyze her, ruin the moment. Tentatively she raised a hand to the crease in his cheek and smiled.

Time stood still as they stared into each other's eyes. She hoped he found the answers he needed written in her eyes, because she couldn't speak about her past. Not yet, maybe never. But she did want him, and she wanted him to know it.

"Damn," he said. He clenched his jaw and glared down at her like she'd done something wrong. He held his breath for a finite moment, stroked her cheek.

Then he grinned.

***

Connecticut, April 12th

Marsh dragged his hand through his short hair and blew out a ragged sigh of frustration. He drove his black BMW along Interstate 95, past the bustling port of New Haven with the gothic spires of Yale, just visible to the north.

His jaw was clenched so hard he'd given himself a headache. He was as frustrated as hell and getting more pissed by the minute. The number Josephine's father had given him had turned out to be a cell phone, but it was turned off and untraceable. To all intents and purposes, Josephine Maxwell had disappeared off the face of the earth, no ATM or credit card activity, no sightings, nothing, nada, zilch.

She could be dead. But he didn't think so.

Part of him was relieved that she was so hard to find, but he had a bad feeling about it. He'd missed something. His gut instinct was telling him that time was running out, slipping through his fingers like sand through an egg timer. The preliminary hearings on the mob cases were due to start in two days and things were going to happen. Crime families throughout the U.S. were running around like headless chickens, covering their asses and pissed because the feds had got one over on them.

Signs for the exit ramp to New London and Mystic loomed. He suddenly remembered the photograph in Josephine's apartment of the women by the boathouse. *Damn*. He'd forgotten about Elizabeth's aunt. Marsh swung hard across two carriageways, cutting off a sporty little Miata as he left a streak of black rubber on the asphalt.

His cell phone rang.

"Hayes," Marsh answered.

A crackly voice came over a very bad line. "Special Agent Hayes, this is Captain Claremont, Brooklyn PD."

"What can I do for you, Captain?" Marsh didn't have time to deal with another case, but it had to be urgent, otherwise the cops wouldn't involve the FBI. They'd rather suck their own blood.

"I need you down at the precinct. I got some questions for you." The accent was thick Brooklyn, a no-nonsense sort of voice.

"Sorry, Captain, no can do, I'll send one of my team down ASAP." Marsh wanted the cop off the line. He needed to get a name and address on Elizabeth's late aunt. She'd had a house near Mystic—that was all he knew.

There was a muffled exchange at the other end of the line, as if the man had covered the mouthpiece and conferred with someone else.

"You don't get it, Hayes," Claremont said

178

abruptly. "I need to question you in relation to a double-homicide. Your prints were found all over the murder scene."

Shit.

"Walter Maxwell?" Marsh asked. He needed to be sure.

"How'd you know that?" the chief asked.

Marsh nearly laughed at the Colombo-style nature of the interview, but he didn't. Josephine Maxwell's father was dead and he didn't believe in coincidence.

"Because he's the only person I've visited in Brooklyn in the last thirty-eight years. What time did the murder occur?"

"I can't—"

"Who's the other victim?" Marsh cut through the bureaucratic bullshit.

"Can't disclose that at the moment, Hayes, if you just—"

"Was it a mob hit?" Marsh asked.

"Mob?" Claremont clearly hadn't got a clue what was going on.

Forget it. Marsh wasn't wasting his time being questioned by detectives while the mob lined up their next victim. He'd get the information he needed from another source.

"Listen, I met Walter Maxwell this morning for the first and only time. I gave him a bottle of whiskey and three-hundred bucks. It was in relation with an ongoing investigation that I am not at liberty to discuss."

He let his FBI status work for him and put on his most autocratic voice. "If you need any more information I suggest you talk to either FBI Director Brett Lovine or my attorney. My secretary can tell you how to contact them." He ignored the spluttered protests and rang off. Then he dialed his secretary before anyone else could tie down the line. He needed information and he needed it fast.

The FBI had a leak.

It had to be a mob hit. *Had to be.* How else could they have connected an old man in the slums to an upscale curator at MOMA? Marsh knew the OCU had fingerprinted Elizabeth's apartment after she disappeared and had gotten a cold-hit on Josephine Maxwell's prints. That information must have been passed onto the mob, only they hadn't believed the old man when he'd told them he didn't know where his daughter was. They'd killed the bastard.

Marsh didn't believe in coincidence. Josephine Maxwell was up to her slim neck in trouble and time was running out.

Half an hour later, Marsh stood outside the house that had once belonged to Elizabeth's aunt, nestled on the beach just outside the small town of Stonington. He'd been dumb. He should have remembered that Elizabeth never sold property. His black BMW was parked on a grass-verge hidden from view a hundred yards down the road. The house was a two-storey clapboard with freshly painted blue shutters, set deep in leafy gardens, well hidden from the casual passerby.

Marsh wore a black jersey over his white shirt, his 9-mm SIG pistol holstered to his chest. The place was quiet except for the scream of gulls on the wind. Salt stung the air.

Adrenaline hummed through his veins, reminding him it had been a long time since he'd put his own life on the line. Maybe too long. He vaulted the small wooden fence that sided the property and made his way through the garden, not wanting to approach from the drive. Cautiously, he worked his way around to the back of the house and spotted lights on in a couple of rooms.

He stretched up and spotted a blonde woman walking away from him toward what looked to be the kitchen.

Bingo.

Looking up, he saw an intricately carved balcony with the doors standing ajar and gauzy drapes billowing in the wind. An old hemlock stretched gnarly limbs just inches from the white balustrade. It had been years since he'd climbed a tree to get into a woman's bedroom.

Two minutes later he stood in an opulent room and brushed lichen from his pants. A canopied bed, draped with cream silk, dominated the room. It was a bed made for fantasies. Marsh raised his eyebrows, wondering just whom it belonged to. It wasn't a bed he could picture Elizabeth sleeping in; it was far too girly for his gritty agent. A delicate French lady's-vanity stood next to the window, complete with a skirted stool. Covered with dozens of tiny glass perfume bottles and an old wedding photograph in a silver filigree frame, it looked like something his mother would have liked. Checking the hall, he made his way silently downstairs, and headed toward the sound of music that spilled from the kitchen.

Josephine Maxwell stood at a center island with her back to him, opening a can of tomatoes. Long silver-blonde hair was caught up in a simple twist that exposed the graceful line of her neck. Her long legs were covered in skintight black leggings and she wore a figure-hugging black tank, draped with a gauzy green shirt that had some weird ethnic print on it. It floated around her as she moved in time to the music.

He waited for her to turn around, knowing she was going to be frightened when she saw him, but not knowing how to prevent it. Not that she didn't deserve a little shot of terror, the way she'd treated him when they'd last met. But he had to convince her he was one of the good guys. *Somehow.* She grabbed a saucepan, oblivious to him, and his nerves stretched to breaking point.

Dancing to the music, she whirled and froze as she saw him standing in the doorway. She swallowed convulsively and her eyes darted towards the French-doors at the other end of the kitchen. He started to shake his head, to tell her everything was okay, but she hurled the saucepan and its contents at him. He swore, ducked, and narrowly avoided the cast-iron pot before chasing after her. She made it to the doors, but couldn't unlock them before he grabbed her.

He spun her around by the shoulders. "Calm down, I'm not here to hurt you."

The look in her blue eyes suggested she didn't believe a word of it. She raised her chin a notch, but remained rigid beneath his hands, quivering like the string of a violin.

"I've come to get you out of here, you're in danger," Marsh told her. *Understatement of the century.*

"Elizabeth said that if anybody found me it would be you. How'd you do it?" Her voice caught him off guard. It was as soft as a whisper and stroked his nerves like a gentle caress.

"It wasn't easy," he admitted.

Josephine smiled tremulously. "But you found me anyway."

She looked so forlorn that he released her shoulders and was about to explain the danger when she piled her knee into his crotch so hard that his vision blanked. Pain exploded into every neuron of his body, telling him to die now. She was out of the door in a flash, racing across the garden.

It took him a good twenty-seconds before he could move, and then it was just an inelegant stumble. At least he hadn't screamed—or had he?

"Damn." He went after her. *Vicious little cat.*

He could hear her crashing through the bushes as she headed towards the beach. He ran flat-out through the shadows and over the uneven ground, relying on his luck not to break a leg or trip in the blackness. Not that his luck seemed to be doing him much good tonight, but he couldn't let her get away, it was too dangerous.

The noise stopped abruptly and Marsh slowed down, moving quietly around large bushes and trees. Another sound caught his attention, the low throb of a powerboat heading out to sea. He ignored that sound and focused on his immediate target. He could hear the waves lap against the dock. Smell the salty tang of sea air. She was close by, he could feel her. A sliver of moon illuminated patches of garden, but dense shadows shrouded most of it. She wore black, but her face and hair would catch the moonbeams.

He almost called out to her, but decided silence was his best ally. He could explain the situation when they were somewhere safe and the shrew wasn't trying to emasculate him. He rubbed his balls, which still ached from her knee. Patient now, he crouched on the grass beneath an overgrown honeysuckle bush looking for reflections of moonlight across pale skin.

There. Just beside the trunk of a massive oak was the glimmer of a face.

He backtracked behind the honeysuckle and along a lilac hedge, keeping his attention focused on the spot where she hid. He crept forward slowly until he could make out her faint profile against the night sky and see her shoulders rise and fall with each breath.

He caught her from behind, banded one arm around her middle, pinning her arms to her sides, while his other hand covered her mouth to smother her screams. She writhed and struggled violently, trying to bite his hand and scratch him with her nails.

Damn, for all she was slight she was fierce.

Other sounds caught his attention, deep male voices followed by the abrupt cutting of a powerboat's motor. Silence followed, with just the splash of wake causing the dock to bounce and grate against its moorings. Soon even that was gone and the sounds of their struggle carried like bomb-blasts in the silence.

"Hush," Marsh said.

She bit him. He squeezed her chin hard enough to get her attention.

"Goddamn it, I said *be quiet*," he hissed into her ear. "We've got company and it's not the fucking Boy Scouts."

She stilled in his arms and he finally had her full attention.

Marsh pulled them both back behind the oak

184

tree and started to reverse toward the thick vegetation that edged the fence at the side of the property. He froze as three dark shadows crept stealthily toward the house. Josephine flinched beneath his hands as pistols were drawn and magazines inserted. He kept his hand over her mouth just in case she did anything stupid. One man broke off and headed around to the back of the house—to block her escape.

When the men entered the open French-doors, Marsh decided it was time to get out of there. He turned her around to face him. "Look, they're here to torture and kill you. Got it?"

She nodded, her eyes wide with fear.

"My car's parked just the other side of this fence. If I let you go, you have to promise to come with me, to trust me."

She stiffened her spine, but nodded. He let her go, knowing he could never trust her, but she wasn't stupid. He kept a tight grip of her hand, just in case she decided to bolt.

Drawing the SIG from its holster he took the safety off and moved along the fence to the spot where he'd climbed over earlier. They could hear movements inside the house, shouts and the sound of furniture being broken. He jumped the fence and waited for her to join him, but she tripped and fell, cutting herself on a wooden post and crying out in pain.

Marsh pulled her to her feet.

"Run." He hissed and half-pushed her along the road. He could hear feet pounding through the garden. They were still twenty feet from the car when the first mobster opened fire.

Marsh fired back blindly. Bullets whizzed past

his head with only inches to spare. He threw himself into the car at full speed and gunned the engine. Josie still had one leg out the passenger door when he floored it and tore down the road with grit spitting out behind the tires.

They'd made it, for now.

Chapter Twelve

Mount Vernon Street, Boston, April 12th

Josephine Maxwell's silver blonde hair fell down from its twist, making her look younger than her twenty-seven years. Marsh untangled the knots gently with his fingers, tentatively traced the outermost shell of her ear. Delicate features in a heart-shaped face denied the ice that flowed through her veins—making her look as soft and innocent as an angel.

But she was a player and he shouldn't be fooled. She'd kicked him in the balls a split-second after she'd conned him with those big blues. If he underestimated her again it would be more than his manhood at stake, it would be her and Elizabeth's lives.

At least now he had her under control.

Drugged.

They'd made it back to his family's Louisburg Square home without incident and he'd carried her up the wide staircase to the guestroom closest to his own bedroom.

To keep an eye on her.

Sitting on the satin coverlet, he pulled a wide-bore syringe from the little surgical kit he kept in his office. Josephine would escape from him at the first opportunity, but he intended to be ready for her. In fact, he needed her to escape. He was relying on her to lead him straight to Elizabeth.

Heavy bronze-colored drapes were closed against prying eyes. The lights were on, but he was confident that Josephine wouldn't rouse, and he needed to see exactly what he was doing. Carefully, he turned Josephine onto her front, gently moved her arms to the sides of her body, turned her head to the side so that she could breathe more easily. He pulled up the black top she wore, exposing her back, ready to swab the insertion site with alcohol.

Her skin was as pale as alabaster and she wasn't wearing any underwear. That was the first thing he noticed. Then his gaze lit on the first scar and his mouth twitched. He pulled her vest higher and saw that she was covered in evil lines of old pain. They formed an 'X' in a series of crisscrosses over her back.

Heart thumping unevenly in his mouth, Marsh swallowed and turned her onto her back, lifted her top and traced the pale jagged lines that ran from just below her collarbone to her navel. One sliced the edge of her nipple, furrowing its edge. Desire surged within him at the sight of small pert breasts and a lean soft stomach, but he ignored it, concentrating on something more important. Six scars ran the length of her torso, in long straight lines. Smaller ones flashed across her skin, pearly white in the bright light.

Jesus. He sat stunned and it took a moment to realize the pounding in his ears was blood blasting through him like a juggernaut down a ravine.

He'd forgotten about the report. Forgotten about the fact she'd been knifed, almost to death, as a kid.

Son of a fucking bitch. And he'd wondered why she was so bitter and angry. Pulling her shirt down, he covered her up and smoothed the material at the edges.

How could anyone do that to a small, defenseless child?

If I ever get hold of the bastard... But he wouldn't. Life was never that neat and tidy.

Marsh looked at her sleeping form and shut off the guilt and anger that hummed within him. He rolled her onto her front where she flopped like a giant rag doll. Trying not to think about the violation, he pulled up her vest, picked up the syringe and inserted the tiny transmitter, subcutaneously, just below her shoulder blade.

There was no time for sentiment. Neither woman would applaud his methods, but he wasn't looking for thanks. Standing back he gazed down at her. She would hate him if she found out what he'd done, but he'd deal with that. If he had any hope of keeping Elizabeth and Josephine alive, he didn't have a choice.

***

Eliza stood on the porch with two hands wrapped firmly around a mug of hot coffee. She'd pulled on a pair of baggy sweats under her nightshirt and was wrapped up in her bathrobe. She was watching a bizarre scene play itself out in the yard. Blue and a couple of other ranch dogs were rounding up a bunch of stray cows that had somehow managed to get into Rose's garden. Rose ran around, waving a tea towel like a red flag. But, most incredible of all, two kittens had joined in the chase and cornered a large cow against the back fence.

Despite her sour mood, Eliza couldn't help grinning. The kittens thought they were tigers, not half-pound bags of bones. Snarling, sharp-clawed bundles of fur, they hissed and spat until the cow dived for the gate and ran back into the meadow. Eliza laughed out loud and Rose noticed her for the first time.

The older woman wasn't long out of hospital. She must have spotted the cattle from her bedroom window and rushed out to defend her precious flowers that were just starting to sprout. She wore a navy bathrobe over flannel pajamas, bare feet stuck into heavy work boots. Iron-gray hair flew haphazardly around her face, softening the heavy wrinkles carved into her narrow mouth and wide forehead.

Rose waved her over. Reluctant to disobey a direct command from the matriarch of the Sullivan family, Elizabeth grudgingly went.

"They breed them fierce around here," Elizabeth said, pointing to the kittens with her coffee mug. She clutched it like a shield, wary of the older woman's regard.

Rose gave a husky laugh as she slammed the gate behind the cows. "They do that," she agreed.

Elizabeth shivered and wrapped her robe more tightly around her shoulders. It was cold out here in the open with the wind blowing.

A ruddy glow spread across Rose's cheeks, emphasizing her otherwise pale complexion. Rose grimaced as if in pain and took time to catch her breath. Elizabeth put a hand on the older woman's arm, but Rose patted it away with a half smile.

Eliza wondered where Nat was. She'd wondered where he was all last night. In fact she'd lain awake for hours, expecting him to turn up at her door and take her up on her offer of 'no-strings' sex, half dreading it, half desperate to get it over with.

He never came.

She'd given him a massive green light yesterday, but obviously he'd reconsidered.

"The boys spent last night foaling another mare," Rose said, reading her mind. She folded the tea towel neatly into quarters and slapped it against her thigh.

Elizabeth spun towards the older woman. "Was everything all right?" Her sense of relief was tempered by the grisly memory of Banner's carved-up body.

"Yeah." Rose nodded towards the stables where Nat and Cal appeared out of the gloom, grimy and rumpled, but both smiling.

Eliza caught Nat's gaze, and even at this distance, the air sizzled.

Rose obviously felt it too. The woman's expression turned pensive, her lips drooped down at the corners. "Worst thing about dying is leaving your babies behind." She followed Elizabeth's gaze back to Nat.

Elizabeth looked at her sharply. "Are you dying?"

"Yeah," Rose nodded. "Yeah, I am." The old woman pulled her stooped shoulders straighter, slapped the tea towel rhythmically against her thigh.

Elizabeth watched Nat walk slowly toward them where they stood on the other woman's frost-burned lawn.

"I'm sorry," she murmured to Rose, noting the gray pallor that permeated her skin, knowing her sorrow was wasted. Rose wasn't telling her this to gain her sympathy.

"It'd be nice to see at least one of my babies

settled," Rose said with a gleam in her eye. "I know he's got his eye on you and my Nat is mighty picky."

"It isn't like that," Elizabeth stated, blushing at the same time. She could hardly tell Rose they were only interested in sex—not marriage and babies.

"Don't break his heart, ya hear," Rose muttered fiercely under her breath.

Elizabeth watched Nat move. His long legs covered the ground with an easy stride, broad shoulders strong and sure, blue eyes dazzling. Her breath caught. There was no way she'd ever intentionally break his heart.

"We don't always get to make the choices we want." Elizabeth matched Rose's quiet tone.

Rose laughed and tapped her chest before Nat was close enough to hear, though he eyed them nervously. "You don't have to tell *me* that, girl, I know. But if you hurt him, I'll haunt you all the way back to New York City."

Elizabeth smiled the way Rose had meant her to, but sorrow tugged at her heart. Staying wasn't an option.

"I'm going to put on breakfast." Rose called to the dogs and kittens and headed into the ranch house at a brisk walk. "Come on in when you're ready."

Elizabeth nodded, emptied the dregs of her coffee onto the flowerbed and held Nat's gaze as he approached. She'd spent half of last night scared to death that he was going to show up and the other half pissed because he hadn't. She wasn't backing down now and she wasn't running away—not anymore.

He had on the same clothes as yesterday and he

stopped an arms' length away from her, resting his hands on his hips. The sleeves of his shirt were rolled up to reveal strong forearms, roped with lean muscle and covered with warm, tanned skin. She wrinkled her nose. He smelled musty and sweaty from the work he'd done, looked tired as he stood watching at her.

Elizabeth took a half step toward him, but he held up his hand, palm outstretched to stop her from touching him.

"I'm in dire need of a shower, Eliza," he warned. "I wouldn't get too close if I were you—"

Elizabeth caught his hand in hers and reached up and pressed her lips to his mouth. She muffled his half-hearted sound of protest and wrapped her arms around his neck, kissing him for all she was worth. Nat gave up the fight, folded his arms around her waist and pinned her to his chest. He molded her body to the length of his with firm strokes of strong hands, lifted her up off the ground in an effort to get even closer.

Eliza's head spun from the sensations that bombarded her. His mouth claimed hers with a passion that felt both fiery and tempered. Restrained—like a volcano.

It was heady to realize she could do this to him. His mouth was wild and gentle and as sweet as spring water. She ran her fingers through his silky hair, cradled the back of his head and gave her lips free rein across his rough jaw. He shuddered and closed his eyes. She raised her head, traced the crease that lined his forehead and placed a small kiss at the edge of his mouth.

She rested her hands on his shoulders and looked down into his eyes as he held her aloft.

A shrill whistle blasted the air, breaking the moment and the illusion that they were alone. Nat grinned and threw Ryan a one-fingered salute before he lowered Elizabeth back down on the ground.

"Well." Nat leaned back on his heels, still holding her shoulders in a loose grip, "Good morning to you, too."

She tried to pull away, suddenly embarrassed. "Sorry, it's just..." The feeling that time was running out meant she didn't want to waste a moment of it. "I wanted to do that all night and well..."

Nat laughed, held onto her and kissed her again. "Yeah, apologize, why don't you? Like that wasn't the best damned kiss *I've* ever had."

Warmth spread from her toes to her hairline, leaving a telltale blush that heated her cheeks. Desire skittered below the surface of her skin, reminding her she was a flesh and blood human being, not a husk of womanhood that Andrew DeLattio had chewed up and spat out.

Dawn rays glinted off Nat's hair as he squinted down at her. He seemed to have understood her swift change of mood and his eyes turned serious, full of patient concern.

She knew the difference between sex and violence, knew the difference between force and desire. But she didn't know if her mind was strong enough to cope with making love, or if she would freak when push came to shove.

"We have to talk." Eliza stepped out from his embrace and wrapped her arms across her chest. She might not be able to tell Nat the full details of what had happened to her, but he deserved the

194

basics. She owed him that before things went any further between them.

Nat nodded, looked at the ground for a moment as if reluctant to meet her gaze. "Yeah."

"Tonight," Elizabeth squared her shoulders and forced a smile. Telling Nat what had happened to her was not going to be easy, but she was determined. It was way past time.

"Tonight," he agreed. He reached out a hand and stroked a finger down her bottom lip and along her chin and then tapped her nose lightly.

A sound caught her attention. She saw a car behind Nat's shoulder, just cresting the rise to the rear of the ranch house. Her fingers automatically reached for her pistol, only to come up against the soft toweling of her robe. No holster. No Glock. *Stupid.*

"You've got company," she said, her voice, hard and low.

Nat turned and cursed. "Sheriff Talbot. What the hell does he want?"

***

An hour later, instead of wrapped up in the arms of a handsome cowboy, she sat opposite a local law enforcement officer, Sheriff Scott Talbot, in the Sullivans' den. She'd showered and dressed as slowly as she could, hoping to avoid the man, but it turned out he'd come to interview her—about her little brawl down at the *Screw Loose*.

Somebody had made a complaint.

Just thinking about Marsh's reaction to that fiasco made her squirm. Her boss was a perfectionist and expected the best from his agents, but she wasn't his agent anymore, she reminded herself, she was on her own now.

Sipping hot sweet tea from a bone china mug, she controlled her irritation.

In his forties, with a florid complexion and a belly that strained over the thick belt of his washed-out khaki trousers, Sheriff Talbot had black hair liberally sprinkled with gray and light brown eyes that turned golden in the sunshine. Shorter than Elizabeth by a head, he wore his revolver on his hip like a man with a Napoleon complex.

Elizabeth ground her teeth in order to stop herself from finishing his sentences. And he took notes like a schoolboy, long torturous notes that had her repeating herself a hundred times. If she'd been working with him, she would have pointed out the advantages of a digital voice-recorder, but it wasn't her problem.

Feck.

"So you're from New York City, Miss Reed?"

That was the third time he'd asked her that question and she itched with the desire to call him on it, but at least she wasn't feeling like a victim. She was totally pissed.

"That's right, Sheriff," she replied with a smile, unconsciously flexing her fists. "Need me to spell it for you?"

He hesitated, looked up from his notes.

"Well, ma'am," there it was again, that long pause for no earthly reason, "I can see why these questions might seem like a waste of time to you, but..." he paused for another long breath and she held back a groan, "...that's just the way we work around here." He smiled at her, almost in slow motion.

She held his gaze and forced herself to smile back while he jotted something down in his little book. She craned her head, desperately wanting to see what he wrote.

"You got an address for me, ma'am?"

A false one on Staten Island rolled off her tongue. She released a pent-up breath and placed her cup carefully on the coffee table. Mistake number one. Like a nervous suspect she'd blown it.

She got up and began to pace.

Didn't matter that she'd told him what had happened three times already. He just kept on at her like a damned...cop.

"You sure you handled those boys all by yourself?" Talbot scratched his head with his pen. "I mean we've got a report of a broken nose, broken fingers, concussion, dislocated shoulder. *You* did all that?"

Was he going to press charges? Then suddenly she saw it—he wasn't out to get *her*. He was after Cal, or Nat. Eyes narrowing, she stared him down. He'd figured she wasn't capable of taking on a couple of goons and she was taking the rap to keep Cal out of prison.

"Is Cal Landon still on parole?" Eliza enquired, her voice as hard as flint.

Sheriff shook his head slowly. "No, ma'am."

"You should be asking those bastards why they attacked an innocent man minding his business in a bar."

"Now, I wouldn't exactly call Cal Landon an innocent," the sheriff broke in with a chuckle.

"And you can ask all those so called *witnesses* why they did nothing to help a man who could have been beaten to death."

Small town justice sucked.

The justice system sucked, period.

The sheriff seemed unfazed by her anger. He offered her a piece of gum before he popped a piece into his own chubby mouth. "You wanna make a complaint, Miss Reed?"

"This is your town, Sheriff. You deal with it." Heat burned along her cheekbones and she compressed her lips angrily.

Tilting his head to one side he appeared to consider her answer before nodding. "That's right, ma'am, something you'd do well to remember yourself." His tone went stiff for a moment, just long enough for Elizabeth to reassess Sheriff Talbot's tedious probing.

They held each other's gaze for two interminable seconds before she conceded the point with a cheerless nod.

"You're staying at the Triple H for another couple of weeks, right?" he asked, getting awkwardly to his feet.

Elizabeth nodded. She had to leave sooner rather than later now, but she wasn't going to tell him that.

"Well, ma'am, as they say in the movies, 'don't leave town' without talking to me first, now will ya?" The drawl was still languid and easy, but Elizabeth recognized the tougher steel beneath it.

She smiled sweetly, knew she didn't fox him for an instant. "No, sir, Sheriff."

"Would you mind asking Doc Sullivan to come on in here for a minute, ma'am?" He continued to labor over his notes and she breathed a sigh of relief, escaping as quickly as she could.

***

Nat woke to the faint buzz of the TV. After being up all night, he'd fallen asleep on the couch in the family room waiting to talk to the sheriff. It was obvious from the settled hush of the house that Talbot was long gone and the place seemed empty.

A news channel droned on, and he knew he really should go to bed and get a few more hours of rest before he got back to work.

"Today, seventeen alleged members of the Bilotti crime-family were indicted in front of the grand jury on multiple counts under the 1970 'Racketeer Influenced and Corrupt Organizations' act, RICO for short. The Bilotti crime-family is reputed to be the largest Mafia family currently operating in the US."

Like he cared. The Mafia was about as far removed from Montana, as Brazil was from Iceland.

The dignified, gray-haired newscaster continued in a gravelly voice. "Those indicted today include Julian Galliano, the so-called 'Godfather' of the Bilotti crime-family." A picture of an old man with a large nose hit the screen, followed by pictures of several other well-dressed middle-aged men.

"John-Paul Mallena, nicknamed 'The Lion' and considered by the FBI to be the second-in-command, was also indicted and is being held without bail at a federal facility here in Manhattan."

The newscaster paused dramatically as Nat stretched out his limbs—*thank God the foaling had gone well last night*. He smiled thinking about the smart purebred Arabian filly who'd all but pranced out of the womb. He sat up and rubbed his eyes. *Better check her.*

"If successful at trial, the FBI will have dealt a crushing blow to organized-crime here in NYC. This is the biggest operation since 1991, when John Gotti, head of the Gambino crime-family, was sentenced to life without parole, along with dozens of his associates."

Behind the newscaster's rigidly coifed, poised head, the picture of another man appeared. This time the face was younger with pale eyes and Italian good looks.

Nat put his hands behind his head and closed his eyes for a moment longer.

"The indictments follow the arrest of Andrew DeLattio on charges of insider-dealing and money laundering. Mr. DeLattio is a stockbroker on Wall St. and is also the nephew of John-Paul Mallena. FBI officials refuse to say whether the cases are connected."

The newscaster droned on. "Police are still looking for a former girlfriend of Mr. DeLattio. Miss Juliette Morgan disappeared three weeks ago." The anchorman looked soberly into the camera. "Fears are growing for Ms. Morgan's safety following rumors that she provided key evidence against the Bilotti family. Ms. Morgan was herself accused of switching valuable pieces of artwork with quality forgeries."

"I've no comment," said a voice on the TV. Nat sat bolt upright on the couch and stared at the screen. The voice was unmistakable—a soft Irish lilt with East Coast vowels.

Eliza's voice.

The footage switched to a lithe figure clad in black emerging from a large municipal building. The tall redhead was squeezed between four dark suits, and despite the cold and the gloom, wore sunglasses to hide her eyes.

The redhead flicked a single irritated glance at the cameras and then, chin held high, eyes staring straight ahead, she walked to the waiting limo without another word.

"There you can see Ms. Morgan leaving the District attorney's office three weeks ago, guarded by four federal officials. She hasn't been seen since."

Damn.

What the hell was going on?

***

Elizabeth made a real effort. She wore a dress—black, round-necked, with three-quarter length sleeves—that reached half way down her calves.

Understated.

It was also soft and clingy, revealing the curves she'd so far hidden beneath big shirts and thick coats.

Understated, but sexy.

Not that Nat noticed—there was a sternness to the set of his jaw as he loaded the wood-stove, a seriousness to his expression that reflected her inner thoughts. Absently, she smoothed the material along her thigh, watched his competent hands handle the logs with strength and economy, his mind seemingly absorbed by the task.

The smell of coffee mingled with the acrid taint of wood smoke and brought the down-home feel all the closer. She lifted her mug to her lips and took a sip of the bitter brew.

Van Morrison crooned in the background.

Nat hadn't said much since he'd walked in the door, but she was the one who needed to do the talking.

"There's no chance of getting enough money to pay off the loan without selling that land?" Okay, so she was avoiding the issue.

Nat's hand slowed and paused. He stared down at the wooden floor as if he couldn't bring himself to look at her.

"Nope," he said, voice tight.

"I've got money," Elizabeth offered. She put her coffee mug down on a side-table and took a step forward. He frowned at her, but she carried on regardless. It would be nice to do something for the Sullivans before she left.

And she *had* to leave.

Nat's laser blue eyes told her to back off, but he didn't say the words. His lips were drawn into a hard, straight line, his chin jutted out at a stubborn angle.

Elizabeth was getting nowhere. She pulled her hair back from her face, out of her eyes and knew she should give it up, but she also knew that she could help, because one thing she did have was money and the Sullivans needed a sponsor.

"I could," she hesitated, wary of the cold light that entered his eyes, "...you know, lend you some, until you're back on your feet." The Sullivans could have it with bells on as far as Elizabeth was concerned.

"No." His lips were tight. "*Thank you*," was forced out, cold and sharp between his teeth.

"Why not?" Bravely, she went towards him. "I want to help."

As she got close, he stood up, wiped his hands

on his jeans, his face a remote, hard mask that she didn't recognize.

"Where'd you get the money, Eliza?" A muscle jumped along his jaw. "I didn't realize *law enforcement* paid so well."

Panic fluttered along her nerves, her feet began to backtrack.

"I inherited it." She lifted her chin and stopped moving, determined to do this right. Reaching out, she touched his arm, but he was as responsive as steel.

Blue eyes were glacial—fascinating to watch—even though their inexplicable coldness punched her panic button with a quick one-two.

"I don't want your goddamned money," Nat snarled and advanced towards her.

Backing up fast, her heart sped up as fear clawed all the way up her throat.

Chapter Thirteen

Anger tightened like a bowstring in his mind and then snapped like a bone. Narrowing his eyes, fury burned bright and resonant, scorching rational thought. When she backed up, he followed, livid that she'd lied to him, pissed that he'd fallen for both the lies and the woman. It wasn't the first time he'd been blinded by a pretty face.

He corralled her up against the couch, planted both hands on his hips and bared his teeth in a snarl. "Where'd you get the money?"

"I told you, I inherited it—"

"Don't lie to me!" Nat roared, "I saw you on fucking CNN. They think the Mafia killed you. Does that make it easier to get away with your little art scam?" Bitterness edged his voice, a sense of loss merging with the anger. He took a deep shuddering breath. "You enjoy stringing me along with your little mind games?"

Green eyes were huge in her pale face and she shook her head, whipping her hair across her cheeks. It took him a moment to recognize stark, vivid terror.

Terror aimed at him.

It shook him—knocked the breath right out of him. Anger crashed in a wave and he tried to grab her shoulders, wanting to tell her it didn't matter, that he didn't care, but she flinched, panicked and fell back. She scrambled away from him and then squeezed into a tight ball.

He inched toward her, but she shrieked, "Don't touch me!" And he stood still, breathing heavily and frowning.

She'd screamed *don't touch me* the first time they'd kissed. *What had happened to her?*

"It's okay, honey. Look." He held up his hands. "I don't care what you've done. I'm not going to hurt you." His tone was gentle and he hoped soothing. She cowered in the corner of the couch like a whipped dog, and it didn't make any sense. After seeing her on the news and in that bar fight, he'd figured she'd have gone nose-to-nose with anybody without backing down an inch.

Obviously, he'd been wrong.

Walking over to the fireplace, he gave her time and space to get herself together. He wanted to haul her into his arms and comfort her, but knew it was too soon to touch her.

He'd never raised a hand to a woman in his life, had never even considered it. But some bastard had. Nat tried to hide the dismay that burned like an ulcer in the pit of his stomach. Man, he'd like to get his hands on that bastard.

"I saw you on television, Eliza." Frustrated, he propped his hand against the wall, scrubbed the other hand over his face. "I recognized your voice and I wanted to know what was going on, but I sure as hell would never hurt you."

He followed her with his eyes, stayed perfectly still as she got up and turned off the music with a click that left the room in booming silence.

She spoke in a flat voice, devoid of emotion. "I used to work undercover for the FBI. The art forgery story the press reported was part of my deep cover background that we—the FBI—put together, designed to draw in the crooks. Even though I resigned from the bureau they can't reveal I was an undercover agent because it might jeopardize the other operatives I worked with."

The FBI...Jesus, it sounded crazy but...it fit.

"Okay..." Nat paused and looked for any hint of subterfuge, didn't see anything but naked hurt. "So where did you get the money?"

A brittle burst of laughter splintered into a sigh of resignation. "What does it matter?"

Fear began to sink in. Fear that he might have crossed a line he hadn't even known existed. "I'm sorry I yelled at you." He walked slowly towards her, "I didn't mean to scare you." He lifted a hand to touch her cheek, but she jerked away.

"You didn't scare me, Nat." Her voice was barely above a whisper. "I did that all by myself." She lifted her head and met his gaze head-on, eyes narrowed in warning, voice still trembling.

"There's something else you should know. I was raped. In New York. I was raped and I'm not good at any of this anymore."

He closed his eyes and forced himself to stand very still. Regret poured through his veins that he hadn't been there to protect her, along with fury so potent it blasted his mind. That someone had used her that way, injured her that way, ripped at him. He'd suspected the worst. Shit, she slept with a loaded gun under her pillow. Swallowing hard, he blinked away the tears that burned the edge of his vision. He'd hoped he'd been mistaken...

But he hadn't been mistaken.

Not looking at him, she stared down at her hands fisted in front of her. "I'm sorry, I can't talk about it. You just have to leave."

Eliza was fighting to control her emotions. He wanted to pull her close, comfort her against his chest and hold her safe, make everything better, but rage simmered within him and he knew if he stayed it would spew out like lava and probably scare her.

She didn't need that.

Gently he reached out and rubbed a strand of her dark hair between his thumb and forefinger. It felt like raw silk against his rough skin, and nearly made him choke with wanting.

"What's your real name?" he asked softly. He needed to know.

"I never lied to you about the important things." She glanced up, unshed tears sparkling in her eyes. "My mother called me Eliza."

He took a half step toward her, but she held out her palm to stop him.

"Please go," she said.

He started to protest, gave up when he realized it was useless. She needed time alone, and hell, he needed time to think. He'd screwed up badly, should never have raised his voice to her, no matter how pissed he was. A burst of panic shot through him, but he resolutely crushed it. He'd make it right somehow, but not now. The barriers she'd thrown up would take more than a few careful words to penetrate.

Picking up his hat and old suede jacket, he paused. "I'm sorry. Sorry for yelling, sorry for being a jackass and real sorry about what happened to you, Eliza." There was nothing he could do or say that would heal the wounds, but he needed her to know. "It doesn't change the fact that I still want to hold you, but I guess it does mean I'll back off, until you tell me it's okay."

She didn't look at him, just stared down at her hands twisting the gold signet ring she wore on her pinkie—as unreachable and isolated as a granite mountaintop.

Walking out the doorway, Nat stood outside the cottage, uncertain and dazed. Before he could change his mind he heard the lock turn and the deadbolt slide into place. Placing the flat of his hand against the smooth surface of the door, he leaned against it.

She didn't want him.

And he couldn't blame her.

Rage stole through his system at the thought of someone hurting her, making it hard to breathe. His hands tensed into useless fists that clenched and unclenched at his side. The silver moon rode high and proud in the night sky and he wanted to kick himself. If she ever spoke to him again—and that was a big *if*—he wanted her not to cower with fear if his voice rose a couple of decibels. *And* she was going to learn to trust him enough to tell him all the bad stuff, all the hurt and all the secrets.

Assuming she stuck around...

Visions of her sneaking away in the middle of the night made his heart stutter. It was exactly the sort of sneaky thing that she'd do. Disappear, without a word.

Well, hell. What the heck could he do about it? *Except maybe disable the Jeep?*

Eliza had invaded his senses and Nat didn't want her to leave. Not yet.

She was beautiful, but it wasn't just that. Fiercely independent and violently passionate she seemed held together by nothing more than dogged determination and pure bloody-mindedness. And he couldn't get over the aching vulnerability that shone in her eyes when she lost her defenses.

And he'd scared her.

Nat rested his chin on the smooth wooden rails of the fence that ran along the back of the horse barn. Eliza was the best goddamned thing that had happened to him in a long time, but he had absolutely nothing to offer her.

She'd been violated and hurt. Now she was on the run from the mob.

Christ.

At least she was safe here.

He grabbed the rail, hoisted himself up to sit on the fence and stare up at the moon. An owl hooted nearby. The stars were bright against the inky night sky; the moon glowed like a big, fat, silver coin.

A wolf called out from the hills, a long, drawn out cry. The sound raised the fine hairs on the back of his neck, its loneliness echoed within his heart. Nat looked back at the cottage—dark now, shrouded in complete and utter blackness. The wolf howled again, its loneliness tangible. Only silence answered, silence pierced with longing.

***

Vermont, April 13th

"Where is she?" Marsh leaned over Josephine, clutched the arm of the sofa, rapidly losing patience. Gravelly tones flowed from the stereo, accompanied by the log fire that crackled and spat in the big stone fireplace. Her chin lifted. Her bottom lip stuck out at a mutinous angle.

"Shit." Marsh dropped his head with a slump

and moved away from her. "Exactly how long are you going to sulk for, princess?" He worked hard to keep his voice level and controlled, forced his concentration to remain on the job at hand.

And gave up.

Rubbing the back of his neck where tension had knotted the muscles into painful bands, he slouched down on the leather couch, stared into the bright orange flames of the fire. It was dark outside, pitch black as only a forest can be. The nearest cabin was miles away, across the lake, hidden by trees. He'd been waiting for her to give him the slip for the last forty-eight hours, but so far she hadn't budged an inch.

And I'm stuck babysitting the female from hell.

He watched as she got up and padded barefoot across the hardwood floor to the wet bar. He noted the delicate arches of her feet and the cute toenails painted different colors. *Figured.* She poured two drinks, fussed over the ice bucket and dropped a cube on the floor. It skittered under the table and Marsh averted his eyes from her backside as she bent down to pick it up.

She straightened and carried a glass of whisky over to him, placing it mutely on the table beside him. Then she went and sat back down, sipping a glass of lemonade.

Why was she being nice to him now?

She'd called a cell phone the other day but hadn't gotten a reply. The number had been registered to a Jane Smith, but Marsh was convinced it was Elizabeth's. They were tracking and tracing calls, but so far nothing. Maybe they'd get lucky.

And the way things were going—maybe not.

The names Josephine had called him when she realized he'd drugged her had boggled even his experienced mind—and he'd been in the Navy. Luckily she didn't suspect about the tracking device.

He tapped his index finger against the crystal tumbler. He wasn't going to allow Josephine Maxwell to psyche him out. She hadn't spoken since yesterday morning, after he'd refused to let her attend either her father's, or Marion Harper's, funeral. He couldn't blame her for being upset, but wasn't about to sacrifice her on a sentimental whim.

But now her silence was beginning to irritate him, the childish stunt grating on his nerves like a constantly plucked violin string. However, if she realized he was rattled, she'd never speak to him again.

Steve Dancer, his technician, had bought clothes and supplies. Now Josie was decked out in a utilitarian navy-blue cabled sweater and soft cotton leggings. Dancer brought her a pair of boots, but she'd said she preferred the ugly old black Doc Martins she'd had with her. Everything Dancer had picked up had been black or navy as per bureau mandate, but Marsh had to admit the dark color suited her.

She'd vehemently denied knowing where Elizabeth was or what her plans were. They'd made the switch and disappeared, end of story.

Marsh didn't believe her.

"If we don't find Elizabeth soon, the mob will." He stared trance-like into the blaze, defeat settling over him like a blanket. But this wasn't just about him losing. This was about life and death. And Josephine was playing games.

He sipped his Scotch then put it back down on the side table.

She watched him, always.

"Why are you so sure they'll find her?" She tossed her fine blonde hair over one shoulder. "*You* can't."

He blinked. Suppressed a smile. At least she was talking to him again.

"You. You're the weak link." He carried on staring at the fire, watching her out of the corner of his eye. "I can't lock you up forever." Marsh ignored her smirk. "And as soon as you resurface, people are going to start to ask questions." He turned and studied the perfect bone-structure. "You have the kind of face people never forget."

He wouldn't forget it. She was engraved on his conscience like an etching. And he wanted her, and that aggravated the shit out of him. "Why do you hate me so much, anyway?" Marsh asked her, his curiosity piqued. "I've never done anything to you."

Josie sat quietly and for a moment he thought she was going to resume her silence. "You recruited her, didn't you?" she said finally.

"Yeah." Confused he raked his hands through his short hair. "But she wanted to do it. I didn't force her or—"

"Of course she wanted to do it! Her parents were blown to bits by terrorists when she was a child. What kid wouldn't want to get a chance to get back at the bad guys?"

"She wanted to do it," Marsh repeated.

"It was like recruiting Peter Pan or Ariel—"

"She wasn't a kid when I took her on," Marsh cut in.

"I'm not talking about her age," Josie snapped,

sounding frustrated. She blew a strand of hair out of her mouth. "She was an innocent. You took that from her."

Maybe she was right. Christ, maybe that was why he felt so damn responsible for Elizabeth. *No*, he'd have felt the same way about any of the agents on his team.

"Why'd ya do it anyway? Why her? So you could sleep with her?"

What the...? "I don't sleep with colleagues." Marsh refused to get angry. She was trying to rile him and he wanted to know why.

"You should have gotten someone mean, someone who knew the rules of the street. Someone who knew what happened when you crossed a wise guy."

"Like you, you mean," Marsh smiled a cruel smile. Josephine thought she was so goddamned tough. "Elizabeth was a trained agent, but she was never supposed to get mixed up with the mob. She was supposed to investigate art fraud, not go undercover for OCU."

"Surprised you with that one didn't she?" Josie sipped her lemonade, still watching him closely. "More guts than brains."

"She's a smart girl, but obviously not smart enough." Marsh felt cornered and pissed off. When had this become about him? "It was her innocence that appealed to me. I needed someone clean, someone fresh."

"You needed a devil in sheep's clothing." Josie looked him in the eye. "You should have recruited me."

Marsh laughed. "No way." He looked away. "I would never have recruited you."

"Why not?" she asked.

He'd already told her, but she hadn't been listening. He didn't sleep with colleagues—and he wanted to sleep with Josephine Maxwell so much it was starting to hurt.

He'd brought her out to his family's cottage in rural Vermont. There were no neighbors to speak of and his parents were cruising halfway around the world. No witnesses, no innocent bystanders to get caught in the crossfire should the mob track her down.

From here she'd have a better chance of a clean escape, and he'd have a better chance of following her without a mob guy spotting her first.

But for all his lax security, for all his open doors, Josephine Maxwell hadn't budged an inch and he'd been forced into close confines with a woman who drove him crazy in more ways than one. He had sworn to protect her, whether she wanted his protection or not, but she was as stubborn as a two-headed mule. And while he appreciated the bond of friendship and loyalty the two women shared, it forced him to do something he'd rather avoid.

And so, here he was, holed up with this incredibly sexy woman, about as miserable as he had ever been in his whole life. His fists tightened reflexively, thoughts hardened. She might be a hellcat, but she was on his territory now. Playing in his world, by his rules. He took another sip of Scotch and felt Josephine's gaze follow his hand. He fought to keep from turning to face her. Didn't want to stare at her like a lovesick puppy. Maybe the drinking bothered her because of her father, but he wasn't about to get drunk.

Shit. Thinking about her father didn't help. The mob was looking for this woman and they'd already killed to get the information they sought.

Out of the corner of his eye he saw her stand and walk toward him. He braced himself for trouble as she slowly knelt at his feet.

Every man's sexual fantasy.

Sprawled back against the couch, he watched her with narrowed eyes.

"Kiss me," she said, putting her hands on his knees and leaning into him.

Marsh raised an eyebrow; thankful he had the sense not to drool like an idiot. He said nothing, made no move towards her. She looked at him solemnly, her blue eyes dark with secrets. When she wasn't spitting fire she looked as serene as the Madonna.

She licked her bottom lip and Marsh watched the progress of her pink tongue like a flare in the night sky.

"What are you up to, Josephine?"

Uncertainty flickered across her features as she started to withdraw her hands, but he caught her wrists and pulled her slowly, inexorably, towards him.

"Nothing," she murmured, watching his lips as if she actually wanted to kiss him. Even though she was more likely to bite him. It wasn't an idea he minded.

She didn't pull away. And one kiss wouldn't hurt...

"I don't believe you," he mouthed against her lips, "but let's see what happens." He kissed her gently, released her wrists and slipped his hands into hair.

215

The kiss was heady, like a starburst. Tentative lips met, sampled and tasted, heated and wanted more.

Josephine pulled back from him, broke the kiss and swallowed hard. "I think I may need a real drink after all." She took the glass from his hand, the fleeting contact making his fingers tingle. He watched her take the tiniest sip.

She seemed to be building up to something, but he didn't know what.

"I want to make love with you." She ran her index finger around the rim of the whisky glass and watched him from beneath heavy lids.

"Yeah, right." Marsh didn't mask his disbelief. One minute she was pissed at him, the next he was irresistible? He breathed in and held it. Waited. Tried not to get turned on because there had to be a catch. He wasn't stupid enough to buy it, but God, he wanted to.

"I want you to make love to me." She passed the glass back into his hand and slid her palm along the top of his thigh. "I dare you." Her eyes looked into his with intense concentration and her hand rested on his thigh, kneading the muscles in a smooth massage that had him as hard as rock before he could count to three.

"Drink your whisky, Mr. Special Agent, and then maybe you'll have the nerve to seduce me."

Marsh lifted the Scotch and swallowed it in one go. The single malt burned all the way down to his gut and he held on to the sensation, wanting to think about anything other than sex. He put the glass down on the side table and watched her, trying to decide whether or not she was serious.

Did she want a bout of sweaty sex to relieve the

216

boredom of their stay? Did she look at him and feel her mouth go dry with desire, unable to look away? Or did she want to manipulate him in the age-old fashion of Eve? He wasn't so easy—was he? Yesterday he wouldn't have thought so. Today...

She knelt between his legs, her forearms pressed along his thighs, his knees brushing her torso and the soft swell of her breasts. Her lips were rosy from their kiss, slick with moisture that glimmered in the firelight.

Her hand moved higher, just a fraction, just enough for him to imagine how good it would be for her hands to be on his naked skin. And then the fire within him exploded, snapped his control and unleashed his desire. *To hell with her motives.* He pulled her up onto the couch beside him, laid her along its length and came down on top of her.

He trapped her face between his hands and dipped his head to kiss her, his tongue tasting the sweetness and nervousness of her mouth. She responded tentatively, returning each touch with short sweet darts that teased and fled.

It was unbearably erotic.

Still kissing her, Marsh slipped one hand down the length of her body and then dipped beneath her sweater. He caressed her breasts, brushed nipples that turned to rigid pebbles at one stroke, and moved gently around them. Teasing her with elusive touches that made her moan as she slowly began to wriggle. Subtle tremors ran through her body and built to unconscious rolling motions that grew stronger as her body strained against his hands. Incoherent pleas for more came out in breathy whispers. Watching her eyes, he rubbed the pad of his thumb across each delicate silk-covered nipple, first one and then the other. Her pupils dilated and she gasped and closed her eyes, throwing her head back and exposing her throat to his lips.

"That feels amazing." She swallowed and he followed the reflex with his tongue.

Impatient with the clothes that hid her body, Marsh wrestled the sweater over her head, but she shook her head and grabbed the bottom edge when he started to lift her T-shirt. Frustrated, but not defeated he slid his hands beneath the cotton and unclasped her bra with a flick of his fingers and slipped it from her shoulders. She looked startled by the move, but Marsh figured she was nervous about the scars—scars she didn't know he'd already seen.

Her curves were subtle, hidden, but all the more alluring. Bunching material in one hand he pulled the T-shirt tight across her breasts. His fingers traced the outline of her nipples through the thin cotton. He dipped his head and suckled them through the material. She groaned, her back arching off the couch and her head falling weightlessly against the cushions. Tiny sounds escaped her mouth as she breathed heavily. Marsh trailed kisses up her neck, slowly, gently, grazing her cool skin, enjoying making her shudder.

He looked up and found her watching him with shocked eyes; embarrassment and uncertainty mixed with mounting desire. She looked like a virgin in the first flush of passion.

Like hell. No woman that beautiful would make it to twenty-seven untouched and Josephine Maxwell was too tough to play the vestal virgin.

Marsh wanted to make her scream with pleasure before the night was over. He wanted to affect her the way she affected him. He slid his hands beneath the T-shirt, moved lower and outlined the waistband of her leggings with one smooth touch.

She tugged at his shirt and he pulled it over his head and flung it to the floor in an impatient move. Then her hands began to trail over his body, stroking the muscles on his back, down his chest.

"Let's go to the bedroom," she said unsteadily.

Oh, yeah.

He stood, tugged her hand and led the way down the corridor. His feet dragged, felt heavy, but he didn't want to stop. The whisky had gone straight to his head.

Sinking with her onto the bed he kissed her again, needing to feel her lips against his. He nuzzled her earlobe, making her writhe as her fingernails bit into his upper arms. She breathed his name and his head whirled, discipline nearly deserting him.

After another long, drawn-out taste of her lips, he inched her leggings and panties down over smooth satiny thighs, and followed the revelation with his mouth. She tensed, but he wasn't about to let her get away from him this time. She'd put him through hell and he was going to repay her with torture.

Tossing her clothes aside, he moved her thighs apart and lifted her hips high.

She squirmed with self-consciousness, totally exposed and vulnerable, tried to say something as he sank his tongue into the hot secrets of her sex. Her eyes blanked and she folded in shock. He slipped his finger inside her, his thumb gently rubbing the tight kernel of flesh that begged wetly against his fingers.

Marsh's control began to slip, and his objectivity had long since flown out the window, but he didn't give a damn. He felt light-headed with the pleasure of finally getting his hands and mouth on Josephine Maxwell. He was damned if he was backing out when she was begging him to be inside her. Her hands pulled at his hair and her hips rose off the bed with hunger.

He desired her more than he'd ever desired anything in his life. Slipping between her legs, he moved slowly against her, arousing her with his hard and ready body. She squirmed and twisted, ran her hands over his skin, then lower over his buttocks. With a muffled oath he kicked off his pants, all the while focusing his entire being on making Josephine blind with lust.

Marsh breathed hard, but still couldn't think properly. His head felt thick and heavy, but he didn't care. His penis pressed up against her center, every inch of him aching with need, drowning out rational thought and common sense. He kissed her mouth, mating his tongue with hers and trying to restrain the need to drive into her until she was completely ready for him. Her thighs opened, her hips arched against him.

He thought he might die when she wrapped her legs tight around him. He'd meant to hold back, to take some precautions, but all he could think about was burying himself in her tight folds. *Now.*

He slipped a hand between them, positioned himself and thrust his hips. Something gave as he buried himself fully inside her with one long stroke. He froze even as she came around him.

A virgin—she's a virgin?

His vision dimmed to gray; her body pulsed like

a glove fitted tight around him. Her surprised cry made him smile even though he couldn't open his eyes.

Something wasn't right.

He gritted his teeth as he tried to hold still for her, to think, to let her get used to him. But she was so damn tight and arousal seared his brain. His head felt fuzzy. Swirling images dislocated his mind as he felt every quiver and clench of muscle around him.

She tilted her pelvis, took him deeper and he knew he was lost. He moved his hand down, between them and stroked her swollen flesh. His head dropped to her shoulder, his weight pinned her, and drove into her deeper and deeper, over and over again. He knew he was finished, game over, but as he felt the edge of his own release she stiffened again, her mouth falling open in a cry of pleasure and surprise. His climax hit him with the force of a hurricane, drowning him in sensations so startling he thought he'd exploded. His mind went blank, dazed by wonder, his body so sated with pleasure he couldn't move.

Sex had *never* been that good before and he'd had plenty.

Josephine's eyes were round and startled. "I can't believe we actually had sex." Her voice came out like a squeak.

Neither could he. He rested his head beside hers on the pillow. Something was wrong with him but he didn't really care. He couldn't move. His lips felt like wool.

"You okay?" she asked.

"Fan—" Marsh yawned, "fucking-tastic." Fatigue whipped away his energy like a thief. He passed out still inside her.

Chapter Fourteen

Eliza kicked Tiger on with her heels, ignoring the insecurities that clamored through her brain and urged her to turn back. She'd frozen Nat out last night. Shut down and shut him out. She been scared, caught up in her own terrifying memories of rape, and had ignored his rights to a few answers. Well, now he was going to get all the answers he wanted, and quickly, because she was leaving the ranch. Today.

Sweat trickled between her shoulder blades, rolling along her spine as the sun beat down mercilessly. Andrew DeLattio would come for her, and she didn't want him to find her where so many people she cared about might get hurt.

She'd have left already, but the damned Jeep hadn't cooperated. And she'd realized then, as she'd turned the key in an ignition that refused to fire, that she'd been taking the cowardly way out. She'd been so busy running from her past that she'd never given a thought to Nat's rights. He was a good man, not a deviant. He'd seen her on TV—hiding out under an assumed name—and had had every right to be suspicious. She sure as hell would have been. He deserved an explanation and she was determined to give him one—just as soon as she found the damned cowboy.

Reluctantly, very reluctantly, Cal had given her directions to where she could find Nat.

Cal had owed her one—and she'd collected. He

223

was still moving stiffly from his beating, but it turned out nothing had been broken. Cal had directed her up in the hills, about a mile north of the glade where she'd first tested out her rifle. Told her to make enough noise and Nat would find her. He was photographing the wolves in their den and had planned to be gone most of that day and maybe overnight. Eliza couldn't wait that long. The agitation in her chest already made her feel sick.

Tiger stopped and sniffed the air, dancing sideways as his gaze locked onto a stand of lodgepole pines. He jerked his head against the reins, snorted, dug his heels in and refused to go any further.

The horse was spooked.

Eliza peered into the trees but couldn't see anything through the densely interlaced branches. Her palms grew damp and she swiped them along her jeans.

Was it animal or human?

Nat had assured her the wolves were 'more or less' harmless. She wasn't so sure. She unslung her rifle from her back and tried to soothe Tiger with encouraging words as she loaded the magazine with cartridges. Not so easy with the horse dancing beneath her.

Should have done it earlier.

Tiger jerked and she dropped a cartridge into the short grass that edged the deer track she'd been following. She left it. Tiger was close to bolting and she couldn't risk the horse getting away from her. She chambered a round, left the hammer half-cocked. She didn't know what the danger was, but she also didn't want to shoot some hapless hiker taking a leak. Her heart hammered so hard she could hear the pounding of blood in her ears. She managed to load three cartridges before she was forced to give up and try to control the horse.

Her stomach dropped and rebounded to her throat as a massive brown form shouldered its way through the branches, out into the open. The grizzly ambled towards her, head high, nose keen, black eyes beaded directly on her.

Shit.

She'd never encountered a bear in the wild before, but she knew what the experts advised. Don't panic. Don't run away.

Yeah. Right.

Tiger reared up with a loud squeal and plunged into the trees at a gallop.

Eliza clung one-handed to the horse's mane, gripping her rifle with the other hand. The reins dangled dangerously loose, but she didn't dare reach for them.

Feck. Feck. Feck.

The bear followed, giving chase at breakneck speed through dense forest and over rocky ground. She'd had no idea that anything so large and cumbersome could shift like a rocket. Tiger seemed to know though, reminding her that instinct was a powerful thing. The horse stretched out his legs in a flat-out gallop. Eliza, lying along his neck, hugged the saddle like a limpet.

She saw it a split second before the horse did, a sudden drop over a sheer cliff. Eliza compensated by leaning hard to the left, but she had no chance of staying on-board as Tiger made a right-angle turn at top speed.

Eliza sailed through the air, gripping her rifle like a lifeline. Self-defense training kicked in as she hit the dirt, dropped into a roll and careened down a grassy bank more than ten meters from where she'd left the horse's back.

Seeing stars as her teeth jarred on impact, the side of her head rang with bludgeoning pain. Blasts of light assaulted her brain. She still held the rifle, but released it onto the grass as she lay back and tried to regain her breath. Her ribs felt flattened, her chest squeezed so hard the air had been knocked right out of her lungs.

She could not move.

Sucking up a rough breath, she squinted between pain-filled lids and saw the grizzly peering over the edge of the cliff. He seemed to grin as he started forward. Still on the move. Still after her. She reached for the .30-30, knowing it was no match for the huge creature. Cocking the hammer with her thumb, she rose slowly to her feet.

***

Nat was having trouble concentrating on the wolves. He'd taken a few rolls of film just after sun up, when the pack had brought home a kill for the alpha female who was holed up in the den. But since then he'd gotten nothing. The wolves were mostly out of sight, lying about in the hot sun. A couple of last year's pups were still visible, but they hadn't moved much beyond the flick of an ear to remove a pesky fly.

The hide he'd constructed two winters ago was a good hundred yards from the den, with a clear view into the dark recesses with his telephoto lens. He sipped coffee from a thermos and tried not to think about Eliza.

Hell, the woman was trouble with a capital T. He'd known it the first moment he'd seen her and still he'd been unable to resist the draw.

If what she'd told him was true, then she was on the run from the mob. His mind staggered at the possibility that someone out there might want to hurt her. That somebody had already hurt her. *Damn.* He swallowed hard, feeling liked he'd failed her even though he hadn't even known her then.

And what if they tracked her here? He locked his teeth together so hard the enamel grated. Give him ten minutes alone with the bastards and see how they felt to be on the receiving end of violence.

But there wasn't just him to consider. He had his mother, his sister and his niece to look after.

A young wolf's ears pricked up a second before the alpha male came to the opening of the den. The male was big, easily 130 pounds, maybe more. His sharp ears pointed straight at Nat, and his yellow eyes glowed. He was a magnificent animal, his pale silver coat glinting in the sunlight. The pack began to gather around him, others coming out of the den to wheel around in agitation.

The small, sleek, black female rose to stand shoulder to shoulder with her mate.

Something's happening.

Nat's spine prickled as he shot off a few frames of film. The wolves turned as one unit and looked down the narrow valley. They bristled and started yapping, just before Nat heard the unmistakable growl of a grizzly. Automatically he reached for his Remington, tucked neatly against the wall of the hide. Still shooting film, he cycled the bolt and lowered the safety on the gun. Leaning over as far as he could, he tried to see what was going on, but that edge of the valley was out of his line of sight.

His horse, Winter, wasn't far away, left loose in a tiny glade about a quarter of a mile away. The horse wouldn't go anywhere. Unless the bear attacked it.

One by one, the pack peeled away, heading down the gorge, toward the bear. Protecting the den and the newborn pups. The female went back inside.

Nat grabbed the camera from its tripod, hung it around his neck and raced out the door as he heard the bear growl again. But his heart damned near stopped when it was answered not by barks, but by a shot from a small caliber rifle.

***

Marsh woke to bright sunshine, white light burning red against his eyelids, and wondered just how much he'd had to drink last night. He squinted at the time displayed by the square digits on the radio alarm. Nearly eleven a.m.

Christ—how long did I sleep? What day is it?

He stared groggily at the apple-green bedroom walls with less energy than a dehydrated slug.

Josephine. The truth came to him in a blinding flash. *The witch had drugged him.*

Marsh swallowed convulsively, his throat raspy with dryness, his tongue like thick cotton wool. He didn't know how she'd found the GHB locked in his briefcase, but she was a more accomplished thief than he'd given her credit for. Should have known better than to underestimate a street kid.

His memories seemed intact though—too freaking intact. The room smelled of sweat and sex.

What the hell had he been thinking? But memories of her running her hands along the insides of his thighs had his body reacting all over again, which told him exactly where his brain cells had fled to last night.

At least she'd only given him a small dose of the drug. Any more mixed with alcohol could have had him passed out for days.

Shit, what day was it?

Maybe she didn't give a damn if he died. Except she wanted to disappear off the radar not get put on the FBI's most wanted list for the murder of a federal agent.

Ignoring the fuzziness of his brain, he tried to sit up, only to be pulled short by something rigid attached to his wrist. In horrified fascination he stared at the metal bracelet that secured him to the cast-iron bedpost. Then he fell back on the bed and laughed so hard he nearly cried.

Seduced and abandoned.

Handcuffed to the fucking bed.

Goddamn. You had to admire those women.

Wiping the tears from his eyes, he recalled making it to the bed, just before they'd made love. *Had sex*, he corrected himself, they'd had sex—not made love.

He should have suspected something was up from the first moment she'd smiled at him and said "kiss me."

Hah!

Humor seemed preferable to screaming down the walls. He sat up, the metal clattering against metal as he checked out the bedstead. She'd been surprised as hell when he'd gotten her naked and, he realized with sudden clarity, Josephine had gotten a damned sight more than she'd bargained for last night. She'd screwed up the dosage—had expected him to collapse long before he had done—and he'd screwed her in return.

At least he'd gotten something out of it.

Shit. He hadn't used a condom. Gripping his head with his free hand, he sank back to the pillow. *Fuck.* Disease shouldn't be a problem although nothing was guaranteed. He was clean, she was a virgin.

But a baby?

Damn.

Maybe she was on birth control, didn't seem likely, but... Marsh wrapped his free hand around the back of his neck, tried to rub away the unease. The thought of Josephine swollen with his child didn't scare him the way it should. He was surprised by the feelings the image evoked—even though he could murder the woman.

The bed was antique and solidly made. He was stuck. There was nothing for it. He had to call Dancer. Marsh was going to be the laughing stock of the division—if they ever found out.

Marsh dragged the bed across the floor, leaned into the movement with all his might to keep up the momentum. He ignored the screech as it scraped, inch by reluctant inch, across the polished wooden floor. Sweat dripped down his back, slick and hot as he reached the jacket that hung behind the door. He grabbed his cell, thankful that it, at least, was still there. He didn't know what he'd have done if she'd taken that with her.

He put in the call and figured there might just be a way for him to extricate himself from the bed in the next thirty minutes before Dancer arrived. All he needed was a screwdriver.

***

Eliza glared up at the bear. She'd wasted her first shot firing over the animal's head in an effort to scare it away before she became lunch. The bear just growled a laugh. A noise that rumbled along the ground like a minor quake before it rested at her feet.

Dogs yapped in the distance.

Weird. Her attention was pulled away from the massive creature for a split second.

Then she realized it wasn't dogs, but wolves.

Great, two of nature's top predators right on her heels. The bear was about thirty yards away working his way around the edge of the cliff, lumbering towards her like a slow moving freight train.

"Shoo, bear!"

If Nat were anywhere around here, he'd have heard the shot. But judging from the bear's stance, it wouldn't make a blind bit of difference. He was pissed and hungry. And she was dinner.

The irony didn't escape her. All her plans and plotting, wasted. Her Glock was back at the cabin and her hand-to-hand combat skills were successfully neutralized by a thousand pounds of teeth and claws.

Sweat gathered along her brow as she took aim at the huge beast. She didn't want to hurt it, but didn't know what else to do. The bear seemed to immediately realize it had become a target, for it sidled off and reared up to its full height. Eliza kept looking up. Nine feet of solid power, fur and muscle.

Hell. Her little gun wasn't going to do much damage to this sucker, but she was damned if she was going to just lie down and die. A tear escaped and ran down her cheek. She wiped it on her shirt cuff. Kept her aim steady.

A wolf appeared at the edge of her vision, pale gray and huge. She dared not turn towards it, but could feel its energy focused on the bear.

Not her, thank God.

She was relieved to have an ally. Not that the presence of the wolf seemed to bother the bear. He ignored it, edged closer to her, and she knew he was going to charge in the next few seconds.

This was it.

She braced herself for the moment, knew that this was where it was going to end. On an isolated hillside in Montana—a meal for either the wolf at her side, or the bear that stalked her. Nat would never get the answers he deserved. She'd never get her second chance...and she suddenly realized she didn't want to die. Her heart cried out against the unfairness of it all.

The bear wheeled, charged. Eliza fired her rifle, levered the last round, and fired again. The bear flinched, but kept on coming, furious, irritated by the bullets that peppered his hide. Elizabeth threw herself to the ground and curled up into a ball, braced for the blow that had to come.

A shot rang out, followed by a second a moment later.

She heard the bear fall, felt stones and dirt pelt her skin as the huge creature smashed to a halt. A hot gush of breath grazed her cheek. The musty smell of damp fur and fresh blood overpowered her nostrils. She opened her eyes, stared into the blank eyes of the massive beast that had hunted her. And started to shake.

Tears of relief wet her cheeks as she heard someone scramble down the rocky cliff towards her.

"Eliza!"

It was Nat.

She tried to rise to her feet, but her knees wobbled too badly. She staggered away from the body, stumbled and scrambled backwards, unable to believe the animal was dead and not about to charge again. She flung her empty rifle to the ground and launched herself into Nat's outstretched arms and hung on. He wrapped her up with a warmth and strength so solid that she wondered how she'd ever be able to live without him.

She clung to him with every ounce of strength she possessed.

"Oh my God, I was so scared." Easy to admit now.

Nat pulled her closer so their bodies clicked into place at every curve.

"I've never been so terrified in my whole life." His breath whispered through her hair as he spoke.

She pulled back, looked up into blue eyes that were dark with emotion. Her gaze lowered and she stared at his full bottom lip and knew she wanted to kiss him, desperately. She wasn't good enough for him, but still...

The hard lines around his mouth faded as he attempted a smile.

"Oh hell." Nat lowered his mouth to hers and kissed her.

Eliza's head whirled as she pressed her mouth against his in a kiss that bled into her soul. She held on so tightly her muscles locked, unwilling and unable to let him go.

His arms were steel, supporting her back, his legs pressed against every inch of her own. She wanted to drown in the sensation of safety and strength, dive deep into the friction of physical release. Memories jabbed her conscience, but she shied away and sank deeper into the feel of Nat's warm lips, the subtle rasp of stubble against her skin. Her arms crept up around his neck, she wanted to throw herself into this man, reaffirm all that was good about life. Discover, before it was too late, what she'd been missing.

Coming up for air, she blinked at the bright sunshine, was surprised by the sound of birdsong.

Nat let out a deep sigh, combed his fingers through her tangled hair and framed her face with his big hands. He rested his forehead against hers and laughed. The sound of a deep blast of relief that warmed her heart.

"You sure do have a fondness for trouble."

Elizabeth bristled in his arms. "I do not—"

She felt his laugh rumble through his chest again, saw him swallow hard. "Yeah. You do."

She sagged against him, eyed the poor creature that had stalked her with deadly intent just moments earlier.

"I do seem to attract it," she admitted, rubbing her cheek against the soft cotton of his shirt.

Nat relaxed his grip, turned his head to look at the wolf pack that hovered a short distance away.

Elizabeth noticed them and stiffened.

"They won't hurt you." Nat read her mind, nodded his head towards the bear. "They're eager to start lunch."

Elizabeth shuddered, knowing she'd almost been lunch.

The big silver wolf sat in the dirt no more than ten yards from where she and Nat stood. He panted lightly, his teeth flashing white against the black of his lips.

Elizabeth backed up a step. Nat wrapped his arm around her shoulders, leaned down to pick up her rifle and pulled her away, back down the valley. The wolves parted around them, sidling in half circles to let them pass. If anything, they seemed amused rather than threatened by the human interlopers.

"A lot of ranchers shoot them on sight," Nat told her as the big wolf followed their progress with his yellow gaze.

Elizabeth walked quickly. She'd had enough wildlife to last her for a lifetime. Snarls and growls filled the air behind her as the pack began to tear up their enormous meal.

Christ. Images of her own death lurched into her mind and made her stomach turn. She shuddered. Nat pulled her closer and held on tight. Without him she'd be dead. Without him she didn't want to live.

***

When Steve Dancer walked into the cottage, Marsh had his pants back on. He was standing in the middle of the lounge, still handcuffed to a very large, very bent, cast-iron bedstead.

Marsh's hair was slick with sweat. His arm badly wrenched at the shoulder. Blood trickled from his wrist and stained the floorboards beneath his toes. The smaller man grinned. Got out his phone and took a photograph.

"Give me your keys." Marsh's breath was short, his temper shorter. His own keys had disappeared and he'd bet the bank who had them.

He'd used a nickel and colossal amount of determination to dismantle the bed. He was going to melt it down for scrap, first chance he got. He glared over at Dancer who lounged against the doorjamb. *Grinning bastard.*

Steve Dancer looked like the archetypal boy next door. Straight floppy hair, the color of burnt ginger. Marsh snorted. Women seemed to think he was 'cute', much to the male disgust in the division. The crazy freckles and light blue eyes didn't seem to hinder his appeal either.

Guy was about as 'cute' as barbed wire.

Marsh took one look at the eyes that were bursting with glee and a reluctant grin tugged his lips. "Just give me the keys, okay?"

"Jeez boss, I hope she was worth it." Dancer pulled out his keys and threw them to Marsh.

He caught them in a firm one-handed grip.

"I haven't decided yet." Christ, he was going to pay her back for this. She was probably laughing her ass off right now. Just so long as she was safe. He undid the handcuffs, threw the keys back to Dancer and slipped his own cuffs back into his pocket. He'd deliberately placed her in danger, *and now she might be pregnant.* The nagging worry wouldn't go away.

"Everyone all right?" Marsh asked. He'd been out of touch for twelve hours, and a lot could happen in that time. Elizabeth wasn't his only responsibility.

"Sure." Dancer moved away from the doorjamb

236

to wander towards the view of the lake. "Aiden's champing at the bit though. He got a sniff of a Manet that's been missing since WWII, wanted me to go to Texas to help him check it out."

Marsh swore, annoyed with the delays, which were costing their operation. They worked long hours to catch thieves and fraudsters—had to be ready to move at a moment's notice. But Elizabeth was one of his team, and she was in danger. The Manet could wait. The Forgery and Fine Arts Division looked after its own.

"He can do the initial examine on his own." Marsh hoped this business was over soon. Mob trials were coming up and things were coming to a head. Rumor had it that the assassin, Peter Uri, had been on the move again, but nobody could get a solid lead on the man. He was like a damned ghost. Marsh's gut clenched at the thought of the danger the two women faced.

Dancer moved behind the couch to peer out the window. He bent down and picked up a scrap of lace. Josephine's bra.

Marsh held out his hand and Dancer passed it over, smirking with his eyebrows raised. He stuffed it in the pocket with the handcuffs.

"So where is she?" Marsh tried not to sound anxious, busied himself by examining the cuts on his wrist. Despite the blood they were nothing serious.

He followed Dancer into the cabin's oak-lined kitchen and watched him boot up his laptop.

Seconds felt like minutes as Marsh dragged his weary hands over his face and tried to rub the after-effects of the drug from his vision. "She's had twelve hours to get where she's going. Shit." Panic gripped him, "What if she's out of range?"

"She could be on the moon and she'd still be in range of this baby. Quit worrying."

Marsh avoided the look Dancer threw him. They'd been colleagues for over a decade now, and knew each other well. They'd worked in countless dangerous situations, and some god-awful funny ones. Marsh was well aware his customary cool had moved way beyond frayed.

"Get some coffee before you fall over and eat something too." Dancer took over, clearly enjoying turning the tables for once. "If I have to get into that chopper with you, you'd better be one-hundred-percent fit." Dancer shuddered. "Man, I hate those things."

Marsh grunted, leaned forward eagerly as a beep sounded in the room. Dancer turned down the volume on the laptop and angled it toward him.

"Got her, she's moving across Pennsylvania at a rate of approximately 500 mph. I guess it's safe to assume that even though she stole your car..." Dancer grinned as Marsh winced. "She's airborne." Dancer pointed to a second, stationary signal. "Car's at Logan Airport. I can get Dora to pick it up for you."

Marsh shook his head. "Leave it. The bomb squad better check it out before anybody goes near it." *Just in case the mob had made Josephine.*

Wearily, he moved away from the beeping noise, put on the coffee and broke out the eggs for an omelet. He had a jet and a helicopter waiting at an air force base twenty miles away. They had time for breakfast and he needed food.

"Keep on her," he ordered over his shoulder. "You get anything on that cell phone she called?"

Dancer shook his head, fiddling with the laptop.

"But you traced the original signal to the Midwest or the southern Canadian Rockies right?"

"Yep, and it looks like that's where our little bird is heading right now, doesn't it?" Steve nodded to the steadily blinking light.

"Josephine can't cross the border. She doesn't have a passport with her." Marsh rubbed at the day's growth of stubble on his chin, "But she could have set up a locker at the airport with spare ID." That's what he'd have done.

Elizabeth would have done the same.

"Doesn't matter where she goes, boss, we've got her." Steve glanced at his watch. "We've got a break in transmission coming up in a few minutes when we switch satellites."

Looking smug, Dancer grinned at his boss. "So how much is that photo worth, boss? And where the heck is my coffee?"

Chapter Fifteen

It was dark by the time Eliza and Nat got back. Cal was waiting for them by the stable door, anxious, despite the call Nat had put through over the radio.

"Tiger came back over an hour ago," Cal said. "He's fine." The cowboy eyed Eliza critically, blew out a thin stream of cigarette smoke. "Should never have let you go out on your own."

"Like she ever does what she's told." Nat spoke with a grin to ease the other man. No need to tell Cal what a close call it had been. He had enough guilt on his conscience

Eliza placed a hand on Cal's arm. "Sorry I worried you."

Cal looked down at the ground, eyed his boots and kicked the dirt. "Shit, Eliza."

Without another word, he took charge of the horses, led them away into the horse barn.

Nat took Eliza's hand and pulled her toward the cabin.

"We're not going to see the others?" she asked. She sounded weary. Her voice wrung out from too much drama.

Nat shook his head, kept on walking. There was only one place he wanted to be right now and it didn't involve his mother.

He took the steps in one long stride, held the door and let her pass. She kept her head down, feet dragging. Inside was pitch black, the light of the moon slicing through the curtains in thick wedges.

Eliza turned to face him. She was wrapped up in her lumberjack coat, huddled into it, hands pushed deep into the wide pockets, chin buried deep into the collar. Finely winged brows lowered over green eyes and her teeth gnawed at her bottom lip. Bad memories seemed to simmer just below the surface, and she looked as skittish as a colt, but not scared, he realized, just tired and nervous.

Well, hell, he was nervous.

His rubbed the back of his neck, his mouth tense. Talk about putting pressure on a guy not to screw up.

He walked over to where she stood, and slowly undid the buttons of her coat, one at a time, while she watched each single movement. They weren't on solid ground here. Neither of them knew how it was going to play out, or where it would lead. He'd never felt this strongly before and his hands damn near shook with the effort to take it slow. All the while she watched him with those feline eyes of hers, solemn and silent. He didn't want to scare her; he didn't want to screw up. He removed the coat from her shoulders, hung it up on the peg on the back of the door and took her hand in his.

"Come sit with me." He tugged her over to the couch.

"Nat..." Eliza began.

His heart sank. Rejection curdled in his gut. Not that he couldn't wait, not that he didn't understand, but he didn't want to leave her alone tonight.

Who was he kidding? He didn't want to leave her alone, period.

She squeezed his fingers. Whispered. "Come to bed with me."

Surprise held him still. Nat took a breath—then

another, as he tangled his fingers with hers, palm to palm, and pulled her close. Desire mingled with a gentler emotion that he couldn't name, didn't want to examine.

She was stubborn and reckless. And hurt. And he wanted her. Didn't matter that she wasn't right for him and wouldn't stay, didn't matter that they might lose the ranch next week. He wanted to be inside her, and not think about anything else except her for as long as possible. He kissed her, gently at first and then took it deeper, tasted, explored with his lips, his tongue. Passion flared like a flame, spreading wildly, branding them both with heat.

They were linked hands and mouth, bodies close but not touching. Nat needed her to know this was her decision. No one was forcing her this time.

"I wanted you from that first moment I saw you," he admitted and kissed the freckles that marched across her nose, her temple.

She moaned, sought his mouth with her own.

Her hands begged for release from his hold, but he held them lightly in his own as he nuzzled the soft white skin below her ear. Her hands strained, but he didn't let go.

"You're so goddamned beautiful. Exactly what I don't need."

"You prefer ugly?" Her voice cracked. She arched her head back. Sighed. Her body moved into him, closed the gap and fused with his.

Nat felt her melt, felt her reserve crumble to dust. He wanted that. He cupped her cheek with his hand, slid the other slowly over her body, over her narrow ribcage, around the underside of her breast—teasing touches that made her sigh into his mouth, as she began to touch him too. He palmed her breast, marveled at the weight, the softness. Gently, he rubbed his thumb across her shirt, raising her nipples like pebbles through the soft white cotton. She didn't object. Instead she burrowed deeper into his embrace and returned his kisses— nibbled at his bottom lip.

A growl worked its way loose of his throat and rumbled through his chest. Nat raised his head, looked down at the passion fed turbulence that stormed through Eliza's eyes. He wanted to lose control and sink himself into this woman without rational thought or feeling. But he had to be careful. He had to take it slowly.

"Tell me if I do something you don't like." He worked hard to keep his voice even. "Tell me if I scare you."

Eliza looked up at him with eyes so dark they glinted black. "You won't."

***

Something hard loosened inside her, shifted and melted away. The nerves were gone, her pain nothing but a distant echo. Tears welled up at the beauty of the moment, but she forced them back. Tears weren't what she wanted to show Nat Sullivan tonight. She concentrated on her growing hunger, hunger and urgency. Elizabeth reached up and smoothed a lock of hair back from Nat's forehead, surprised at how softly it stroked her fingers.

Subtle traces of lemon soap clung to his skin, overlaid by the warm scent of working man. She nuzzled the thick cord of his neck, absorbed his essence like a balm. His cheeks were rough like sandpaper beneath her lips. She groaned, wanted to feel more of him, but hesitated...afraid. She wrapped her fingers around strong biceps. He felt so right, so perfect. He was taking everything slowly, being incredibly gentle with her—touching her like she might shatter into a thousand tiny pieces if he pressed too hard.

Her heart hammered too fast. Elizabeth didn't want gentleness now. It touched her too deeply and she didn't think she could stand it much longer. She bit her bottom lip, swallowed her uncertainty. Pulling him closer, she tugged at his shirt until it was loose and she could slide her hands beneath it and over firm flesh. His body felt so incredibly hard and yet his skin was as smooth as satin.

She put a hand to his cheek, loved the feel of rough stubble against her palm. Despite shaking hands, she took a step back, pulled her shirt over her head and dropped it to the floor. His Adam's apple bobbed up and down as he swallowed hard. Standing immobile and trembling, she undid the tiny buttons on his shirt. He shrugged out of it. Let it join hers on the floor.

Moonlight brushed his body, carved by constant labor into planes of hard muscle and sinew, the soft light gilding the broad shoulders with silver. Crisp blond hair covered his chest and upper body, ran down his stomach in a straight, thin line. Unconsciously her fingers balled into tight fists at her side.

She'd always appreciated beauty and Nat's was flawless. Strong and rugged like the mountains that had bred him.

She forced her hands to relax, reached out and danced one fingertip across his skin, fascinated as

244

his muscles contracted. Elizabeth looked up. Found he was watching her with an unblinking gaze. Eyes of midnight blue drilled into her, but he held back patiently, let her take what she wanted at her own pace.

She blinked back tears, along with memories of another man's eyes.

He held her loosely as if he thought she might turn and run. Scared to let go and scared to hold on too tight. Fears she hadn't realized she still harbored washed away with the gentle pressure of his hands. She wrapped her arms around his neck, kissed him, and reveled in the feel of his bare flesh against her own. Raw silk gliding against raw silk. Hot, where she touched him—like a fever. She gasped as he undid the clasp on her bra, slid his fingers beneath the white silk.

Shock waves rippled through her body as his touch became more demanding. Her knees buckled, urgency clawing through her and making her oblivious to everything but the heat building between them. She forgot the past, the grief, forgot to worry about the future, and instead let him fill her with sensation. The room spun as he picked her up and carried her through to the bedroom. She laughed.

***

Nat tried. Really he tried. But her fingers raced over him, defeated his resolve, stole his balance with dark touches and sharp nails. Then the sound of her laughter, like warm sunshine, touched him on the inside.

He was lost. Crazy about her—completely

captivated. He drank in the sight of her bare flesh and lush curves. Full breasts that his hands itched to touch. Dark nipples that begged his mouth to taste. Soft, resilient, strong.

A bruise darkened her ribs, but she'd made no mention of it. Nat stopped still for a second, tightened his grip and closed his eyes, realizing he'd nearly lost her today. With a quick prayer of thanks he eased his grip but didn't let go.

Her scent enveloped him, calmed his fears with the solid thrum of her heart beneath his fingers. Walking to the edge of the bed, he was glad that the moonlight flooded in from the open curtains so that he could see her. He sat down, careful not to jar her side, cradled her in his arms, and kissed her again. Deep narcotic kisses that thickened the blood and quickened the pulse. He seduced her with his mouth until she whimpered with need and then he laid her on the bed to undress her.

First, he pulled off her boots. Then slowly drew her jeans down her long legs and dropped them to the floor.

She lay silent. Watching him. Her eyes glowed like a warm ocean, her lips slick and wet from his kisses. And her body...full breasts, softly curved hips and legs that went on and on and on.

Grazes marred both knees.

He ground his teeth, his mouth clenched tight against the fear.

If I hadn't been there... If I'd missed...

"Don't stop," Eliza whispered. Her hands sank into his hair, anchored him to her. Determined. Urgent. Her breath taunted his lips.

He shifted his weight onto his elbows, kissed her again, his mouth moving lower as he grazed her breasts, teased her nipples. An exploration that begged for thoroughness and speed—contrasting needs that pushed and pulled him.

He moved lower to kiss her stomach, the sensitive area at the crease of her thighs before returning to her mouth like a bee to a flower. Her body arched beneath his, quivered with each touch. Tension strained within her muscles and answered the need growing within him.

She pressed toward him. Her eyes gleaming with desire, her mouth breathing his name like a litany. Her hands streaked over his body; pointblank lust driving him to the brink. He gasped, gripped her hands once again in his own, holding them gently above her head. He trailed a finger down the delicate skin on the underside of her arm, followed the shiver with his lips. Their breathing was labored and quick. She looked at him with wild eyes that urged him on.

He slid to one side so he could see her better and slow things down. He felt like he'd waited forever for this moment and he intended to savor each instant.

He ran a single finger down her body as he watched her watching him. His hand moved lower, slipping beneath her panties and into her hot wet core. She tightened against his fingers, eyes blanking as he rubbed them against her. But she didn't freak. She didn't shoot off the bed and run for the hills.

The rhythm built higher and higher; he could feel it, see it on her face and hear it in her breath. This was where he wanted to send her. This was where he wanted to go. He gritted his teeth against his own desire and the need to join her there.

She plunged her hands into his hair and pulled him closer, kissed him, ran hungry hands over his hot flesh. Sensation built upon sensation, careened out of control. She shuddered, body bowed as she cried out. It was too much and it still wasn't enough.

She tugged at the catch of his jeans, helped him to scramble out of them, all without letting go of his mouth. They removed the last of their clothes in a tangle of arms and legs, and sank back onto the bed, rolling and groping, their breath shallow pants of pleasure.

He came into her in one powerful thrust, filled her hard and deep. The intense shudder of pleasure rocked them both. He held himself still for one long drawn-out moment as he looked deep into her eyes. She stared back at him, wide-eyed. Blinked.

"Damn." Nat said, "Condom."

Nat closed his eyes, clenched his teeth, and withdrew. Snatching his pants off the floor, he grabbed a square packet and tore into the foil. He needed to be inside her.

The second time was just as incredible as the first. She was hot, tight and wet. And when he began to move, slowly, firmly, she wrapped her legs around him and pulled him deeper inside. His mind blanked as he was enveloped in hot wet heat that flowed around him like lava, tightening the noose around his emotions.

He held onto his control with a single iron neuron.

The rhythm built, changed pace, and then blasted him like an inferno. Their gazes caught and locked, drowning each other in need. Eliza's nails dug sharply into his back, but Nat didn't care. Her body tightened powerfully around him, pulsed exquisitely, drove him towards that velvety edge. He hung onto his control with every ounce of willpower, slowed everything down to a lazy caress that held back more than it delivered. Her breath hitched, muscles clenched demanding more.

Raw dark feelings tore at his gut as he buried himself into her one last time, and felt her explode around him as he came in a rush that seared his mind with white-hot flames.

They fell hard together, unseeing into the darkness.

***

New York City, April 14th

Nerves strung tighter than clock springs, DeLattio paced the plush blue carpet in his hotel suite. He took a drag of a cigarette, noticed the nicotine stains on his fingers were getting deeper, creeping around his knuckles and working their way down each digit.

Like rot.

He rubbed at the mustard colored skin, but it made no difference. The stain remained.

He ground his jaw and started to swear. The discoloration irritated him, nagged at his temper. Snorting, he gave up. Sucked the smoke from his cigarette deeper into his lungs and laughed it out. His uncle, John-Paul Mallena, had put a seven-figure contract out on his life. If Charlie Corelli was to be believed he was already a dead man. The color of his fingers wouldn't bother his corpse.

No reason not to believe Charlie. He'd been

Andrew's bodyguard-cum-personal-assistant for the last eight years. Charlie had been a present from his uncle the day he'd graduated Harvard. Probably the most useful gift a man could get.

But Charlie was also a made-man, a *sgarrista*, on the Bilotti family books. He was one of John-Paul Mallena's original work-crew, who'd taken a blood oath to work for the good of the family. A blood oath Andrew hadn't been allowed take because his father hadn't been Italian.

Andrew stubbed out one cigarette and lit another. He hid the tremors in his fingers by giving his hand a shake. His father had been a French/Slavic cross whom J.P. had gotten rid of years ago. His mother had never suspected, but Andrew had known—known and been grateful not to have been disposed of the same way.

He glanced towards the two federal agents who'd been assigned guard duty that night. Neither man liked him; not that Andrew gave a fuck. They were typical feebs—smarmy, arrogant.

He'd always known he'd have to run one day—Christ, he'd been scamming the mob since tenth grade. And he'd prepared. But he hadn't expected to be screwed over by some sniveling bitch.

He inhaled deeply, held the smoke in his lungs until it filled every space and he couldn't hold it any longer. Exhaled slowly, brooding. He'd shared the profits with Charlie, but Andrew didn't know where Charlie's loyalty would lie when push came to shove. Andrew loved the guy, but chances were Charlie would be the hit man.

In his world, life and death were flips of the same coin.

One of the agents, Wade—tall and skinny with a

buzz cut—played a game on a laptop, while Butler—his shorter, darker partner—snoozed on leather upholstery under the *New York Times*.

Looking at them, Andrew wanted to smile because he knew they were dead.

Crushing out the cigarette, he paced the floor, went over to the mini-bar and poured himself a shot of bourbon.

He was smart. The plan was set. Very, very soon.

Andrew was looking forward to killing Juliette Morgan. The need stabbed at him, distracted his mind when he should have been concentrating on escape. Tapping his fingers on the soft leather on the back of the chair he remembered the last time he'd seen her—spread-eagled and naked on the bed.

His nose itched from where she'd kicked him in the face. Everything he'd done to her and the only thing he could recall was that sharp rush of pain as the bone snapped. Anger narrowed his eyes and tightened his mouth. He gripped his glass so hard he thought it might shatter.

There was a knock on the door and he jumped, nerves as taut as tripwires. The feebs stood, unholstered their weapons.

"Get in the john," Butler, the short one, ordered him.

Andrew walked away to the marble-tiled bathroom shaking his head. He hated these guys. The FBI thought they knew everything, but he'd show them. And he wanted to know her real name before he did her again, wanted to destroy Juliette and her alter ego once and for all.

From behind the door he heard the agents greeting his lawyer, Larry. Andrew came out, wiped the thin sheen of sweat from his brow with a handkerchief. Larry was performing small miracles for him with the District Attorney's office. Stupid schmuck. The lawyer juggled his briefcase in one hand and a large box of takeout pizza in the other, along with a plastic carrier bag.

"I met the delivery boy in the corridor and thought I'd better bring it in." Larry gave the agents a frown of disapproval as he handed over the food. "I have to go over a couple of points with my client." Larry nodded towards Andrew, but avoided eye contact.

Intimidation got the best results.

"We'll go into the bedroom to discuss them, if we may?" Larry's voice was even thinner than usual.

The feebs searched him, a quick up and down of hands and brief inspection of his briefcase. Then they turned away, eager for their food while it was still hot. They sat at the dining table that overlooked Soho's bright lights and cracked open some soda.

Andrew led Larry into the bedroom, closed the door on the other men. Larry's hands shook so badly he could barely undo his briefcase.

"I have your word my family will no longer be in danger?" Nervously Larry pulled a letter from his briefcase. Held it pinched between two fingers like it was contagious.

"You do everything Charlie told you?" Andrew grabbed the letter, his eyes gleaming in anticipation.

Larry nodded.

"Then your family will be fine."

He read the letter. Scanned the contents in one quick motion. Charlie told him not to worry. He told him he'd organized a little surprise for the feds.

Could mean anything.

Andrew shrugged and figured he had no option. Right now he had to trust Charlie.

His fingers itched. He wished to God he had a gun. The springs of the mattress squeaked as Larry sat down heavily. The old man hung his head in his hands. He looked like he was about to crumble.

Having your family threatened was hell on a person.

Andrew walked back to the door. Listened carefully. A crash sounded and Andrew opened the door a crack. Both agents lay on the blue carpet convulsing.

What the fuck?

They were breathing heavily. Holding their throats.

"Charlie." It came out as a whisper of blessed relief. Andrew didn't know what the man had poisoned them with, but he was grateful he'd never liked pizza.

Cautiously he walked across the thick carpet to look at the men who lay dying. Butler had stopped breathing and looked dead already. Andrew pushed him with his foot, but the guy didn't even blink. Wade made gurgling noises that rattled up from his lungs. Andrew thought about shooting him to put him out of his misery, but decided not to. Too loud, too noisy.

And why waste a bullet?

He hunkered down. Lifted the SIG-Sauer from Butler's belt, raided the man's pocket for ammo. Andrew's own pulse settled and the tension in his shoulders relaxed as he handled the gun. Now he could defend himself. Now he had a chance. He flipped open Butler's wallet, found baby photos on the inside flap.

Andrew raised his head as Larry came to the bedroom door.

"Oh, my lord." His lawyer held his hands to his throat as if he could feel the poison at work. "I didn't know...I mean the pizza boy was just there. I offered to bring it in..."

"Sure you did, Larry." Andrew walked into his bedroom, grabbed his coat. "Tell it to a judge."

Larry gaped open-mouthed. "I, I, I—"

Andrew shot him in the temple, watched the man crumple to the floor. He walked over to take another look at the agents who'd insulted and derided him. Wade was still alive, gasping those last little breaths with slow torturous desperation. Andrew saluted him mockingly, felt the man's eyes follow him as he left the room.

Now he'd keep his promise to sweet little Juliette. He could hardly wait.

***

They lay silent as her heartbeat slowed to a quiet cadence. A wolf howled in the hills, a desolate lonely sound, competing with the wind that whispered quietly against the window. The wolf's plea resonated through her, melancholic and dramatic, making her quiver—reminding her how close she'd come to death.

And death still stalked her.

Nat reached for the bedcovers and pulled them over Eliza, keeping her warm and holding her tight.

He wasn't asleep then.

She wished he were.

She brushed her lips against his chest, trembled,

hugging him firmly for a second, before releasing him. He'd changed things for her and she wasn't sure how to deal with it. There was a quality about Nat Sullivan that touched her soul and scared her down to her toes. She was healing—and that scared her almost as much as the thought of dying. Her fists balled uncertainly, lying rigid and tight against his flesh.

He'd pulled her back from the brink of self-destruction and taught her to trust again. To love.

Could it be love?

Restlessly she moved away from his warmth, climbed out of the tangled covers and walked through to the lounge to lock the front door. Pulling the drapes, she shut out the moon, preferring the dark now, and leaned her forehead against the coolness of the wall.

"Come back to bed, else I'm gonna have to come and hunt you down." Nat's voice rumbled through the open doorway.

Elizabeth knotted the thick drapes around one hand. Nobody in Nat's world would hunt down and kill anybody, but in her world—for a price, or revenge, or kicks—they'd do it without mercy.

What had she done by coming here? Closing her eyes, she ran her finger against the hard edge of the casement window. She bit her lip. If DeLattio found her here, they were all as good as dead.

But he wouldn't. Swallowing back the pain, she knew she couldn't stay, but the thought of moving on, of leaving Nat, tore her in two.

Returning to the bed she stood quietly at its edge. Nat took her fingers in his palm and kissed each fingertip, her knuckles, the fragile blue veins on her wrist. He pulled her down beside him.

"Wanna talk about it?" His voice was deep and even. She concentrated on the timbre, wanted to imprint the sound on her memory.

Her rape. Did she want to talk about being raped?

A shiver worked its way through her shoulders and vibrated through her frame. *No fecking way.* The memories that stole through her mind made her burrow her nose deeper into the curve of his shoulder.

Bound wrists. Blurry images of sex with fractured flashes of clarity. The drugs had blunted the pain and the details. Dulled the degradation except for the sound of DeLattio laughing at her. His laughter still haunted her dreams.

She didn't *want* to talk about it, but knew she had to.

"I worked undercover for the FBI, but not organized crime. I worked in art theft." Eliza squeezed his arm, felt him squeeze her in return.

"I was at a gallery opening when this guy started hitting on me." Her voice shook. "He made me nervous—not something that happens very often. So I left. Avoided him." She circled a finger on his chest in a nervous gesture.

"Turned out he was some big time mobster." Her finger stilled, pressed gently into his skin. "The Organized Crime Unit approached me the next day and asked me to go out with him on a few dates. Plant a few bugs." She shrugged. "The usual thing."

Her fingers sifted his hair, contrasted the softness with the solid muscles of his body. She liked touching him, liked having that freedom. "They promised to protect me, but they didn't."

A knot formed in her throat, constricting the

words. Nat seemed to realize she couldn't go on and pressed her head against him, comforted her with the soft weight of his hand against her skull. She breathed deep, inhaled his scent. Heard his heart beat slow and true, next to her ear.

Trembling, she embraced him and swallowed down the tears that wanted to escape. She had no business making love to this man, pulling him into her web, into the mess that her life had become. Whatever it was that burned between them should have been left to die. But it was too late for that now. She hadn't been able to resist the attraction and it killed her to know she'd have to leave him soon.

But not yet.

Determined to get away from the confessions about her past, she reared over him, smoothed one hand across the firm planes of his chest.

"So who are you, Nat? Cowboy, photographer, sharpshooter? Just who is the real Nathan Sullivan?" She tried to smile, silently begged him to change the subject. The pain-filled memories were in the past, she wanted them to remain there. He grabbed her before she could move an inch and rolled her beneath him in one smooth move.

"You forgot demon lover." Nat nibbled her bottom lip. "You've just met the real Nathan Sullivan, ma'am. He was the one sweating all over you. Maybe you've forgotten him?"

"Maybe I have," Elizabeth said, tracing his lips with her fingertip. "Maybe you'd better remind me."

Her hands moved lower, ran over his flesh to play with flat brown nipples. The muscles of his abdomen clenched against her tummy, the hardness of his erection pressed against her thigh. Bending her head, she teased him with her tongue, licked his nipples and sucked them gently. His breath tightened and his hands gripped her.

She couldn't answer many of his questions and she wouldn't lie to him, but perhaps she could make him happy for a little while longer. Make him mindless with lust—exactly what she wanted to be.

Chapter Sixteen

Stealth shifted agitatedly beside him, scenting the mare waiting patiently ahead. Nat wiped the sweat off his forehead as raw energy poured from the black stallion in hot waves that stank of excitement and eagerness. The brood mare was a Morgan, quiet and experienced and in a strong standing heat. Nat had chosen her for Stealth's first breeding partner, having collected semen from a phantom mare in the past.

It was an edgy time.

Inexperienced stallions tended to switch off their brains and act stupid the first time they met a mare in heat. Pretty much like most guys. Nat glanced over at Eliza who was helping Ezra put salt licks onto the back of the pickup. Dressed in work jeans, with her jacket buttoned up to her chin, she still looked cold despite the warm wind that blew down from the ridge. Dark circles rode her eyes and fatigue wore down the edge of her smile. She laughed at something Ezra said and the sound rippled along his nerves, reminding him of how they'd spent most of last night.

The stallion snorted, velvet nostrils flared red as he danced around, jerking back on the lead-rein. Stealth's first sexual intercourse was fraught with potential danger—most things depending on the mare. If she kicked him during mating he could become gun shy and be too afraid to ejaculate. Or she could bolt and make the stallion prone to rush to mount mares in the future, to hang onto them too tight.

Shit, Nat could relate. There was nothing simple about dealing with females.

Sweat gathered on Stealth's back and withers, a sure sign he was geared up for action. Eliza raised her head and looked over at him as if feeling the weight of his thoughts. Then she looked over at the mare who stood lined up against the breeding wall.

Did she compare servicing a mare to rape?

He stumbled slightly and Stealth jerked fussily on the end of the rein.

Nat forced himself to relax. Knew that his own anxieties were easily transmitted to the young stallion. He led Stealth towards the mare, put gentle pressure on the breeding halter, and was pleased at how the stallion responded to him, despite the mind-numbing distraction of imminent sex.

No, Nat didn't equate the two. A mare that didn't want to be bred would be damned difficult to force, even by nine hundred pounds of teeth and sex hormones.

Nat swallowed the bitter taste in his mouth and tried to concentrate on the job in hand. The mare angled sideways slightly, took a long look at the young stud that approached her, deciding whether or not she was going to accept him. Nat let her look, but sensed no reluctance. Cal nodded and Nat brought Stealth up to the rear of the mare and eased the stallion over her haunches. The mare braced herself against the added weight of the stallion, but didn't swing around or kick out.

She was a good mare.

Nat glanced at Eliza, felt the air go sultry between them. Stealth needed no help guiding himself into the mare and Nat stood to one side and tried not to get turned on by the thought of doing something similar with Eliza.

Jesus, this was routine, a normal job on a busy working farm, but today it felt...personal. His nerve endings were on fire and his body in a heightened state of arousal. *Damn. It was embarrassing.* He scrubbed his hands over hot eyes, and felt like a pervert, lower than the lowest scumbag.

Ezra said something to Eliza and she turned away.

A car crested the hill behind the main house and Nat cursed, knowing the timing couldn't be worse. The mare shifted nervously as Stealth strove for completion.

The driver gunned the engine and Nat used every ounce of willpower he possessed to calm the mare and urge Stealth to get the job done.

His mouth thinned. He wanted to yell at the driver, but he didn't dare glance away from the bonded pair. With an inelegant snort Stealth ejaculated and collapsed on top of the mare.

Cal held the mare steady as the stallion slid down, and was already leading her away by the time Nat eased the stallion to the ground.

The horses are fine. Everything is fine.

Nat breathed out a sigh of relief, still as uncomfortable as hell in his snug jeans.

Figured.

He stroked Stealth's nose, rubbed his ears and told him he'd done a good job. Even if the mare didn't conceive, the event had been a success. He turned to the newcomers and kept his face carefully neutral when he saw Troy and Marlena Strange, standing next to a new model Mercedes four-by-four.

Tomorrow was the day of the auction.

Nat stopped himself from grinding his teeth. Chances were that by tomorrow evening, Troy Strange would own a piece of his heart.

Okay—so maybe things weren't so fine.

Marlena glanced at Nat's crotch with a wicked smile that killed his arousal stone dead. The woman was stunningly beautiful, but she left him colder than a gravestone.

"What do you want?" Nat asked. It wasn't exactly neighborly, but he didn't give a shit.

"Thought you might be ready to let me take another look at that stallion of yours." Troy flashed a phony megawatt smile, the accent pure Texas, but thick with insincerity. "And here he is all ready for me."

Troy moved toward Stealth, who stood quivering from exertion, and raised his hand to stroke the black stallion's nose. The horse bared his teeth and rolled his eyes until their whites gleamed like bloodshot crescents in the afternoon light.

"Touch him and I'll put my fist through your face." He didn't raise his voice. He didn't have to. With one step he moved between Troy and the stallion.

Troy hesitated, dropped his hand. "You can't afford to be choosy, *neighbor*."

As if Troy had a say in how Nat felt.

"If you go belly-up, I'll have this place for peanuts, the horses too." Troy snapped his finger and thumb together for effect. He took a cigarette packet out of his shirt pocket and offered one to Nat.

Like they were friends having a conversation.

Nat kept his silence though he wanted to smash Troy so hard, he could barely hold back. His fists rounded into solid blocks by his side, but he didn't need a lawsuit on top of everything else, and Troy Strange *would* bring a lawsuit.

Nat said nothing, stood absolutely still and stared down at Troy like he was a bug on a pin.

"You know it and I know it," Troy continued, ignoring the silent warning. "Why don't we just cut the crap and I'll buy the horses and the ranch now for a fair price." He named a ridiculously low figure, tapped the cigarette on the packet and lit up. He breathed the smoke deeply into his lungs, blew out, straight into Nat's face.

Nat didn't blink.

Troy thought he understood the code of the west, thought he knew how to be a real man, but he wasn't even close. If Troy had been bigger Nat might have taken him on, lawsuit be-damned, but he was only medium height with a slight build. It would be like punching out a child.

Marlena strolled over to stand beside her husband. She towered over him, slim and lithe, long dark brown hair flowing in waves to halfway down her back. Troy placed a possessive arm around her waist as if to rein her in.

Sneering, Nat figured she needed a leash. She eyed him like he was on the menu, her tongue just peeking out of her oversized lips.

Great. Freaking great.

Troy glared at him even though Nat kept his face impassive. Nat threw Eliza a quick glance, but she'd disappeared.

"Get off my property," *asshole,* he bit down on the insult, "before I call the sheriff." His voice remained flat calm, like the surface of a lake before an electrical storm. Inside he seethed, resentment curling through him like an ember on slow burn.

"Sheriff Talbot would be a little upset if he had to come out here two days in a row." Strange smirked and suddenly Nat knew. Troy had set up the whole thing—the fight, the visit from the sheriff. He was trying to drive the Sullivans right out of town. Sonofabitch.

What the hell had Marlena told her husband about him?

"How's the convict?" Strange smirked again. As if he was too goddamned stupid to figure out he was being screwed by the Texan.

Nat sensed Ryan come up to stand beside him. His brother moved quietly when he wanted to and Nat sometimes forgot he wasn't the only Sullivan who stood to lose the ranch.

"Did you know half the town's fucked your wife?" Ryan asked Troy with a slow friendly smile. "Only the male half, mind." Ryan laughed at his own little joke, as if he thought it was funny.

Nat didn't. He hated where this was going, cringed before Ryan opened his mouth again.

"She even offered Nat a blowjob a couple weeks ago, but he was kinda rushed so he couldn't take her up on her offer...I took her up though," Ryan spoke in a low dead whisper, the king of easy-going, suddenly pissed. "She tell you about that?"

Crap.

Troy's frame buzzed with temper. His fists clenched and unclenched by his side.

"Maybe you need the stud for her?" Ryan smiled, but Nat had never seen him look so deadly. "Because I know she likes it hard and fast, and maybe you're just not up to the job?"

Marlena started to splutter a defense. Troy cut her off with a sharp slice of his hand and a hard grip on her wrist. "Don't think I don't know what you're trying to do." He glared at Ryan with unrestrained fury. "This from the king of screwing around? I bet your dead wife turns in her grave, the way you nail anything that—"

Troy never saw it coming. He was flat on the ground, nursing his face with both hands before he could say spit.

Nat was just sorry Ryan had got there first.

"Don't *ever* mention my wife again," Ryan spat between gritted teeth.

Maybe he should have warned Troy about Ryan's sore point.

Marlena must have decided that the best defense was a good offense because suddenly she was shouting. "I didn't come on to him. He attacked me!" She was pointing at him, *Nat*, and there were actual tears in her eyes. He just bet she'd spun a great tale that hadn't included going down on him as a tip for a ride home.

The woman was spitting mad, her revenge foiled by a man she thought she'd already nailed. "And don't think I have to take these accusations from you." She pointed at Ryan. "You'll hear from my lawyer."

Nat stared at Troy who still rolled around in the dirt and shook his head—*mention the freaking lawyer now, why don't you.*

Ryan laughed, but it didn't sound pretty. "I can get signed affidavits from half the cowboys in town, *sweetheart,* regarding your favorite sexual position. And they're just the ones who can write."

Troy climbed to his feet nursing a split lip. "I'm going to destroy you, you bastard." Troy thrust his face closer to Nat's.

What? *Why him*? He crossed his arms over his chest and stared Troy down. "Just try it."

Did he really believe he'd go anywhere near his crazed wife? Nat glanced across at Marlena and swore. She was reeling against the four-by-four, crying as if her heart had been broken.

His hands itched with the desire to start clapping and shouting *Bravo*.

The bitch was completely loco. He could lose the family ranch because some bimbo didn't like the fact he'd rejected her?

"Nat!" Eliza shouted, "NAT!"

What the…? Nat looked across to see Eliza standing on the porch of the main house, trying to hold his mother upright.

He started running.

"I hope the old bitch dies—" Troy shouted after him. Nat knew Ryan hit the little bastard again, but he didn't stop to look.

By the time he'd reached the porch, Eliza had laid Rose down on the floor and dashed into the kitchen to phone 9-1-1.

His mother's complexion was a ghastly gray and her skin clammy when he touched her cheek.

"Nat," she gasped. Her right hand clutched at her left breast as her back arched off the floor. "Hurts..." She was having another heart attack. Panic screamed inside his head, but reason drowned it out. Her blue lips were pulled back in a grimace of pain, her breath shallow. His own heart shriveled and died inside his chest. He couldn't lose her now.

"It'll be okay, just try and lie still." Kneeling, he

pulled a blanket off his mother's rocking chair and placed it as a pillow beneath her head. The emergency services would take too long to get here.

Sas was at the ER.

"Phone the ER, Eliza, number's on the board," Nat shouted through the screen door. "Ask them what to do."

She held her chest and grimaced hard. She shuddered, took a sharp, jerky breath. "Don't. Let them. Take the ranch. Nat."

"No one's taking anything, Mom, so—"

"Promise me." Rose gripped his hand so hard it hurt. "Promise. Me." She gazed into his eyes and Nat's whole body filled with dread.

Swallowing the knot that formed in his throat, he nodded. "I promise."

Eliza ran through the door at the same time Ryan pulled Nat's truck up to the porch steps.

"Doctor says get her to the ER as fast as you can." Eliza held out a strip of tablets. "She told me to put one of these under her tongue and then get yourselves down there ASAP."

Eliza tore out a tablet and passed it to Nat.

He placed it under his mother's tongue and picked her up, cradled her silver-haired head against his chest. She'd drifted into unconsciousness.

Grimly, Nat held Eliza's gaze as he climbed into the truck. He hugged his mother close to his chest as Ryan gunned the engine, but the chances of Rose making it to the ER alive were slim to none and they all knew it.

***

Five hours later, Elizabeth waited at the kitchen

window, looked out at the moon, past little pots of herbs that lined the windowsill. Nat had phoned.

Rose was dead.

Elizabeth felt sick. She'd finally figured out that her whole damned life was cursed.

She wasn't in denial anymore; her eyes were wide-open. She loved Nat Sullivan to the depths of her soul and there was nothing she could do about it. Now his mother was dead, but she couldn't even stay to comfort him.

Despair dragged like lead in her chest—pulled her shoulders down in defeat. She was going to leave tomorrow, abandon him as if he meant nothing to her, with that bitch and her husband ready to drive nails into the coffin.

But she could help. She would help. She'd already set the wheels in motion and hoped there was time to make it work. Nat wouldn't like it, but then he didn't have to know.

Heartache choked her and she couldn't breathe, couldn't get the air past the weight of guilt and misery that blocked her throat. Elizabeth stumbled to the door. Threw it open and staggered outside. Ran from the house into the cold night air and reached the corral, climbed the rails and stared up at the stars.

Stealth trotted over, a zephyr of air in the darkness, and rubbed his velvet soft nose against her arm. The misery didn't stop. Desperate, she did something she hadn't done since she was a little girl. She found the North Star, wished upon it, like a child the night before Christmas.

***

Nat's shoulders slumped forward; his throat constricted so tightly that no matter how hard he swallowed, grief still suffocated him like a garrote.

Sarah—hell, he didn't even want to think about the look in her eyes when she'd realized they'd lost the battle. All that medical knowledge and she was still impotent against death. He held on to the edge of the kitchen sink, squeezed his eyes shut, but only saw the hollow reflection of grief in her eyes. He'd known before she'd told him that Rose was gone.

Hell.

Standing in the kitchen, encircled by darkness, the sound of his breathing was harsh in the noiseless room. The house was silent as if in mourning. Hell, it was.

Sarah had stayed at the hospital to make the arrangements for the funeral. He'd dropped Ryan and Cal at a bar then he'd come home for Tabitha. And for Eliza.

He didn't remember the house ever being this quiet before. Not when his dad had died, nor when Ryan's wife, Becky, followed just a few months later. Maybe it was because there'd been a baby to take care of, or maybe, this time, death had finally stolen the heart and soul of his family.

Not wanting to think about his mother, he methodically finished his drink of water, washed the glass, and towel-dried his hands. Walking upstairs, he listened to each footfall echo off the wood before taking another step. It sounded cold and lonely. At the top, he moved along the landing until he reached the last room at the end of the house.

The door was open a crack and he pushed it wider. Eliza lay in a dim pool of light, asleep on top of a *Winnie-the-Pooh* bedspread. Her legs dangled off the side of Tabitha's tiny bed, dark hair loose and tangled around her face, lips slightly parted. Tabitha curled toward her, a kangaroo clutched in a headlock beneath her chin.

Nat forced back tears. He didn't want to have to tell Tabitha that her grandma had died—he could barely comprehend it himself. But Sarah had enough to cope with, and Ryan...well Ryan didn't deal well with death.

Nat rubbed his hand over his face, gnawed the inside of his lips against the edge of his teeth. He didn't really have a choice. Maybe she'd be too young to understand anyway. And that thought brought a rush of sorrow that welded his throat shut. Tabitha wasn't even three years old and she'd already lost three of the most important people in her life. Four—if you counted Ryan's stony detachment.

The nightlight coated the curve of Eliza's cheek with soft peach and darkened the golden freckles that stood out on her nose. Another orphan, raised by strangers.

How did you survive without a mother to love you? A mother to wipe away the tears, soothe the hurt and scold the misdeeds? A mother to make you wear sweaters when you weren't cold and wash up when there was nothing wrong with being dirty?

He watched the gentle rise and fall of Eliza's shoulders as she slept. Wanted to reach out and touch, but couldn't get his hand to release the death-grip on the doorknob.

Rose Sullivan had been a hard woman, bred for toughness in the high mountain valleys, but she'd had a soft side too, a side that had loved her children as fiercely as a wildcat defended her

270

young. Just the way he'd loved her back. But now his grief weighed him down like a boulder, twice as heavy because of the promise he'd made before she'd slipped away.

He'd save the ranch. Somehow.

The auction would go ahead tomorrow morning. The woods would probably be sold before most people knew Rose was dead. *Shit*. Nat let go of the door, rubbed his eyes and straightened his shoulders. Eliza whimpered and her hand burrowed beneath her pillow. Protectiveness hit him in a wave that rocked him. Pushing the door wide open he walked into the room and stepped over the stuffed teddies that lay scattered across the carpet. He covered Tabitha with her favorite blanket, brushed a fine blonde curl back from her forehead and kissed her cheek.

The little girl stirred but didn't waken. From an early age, neither Eliza nor Tabitha had experienced a mother's love. He wasn't going to waste time feeling sorry for himself. Rose had always hated whiners, had always hated being the center of attention.

Nat walked around the bed, slid his arms beneath Eliza and lifted her up. Thankfully there was no gun tucked under the pillow. She snuggled closer to his chest, burrowing into his arms. Leaning down, he kissed her hair and caught a hint of her scent.

Nat carried her through the empty house and placed her carefully on his bed. He was too numb to feel rage and even misery was moving beyond him. Too battered to want to do more than search for comfort any way he could.

He undressed, dampened down the stray

emotions that threatened to fill his chest, slid into bed and pulled Eliza close. Murmuring something unintelligible she snuggled closer.

Nat lay awake, staring up at the ceiling. His mother had been the mainstay of his life. Now she was gone. He'd known she was ill—hadn't wanted to acknowledge the reality that she might actually die. Rubbing his chin in Eliza's hair, he reflexively tightened his grip, he didn't know what he was going to do about Eliza, but he didn't want to let her go, not yet.

Maybe not ever.

He'd gone and fallen in love with her and that scared the shit out of him. God knows, he'd been hurt by Nina's betrayal, he didn't want to go though that annihilation again.

His jaw ached from the effort of keeping his emotions in check and his heart thudded against his ribs. He'd promised his parents that he'd save the ranch and he wouldn't give up. Debt was his middle name, encumbered by a family that was splintered around the edges. He could never leave.

Nat growled softly under his breath. What about Cal? Ezra? Who'd employ an ex-con, and an old man who should've retired years ago?

Eliza moaned in her sleep and he soothed her with a kiss on the temple.

Tomorrow's sale of Venus' woods might generate enough money to get them out of this year's mess, but what about next year? Where would he get the money to build the indoor arena he needed to train other people's mounts during the winter? The vultures were circling and Troy Strange was the most ravenous one waiting to pick over the bones.

Hell. The son of a bitch was the last person Nat wanted taking anything from him. His stomach pitched and rolled with a mixture of hate and dread.

Eliza whimpered and twitched in her sleep, pulling him back from his thoughts. He wished he could dispel the sadness that crept upon her, darkened her eyes and doused her happiness.

It would take time. The one thing he figured he didn't have with Eliza.

The tempo of her breathing changed, tension invading her muscles as she started to writhe under the covers as if running away.

He leaned over her, brushed a strand of hair off her forehead. "Eliza, wake up, honey."

Green eyes opened, wide and shocked, but she relaxed on a sigh. Realization crowded her gaze and chased away the vestiges of sleep and tears formed on her lashes. She reached up to cup his cheek.

"I'm so sorry about your mom."

Tears slid down the sides of her face, staining the pillow. Nat held her gaze even though he didn't want to. He traced a tear with a blunt finger and wiped it away. Some things were too important to avoid. Nodding, he let the misery slide through his mind and acknowledged the pain.

She tried to smile at him, but her lips trembled too badly to pull it off. He couldn't read the emotions that shone in the depths of her eyes, but reminded himself that sympathy was a poor substitute for love.

Now wasn't the time to figure it out.

She leaned up. Pressed her lips to his in a gentle caress. Time hovered slowly and she drew out the touch until it was saturated with longing. Nat savored the feel of her lips against his. Tasted each kiss, and let them feed his sorrow.

He undressed her slowly. Lay back when she moved over him. Let her soothe his hurts and absorb his misery with kisses and unbearable gentleness. Oblivion loomed over him with an intensity that burned white behind his eyelids. He grabbed onto the passion, ignored death that hovered in the background like a soundtrack. He didn't want to feel anything but Eliza's breath on his body or her touch on his skin. Pain and heartbreak could wait.

Chapter Seventeen

Learjet, April 16ᵗʰ

"**De**Lattio escaped?" Sick with dread Marsh paced the passageway of the jet.

Half an hour ago he'd been feeling great, wide-awake and alert after a few hours sleep. The anticipation of finding Elizabeth and Josephine had zinged along his nerves like electricity. Now his good mood sank below a rising tide of fear.

"Someone poisoned the agents assigned guard duty—Bob Butler and Peter Wade." Dancer grimaced, tapped more keys on his laptop. Marsh hadn't known the agents personally, but his stomach twisted anyway.

"Sodium cyanide. DeLattio's lawyer was found with a 9 mm gunshot wound to the head."

"Christ," Marsh stuffed his hands in his pockets, alarmed at the turn of events. "And Ron Moody said *Stone Creek*, Montana?"

A sheriff from a small town in Montana had put in a request for an ID on fingerprints that turned out to be Elizabeth's.

"Yeah." Steve Dancer pointed to a GPS map on the computer screen. "Gave me the usual bullshit, but that's where he said. And it lines up with Josephine's route. She's heading north on Highway 15. If we fly straight to Kalispell we could be waiting for her when she arrives."

Marsh thought about it and liked the idea. He'd

275

love to see the look on her face. Turning, he gave the orders for the pilot to change the flight plan. Still restless, he paced up and down the corridor, examining their plan for loopholes.

"How do we find Elizabeth once we get to this place?" Marsh grabbed an apple from the complimentary bowl, thought about the effects of cyanide and changed his mind.

"The local sheriff is a guy named Talbot. I figure we contact him first, find out what he knows." Dancer reclined in his leather seat, stretched his arms over his head and yawned.

"What if she bolted?" Marsh felt uneasy about this. Elizabeth wouldn't have stayed in one place for so long, not when she'd had a run in with the local sheriff.

"We just keep on tracking Josephine." Dancer nodded to the red dot moving across the screen. "Sooner or later those two gals are going to hook up."

And they'd be ready...you betcha.

Marsh prayed it was sooner.

If DeLattio being on the loose wasn't bad enough, he'd also got a call from Director Lovine telling him Peter Uri had given his surveillance team the slip. Marsh didn't like the timing, didn't believe in coincidence. The assassin seemed to know DeLattio's moves before he did. Or maybe Uri had a different agenda.

The FBI had to have a leak, but no one had traced it yet. That meant chances were Peter Uri was on his way to Stone Creek, Montana, just like they were. Marsh peeled a banana and ate without enthusiasm.

He'd baited a trap with a woman who might

well be carrying his child, never expecting two predators to be unleashed into the fray. Throwing the banana peel in the trash, he settled into his seat to try to get some sleep. Reaching Eliza before anybody else did was the best they could hope for. Even with that bastard DeLattio on the loose it was still the best they could do.

***

Nothing had changed. The ranch house still stood. The world still spun on its axis and the mob still wanted to kill her. But she'd changed. She'd changed beyond belief.

She was stretched out naked on the bed, breathing hard. The soft wool of the blankets tickled, making her shiver, so did the sweat that was growing cold on her skin. Nat lay beside her, face down in the covers, unmoving.

Slowly her heart rate returned to normal and she raised her head, laid her cheek against the warm muscles of his broad back and tasted the salty dampness of his flesh.

"Again?" Nat's voice rumbled through the pillow. "Already?"

She laughed and kissed the flat hollow between his shoulder blades. "I'm so exhausted I couldn't move if there was an earthquake."

She trailed a finger down his spine, over each bony indent, and marveled at the strength of the man, tempered by gentleness. She savored the freedom she had to explore his body—those strong wide shoulders and long muscled limbs. His skin was smooth beneath the pad of her finger, made her tingle with want.

There was only a little time left. She didn't want to waste it.

She'd made him laugh, tried to make him forget, and had comforted him while he'd cried. Then, as she'd been wrapped securely in his arms, he'd told her how Rose had fought valiantly for life and how hard it would be to let her go.

She remembered that. Remembered the pain of being left behind, remembered being told her parents were dead. She'd been scared and lonely until her aunt had come to claim her. Then she'd been scared and lonely in boarding school.

"Rose told me she was dying," Eliza told him quietly. He lifted his head off the mattress to stare at her.

"What?" Nat asked her. An incredulous note overrode the roughness of his voice.

Eliza studied the way the dim light flowed over his back and avoided his eyes. "She told me she was dying. She wanted to make sure you were going to be okay. For me to promise I wouldn't hurt you."

"What did you tell her?" His blue eyes were intent on her face.

Moisture dried up in her throat as Eliza forced herself to meet his eyes. "That we don't always get to make the choices we want."

He rolled over, snagged her to him so that she lay across his chest. She tried to pull away, but he held her effortlessly.

"How come you joined the FBI?" He watched her eyes intently as if looking for secrets.

"Marshall Hayes, a friend of mine." Elizabeth relaxed on a sigh. "I'd known him for years." The details didn't matter anymore. "He recruited me when I was still too stupid to know better."

She remembered how easy it had all seemed. "We had a lot of fun over the years, caught a lot of crooks."

With three agents working deep undercover and very little backup they didn't have time for the usual bureau politics. They didn't apprehend the criminals, just collected information then called in the field agents for arrests. An easy job, for the most part.

"What made you become an agent?" Nat caressed her cheek with his index finger and caused a shiver of reaction to flutter all the way down to her toes.

She shrugged, unconsciously played with the crisp hair that sprinkled his chest.

"I don't really know...I guess it was all tied up with losing my parents." She looked up at Nat, touched his hand. "I still have a lot of baggage up here." She tapped her finger against her skull. "I wanted to help people, to make a difference and my specialty subject was art." She laughed at how young she sounded. "When Marsh offered me the chance to join his team it seemed like the perfect opportunity. And I was good at it too. Thought I was finally doing something that mattered."

She looked down into dark eyes, absorbed the contrast with the pale lashes and golden skin. She could feel the hard length of him beneath her, the solid planes of sinew and bone that made up his body. Heat radiated from him like a furnace and she wanted to remember him this way forever.

"I was very good at it until I started work with the Organized Crime Unit."

A chill glanced against her skin and she pulled the covers up around her shoulders. Nat watched her, quiet and somber.

Bitterness swept through her like poison. "OCU couldn't believe it when they realized I was an undercover fed and that Andrew DeLattio had asked me out on a date. They orchestrated a second meeting and this time I agreed to go out with him." The bastards had moved heaven and earth to throw them together again.

Holding herself very still, as if a single movement would shatter her control she continued. "He was very polite at first, a real gentleman." She didn't want to remember how he'd become less polite and more insistent. More forceful.

"I planted bugs in locations other agents couldn't infiltrate." She tapped her finger against his chest before she caught herself. "I witnessed some incidents and helped OCU work out who worked for whom." She looked down, held his gaze. "But I got nervous and bailed."

"You didn't want to sleep with him." It was a statement, not a question.

She nodded, moved her gaze to his lips and dropped a quick kiss there for good measure. "OCU begged and threatened, but I stopped seeing DeLattio and tried to return to my other duties."

Pulling the covers around her shoulders she sat up. "I guess I was feeling pretty damned proud of myself." Her fingers clenched the blanket. "He came to the museum's Christmas party, spiked my drink, and carried me out telling everyone I was drunk and needed to go home." Her voice shook with both anguish and anger. "He took me up to my apartment, tied me up, beat the crap out of me and then raped me."

Nat put a hands on her shoulder, touched her as

if she were fragile.

"You don't have to tell me if you don't want to." His gaze was full of empathy and rage. She understood the rage.

"You deserve to know." Elizabeth let the blanket hang loosely around her shoulders, stretched her hands and arms out in front of her. "I don't remember most of the attack. But for me, the worst thing was having the other agents find me tied to the bed." Her voice cracked. "The special surveillance group had stood down when I stopped seeing DeLattio, but my purse was still wired and monitored by OCU. They recorded every scream I made, taped me begging for help and pleading. And they used it. Used it to make him turn state's evidence and give up his crime connections. Can you imagine?"

Elizabeth could see that Nat imagined all too well.

She held his gaze. "I spent two days in hospital before my friend Josie broke me out." God, she'd have been lost without Josie. "When the bruising on my face faded enough, I covered it with makeup and went back to work."

She ignored the ache in his eyes. It was a reflection of her suffering and she wanted it to end.

"I made a lot of mistakes, Nat. I ignored the advice I was given. Refused counseling. Refused to let OCU tell Marsh or any of my other colleagues what happened." Tears spilled over. "I was too humiliated for them to know."

Nat wrapped his arms around her, silently gave her his strength.

"I walked around like a zombie for weeks, terrified, absolutely terrified he would come back. I barely slept or ate, carried a loaded gun wherever I went." She laughed when he raised a brow. "Even worse than I am now."

Elizabeth ran a hand through her hair, brushing it away from her face. "Then one day I quit—left Marsh in the lurch and ran. Like a coward."

Tears formed on her lashes, but she dashed them away. "I was so scared for so long..." She didn't know how to go on, but Nat silenced her by placing two fingers gently on her lips.

"You did what you had to do." He wrapped her up tight in his arms, kissed her cheek. "What are you going to do now?" His directness startled her.

She avoided his gaze and made a part confession.

"Every day since then I've fantasized about killing Andrew Mario DeLattio." She closed her eyes and hid the emotions that might reveal the plans she'd put into action. He couldn't begin to understand. "I have to leave here before I put you guys in danger."

Nat leaned his forehead against hers. "Listen to me, Eliza, it doesn't matter. None of the past matters." He took her hands in his. "I don't care who's after you. I don't care what you've done. We'll figure this out."

She stared back at him. Sadness drowned what should have been pleasure. It wasn't the past she was worried about.

"I need you to stay." Nat's eyes burned fierce and bright in the lamplight while his hands were as hard as steel. "Please stay."

The words jolted her, like unexpectedly stepping off a curb. She looked up at him, a quick glance that read the truth in his intensity. In the stark vulnerability of his gaze. Anguish and hopelessness burst the euphoria of finally finding love. He was everything she had ever wanted. Good and honest. Strong and brave. Integrity matched with an innate sense of honor.

Another tear formed and overflowed down her cheek. She didn't want to leave him, but she had to. She wiped away the tear, pulled the blankets back up around her shoulders.

The world was caving in around her. It was happening so fast now that she couldn't stop it, couldn't plug the gaps with lies anymore. Every day she spent on the ranch increased the danger to the others. Nat had already lost his mother, she didn't want to bring more disaster down on him.

He'd told her once she was trouble and he was right.

I love you, whispered through her mind, but she couldn't say it. If she did, she'd never be able to leave him. He didn't care what she'd done? Well, he should care. She was beyond redemption. Not that it mattered. She wouldn't put him at risk.

The scent of their lovemaking filled the air, reminded her of the bond they'd forged, but the words dragged out of her mouth anyway.

"I can't stay. I'll leave today." She hadn't wanted to tell him—had wanted to creep away like a thief in the dark.

"What?" he jerked as if he'd been bitten. "What the hell did you say?"

Elizabeth bowed her head. "After the auction."

Nat jumped off the bed, paced up and down.

"*Jesus!*" He rubbed his hands through his flaxen hair, so upset he was physically shaking. "My mother *died* and you can't even wait a couple of days?"

Elizabeth was silent. Nothing she said would make this any easier. She could only screw it up.

His anger didn't scare her. She'd rediscovered the courage that had deserted her for so long—thanks to Nat. He stared at her, his jaw set in a hard line. "You're not telling me everything."

No, she wasn't.

Nat stood at the end of the bed, oblivious to his nakedness, legs spread, arms folded across his chest. He tucked his chin in, narrowed his eyes and frowned down at her.

"You could stay here couldn't you? No one knows you're here."

The idea was so tempting...and drove home every reason she had to leave. She desperately wanted to stay. Desperately.

She shook her head. "Talbot knows. I have to go."

"Why?" Nat asked.

She could see Nat's mind at work, trying to fit all the pieces of the puzzle, trying to solve the problems she ran from, but he didn't have all the pieces.

"Why?" he demanded, louder this time.

She didn't answer, just stared down at her hands spread across the coverlet. The ring her mother had given her on her seventh birthday glinted on her finger.

"You think the mob will find you here?" Nat asked.

Elizabeth nodded, biting her lip against the need to stay.

With quick jerky movements he started to get dressed, doing up his jeans, pulling on a shirt.

284

This was goodbye, she realized suddenly. Nat stood by the edge of the bed and looked down at her. Elizabeth lifted her head to meet his turbulent gaze.

"It doesn't have to be like this, Eliza," he said softly.

"Yes." Elizabeth straightened her back. "It does."

Nat cursed and left, closing the door behind him with a quiet click that sounded like the final nail being driven home in her coffin.

A bitter draft streamed through the air and swept goose bumps across her flesh. Nat's scent clung to the pillow and she hugged it to her, trying to commit the smell to memory, but she knew it would fade. Given time, everything faded.

***

Nat shoved the truck into third gear, going down the steep incline towards the lower river valley, and again, down into second. The engine roared in protest, but the truck slowed a little. The old Ford shook in time to Dwight Yokam and Sheryl Crow singing *Baby Don't Go* and made his teeth ache.

Every time he went over a rut his brain jounced and he braced himself on the steering wheel and hung on for the ride. He was glad he needed to concentrate and wasn't able to think much. Sas had come home around eight a.m., grief-stricken and worn, her eyes puffy from crying.

She was holding up, but barely. Ryan had been unconscious in the bunkhouse, Cal and Ezra each nursing coffee, subdued and silent. Nat had left them. Refused their offers of help and headed out to the auction on his own.

Rose would have wanted it this way.

The trail was only marginally quicker than going back down onto the main road and heading along the highway. It was just a tractor rut truth be told, a double indentation of bare gray earth surrounded by the crush of wilderness. But Nat wanted to use this route—it might be the last time he'd have the right.

He didn't know if Eliza would be there when he got back. It burned his gut to think about her so he stamped down on his thoughts and even harder on the truck's lousy brakes. He wanted to help but she wouldn't let him. It was driving him insane.

Going too fast, he hit a big rut and just managed to jerk the steering wheel back before he smacked the verge. Punching the dashboard in frustration, he tried to concentrate on the drive. He entered the cool and shaded forest and rolled down the window to let fresh air flow around the airless cab.

This land was no good for ranching and cost them a heap in taxes. Didn't matter how beautiful the place was, sentimentality didn't pay the bills.

The light inside the forest was sharp and bright and a gentle breeze brushed shadows across the lush grass. Bluebells and dog daisies covered the underbelly, popping up along the edge of the trail like brightly colored pennants.

Breathing deeply, he smelled the fresh earth and tasted the essence of life as nature took advantage of the short summer. Birds sang in the trees and he heard the tentative buzz of newly hatched insects.

He'd lost his virginity in these woods, in this very truck. His hands tightened on the steering wheel. Him and Adele Black, a pair of sixteen-year-olds with their heads full of hormones and curiosity. Adele had been a tiny little thing and he'd been a good deal smaller back then too. He couldn't imagine doing it in a truck anymore. The image of Eliza stretched naked on the burgundy upholstery made his heart hammer and his blood pound.

Shit. He had to deal with this. The woman was leaving him.

He neared the old gate that led through to a meadow at the bottom of his property. It was the ideal location to build that picture-perfect little holiday home, if you had the cash. Nat hoped to God someone other than Troy Strange had the cash.

Bracing his shoulders, he looked down to the bottom of the meadow, through the gate that led onto the highway where cars were parked. He spotted Strange, deep in conversation with their local bank manager. Nat parked the truck behind the gate, got out and vaulted the old five-bar.

Though he wanted to kill Troy Strange, he clamped down on the urge for now.

Marlena lounged against the Mercedes in a clingy top, micro-shorts and high-heels, looking as out of place as a hooker at kindergarten. She spotted him, eyeing him like a piece of meat and he grimaced, figuring maybe those feminists were onto something after all.

He spotted Molly Adams, another old high school girlfriend, sitting on the fender of a little Honda. She was plump, but still pretty, and ran an old fashioned saloon that drew in the tourists. She smiled, waved a half-eaten apple in his direction. She obviously hadn't heard about Rose's death yet, but it was still early. Feeling grim, he nodded, but stayed back, in no mood for pleasantries or conversation.

Several lawyer-types clutched cell phones like substitute personalities and he recognized some of Sarah's co-workers from the hospital. Nat smiled woodenly and tipped his hat to a couple he'd met at a wedding about a year ago. He hoped his smile didn't look as sour as it felt.

Nat crossed over to where the auctioneer, Rich Willard, a short, beefy man, stood perched on some sort of wooden podium. Rich had been a great friend of his dad's, a good man to know in a crisis. His belly protruded over tightly buckled trousers and a stray piece of food dangled from his moustache.

Nat had always liked him.

"Sorry to hear about your mother, son." Rich's watery blue blinked repeatedly. "We can do this another time if you want."

Nat looked out over the crowd of people gathered nearby. No way did he want to go through this again. Ever.

"No. Today." Nat cleared his throat. "Appreciate you doing this for us."

"Don't mention it. Just glad I can help." Rich looked at his wristwatch. "You ready to start, son?"

The compassion in Rich's eyes made Nat grimace. This wasn't easy for him, but he'd be damned if he showed that weakness in front of anybody here today.

"Let's do it," Nat said.

"If it makes you feel any better I have Atty in the crowd and we're prepared to pay at least the reserve price." Rich peered out, searched for his diminutive wife somewhere in the crowd.

Nat swallowed, his voice thick with emotion.

"You don't have to do that, sir."

"Hell, we'd love to own this land, Nat." Rich lowered his head conspiratorially. "You know women, son, once they get an idea into their heads." Rich laughed, a funny belly gurgling sound that was as forced as Nat's smile. "If she gets carried away I'll pretend I don't see her."

Nat went and stood beside the top gate. Marlena watched him and he hoped she didn't cause more trouble; he didn't want to have to deal with her today. Strange slipped a hand around his wife's waist and pulled her closer. Nat hoped he had chains.

Rich started the show with an outline of the land and what it contained. The stream with its waterfall, fishing rights, hunting rights. Seven acres of mature forest, mainly yellow pine, quaking aspen, and some red cedar. And three acres of lush spring meadow. Each word struck a nail in Nat's heart. Bids started at $100,000.

Nat watched as the smaller players upped the ante, slowly, inexorably towards the $300,000 mark. That was what he needed to clear his debts. That was enough to pay off the bank.

Slowly the small time bidders fell away and the serious combatants began to show.

Nat tried to be dispassionate. It was just land after all. But his mother had always loved this patch of ground... A guy who looked like a rumpled tourist bid $400,000, which surprised him. Nat wondered if the man was just dipping his toes into the action to add to the excitement of his day or if he was serious about owning a piece of Montana.

Troy Strange had the smug look of a man who knew he could buy out everyone there twice over and upped the bid to $450K, and went back to his conversation with the banker.

Damn it.

Nat wanted to kick a rock but stuck his hands in his pockets instead. One of the local doctors upped it to $460,000 and Nat began to hope.

Strange upped it again, his grin tighter this time. Rich looked back to the doctor who shook his head. His wife whispered fiercely in his ear, but the doctor just shook his head and folded an arm around her shoulder.

Nat's heart began to pound in his chest.

No. No. No.

He stared into Troy's smirking face, gritted his teeth and set his mouth into a hard line. If the bastard bought it he was going to deck him.

"Any more bidders?" Rich asked in a hopeful tone. He knew how much the Sullivans disliked their Texan neighbor.

One man raised his hand, all the while talking into a cell phone.

Rich tilted his head in polite inquiry as the guy held up his hand again in a quick moment of consultation.

"But that's ridiculous..." was all Nat could catch at this distance.

Impatient, Nat crossed his arms over his chest and breathed out a heavy sigh. He wanted to get this over with, find out if Eliza had left him—and bury his mother.

"One million dollars," the guy on the cell shouted. "One million American dollars." He looked liked he'd swallowed his tongue.

Nat wished he'd had the pleasure of watching Strange's mouth sag, but his own was gaping in surprise.

"That's one million going once," Rich stared at Strange who ground his teeth and glared at the little guy with the phone, "Going twice," Rich waited a heartbeat, "Gone!"

Nat sagged against the five-bar gate. One-million-dollars? His legs recovered slowly, but his ears still rang. *One-million-fucking-dollars!* He wanted to laugh, would have, if his heart hadn't been ripped out and his pride trampled into the mud like trash.

But Troy Strange hadn't bought it. That was the *other* good news. Nat pushed himself off the gate and walked down the hill to where his banker stood in his Sunday best. "You'll get your money tomorrow, Brent." Nat tipped back his hat and couldn't hide the satisfaction in his voice.

"Obviously I know something you don't, Sullivan." Brent Whittaker's tone implied an *as per usual* that hung in the air like a red flag.

Nat studied the man, and wondered if he could punch Brent in the nose without getting sued. *Not with this many witnesses.* The prick always managed to sound supercilious whatever the subject. He was a money-man who cared about little besides wealth and power.

It was all bullshit.

"Your loan was bought from the bank—"

Nat grabbed him by the throat one handed and squeezed. "Who?"

"Don't...know—" Brent choked.

Nat let go, but leaned closer. "Who bought the loan?"

"Maybe the same person who bought the land." Whittaker rubbed his sore throat and looked over to the guy who'd bid a million bucks. "Maybe they're trying to force you out."

Nat didn't give a fuck what they were trying to do. With a million dollars in the bank the ranch could survive for a good few years. Maybe long enough to get the stud farm up and running.

It was almost worth losing the woods.

"How do I find out who holds the debt?" Nat demanded.

"I expect they'll let you know soon enough." Whittaker's lips twisted into a smirk that suited his pinched autocratic face before he turned and scuttled away.

Jerk.

Nat shrugged and walked over to where Rich was exchanging details with the guy on the cell phone. Sticking out his hand he introduced himself.

"Nice to meet you, Mr. Sullivan." The man juggled the phone, some papers and a briefcase between his knees. "I'm Arthur Nugent."

The accent sounded English to Nat. "You going to build a home here, Mr. Nugent?"

The man laughed sounding tired, and bobbled the cell. "No, no sir. I'm acting on behalf of a client." The man nodded towards the phone like it was a real person. "A client who wants to remain anonymous, so that's all I can tell you, I'm afraid."

Feeling uneasy, Nat thanked both Rich and Arthur Nugent and agreed to meet up the next day in his lawyer's office. He signed the papers and walked back to his truck, unable to shake the disquiet that tingled at the back of his mind.

There was no way anyone would get their hands on his ranch.

No way.

He vaulted the gate, jumped into the truck and reversed to drive back up the lane. Suddenly the euphoria of the sale receded; money was only one of his many problems.

Chapter Eighteen

Elizabeth took her rifle from the top of the wardrobe where she'd placed it for safety. She loaded it, left the hammer half-cocked and the chamber empty, then slid it into its carry case and propped it next to her rucksack. Back in the living room she packed the rest of her gear, piled some emergency cash, a spare passport, and a change of clothes into a small tote.

Just in case.

She tried to focus her mind on the job, not on the stabbing pain that shot through her whenever she thought about leaving Nat, but her presence here put them all in danger.

The trials were due to start any day. The newscasts continued to harp on about her disappearance and she felt uncomfortably exposed. Not that she resembled Juliette anymore, but Nat had pieced together her identity pretty damned quick, which meant others could too.

Nat...

She swallowed then determinedly zipped the tote. Maybe she should disguise her voice—quash the Irish lilt that lingered? Prickles of unease tapped along her spine. Had she missed something? Screwed up and given something away?

DeLattio was after her.

She knew it. She almost felt his fingers clutching at her back.

She checked the Glock, then slid the gun into

the shoulder harness she'd strapped on over her T-shirt.

A navy baseball cap was pulled low over her hair. She picked up her black shades and carried her stuff out to the Jeep. Blue hovered next to her, tried to jump inside, but couldn't quite make it.

"Sorry, buddy, you can't come with me." She rubbed his head, lingered over the soft velvet of his ears and swallowed the lump in her throat. She gazed up at the mountains in the distance. The sky was a relentless blue. Deep and clear like the depths of Nat's eyes. She tried to absorb the scene. Knew she'd never set foot in Montana again.

The yard was peaceful. The cattle had been moved up to higher pastures. Foals gamboled besides their dams. The kittens chased strands of hay by the open barn door and Stealth whinnied from his stall.

There was no one around to say farewell. They were all busy. Just the way she'd planned it.

Loneliness pressed against the edges of her mind. It was an emotion she was well acquainted with. *Heartbreak wasn't.* She hefted the last bag, pushed it further into the dark recesses of the rear compartment.

She didn't want to go.

A chasm of grief tore through her so wide it threatened to swallow her whole. Emotions that had been buried deep surged and overrode the need to run. Sagging against the side of the Jeep, she held her hand across her eyes and tried not to weep.

The sun felt warm on her skin. Metal, hard beneath the press of her hand, gleamed dully in the midday sun. Birds sang and darted around the cabin. The breeze rustled the tree branches in a familiar refrain. She'd found a home here, a family to love. Fear and revenge seemed petty cousins to such riches. But she wasn't leaving for her own safety, she reminded herself. She was doing it for the Sullivans. For Nat. If she didn't leave now they could all die.

Elizabeth pushed herself away from the warm metal of the car and blanked her thoughts. Taking a step back, she reached up and closed the trunk with a sharp bang that echoed off the distant hills in a final volley. Moving quickly she went back to check the cabin one last time, and Blue followed every step she took.

***

Marshall Hayes sat behind Dancer in Sheriff Talbot's beat-up old Blazer, anxiously gripping the back of the headrest.

"You say you interviewed Elizabeth Reed three-days ago?" Marsh asked Talbot.

"Yes, sir." The sheriff's drawl was pure Midwest. "Knew right off there was something funny about her. Looks like I was right, don't it?" He looked at Marsh, clearly expecting an answer.

The sheriff wanted to know what sort of criminal he'd tracked down.

"We really appreciate the ride, Sheriff." Marsh avoided answering the question. He needed to keep the guy on his side, but without risking any leaks to the press.

A tree-shaped air-freshener jiggled as the sheriff turned his attention back to the road. Elizabeth should have been smart enough to leave the ranch after the sheriff questioned her. Even if he wasn't suspicious, she'd have moved on—*right*?

He tried to focus on what the sheriff was saying. "Pardon me?"

"I just wondered if any of you high-rolling federal agents," the drawl carried an edge of irritation, "were ever gonna tell a hick country boy like me what the hell is going on?"

Marsh smiled at the man. Pissed off law enforcement officers were his forte. "Later, Sheriff, I promise you." Marsh caught Talbot's gaze in the rearview mirror. The sheriff's eyes flashed hot for an instant, but then he nodded, apparently satisfied.

For now.

Marsh glanced at the scenery through the windshield. Took in snow-capped peaks, deep valleys, and long swathes of uncut forest. The land was ripe with spring. Bright greens splashed against mountainous backdrops, wildflowers intermittent along the margins of the road.

A pretty spot.

"Triple H is just over the next ridge." The sheriff nodded towards the approaching rise.

"What are the owners like?" Marsh asked.

"The Sullivans?" The sheriff looked grim. "Rose Sullivan, the mother, died of a coronary just yesterday, so they're not really accepting social calls."

"This is far from a social call, Sheriff."

"Right." Talbot nodded, threw a measured look over his shoulder. "Well, Nat Sullivan is a big guy, and I wouldn't wanna rile him. But he should be down at the auction right now. They're selling off a piece of land down near the reservoir." The sheriff tapped sausage-like fingers on the steering wheel. "They're good people. Been here for generations.

297

Nat's got a brother and sister that live on the ranch too. She's a doctor down at County Hospital." The sheriff shrugged. "Regular folk."

Talbot wound down his window and leaned his forearm along the sill. Adjusted his mirror. "It's just a small place. They're struggling to keep it afloat, but they're stubborn. Too damned stubborn to go down without a fight."

They crested the ridge, and the ranch spread out below them in the small valley. Marsh took in the large central ranch house with its L-shaped frame. A big orange Dutch barn dominated the yard and a long shed, probably stables, crouched close besides it. There were three circular wooden corrals and horses dotted the meadows all around the valley.

"Turn off the engine and coast down the hill," Marsh said. He spotted a cowboy riding away from them on horseback up on the far ridge. Two small cottages were just visible at the edge of the trees, beyond the furthest corral. A Jeep and a red Explorer were parked beside the barn. "Everything look as it should, Sheriff?"

Talbot stared at Marsh for a moment before the import of the question sank in. The sheriff turned back and examined the scene through law enforcement eyes.

He pointed to the cowboy on the ridge. "That's old Ezra Jenkins, one of the hands, heading to the upper pastures by the looks of it."

His gaze shifted to the ranch itself. "The Jeep is Eliza Reed's, or whatever the heck her name is. The Explorer belongs to Sarah Sullivan. Don't see Ryan's truck. Could be parked in the old barn though." He pointed to a ramshackle building on the far side of the ranch house. "Cal Landon, the other cowpoke who works here, doesn't own a vehicle so he could be anywhere." The sheriff brightened. "You here because of him?"

Marsh shook his head.

Talbot's face dropped.

"Oh, I almost forgot, there's a little girl about the place too," the sheriff added.

Marsh and Dancer exchanged a glance. *Shit*. A kid to worry about as well as everything else.

Marsh took out his SIG, bullet in the chamber. "I'm going around the back. You two drive around the front and check it out."

He slipped out of the car and ran across the gravel track, vaulted a wooden fence and sprinted to the side of the house. DeLattio could have come and gone already. Wasn't likely, but it could have happened. Sweat beaded on Marsh's brow and he swiped at it with the back of his hand. He didn't want Elizabeth in that man's clutches. The medical report had been bad enough and next time, Delattio wouldn't stop until she was dead.

Next time...

Marsh gritted his teeth. *Not if I can help it.* He skirted the house. Trampled some shrubs and cut his hand on a rosebush. Sucking blood from his finger, he checked the windows. Didn't see anyone. Ducking his head, he ran across the neatly trimmed back lawn to the far side of the house. At the corner he paused for a moment, scanned the area before running down the side of the house. The sheriff and Steve Dancer stood on the porch, knocking on the door.

Dancer had his hand in his jacket pocket, weapon concealed.

Marsh heard someone answer the door.

"Hey. Sheriff Talbot, you back again?"

"Sorry to impose, Ryan. Condolences on your ma." Talbot placed his hands on his waist, formalities over. "Miss Reed around?"

"What do you want her for this time?"

Marsh heard the frown in the young man's voice.

"Just answer the question, Ryan."

Marsh measured the hesitation, knew with certainty that Elizabeth was around somewhere and then froze at the sound of a bolt chambering a round close to his ear.

Shit.

He balanced on the balls of his feet, ready to dive, held his SIG up in the air. Didn't breathe as he turned to face a blond cowboy who scowled down the length of a .308 Winchester.

Marsh exhaled in relief. At least it wasn't a gangster who'd gotten the drop on him. Not that the cowboy looked particularly friendly, but at least he had no reason to want him dead.

Marsh looked the man over, tried to assess the light in the man's blue eyes.

Sharp, cool, focused.

"Drop the gun and move out into the open where I can see you." The cowboy's voice was deep and flat. Calm. Not easily panicked.

Good.

Marsh threw his weapon into the yard, near the parked vehicles. He placed his hands on his head, and walked out from the side of the house.

The three men on the stoop watched him, slack-jawed. The cowboy followed him, but kept close to the house for cover.

"Jesus, Nat, what in the fuck are you doing?"

Sheriff Talbot fumbled with his holster.

"Touch that gun, Talbot, and I'll nail your ass and bury you so deep, not even the bears will find you." His attention never left Marsh. "Get your hands up, all of you, before somebody does something he regrets."

Talbot must have seen his career slide down the toilet and gasped. "He's a goddamn federal agent."

Marsh saw no surprise on Nat Sullivan's face. Now wasn't *that* interesting? And he didn't lower the rifle.

"Get your hands up," Nat repeated. "Now."

Marsh gave Dancer an imperceptible nod. Dancer raised his hands. The sheriff followed suit reluctantly.

"What do you want?" Nat asked Marsh.

"He's a freaking federal agent, Nat. Doesn't matter what he wants." Sheriff Talbot's voice cracked. "Put down the goddamned gun."

"I don't care if he's the President of the United States, *Sheriff*." His voice was hard as steel. "What the hell is he doing sneaking around my property with a drawn gun?"

Silence hung in the air. Marsh felt the weight of it as the others watched him, waiting for answers.

"He's looking for me."

Marsh glanced behind him and felt a flood of relief so strong his knees nearly buckled. Elizabeth moved from behind the stable doors, pushed her black Glock into her shoulder holster. She wore jeans and a faded shirt, draped over a faded University of Montana T-shirt.

She looked tired and thin. Dark hair was scraped back into a ponytail and hidden under a ball cap. Cheekbones were stark above hollow cheeks and her lips, normally smiling, were bloodless and grim.

It had been a long time since he'd seen her as anything except the highly fashionable Juliette Morgan. Eliza Reed was a different kind of woman.

"Elizabeth."

Dancer bolted over the rail and ran to her. The guy picked her up and twirled her around. Marsh held motionless as Dancer crushed her in a fierce hug and kissed her full on the mouth. Tension radiated from Nat Sullivan in solid waves. He held the rifle pointed straight at Marsh's heart.

Way to go, Dancer.

"I'd forgotten how butt-ugly you really were." Dancer pulled off Elizabeth's cap and ruffled her brown locks.

Some of the tension eased from her stance and her lips curved into the smile Marsh remembered.

"Jeez, Dance, get your hands off me." Elizabeth laughed and shoved him away. She wiped her mouth with the back of her hand. "When was the last time you shaved?"

"I thought you liked the rough and ready type." Dancer threw his arm around Elizabeth's shoulders. Raised his eyebrows as he stared at the tall, angry cowboy who still held the rifle trained on Marsh.

***

"Not as rough as you, idiot." Elizabeth followed his gaze and her smile slipped. "Nat." His name was a whisper on her lips.

He was shockingly handsome in faded denim that brought out the blue of his eyes. She blinked away an image of him covered in blood.

"Let me introduce Special Agent in Charge,

Marshall Hayes," she put a hand on Dancer's shoulder, "and this *fool* is Special Agent Steve Dancer. Both work for the Fine Art and Forgeries Division of the Federal Bureau of Investigation."

There was a second's pause as Elizabeth stared into Nat's steady eyes. "Marsh is my old boss." Elizabeth ignored the gapes from Ryan and Sheriff Talbot, concentrated instead on the man in front of her. *The man who cared enough to aim his rifle at a top government official.*

Both men were important to her. Both wanted to protect her. Nat was as blond as Marsh was dark, the planes of his face harder and leaner compared to the square-jawed Bostonian. Both men were tall and fit, Nat having the extra bulk across the shoulders from hard manual labor he did every day of his life. Marsh's suit contrasted vividly with Nat's old denims, but both men held themselves with the natural grace of born leaders.

Storm clouds had begun to gather in the distance. They grazed the jagged tips of mountaintops with ominous portent.

"You can put the rifle down, Nat, he's one of the good guys," she said gently. Sweat gathered on her brow, beaded and slid down the side of her face.

"Sure of that, Eliza?" Nat asked.

Elizabeth shrugged away from Dancer and walked over to Nat, laying her hand on his arm. His pulse beat warm and vital and *alive*. She wanted to keep him that way. "Yeah, I'm sure."

Nat searched her eyes for doubt and finding none finally raised the rifle. He reached out a hand to cup her chin, rubbed her bottom lip with his thumb. Elizabeth leaned into the touch, wanted to throw herself into his arms, but held back. Nothing had changed. She still had to leave. Nat dropped his hand. He seemed to sense her withdrawal and she watched as he hauled his gaze back to Marsh.

Nat walked over and picked up the SIG that lay on the ground. He balanced it in his free hand, blew off some of the dirt and hesitated.

"Here." He held it out for Marsh to take.

The two men stood a couple of feet apart, weighing each other. Elizabeth watched them, amused and a little sad. *Alpha males at play.* Another time and they might have become friends.

"Is someone going to explain this shit to me?" Sheriff Talbot barked. The slow drawl was gone. An aggravated rumble filled its place.

Elizabeth ignored him and approached Marsh. She felt like a truant schoolgirl finally being called before the principal.

"Hey." She didn't know what else to say after all the trouble she'd caused. Not that he'd had to track her down, but she'd known he'd try.

"Hey yourself." Marsh pulled her into his arms and squeezed her in a fierce hug. She could feel Nat's gaze rake her back. Angry and tense. Demanding answers.

"DeLattio's escaped," Marsh murmured into her ear.

Her breath hissed out of her lungs and her stomach clenched. Pulling back she withdrew from his arms, her body a solid block of trepidation.

"When?" Her voice was reedy and weak. God, she hated the effect the bastard had on her.

"Night before last." He re-holstered his pistol.

Uneasy, her eyes flicked to the trees. *Shit. He could be here already.* Terror and hatred warred in her head. Blanked out all other thoughts. She

304

scanned the woods. Picked out patches of shadow so dark they could have hidden an elephant. She backed away, the desire to flee as powerful as a shove in the back. Her hand crept up to the Glock she'd just holstered. Automatically, she loosened the clasp and pulled the gun free again. Sweat drenched her upper lip. Her heart hammered. She couldn't sense anything evil from the woods. She couldn't sense a damned thing, but hell, he could still be there.

"I was about to leave." She'd been saying goodbye to the little foal, Red, when the sheriff had rolled up. Stupid to hang around.

Stupid. Stupid. Stupid.

She'd get them all killed.

Nat's questioning stare drilled her, but she ignored him. She hadn't meant to be here when he got back from the auction, couldn't bear to witness his pain.

Marsh glanced from her to Nat then leaned towards her, hands on hips. "So how about we catch this bastard?"

Shaking her head, she rubbed the gooseflesh that crawled across her skin.

"We'll set a trap. Draw him here." Marsh regarded her with a small smile, like it was already accomplished. "Who knows? Maybe the bastard will get killed in the crossfire."

Her gaze wavered under Marsh's intense scrutiny and she looked away. The urge to put a bullet between DeLattio's eyes was so strong it was a physical pain in her chest. But the Law demanded judicial process. And she wanted Old Testament reckoning.

"No." She shook her head, set her jaw,

impatient at the delay.

"So you're just going to run away from this asshole?" Marsh demanded.

Elizabeth's eyes went wide at his tone before logic took over. He was riling her. It was a technique that had worked in the past. "Him, the mob, just about anybody else who wants to put a bullet in my head."

Or worse—in somebody else's head.

Marsh was spoiling for a fight, but she didn't have time. She started to walk away. Had to get out of there. Marsh grabbed her arm and swung her back to face him, his fingers bruising her flesh.

"Which may include me if you don't sort out this goddamned mess!" His shout blasted her eardrums about an inch from her face.

Fury seared her, like he had any right to be angry.

Laughter rang out, bounced off the trees and up the valley. Nat was almost bent double with amusement. The rifle rested across his thighs.

"What the hell is so funny?" She raised a brow and glared.

"You are," Nat said bluntly. "You're the most mule-headed stubborn female I have ever met." He was still laughing and Elizabeth didn't know whether to kick Marsh in the balls or slap Nat on the head.

Her heart pounded with the adrenaline surging through her system. Fight or flight. Looking at Nat she knew what she had to do. She shook off Marsh's hand and turned back towards the Jeep.

"So that's it? You're just gonna leave?" Nat's voice was filled with anguish.

She froze, but couldn't turn around. Tears were

too close to the surface. She squeezed the grip of the Glock, her knuckles straining against the molded resin. "I've never had anything to lose before, Nat. Don't make this harder for me."

She climbed into the Jeep as tears blinded her. She slammed the door shut and started the engine.

A blast rocked the SUV, jerked her against the window so hard she banged her head. Her jaw dropped as she watched Marsh point his SIG at the back tire and pull the trigger again.

He blew out the second tire.

Son of a bitch.

He started to walk around the front of the Jeep as Eliza pushed the door open and climbed out.

"You sonofa— Stop!"

Marsh pointed the gun at the third tire, his eyes flat as flint. "You staying?"

Fear warred with anger and anger won. "Do I have any choice?" She glared at Marsh, wishing she'd never met him. Stuffing her Glock back in its holster, she turned and stalked back to the ranch house, careful not to look at Nat. The foundations shook as she slammed the door behind her.

Chapter Nineteen

"So what do we call you, Slick?" Ryan asked. Evidence of grief and a hangover hovered around his eyes and roughened his handsome edge. He sat at the kitchen table, a mug of coffee clutched between his palms as if that would stop them shaking.

"Eliza, Elizabeth, whatever, it's all the same to me." Elizabeth shrugged and glanced toward Nat, who leaned against the far wall—expressionless, unreadable. "My parents called me Eliza."

Methodically, Nat began checking his rifle.

The kitchen was crowded, but she had nowhere to go. *Too many people and not enough air.* She sat down heavily in the chair next to Ryan, her anger spent, took a sip of hot sweetened tea.

"Special Agent Elizabeth Claire Paden Ward," Marsh interrupted. "Aka Juliette Morgan, aka Eliza Reed." He'd filled them in on most of the details, but she didn't like being the floorshow.

Marsh was trying to remind her who she'd been and what she'd done with her life, but she wasn't proud of it anymore; the price had been too high.

"*Former* Special Agent. I resigned." She looked up, gave Marsh a bitter smile. "Look, I don't have time to discuss ancient history with you, Marsh. We both know I have to get out of here."

Marsh was checking his laptop, but she couldn't see what he was looking at. Whatever it was made him smile and that irritated the crap out of her.

Nothing about this situation was funny. Dancer was supposed to be changing her tires. If she knew him he'd be setting up gadgets first.

Damn.

She scowled at the sheriff who leaned against the sink with a mug of coffee in hand. "So what did you do, Sheriff? Broadcast my address on the national news?" Turned out the lawman had 'borrowed' her cup the day he'd interviewed her and run a search on her fingerprints.

Talbot glowered at her, his golden eyes narrowed over a pudgy nose. "I never gave out your address to anyone, ma'am, not even my deputies. The feds jumped all over me the second I put in a request for the fingerprint ID." He gave a short disappointed laugh. "Thought I'd caught another Unabomber."

Nat loaded four rounds into his rifle, sliding each one in smoothly. He held the rounds down with his thumb and slipped in a fifth, closed the bolt.

Eliza gripped her mug harder, looked away before he caught her staring. "What now, Marsh? If I don't get out of here soon, innocent people could get hurt."

Nat straightened away from the wall, placed the rifle on a rack above the door. "You're not going anywhere."

His gaze pinned her where she sat and for a second her heart stopped. Why didn't he understand that he was one person she would never risk? She forced her expression to remain impassive. Cold.

"You don't understand—" she began.

"Don't patronize me." Nat's tone inflexible and clipped. He raised himself to his full height and rested his hands on his leather belt. Warm and tender Nat was gone. Big and pissed Nat was in his place. "I understand just fine. You've got some bastard after you and you're too stubborn to let anybody help."

Unable to remain still, she sprang up from her chair, had to maintain the perpetual motion that kept the demons at bay. "The mob doesn't just give up and forget, you know. They'll kill anyone who gets in their way."

She paced the kitchen floor, needing more space, unable to breathe properly or think quickly enough. Too many people...why didn't they understand? "What about Sarah? Tabitha? *You* for Christ's sake!"

"They can go away for a little while." His gaze was resolute as if the decision had already been made.

"No." Elizabeth dragged her hands through her hair, clasped her skull with rigid fingers. "I will not screw up other people's lives like this. I will not put other people at risk from that monster."

"But you'll screw up your own life? Mine?" Nat spoke so softly she had to stop pacing to hear him. Reluctantly she turned to face him, hypnotized as he stepped towards her. "Ours?"

Tears made it hard to see.

How could he think they had a chance of a future together? She was as good as dead. If she didn't get out of here soon, he could be too.

Nat stood quietly, patiently, waiting for her answer.

"Don't you understand?" The tears brimmed over, ran down her cheeks and dripped onto her shirt. "I don't want you to die."

Nat took the remaining step to touch her, cupped her face with his hands and wiped at the tears with his thumbs. His hands were warm and comforting. She gazed up at him, knew her vulnerability was exposed like a raw nerve.

"I've never had anything to lose before," she whispered.

"Leave now and he's won. Hurt you—again. Scared you—again. Beaten you—again." Eyes darkened to midnight, a smile curved his lips, but his expression was lost. "Look around. You have people here who want to help you, who *care* about you. Don't throw it all away just because of what he did to you."

She pressed her hand against his heart, cherished the solid beat beneath her palm. Stalling for time she traced the edge of a mother-of-pearl button and moved to touch the "v" of skin that was just visible. She tried to block out his words. Tried to distract him with her touch.

He grabbed her hand and held it still. "You can't run away forever. No matter how frightening it is to stand and fight. You said yourself we don't always get to make the choices we want."

Startled, she jerked her hand away as her eyes flew to his. He was thinking about his mother, she realized. His pain was still sharp and fresh. *It wasn't fair.* He shouldn't have to deal with this now, shouldn't have to deal with her problems on top of his grief.

Nat stared into her eyes and read her thoughts. "I will *not* let you go." He glanced up, caught Ryan's eye. "Take Tabitha and Sarah into town. Cal and Ezra too."

Cal straightened from his position against the

wall. "I'm not going anywhere."

"You can't stay here—" Eliza said.

"I owe you." Cal never took his eyes off the sheriff. "I pay my debts."

Talbot stiffened. "You ain't carrying a gun."

Cal gave a dark laugh and stared the sheriff down. "I don't need a gun."

Ryan argued too, despite his red-rimmed eyes and weary as hell expression. "I could take them to Atty Willard's," he said. "Come back here and help."

"No." Nat's tone was flat and firm. "I need to know they're safe, really safe, no matter what happens."

"What about Mom's funeral?" Ryan didn't look fit to drive a car, let alone handle a gun.

"It can wait a couple of days." Nat must have thought it through. "Rose would have wanted us to help Eliza."

"I'm staying." Sarah stood in the doorway. "I want to help too." Tabitha clutched at Sarah's knee, watched the adults with wide blue eyes.

"No," Nat and Elizabeth said together.

"You might need a doctor..."

"No." Elizabeth was fierce. She didn't want to put anyone else at risk. Marsh shook his head, and stood.

Sarah crossed her hands over her chest, ignored the feds and concentrated on her brother. "This is my home."

Elizabeth was quiet. Sarah was right and she should leave. The pressure of Nat's fingers on her shoulder stopped her from going anywhere, and then he hunkered down and held out his arms for Tabitha. The little girl eyed the strangers warily, then let go of her aunt's pant leg and ran to her uncle.

Nat swung the child high up into the air and gave her a kiss. "Hey, Tiger. Wanna go get a treat from the toy store?"

Tabitha smiled, and grabbed his ear with a small hand. Nat caught her fist, held it gently within his own and kissed the delicate dimpled fingers.

"She needs you," Nat told his sister. He turned to where his brother peered determinedly into his coffee mug. "You might not think so, but she needs you too."

For a moment, Elizabeth thought Ryan was going to refuse. He sat immobile, his shoulders stiff and his mouth twisted. Then he took a mouthful of coffee, swallowed and nodded. Finally, he pushed his mug away and walked over to where his daughter hung from Nat's shoulder. Ryan's hands shook as he took hold of his little girl. Whether from the DTs or some other unnamed emotion, Elizabeth couldn't tell.

"Come on, kid. We're going for a ride." Ryan reached over and pressed a quick kiss to Elizabeth's cheek, turned on his booted heel and walked away.

Sarah stared mutinously at her older brother who stood surrounded by strangers in their dead mother's kitchen. She must have read purpose in Nat's stance and the stubborn thrust of his chin because she sighed, shook her head and gave in. She walked over to where Elizabeth stood and gave her a quick hug. The move was so natural, so eloquent, and so unexpected that Elizabeth didn't have time to react before Sarah threw her arms around her brother's neck and kissed him too.

"Be careful," Sarah warned with a tight hug

before following Ryan down the hall.

Elizabeth watched her go, hating herself for being the cause of such disruption to innocent lives. She noticed the silence and looked around. Nat, Cal, Marsh and the sheriff were all watching her.

Alarm crawled up her spine and spilled into her mouth like bile. It seemed the poor little orphan had finally found a place to call home and she was staying, whether she liked it or not.

Unease nudged her conscience as she thought about the assassin she'd hired. He was her backup plan, her failsafe incase DeLattio or the mob got to her first. Her contract had been simple. When DeLattio was free, kill him. She just hoped the assassin got to DeLattio before DeLattio got to the ranch.

***

Stone Creek, Montana, April 16th

"What the fuck are we doing here?" Charlie rubbed chubby fingers across his balding scalp.

DeLattio hunched down in the seat next beside him, a leather ball cap wedged tightly on his head. The waistband of his jeans dug into his gut and the leather jacket was stiff with newness. Charlie was dressed in a snappy gray suit and wouldn't even take off his jacket. He looked like a gangster. Even driving a Dodge Caravan around Montana, he looked like a freaking gangster.

So much for *incognito.*

Charlie wasn't happy. He thought they'd be heading straight to the Cayman Isles. The older man figured Andrew should forget about Juliette

Morgan—or rather, Elizabeth Ward—but Charlie figured wrong. Andrew had a guy inside the FBI who'd been feeding him information for years. The agent had told him some Podunk sheriff in Montana had requested an ID on fingerprints that turned out to belong to the woman who'd made such a fool of him. So rather than leaving the States they'd flown out west in a small plane and were going to the town where she'd been last seen. Andrew didn't care how long it took. He would find her. He would teach her that he kept his promises.

Rubbing his hands along the length of his thighs, Andrew sucked a breath through his teeth.

Elizabeth Ward.

Nice name for a dead bitch.

A willowy blonde struggled with the gas nozzle as she tried to fill a rental car. She was hot and Andrew toyed with going over to help—his dick twitching as she bent over to pick up the gas cap. But someone might recognize him and gas stations always had hidden cameras.

Andrew flinched as Charlie's cell phone rang and all thoughts of the blonde evaporated as Charlie stuck the phone to his ear.

Charlie pulled out a pen and scrawled across the top of a newspaper that was spread awkwardly over the steering wheel. He thrust the paper at Andrew, started the engine then paused as he too noticed the blonde. "Well, look at that."

"What?" Andrew asked. A fat smile curled Charlie's lips, the first in some time. Andrew sat up, gripped the edge of the dash. "*What?*"

"Remember I told you some broad pretended to be Juliette Morgan when she first disappeared? That we whacked her old man, but missed her?"

315

"Yeah." Andrew remembered, but still didn't get it.

Charlie nodded toward the blonde as she headed into the filling station to pay for her gas. "That's her. That's the broad."

***

Elizabeth avoided Nat's eyes and tucked her Glock into the back of her waistband. Mexican carry. With her luck she'd probably shoot herself in the ass. The Kevlar vest she wore under her sweatshirt meant she couldn't use her shoulder holster. Dancer had loaned her another SIG, which she wore as a sidearm.

This wasn't what she'd planned.

Her breath funneled out as she realized the bastard might not even show up. How pathetic was that? But instinct told her otherwise, DeLattio wasn't known for his patience.

The light had started to fade. Storm clouds blocked out the last of the rays of the sun. The kitchen clock ticked loudly against the silence that stretched thin between her and Nat.

He watched her, but said nothing.

Adrenaline hummed through her bloodstream, made her edgy and her hands shake. She rested her palms on the edge of the sink, forced herself to calm down and took two deep breaths. The phone rang and her heart damned near stopped.

She checked the number on her cell, relaxed a little as she answered. "Josie?"

"Did you miss me?" His voice was pure malevolence, noxious and deadly, diseased with evil.

Dread immobilized her spine as nausea robbed her of speech. DeLattio's face splashed through her mind as clear and sharp as a photograph. She sagged against the countertop, watched Nat rise and come towards her.

He touched her arm, a tentative squeeze of support and she drew on his strength, fighting to find her voice and smother the panic that welled up like blood in a wound.

"Where's Josie?"

"You never told me you had such pretty friends. Tut. Tut." The bastard's laugh mocked her, just as it had all those months ago. "And a blonde too. I thought I liked redheads best, but maybe not. But then you're not a natural redhead are you...Elizabeth?"

She couldn't move. Her lips cracked open and words spilled out. "You don't want her. You want me."

Nat's grip tightened on her arm, but she ignored him. DeLattio snickered and she didn't know if she could hold it together.

"You're wrong." For a moment she heard nothing but the rough draw of his breath. "I do want her."

He was touching Josephine. She knew it—could almost feel the slide of his hand—and knew that one wrong word, one misstep and Josephine was dead. Elizabeth gritted her teeth together to stop herself from begging, because begging didn't work.

"But I want *you* more."

Strong arms wrapped around her as if to hold her up. When had her legs stopped working?

"We'll do a swap. I'm on my way to you right now." DeLattio said. "Two minutes. If I see anybody else, I kill the blonde." He hung up, his words echoing in the silence.

Reeling, she looked up at Nat. His face was grim, distorted.

"He's got my friend Josie." Her voice was fragile. She had no time to waste, no time to plan. "He's here. He wants to swap her for me."

How did he get Josie? How long had he had her? Blood tasted sickly in her mouth. She choked it down and cursed the day she'd met Andrew DeLattio.

Palms damp, heart racing, she dialed Marsh, gave him the update, and told him to keep out of sight. She rang off before he could reply.

Nat lifted his rifle off the rack and stuffed a box of ammunition in his back pocket before he cycled the bolt. He looked up and met her gaze.

Headlights swept down the hill behind the house, lit up the dim interior of the kitchen as the car swung into the yard. Elizabeth stared at the door. He was here. Andrew DeLattio was right here outside that door. Lightheaded, she swallowed, touched her hand to the hard jut of the gun that pressed against her spine. She flicked a glance at Nat.

"I have to go," she said.

Taking a step closer, he grabbed her arm. "No. I won't let you."

"I *have* to." Her emotions threatened to swamp her. She had to save Josie. She forced herself to stand straighter and look him in the eye. "I got her into this mess. This is my fault."

Tension crackled to breaking point between them.

"You're not God, Eliza." Nat's hand dropped

away, his blue eyes bleak, desolate, but grimly determined. "You're not responsible for the whole goddamned world."

The van idled in the yard. She could hear the engine thrum quietly like a drum march to her death. Headlights poured into the main house, dazzling them even as they stood in the shadows looking at one another. Maybe for the last time.

Nat's expression turned mean, the planes of his face rigid with bitterness. "Eliza—"

"No." She cupped his cheek with her palm. Pressed a quick kiss to his unrelenting lips. She didn't want it to end this way. "I know I'm not God, but I am responsible for this."

She turned away and braced herself for goodbye. She couldn't endure a lingering farewell—she'd already proven she wasn't strong enough to let him go. Glancing over her shoulder, she nodded towards the rifle. "How good are you with that thing, really?"

"Freakin' deadeye." His eyes gleamed in the darkness. He didn't say another word, no begging, no pleading; he just slid deeper into the shadows.

"I love you." She mouthed the words softly, knowing he couldn't hear her, but needing to say them out loud just once.

She gave him a few heartbeats to get into position and then eased the door ajar. The air smelled like a storm, rain drumming down, electricity crackling through the twilight like a living thing.

The car idled, steam pouring off its hood. Elizabeth opened the kitchen door wide and stood exposed in the beams of the headlights. He might shoot her now but she was betting on a more hands-on ending to his little game.

The car's passenger door was pushed open and DeLattio thrust Josie out ahead of him, using her as a human shield. The car protected his back. He knotted a hand in Josie's hair and dragged her back against him.

Elizabeth's flesh crawled as she looked at him. His handsome face was swarthy and harsh, his wet hair plastered black against his skull. Her personal demon. A laugh bubbled up inside, putting a hysterical smile on her face. He'd always looked like the devil to her. Judging from his bulky frame, the sly son of a bitch wore body armor. They'd need a head shot to take him out.

But DeLattio wasn't going anywhere, she reminded herself. He had at least four guns trained on him and he wasn't going to win this last battle. She'd live or die, but she wouldn't die in vain.

DeLattio stuck a pistol under Josie's chin and Eliza's stomach slammed into her mouth. Josie's head was forced back, her eyes rolling to reveal a mixture of horror and defiance. She threw Eliza an apologetic smile—as if it were her fault they were in this mess. Elizabeth tried to smile back, but it was just a jumbled quiver of lips.

"We meet again," DeLattio shouted over the rain.

Elizabeth blocked out her fears, blocked out his arrogance and worked on autopilot. She stood with her hands loose at her sides, ready to move. "Let her go."

DeLattio shook his head and smiled. "I don't think so. You come out here first, *Elizabeth.*"

Nausea curled in her stomach, hot and greasy. Hearing him say her name was like giving control of her soul to the dark-side. Shivering, she ignored the tiny pellets of rain that stung her skin as she moved out into the open. Drenched within seconds, she was glad of the excuse to shiver. Water streamed down her face and weighed down her clothes like lead.

Josie staggered and cried out. DeLattio jerked her back against him with a tight fistful of hair.

Striding forward, Eliza forced control over her fear-drenched body. Holding Josie's gaze she flickered her eyes to the ground on Josie's right and tried to plant the thought inside her head.

"Let her go," she said again. "She's done nothing to you."

"But you have, bitch. *You* set me up." Andrew hoisted Josie closer and she whimpered. "Throw down the gun." He nodded towards Elizabeth's sidearm.

Elizabeth shook her head, but he tightened his hold on Josie's hair and she cried out in pain. The sound cut through her. Why had she ever allowed Josie to become involved in her mess? She unsnapped the holster, withdrew the weapon and placed it on the ground.

"Did you miss me, Elizabeth?" DeLattio taunted. "Do you think about the night I fucked you stupid? When you begged me for more?"

She'd begged him to stop.

Her eyes betrayed her thoughts and his smile reflected her revulsion.

Elizabeth blocked out his face and his words and thought instead of Nat. She needed to give him a clear shot so he could blow this bastard away. She forced herself past the hood of the car, circling DeLattio to give Nat a better target. She didn't want to die, but it looked like she might have to. DeLattio turned to watch her.

That's it, you bastard. Just give him a shot.

Andrew didn't want her dead. Not yet. Not until he'd had his revenge and a repeat performance. It was weird, but it didn't scare her anymore. She just wanted it to end. And she wanted him dead. Elizabeth inched closer, only an arm's length away. She could feel the fury vibrating from him so powerfully she could actually smell it.

The bastard shoved Josie away, kicked her so hard she went flying into the mud, and then lunged for Elizabeth. He caught her by the throat with one hand and squeezed. Desperate, she scrabbled behind her back for the other weapon, chest burning with the need for oxygen, but she couldn't reach it. *One more try, Elizabeth. Don't let the son of a bitch beat you now.*

He grabbed her arm, wrenched it way up between her shoulder blades and ground his hips against hers like a lover. Panic assaulted her, every fiber going rigid with fear. She couldn't breathe, couldn't suck in a single drop of air. Her fingers were numb and nerveless, her vision beginning to gray. Finally the grip on her throat eased, allowing the smallest amount of breath to leak through. The burning in her throat lessened, her arm was stretched painfully tight but no longer wrenched from its socket. The hand around her throat did a slow, stomach curling glide against fragile skin, then DeLattio slid the cold muzzle of his Beretta flush against her temple. He smiled. *Perfect lips, perfect teeth. No soul.*

Elizabeth's gaze flickered awkwardly to where her friend lay twisted in the mud. "Go to the house,

Josie."

DeLattio glanced over as Josie struggled to her feet.

"Run," Elizabeth urged. The man in front of her would kill just for the fun of it and the pale glimmer in his eyes told Elizabeth he was already thinking about it.

Josie scrambled towards the house—right into Nat's line of fire.

Shit.

DeLattio's eyes turned black with malice and he adjusted his grip on his gun. Elizabeth spat in his face, flinched as raw fury scoured her. He raised his gun into the air for a fraction of a second and she knew he was going to kill her. No reprieve, no repeat performance, no dance.

She grabbed his arm, held the gun upwards and kneed him in the groin so hard she lifted him up off the ground. She wasn't drugged now, the son of a bitch.

A bullet ripped out, shattered the windshield beside her.

She yanked the Beretta out of DeLattio's fingers and flung it hard beyond the fence. Still holding his hand, she twisted his fingers in a parody of affection, then kicked him in the kidneys. Hatred filled her as she watched him go down, rolling in agony. Using her boot she flipped him onto his back, straddled him, her knees sinking into the cold wet mud, her hand wrapped tight around his windpipe.

Elizabeth had no trouble retrieving her gun this time. She pulled it free, stuck it in his mouth and DeLattio flinched as the metal struck his teeth.

Revenge had never felt so glorious or

redemption so far away.

Her lips curled into a smile that stretched her skin tight. "What do you think, Andrew? How do you like it?"

Blood drained from his face and his pale eyes went wide with the knowledge that he was about to die. Why shouldn't she kill him?

A blur of movement at the edge of her vision caught her attention. Marsh stood watching her.

"It's not worth it, Elizabeth."

"Isn't it?" She never took her eyes off her prey. She craved his death so badly the idea was like a drug in her system. She just had to squeeze...she just had to squeeze...she just had to squeeze the goddamned trigger.

Puzzled, she studied her finger.

She couldn't do it. Why the hell couldn't she do it?

Slowly, reluctantly, she drew the gun back an inch. Her hands shook as she tightened her grip.

She saw the exact moment DeLattio realized she couldn't kill him. A feral light entered his eyes and he sneered, cruel lips drawn up against pearl white teeth. "Whore."

She fired a shot, blasted the dirt next to his head. The noise was deafening, but she fired another round at the other side of his skull and hoped his eardrums met in the center and detonated.

Rolling off him, her ears ringing with a high-pitched screech, she staggered away, stumbling and tripping when her feet didn't work. Marsh could deal with the bastard, she never wanted to see him again.

She kept moving, breathing shallow pants that grounded her. An emotion suspiciously like forgiveness, swelled in her chest. Not for him—but for herself. Nat was ahead of her, illuminated in the headlights, rushing out of the house with his rifle in hand, everything good and right with her world. He smiled, those gorgeous eyes crinkling with relief, before going wide in alarm as his gaze slid beyond her. His face shouted a warning, but no sound penetrated her world.

She turned as if in slow motion, her heart beating so loud in her ears she knew the precise moment it stumbled. She toppled back from the impact, pain like a thousand volts of electricity bursting through her leg.

Why hadn't she searched him for a backup weapon? A rookie mistake, one drilled into her at the academy. *Stupid, stupid mistake.*

Her thoughts dulled, slowed like ice.

DeLattio grinned, mud streaking his face as he lay on the ground. He aimed the gun beyond her to Nat and she screamed, her heart pounding with almighty fury as she tried to raise her weapon.

DeLattio's face was taken off by a high velocity bullet that shattered his skull on impact.

Part of her wanted to cheer. Part of her wanted to raise her arms into the air and chant a Hallelujah chorus, but then the pain was too great, white-hot spikes of agony, driven deep into her body, laced with mercury, acid and poison.

DeLattio's blasted features seared her vision. She did not want to meet him in hell.

Where was Nat? Was he hit? Where was he?

Then she saw him, the man who meant everything to her. The man who'd made her feel whole after a lifetime of being broken. The man who'd given her a chance at happiness even though she was condemned to misery.

"I love you." She hoped the words came out. Hoped he could hear her even though her ears were still ringing and pain blocked her senses. She tried to lift her hand and stroke the rough line of his jaw, wanted to erase the anguish that sparked in the depths of his eyes, but she couldn't get her hands to work properly.

She wanted to thank him for loving her. He hadn't said the words, but she knew. No one had ever loved her like that before. Regret tugged at her as he was pushed aside and Marsh tried to stem the flow of blood. It was too late. She tried to move her lips into a smile, into a phrase of solace that would let them forgive themselves—and maybe her. Then the darkness came. She fought the sensation until her eyes couldn't fight it anymore. Peace and a hazy contentment had her drifting away where pain couldn't reach her anymore.

Chapter Twenty

"Eliza!" Nat shouted so loud his chest hurt. "Eliza!"

Blood soaked the front of her thigh, darkened her jeans to black. He sat useless, gripping her shoulders as Marshall Hayes ripped off his belt and used it to tourniquet the top of Eliza's leg.

"Got a knife on you?"

Nat fumbled in his pocket and pulled out the tool he kept there. He'd been too late, too slow to save Eliza.

Marsh passed him the end of the belt. "Pull tight."

Numbly, Nat pulled, watched the other man lean down to put an extra hole in the strap. He tried not to stare at the flesh that gaped, or the sheen of shattered bone that worked its way through the pooling crimson. The hard edge of leather bit into his hand and the bleeding slowed. But the blood was *everywhere*. Hands, face, legs, arms, ground. Spread like syrup across the Kevlar vest that she wore for protection.

Wordlessly, he took the tool back from Marsh's hand and slipped it in his pocket, released his grip on the belt. Nat said a quick prayer as he watched the shallow rise and fall of Eliza's chest, a reflexive jerk as her lungs demanded oxygen.

She was breathing, just.

Please, God, let her live.

Her face was pale, so pale he thought she was

fading away. *Christ.* He touched her cheek, licked his thumb and wiped away a fleck of dirt. Her flesh was warm, soft. His fingers shook as he cupped her cheek. He'd never told her he loved her. Not once had he said the words. Fear had held them back, kept them locked up, he'd been too goddamned scared to tell her.

"I love you, Eliza." He brushed the hair off her forehead and kissed her. "Don't you die on me. I love you."

Cal stood behind him, placed a hand on his shoulder in support. The blonde woman rushed over and fell to her knees beside them in the mud. Nat wanted to scream that this was all her fault, but he knew better. He glanced over to the corpse of the man who'd terrorized Eliza and wished he'd been the one to take the shot.

Marsh pulled out a cell phone, turned it on and swore. "How long does it take an EMT to get here?" He shoved the useless phone back into his pocket. Stared at the blonde who wept in the dirt.

"Too goddamn long." Why had he sent Sarah away? Shaking his head, he bent to pick up Eliza.

"No." Marsh seized his arm, ignored his flat-eyed stare. "Don't move her. We need to splint her leg first."

Nat slumped back on his heels. He closed his eyes and squeezed away the tears. "It can take an hour sometimes." They needed a miracle.

"Damn it." Marsh looked around. He grabbed a couple of planks that rested against the side of the house. "I need rope or some tape. Then get some blankets and your truck..." Marsh focused his attention on Cal, as if he'd already figured out Nat was incapable of action.

Eliza was dying. Nat just wanted to be touching her when she did.

***

County General Hospital, April 17th

Nat couldn't sit or stand still. Dread kept him moving. When he stopped even for a second, his sanity started to burst. When he closed his eyes, all he could see were his hands trying to stem the flow of Eliza's blood and despite his efforts, it pumped out of her irretrievably.

Bracing his arms against the wall, he said, "What the hell is happening in there?"

The nurses ignored him. Doctors went on their way, treating patients and saving lives. He pushed away from the wall, slumped down in a brown box-like chair, rested his hands on his knees and leaned back. Stood up. Unable to keep still. Unable to bear the sight of his blood-stained jeans. Tunneling a hand through his hair, he loosened the dirt that caked it, brushed it onto the gray linoleum floor. Frustration and fear mixed within him, a cocktail of despair. He clenched his fists, his jaw. Stared up at the ceiling as if the gray tiles could give him answers. He'd spent way too much time in hospitals waiting for people he cared about to die.

Sarah was observing in the OR. They were trying to stop the bleeding and pin Eliza's shattered femur back together. He'd given blood. Shit, he always gave blood, but it never seemed to save the ones he loved.

Nat glanced down at his clothes. He was filthy and raw. Hell, he must look like a lunatic, but the only thing he cared about was Eliza fighting for her life on the operating table. Cal rose from his seat, laid a hand on his arm that was meant to comfort. Nat shrugged it away, unable to bear the thought of solace in such a desolate place. Cal moved away to the window, his mouth tugged down by worry.

Was this how Ryan felt? Nat massaged his thumb across the palm of his other hand. Was this why he lost himself in alcohol and sex? Ezra was here too, waiting for news like the rest of them. Nat didn't know when Eliza had stopped being a guest and had become, instead, a part of the family, but Ezra's crinkled old face was in his hands as he slumped in the chair.

The feds were gone, filling out reports and helping the locals process the crime scene. Abandoning Eliza in her hour of need. Again. He twisted a magazine in his hands.

Josephine Maxwell had gone with them. Nat didn't know if she went willingly or not, but he was glad she wasn't waiting here with him. He hated the fact it was Eliza and not her in the OR. It didn't make him proud, but he'd deal with that later. Right now he'd bargain with the devil himself to keep Eliza alive. His heart felt like a blade of ice, his head a volcano about to explode, and all he could feel was a premonition of death.

If only he'd been quicker this would never have happened. If only…

A flurry of activity started around the nurse's station as the night-shift buzzed around in organized chaos. A nurse approached him, someone he'd never seen before. A large African-American woman with big brown eyes and hair cut close to her skull. Kind eyes. *So why do I want to run away from her?* She was going to tell him Eliza was dead. That was why.

"Come this way, Mr. Sullivan."

He followed her like a small obedient child.

She led him through the double-doors at the end of the hall and down a gleaming corridor lined with glass windows. Nat hated hospitals, the smell, the lights, the concrete walls. She took his hand, wrapped large warm fingers around his. Nat closed his eyes not wanting to look through the window.

"She's alive, Mr. Sullivan, but barely."

Surprise blasted his eyes wide open and he gazed through the glass. Eliza lay swathed in bandages, a cast. Her skin was pale against the crisp white sheets. Drips and tubes flowed into her body and monitors beeped and buzzed with a frail life force.

She looked waxen and fragile, *but she was alive.*

"It was a clean break. The bullet passed straight through the bone, but the artery needed work. She's lost a lot of blood and is in very serious condition. If she lasts the night..."

Nat stared, didn't realize he'd slumped against the glass until the nurse patted him gently on the back.

"We gave her a transfusion and she's stabilized, but we'll have to monitor her constantly until she's out of danger—"

"Can I sit with her?" Nat cut in. Embers of hope stirred in his chest and he needed to touch the woman he loved.

The nurse wrinkled her nose and narrowed her gaze over his dirty clothes. "Well, normally it's relatives only..."

"Please." Nat would beg on his hands and knees

if he had to.

"As you're Dr Sullivan's brother I suppose so." She eyed him up and down, chewing a ruby lip as she considered his destiny. No one was keeping him out of that room; he jutted out his jaw and stood tall.

The nurse seemed to sense his determination. "Look, she's still unconscious from the anesthetic and will be for the next little while, and she's going to be weak." The nurse pursed her lips and made a decision. "Come with me," she ordered.

Nat glanced back at the pale figure with her dark hair fanned out on the pillow. Reluctantly, he followed the nurse to a shower room in the doctors' quarters, and she gave him a clean set of scrubs.

Ten minutes later, fresh and clean, he followed the nurse back down the spotless corridor. He ignored the antiseptic smell, the dull whisper of the nurse's soft-soled shoes. Hope was beginning to trickle into him and he didn't intend to let it go.

Entering the double-doors of the ICU, he looked at Eliza. Swallowing hard, he went and stood on the left-hand side of the bed and looked down at her face. She was so very pale, her skin almost transparent in the subdued lighting of the ward. Her heartbeat thumped steadily on the monitor and she had tubes running into her nose and arms. She wore a hospital gown, the sheet pulled up high across her thigh. A glistening white cast encased her leg. Nat reached out a finger, stroked her hair and tucked a stray curl behind a perfect ear. He pulled her limp, cool hand into his and sat down next to the bed.

"Don't you die on me, Eliza." His voice was gruff. He ran the tips of his fingers lightly across her temple. And suddenly it didn't matter he had nothing to offer her. It didn't matter she'd been going to leave him. Now he knew why, and he wished to God he'd let her go.

"I love you, Eliza. Please don't die."

***

Marsh stood over the remains of Andrew DeLattio as they zipped up the body bag. The bullet had entered his left temple, exited through the right and obliterated everything in between. Marsh felt no grief or remorse, just a cold sense of justice that the bastard was finally off the streets.

Andrew DeLattio couldn't hurt anyone else.

Charlie Corelli had been killed by that first shot through the windshield, and his body carted away to the morgue. Dancer had used the dead men's cell phones to uncover the identity of an agent who'd transferred from New York to Quantico about a year ago. The guy had been feeding DeLattio information in exchange for regular contributions to his personal pension fund. He'd already been picked up by his colleagues at the training academy and charged. Marsh let out a sigh, stuck his hands in his pockets and looked up at the sky. Sun was rising on a new day. Thin streaks of red, pink and gold blooded the sky in ribbons of melting color.

Eliza was out of surgery and the doctors were optimistic for a complete recovery. But it was all his fault she got shot in the first place.

The chill found his skin beneath his shirt and jacket, made the hairs on his chest contract. He rubbed his arms to ward off the cold, stared up at Eliza's cabin at the edge of the trees and across towards the horse barn. Wherever the shooter had been it had been a damned fine shot. *Peter Uri. Had to be.* No one else could have pulled it off.

Elizabeth hadn't been the assassin's target. DeLattio had.

Marsh hadn't even twigged there was another shooter until after they'd got to the hospital, and by then Uri would have been long gone. Elizabeth had still been fighting for her life.

Marsh held his emotions in check, betraying no outward sign of distress. Josephine Maxwell had completely screwed with his brain.

Uri had fulfilled his contract only yards from a bunch of law enforcement personnel and no one had even noticed. Marsh flexed his fists. His breath curled up in a cloud of vapor and floated away like a wraith. Uri was famed for his ingenuity, discretion, and high prices; a regular high-flyer on America's Most Wanted list. But the FBI couldn't catch him and Marsh had to wonder if there was a reason behind that. Did the FBI use Uri for their own purposes? Uri had known where DeLattio was going to be before DeLattio had even known. How had that happened? Leak? Or insider information?

Marsh had a horrible suspicion he knew.

Sidling away from the sheriff and deputies who stood around talking loudly, excited by the day's happenings, Marsh ambled toward the pasture where a couple of chestnut horses grazed. Just a man taking some time to recoup after a long night. He lit a cigarette, tilted his head back and expelled the first lungful of smoke up into the air. Like he hadn't a care in the world.

But his mind was racing. He climbed the fence and slowly began scanning the siding of the big orange barn. His feet sank into the grass, morning dew soaking his pant legs and seeping into his expensive shoes. His toes curled against the sensation of wet sock.

One of the horses trotted over, head held high, white nose outstretched. Marsh stroked the soft velvet whiskers as his other hand rubbed across the wood of the barn, brushed away some flakes of paint and moved on. The horse followed, curious and affable, seemingly eager for human companionship.

The local sheriff was running the show and Marsh had no desire to take over the investigation.

Cut and dried, wasn't it? We shot the bastard. Didn't we?

Sheriff Talbot had never heard of Peter Uri and Marsh hadn't enlightened him. Marsh walked along the side of the barn, the horse following two paces behind. Half buried in the dirt a soft glint of copper caught his eye, reflecting the oblique rays of sunshine. The bullet that had traversed DeLattio's brain.

Marsh lived his life following every nuance of the law. Chain of evidence was a major part of that process. Stooping to tie his shoelace, he surreptitiously bagged the bullet and placed it in his pocket. Maybe the mob had hired Uri. Maybe DeLattio's source inside the FBI had worked more than one angle and had gotten the address in Stone Creek faster than he and Dancer had, and surreptitiously passed it on to Peter Uri.

But then again maybe not.

Catching a movement out of the corner of his eye, he turned to see Josephine padding across the field toward him, tracking a second line through the sodden grass. Silently he cursed. He didn't need this. Inside his jacket pockets his hands curled into fists and the muscles around his mouth tightened.

Last night, when Elizabeth had told him over the phone that DeLattio had kidnapped Josephine, he'd gagged. It had been Marsh's fault Josephine had been taken. *His* fault. His stomach had twisted until it was dry.

And when DeLattio had been lying defeated in the mud and muck, the sheer relief of knowing Josephine was safe had blurred his instincts and given DeLattio the split-second he'd needed to pull the other gun. Everything had happened in slow motion and Eliza had nearly lost her life because of his incompetence.

Narrowing his eyes he fought his reaction to the woman who'd caused him more grief than a thousand stolen Mona Lisa's. Josephine sure as hell hadn't turned to him afterward the shooting. She'd given him a look that could sour milk and retreated behind her ice-princess façade.

He smiled at her, but inside he felt empty.

"I bet you think you're pretty clever getting here before me." Dressed in black leggings and a red sweater that rose to her chin, her fingers gripped each other in an intricate web.

"Sure, I wake up every morning thinking just that." He put a glint in his eye to suggest one morning in particular.

She swerved away, avoided his gaze like a car avoiding a head-on collision.

He provoked her some more, a defense mechanism as old as apples. "You should have told me you were a virgin, Josephine. I would have taken it easier on you."

Her gaze swung back to his, embarrassment and indignation on full beam. "What do you mean

336

easier on me?"

"Do you think it counts as date rape?" Marsh mused, taking a step towards her. He couldn't explain the pleasure of seeing her jaw drop or her cheeks pale, but he got a weird kind of satisfaction from pissing her off. Better that than indifference, or pity.

She gritted her teeth. "You were like a dog after a bitch."

"Oh, yeah, I remember that vaguely—the bitch part anyway." He grinned as her fury bubbled to the surface and exploded.

"You're an arrogant bastard. No wonder I can't stand you." Her voice rang out in the clear morning, made the sheriff and his deputies glance over. Marsh flinched, masked his expression before she spotted any weakness.

"So, are you going to arrest me?" She was breathing hard, shoulders rising and falling in short sharp jerks. She held her wrists together, veins upward, in front of her and he was sorely tempted to cuff her. He took a stride toward her, but she backed off a couple of steps.

Not as confident as she appeared then...or maybe she really did hate him.

"Mr. By-the-Book." Her pale blue eyes glittered in an expression of disgust. "That's why Elizabeth didn't turn to you after the rape. You'd have never..." She clamped her lips shut, seemed to realize she'd said too much.

"Yeah?" The question was lazy, like honey in a jar. "Never what?" He walked up to her until he was so close he could have touched her. He leaned down so his lips hovered near her ear. She stood her ground, but her pupils dilated in alarm.

Keeping his voice low he said, "Never realized that Elizabeth hired an assassin to kill DeLattio? Never figure out that she lured DeLattio here to his death?"

"She didn't lure that bastard *here*." Josephine's eyes widened and she shook her head. "She didn't know where it would happen."

He laughed, a harsh bitter sound that had her mouth opening and shutting like a stressed fish. Her surprise didn't last long. The expression on her face turned stubborn, the way it had before she'd given him the silent treatment for twenty-four hours straight. "You can't prove anything anyway."

"Dream on little girl." He tweaked her nose and brushed past her, moving away from her scent and her beauty. He might want her, but she'd never want him and he wasn't going to put himself through that misery. Turning around he walked backward, away from the only woman he'd ever truly desired. "Let me know if you're pregnant."

Her face drained of color, even her lips turned milky.

"I want to know." He stopped and watched her until she nodded, and then he turned away. Josephine Maxwell was a mistake he never intended to repeat. Vaulting the gate, he signaled to Dancer who'd watched the whole exchange from the deck of the house. Marsh needed to see Elizabeth. Josephine could look after her own ass from now on.

***

Eliza came to through a whirl of sensations that felt like she was floating. *Was this heaven?* Surely heaven wouldn't smell so strongly of disinfectant and overcooked bed linen?

Had to be a hospital. *And a shit load of pain meds.*

A beeping noise irritated her, until she cracked her eyelid and realized it was her ECG. All of a sudden it didn't bother her so much. Unbelievably, she was alive. Her heart pounded and she heard it echoed in the pace of the machine. Forcing herself to breathe steadily, she relaxed her fingers one at a time.

The horror of the night before stumbled through her mind like a fast-forwarded movie. She'd thought she was dead. She'd thought she'd lost Nat. But there he was fast asleep, slumped with his head next to her arm on the bed. Rumpled and tired. His chair pulled as close to the bed as it was possible to get. Raising her hand, she ran it through his blond hair that glistened in the morning sun. She shifted uncomfortably as a thousand daggers stabbed her leg.

She groaned, though maybe it was a whimper. Nat jerked awake, nearly falling off the chair in confusion. Recovering quickly, he gave her the biggest, widest smile she'd ever seen.

"Hi," she croaked.

"Hi, yourself." He grinned back. Slowly, he leaned over and kissed her on the mouth. "How do you feel?"

"Like some bastard shot me in the leg and I nearly died." She regretted the humor when she saw him pale.

"Hey," she grabbed his hand, rubbed the calloused palm with weak fingers, "I'm okay."

He looked down at their clasped hands and

squeezed. "You are so much better than *okay*, Eliza."

Emotions squeezed her throat and she blinked back the tears that wanted to flow. Good tears this time.

"I've got a question for you," he said, suddenly serious.

"What is it?"

He picked up the control that raised and lowered her bed. Pressed the button that gently raised her legs higher. "Nurse showed me how to do this. Said it would be good for you once you woke up." He looked out of the windows towards the nurses' station, guilt written in every line of his forehead. "I was supposed to call them when you woke up..." He shrugged and pressed the button again.

She could feel the cast tugging on the stitches, nothing major, just an odd dislocated feeling that should have been painful. Her eyes moved up her cast. Bold black letters were printed upside down in a vertical line so she could read them.

Marry me? It said.

She grinned. "Me?"

Nat blew his breath up across his face in a long exasperated sigh. "Yeah, you. Who else?"

"I..." she blinked, bit her lip, didn't know what to say. She looked down at the white cotton sheets, spread her hand on top of it and swallowed. "I haven't told you everything—"

"Doesn't matter."

"I bought the land."

"I figured that out already. And the loan?" He raised his eyebrows and looked anything but angry.

She nodded. "I've got the money."

"Good, about time this family had some good

fortune." He smiled down at her, looking like a man who didn't give a damn what reasons she came up with.

"And I've done some bad things."

Nat sat down, took her hand and massaged the tight knuckles.

"Eliza, I love you. You've been through hell. We've all done things we're sorry for."

She'd been proud of herself for not blowing DeLattio's brains out, but she wasn't sure who'd killed him in the end. Her assassin? *Maybe.*

Could she forgive herself for that? She thought of Josie and Nat and how DeLattio had dipped his evil into their world. She could live with it. They were both alive, so she could live with it.

She opened her lips to speak, but Nat put two fingers across them. "Remember I told you before it didn't matter what you'd done, or what you were running from? I meant it. I love you. I want to marry you."

"Are you sure?"

Nat threw back his head and laughed so hard even the nurses outside the room heard him. They came rushing in to check everything was all right.

"Yes," Eliza said, peering over the nurses' heads as they hustled him out of the room so they could check her out.

"Yes!" she shouted.

Epilogue

Three days later Juliette Morgan died. The redhead's face was plastered all over the news for about a day, inextricably linked in death to Andrew DeLattio.

Eliza had watched the news dispassionately. She didn't mourn her past.

Marsh had been to see her, wordlessly slipping her the spurious remains of a bullet. She knew what it cost him, that simple action. The bullet might have pointed to her, or it might not have, she didn't know for sure and hoped she never found out. Kissing him soundly on the cheek, she sent him back to Boston and stuffed the bullet in the garbage.

She wasn't ever going back.

Josie stayed at the ranch, looking more tired and skinny than Eliza had ever seen her. Josie swore DeLattio hadn't touched her, more than the quick fumble, but Eliza knew something was bothering her. Eliza resolved to get them both some counseling. It was way past time.

The doctors had told her she was stuck here, maybe for weeks. They were weaning her off pain meds and making her walk a few steps every hour. Nat stayed with her for hours at a time, reading, making her laugh, and mentally spending her money. She couldn't remember ever enjoying her wealth so much and counted her blessings in more than dollars.

Life was good. Nat was great.

Life was great.

Outside the window of the ICU, she spotted Sarah carrying Tabitha in her arms. Cal, Ryan, Josie and Ezra followed in their wake with flowers, chocolates, *Just Married* balloons and a bottle of champagne.

They came in, rowdily, noisily. Ryan shoved Nat's legs off the bed, waking him up from an afternoon nap. Nat jabbed him in the stomach, grabbed his niece, giving her a big squeeze. Then Tabitha climbed into bed besides Eliza and began flicking channels with the TV remote.

Happy tears gathered in Eliza's eyes as she watched her new family admire her gleaming gold band.

Nat leaned over and kissed her softly on the mouth and whispered, "I love you," into her ear.

Life didn't get any better than this.

Want to know what happens to Marsh and Josie? Read an excerpt here...

HER LAST CHANCE
Marsh & Josie's Story
©Toni Anderson

Chapter One

———————————

Her footsteps rapped loudly against Bleecker Street's bustling sidewalk, her swirling black coat creating an illusion of sophistication that usually amused her. But not right now. Josephine Maxwell kept her head down and her stride firm, only the white-knuckled grip on the handle of her art portfolio betraying her inner apprehension.

Her eyes scanned the street. Fear prickled her skin and crawled up her spine. Fear was weakness. She'd learned that before she'd hit double digits.

Stealing a short, hard breath, she figured she should be used to it by now.

The usual Friday night cocktail of locals and tourists milled about in every direction, all intent on devouring the vibrant Greenwich Village scene. Trees lined the avenues, the base of their trunks dressed up in fancy metal grills. The smell of freshly baked bread wafted warm and fragrant on the chill fall breeze. Lights began to glow as the sun started to fade behind Jersey.

And *still* fear stalked her.

Nothing stood out from any other day except the subtle sensation of being hunted. Danger flickered through her and her heart gave a stutter. She ignored it, pressed down the tendrils of panic and kept on walking—nearly home. Nearly safe.

On the patio of a little Italian restaurant, a swarthy dark-haired man in an expensive business suit stared at her with hunger in his eyes. Never breaking eye contact, he tipped back a bottle of beer and took a long swallow. The action brought a childhood memory sharply into focus and a fine shudder ran through her bones. Uber-confident, the guy raised an eyebrow and curled his tongue suggestively around the top of the bottle. Her stomach somersaulted. For one split-second he reminded her of Andrew DeLattio, but thankfully that murdering asshole was dead.

She didn't flip the guy off. The old Josie would have, but nowadays the concrete backbone she'd constructed over the years had started to disintegrate, leaving her less sure of herself, less bold.

She looked away. What the hell was wrong with men anyway?

The memory of one tall, good-looking federal agent flashed through her mind, but she shut it down, determined to forget the biggest mistake of her life. She didn't have time for self-pity or regrets. Life was a struggle for survival, so why waste energy with delusions or fantasies of what-might-have-been?

She kept walking. The odor of wet tarmac, exhaust fumes and damp fallen leaves mingled with hot spicy foods from nearby restaurants. Her stomach rumbled, reminding her she'd skipped lunch. But the need to get home, to escape this irrational fear overrode even basic hunger. Her footsteps quickened and the urge to bolt hit her with every instinct she possessed. She walked faster. Turning the corner to her Grove Street apartment, she watched a piece of litter keeping pace with her boots before being swept ahead on a stronger gust of wind. Fighting the breeze, she shifted her unwieldy portfolio to her other hand. It was heavy, but at least the contents had gotten her another commission.

Dusk was starting to take hold. Sinister shadows hovered between parked cars. Dying leaves rustled as they fell from spindly branches. Finally she was home. A siren went off in the distance as she groped in her coat pocket for the key to the main door of the apartment building. She slid a furtive glance around, saw nothing to justify this uneasy sensation of being watched.

When am I going to stop looking over my shoulder?

Biting back a curse, she shoved her key into the lock and pushed open the heavy black door, wrestling the massive case through the narrow gap.

The lights were off.

A drop of perspiration rolled down her temple. Her hands shook as she turned on the lights and she breathed out a massive sigh of relief when illumination flooded the stairwell. Stepping across the threshold, she closed the door and bent to open her mailbox on the bottom row. A brush of sound was all the warning she had before someone grabbed her around the neck.

She dropped her portfolio. Mail scattered as her attacker swung her off her feet and whirled her around. Adrenaline surged through her bloodstream, sending her pulse skyrocketing. Her fingers dug into cloth and flesh, and she somehow managed to gather enough purchase to stop her weight from snapping her own neck. Her legs smashed into the balustrade, shooting pain through her limbs.

Crying out, she gulped a breath as he dumped her to the floor. Her vision blurred. She lay there in shock. Then survival instinct kicked in. She rolled, scrambling away from the whistle of steel that grazed her ear as the knife hit the mosaic tiles with a sharp crack. On hands and knees she snatched up her portfolio, twisted, falling onto her back, using it as a shield from that sharp hunter's blade. They stared at each other, frozen.

She recognized him.

Recognized the sharp intent in those lifeless silver disks.

Oh, God.

Sickness stirred in her stomach as she stared up at him, helpless. She'd always known he'd come back. *Always known.* The constricted muscles of her throat choked the breath she so desperately needed as they watched each other in silence. Predator versus weak, pathetic, useless prey.

Dressed in black, a balaclava covering his features, he crouched beside her, a dark faceless monster. Ice-gray eyes stared from thin slits, reflecting the gleam of the knife he carried in his left hand. He wore surgical gloves that made his flesh look waxy as a corpse. Blood smeared the latex.

Whose blood?

Moving slowly, as if he knew he'd won, the monster lifted the portfolio from her shaky grasp and laid it carefully against the wall beneath the mailboxes. She couldn't move; just lay there petrified as memories bombarded her.

The predator tilted his head, considering her as if she were already cut and bleeding. He clenched the handle of the knife, strong fingers squeezing the weapon possessively. For all her big mouth and fighting pride she could not move. Because he'd *created* her all those years ago. He'd created her and now he was back to destroy her.

Without hurry he flicked open the buttons on her coat. Lifted her sweater up and over her breasts and terror welded her to the spot. He cut the material of her bra with a jerk of his wrist.

Nausea threatened, but she forced it back. Cold air flicked over her skin. *I can't survive this twice.* The memory of pain crawled over her body like hives. She told her limbs to work, to move, but they wouldn't obey.

Is this what I've been waiting for? For him to come back and finish the job? She flinched as his finger traced a faded scar.

What did he think of his ancient handiwork?

He lifted the knife. She watched as he trailed its razor edge along a furrow of shiny, white scar tissue. From her hipbone, up across her stomach, slowly, over her ribs, *bump, bump, bump.* She held her breath. The flat edge of the knife stroked her nipple, and horror, not desire, had it puckering.

His mouth was hidden by the mask but Josie knew he was smiling. Tears formed. Bile burned the lining of her throat. Their eyes locked and she clenched her fists in frustrated rage as he turned the

348

knife upright and let the weight bear down into her chest. Blood pearled. Pain burst along her nerves with excruciating clarity.

Sucking in a gasp, she braced herself. "You promised if I didn't make a sound you wouldn't kill me." Her voice was ragged, air stroking her vocal chords with the sensitivity of barbed wire.

Time suspended between them like a big fat spider on a whisper of silk. The light in his eyes darkened. "You just made a sound."

She whacked the flat of her hand as hard as she could against his ear and grabbed at his knife-hand, pushing it away from her body. She sank her teeth into his wrist, narrowly avoiding getting a knife in the face. His pulse beat solidly against her lips as she clamped her jaws together until she tasted blood. She didn't let go.

Her other hand clawed at his eye, her legs finally working as they scrambled for purchase on the slick tile. His body fell against her hip, his breath hot and violent against her cheek. Gouging her sharp fingernails into his eye socket, she scratched at the smooth hard shell of his eyeball. Blood filled her mouth, the taste of him bitter and repugnant on her tongue. Her stomach twisted but she didn't ease up. If she did, he would kill her.

With a furious roar, he fell back. Scrambling to her feet, Josie grabbed her portfolio from against the wall and held it in front of her again as a last desperate defense. The predator rubbed his hand over eyes that glowed with malevolence.

In her nightmares he was immortal, unstoppable. In reality, he was just another fucking asshole who liked to hurt people. And God help her, right now he wanted to hurt her.

AUTHOR'S NOTE & ACKNOWLEDGMENTS

Her Sanctuary is the very first book I ever wrote. It was originally published in 2006 by Triskelion Publishing who then went bankrupt. In 2009, it was republished by the lovely people at The Wild Rose Press. However, having dipped my toes in the self-publishing waters in April 2013 with *The Killing Game*, I decided to self-publish *Her Sanctuary* along with the follow-up story, *Her Last Chance* (Marsh and Josie's story).

I feel like I've come a long way as a writer since I started my publishing journey but I hope you enjoy these two stories. I want to thank my editor, Ally Robertson, for doing such a wonderful job and helping me improve the manuscripts.

Thanks always to my critique partner, Kathy Altman, who is my sounding board and my rock. And to Loreth Anne White for being my Skype buddy when we both need a break from the madness of creating something out of nothing.

The biggest shout-out of appreciation goes to my husband and children who put up with the day-to-day minutiae of me being a writer. And to readers who have made my dreams come true!

DEAR READER

Thank you for reading *Her Sanctuary.* I hope you enjoyed it. If you did, please:

1. Help other people find this book by writing an online review. Thanks!

2. Sign up for my "Very Infrequent Newsletter" to hear about new releases and contests. The link is on my website: www.toniandersonauthor.com

3. Come "like" my Facebook Fan Page at: www.facebook.com/pages/Toni-Anderson-Author-Page.

ABOUT THE AUTHOR

Toni Anderson is a *New York Times & USA Today* best-selling author of Romantic Suspense. A former marine biologist, Anderson traveled the world with her work. After living in six different countries, she finally settled in the Canadian prairies with her husband and two children. Combining her love of travel with her love of romantic suspense, Anderson writes stories based in some of the places she has been fortunate enough to visit.

Toni donates 15% of her royalties from *Edge of Survival* to diabetes research—to find out why, read the book!

She is the author of several novels including *Dark Waters*, *The Killing Game*, and *A Cold Dark Place*. Her novels have been nominated for the prestigious Romance Writers of America® RITA® Award, Daphne du Maurier Awards, and National Readers' Choice Awards in Romantic Suspense.

Find out more on her website and sign up for her newsletter to keep up-to-date with releases.

www.toniandersonauthor.com

REVIEWS

A COLD DARK PLACE
(Cold Justice Book #1)

"Toni magically blends sizzling chemistry between Alex and Mallory with lots of suspenseful action in *A Cold Dark Place*. At times I wanted to hide my eyes, not knowing if I could face what might or might not happen! The edge of your seat suspense is riveting!" —Harlequin Junkies.

"Recommended for fans of Toni Anderson and fans of dark romantic suspense. You'd definitely love this one!" —Maldivian Book Reviewer's Realm of Romance.

DARK WATERS
(International bestseller and 2014 National Readers' Choice Award finalist in Romantic Suspense)

"In this action-packed contemporary, Anderson (*Dangerous Waters*) weaves together a tapestry of powerful suspense and sizzling romance." — *Publishers Weekly.*

"The pacing in this book is superb. The tension really never lets up … I never felt there was a good 'stopping point' in this book, which is probably why I was reading all night." —Smart Bitches, Trashy Books.

DANGEROUS WATERS
(International bestseller and 2013 Daphne du Maurier finalist)

"With a haunting setting and a captivating cast of characters, Anderson has crafted a multifaceted mystery rife with secrets. Readers will have to focus, as red herrings abound, but the result is a compulsively engrossing page-turner." —*Romantic Times* (4 Stars)

"A captivating mix of suspense and romance, *Dangerous Waters* will pull you under." —Laura Griffin, *New York Times* and *USA Today* best-selling author

THE KILLING GAME
(2014 RITA® Finalist and National Readers' Choice Award finalist in Romantic Suspense)

"*The Killing Game* is an exhilarating, masterfully-crafted mix of life-and-death adventure and political intrigue. It's also a riveting romance, and with the author's trademark gritty and evocative prose, wily imagination and fierce respect for the plight of the snow leopard and the war-torn country it inhabits, this book is one unforgettable read." —Kathy Altman Goodreads Review. (5 Stars)

"I'd recommend this to any romantic suspense reader looking for a unique, intricately woven story that will really touch you." —Peaces of Me (5 Stars)

"Realistic scene descriptions, endangered species,

and plenty of spies made this a sure fire hit in my reading collection." —SnS Reviews (5 Stars)

EDGE OF SURVIVAL

"Anderson writes with a gritty, fast-paced style, and her narrative is tense and evocative." —HEA USA Today

"... more substance than one would expect from a romantic thriller." —*Library Journal Reviews*

"*Edge of Survival* is without a doubt, one of the most exciting, romantic, sexy stories I've had the pleasure of reading this year and I will definitely be looking for more by Toni Anderson." —Blithely Bookish (5 Stars)

"Sensual, different; romance with a bit of angst, just how I like them; *Edge of Survival* is a romantic suspense not to be missed." —Maldivian Book Reviewer's Realm of Romance (5 Stars)

STORM WARNING
(Best Book of 2010 Nominee —The Romance Reviews)

"... an intense, provocative paranormal romance with a suspenseful twist...This is a book that I am unquestionably adding to my keeper collection." — Night Owl Reviews (TOP PICK)

"It is exactly the way I like my romantic suspense novels to be." —The Romance Reviews

"The plot is full of suspense and some pretty incredible plot twists. ... will have you on the edge of your seat." —Coffee Time Romance & More

SEA OF SUSPICION
(Best Book of 2010 Nominee —The Romance Reviews)

"Deeply atmospheric and filled with twists and turns, *Sea of Suspicion* kept me flying eagerly through the pages." —All About Romance

"*Sea of Suspicion* is one heck of a book! The twists, turns, passion, and many colorful characters give Ms. Anderson's novel a delightful edge." —Coffee Time Romance

"Set along the coast of Scotland, *Sea of Suspicion* is a riveting story of suspense and the depths and heights of human character." —The Romance Reviews

HER LAST CHANCE
(2014 Daphne du Maurier finalist)

"A high intensity story, with action from the first page on, an intricate suspense tale with twists and turns that are surprising and a conclusion that is as near to closure as is possible to come. The characters are deep and rather brooding, but manage to lose themselves in each other. And the writing is clever, hot and altogether fabulous!" —Ripe for Reader

"From the opening scene I was turning the pages totally entranced in the story. I've loved all this authors books but at this moment this has to be my favorite." —SnS Reviews

HER SANCTUARY
(National bestseller)

"*Her Sanctuary* is a riveting fast-paced suspense story, filled with twists, turns, and danger. As the story flows seamlessly between the protagonists and antagonists, the tension rises to fever pitch. Just when you think you know the good guys from the bad, Anderson provides a surprising twist, or two." —Night Owl Romance (TOP PICK)

"Suspenseful, riveting and explosive, this reader absolutely loved this story." —Fallen Angel Reviews (5 Angels)

"Ms. Anderson presents us with one fantastic story that has me wanting more." —Romance Junkies (4.5 Blue Ribbons)

"For a fast paced, enjoyable read filled with secrets and surprises, *Her Sanctuary* will fill all your expectations." —Romance Reviews Today

"Don't miss out on Eliza and Nat's tale. They are just waiting for you to join them in the modern wild west of Montana." —Loves Romances Reviews

CPSIA information can be obtained at www.ICGtesting.com
Printed in the USA
LVOW09s2110030914

402275LV00001B/25/P

9 780991 895